The Wishing Thread

The
Wishing Thread

A Novel

LISA VAN ALLEN

 Ballantine Books Trade Paperbacks | New York

A Ballantine Books Trade Paperback Original

Published in the United States by Ballantine Books, an imprint of The Random House Publishing Group, a division of Random House, Inc., New York.

BALLANTINE and the HOUSE colophon are registered trademarks of Random House, Inc.

RANDOM HOUSE READER'S CIRCLE & Design is a registered trademark of Random House, Inc.

Title-page art from original photographs by Beata Swi
Chapter-opener art from istockphoto/Floortje

LIBRARY OF CONGRESS CATALOGING-IN-PUBLICATION DATA
Van Allen, Lisa.
The wishing thread : a novel / Lisa Van Allen.
pages cm
ISBN 978-0-345-53855-0
eBook ISBN 978-0-345-53782-9
1. Sisters—Fiction. 2. Tarrytown (N.Y.)—Fiction. I. Title.
PS3622.A5565W57 2013   813'.6—dc23   2013021730

Printed in the United States of America

www.randomhousereaderscircle.com

2 4 6 8 9 7 5 3 1

Book design by Virginia Norey

The humble knitter sits in the center
between heaven and earth.
—Susan Gordon Lydon, *The Knitting Sutra*

I have read somewhat, heard and seen more, and
dreamt more than all . . . I am always at a loss to know
how much to believe of my own stories.
—Washington Irving writing as Geoffrey Crayon,
Tales of a Traveller

The Wishing Thread

1

"Long-Tail Cast On"

Mariah Van Ripper had never done things in life on anyone else's time line, and dying had been no exception. On Mariah's last earthly day in Tarrytown, her niece Aubrey had been sitting in the yarn room, the stitches of a lacy mohair shawl waltzing between her fingers. She hadn't realized she'd been dozing, her mind wandering dreamy byways even while her fingers danced through stitch after stitch, until the moment that Mariah appeared in the doorway.

"Oh good. Aubrey! There was something I wanted to tell you."

Aubrey looked up from her knitting. Framed by the doorjamb, Mariah listed slightly to the side like a wide flag waving in a gentle wind. She wore a long shapeless dress made of cotton so crisp and white that it nearly glowed.

"What are you doing back?" Aubrey asked. "I thought you had an appointment with Councilman Halpern. Did you forget something?"

"Yes . . . I believe I did."

"Well, whatever it was, I would have brought it over to you if you'd called me," Aubrey said, chastising a little. "What do you need?"

Mariah didn't answer. Her eyes were wide and confused as a sleepy child's. She murmured between half-closed lips.

"Mariah?" Aubrey stopped knitting at the end of a row, dropped her hands. The shawl lay sunlit and rumpled as yellow fall leaves in her lap. "What is it? What's wrong?"

"Something I was going to tell you . . ."

"Well, let's hear it."

"Something . . ."

"Hey. You feeling okay?"

Aubrey watched her aunt's pupils telescope into tiny black points. She seemed focused on something Aubrey couldn't see, a speck of dust perhaps, dancing in the air, or some secret thought of her own, anchored so deep in her gray matter that her unseeing eyes drifted like boats from their moorings. Mariah was of middling height and impressive girth, with hair like long runny drippings of pigeon-gray paint. Although she had not been a beauty even in her youth, she had kind eyes, a generous smile, and deep, appealing wrinkles. The sun coming from behind her silvered her hair and the white hem of her dress.

"Ah, well," Mariah said. "I guess you'll have to figure it out." She sighed, not unhappily. And then she stepped out of the yarn room and out of sight.

Aubrey set aside her knitting and crossed the wide wooden floorboards. She felt light-headed, caught up in the swill of her own worry. Mariah's health had been in decline for the last few years, and it occurred to Aubrey that her aunt might be having a stroke. The doctors had warned them. Aubrey peered around the doorjamb; Mariah had vanished without the sound of a single footfall to mark the direction she'd gone.

Not even possible, Aubrey thought.

But she called up the stairs anyway. "Mariah?"

She called down the hall. "Hey, Mari?"

She jumped when the phone rang. The hair at the nape of her neck stood on end.

She picked up the receiver very slowly. "Yes?"

"Aubrey Van Ripper?" a stranger asked.

It was then that Aubrey knew—knew before she'd been told—that her aunt had not returned to the Stitchery for some forgotten item. In fact, she was not in the Stitchery at all. And Aubrey thought of how vulgar it was that news of death, such an intimate and private thing, should be borne on the lips of a stranger.

For the first time in her life, Aubrey was alone, fully and finally and unexpectedly alone, alone in that moment and forevermore alone, her knitting needles stilled on a table in the yarn room, her ear hot from the press of the phone, and a stranger's words floating to her from somewhere, not here, explaining a thing that had happened all the way across town.

In his private office not far from the Tarrytown village hall, safely ensconced behind neocolonial pillars and Flemish brickwork, Councilman Steve Halpern poured himself a drink from the small flask he kept for emergency use in his bottom desk drawer. The ambulance had left only moments ago, bearing Mariah Van Ripper's body away from his office for the last time. He leaned back in his cigar-brown chair. It whined under his weight.

"You know, a person never *wants* to see a thing like this happen," he said.

Jackie Halpern, who managed his electoral campaigns, his accounting, his sock drawer, and his blood-pressure medication, smiled. "Of course not."

"But if it *had* to happen—"

"Don't say it," she told him. "I know."

* * *

Slowly, like a thin vapor snaking its way inch by inch through Tarrytown's friendly suburban streets, rumors of Mariah Van Ripper's death spread among people who knew her and people who did not, until finally the fog of bad news wafted thick as raw wool down toward the river, down into the ramshackle neighborhood that Mariah had called home. The dogs of Tappan Square, mangy rottweilers and pit bulls that barked through closed windows, grew uniformly silent and did not so much as squeak at passersby. The oxidized old rooster atop the Stitchery's tower spun counterclockwise in three full circles before coming to point unwaveringly east, and if any of Tappan Square's residents had seen it, they would have known it was not a good sign.

Tappan Square was not Tarrytown's best-kept secret. It did not factor into the region's well-known, accepted lore. When visitors pointed their GPS systems toward Tarrytown and its sister, Sleepy Hollow, they always bypassed Tappan Square. Instead, they flocked to Sunnyside, the ivy-choked cottage where Washington Irving lived and died and dreamed of the Galloping Horseman and Ichabod Crane. They cowered happily at the foot of that tyrannical gothic castle, Lyndhurst, lording over the Hudson River with its crenellated scowl, and they pointed out landmarks from vampire horror movies in its dim, hieratic halls. They trudged among the lichen-flecked soul effigies at the Old Dutch Church, picking their way with cameras and sturdy shoes among tombstones that said BEEKMAN, CARNEGIE, ROCKEFELLER, and SLOAT. They searched for what everyone searches for on the shores of the Hudson River: enchantment. Some of that good old-fashioned magic. And yet, rarely did outsiders make their way to the neighborhood of Tappan Square, where salsa beats blared hard from the windows of rusting jalopies, where illegal cable wires were strung window-to-window, and where magic, or some semblance of the thing, still found footing on the foundation of the building that the Van Ripper family had always called home.

The Stitchery, as it came to be called by neighbors and eventually by the family within it, had always been filled with Van Rippers. To its neighbors, the Stitchery was a curiosity like a whale's eyeball in a formaldehyde mason jar, a taxidermied baby horse with wax eyes coated in dust, a thing that should have been allowed to vanish after the life had passed out of it but instead was artificially preserved. With its architectural hodgepodge cobbled together over the centuries—its temperate Federalist core, its ardent mansard garret, its fish-scaled tower with witch's hat roof—the house did not offer the most welcoming appearance. The latest batches of Van Rippers, most recently led by Mariah, did not believe in renovation. They did not repaint over the awful cabbage-rose wallpaper in the parlor, or fix the scrolling black gate in front of the house that had been knocked crooked during the Great Blizzard of 1888, or replace the sign on the front door that read YARNS even though it was nearly illegible with age. In fact, they vehemently protested such alterations and "unnecessary" upgrades as affronts to history. Mariah Van Ripper was said to have wept, actually wept, when one of the Stitchery's great old toilets needed its innards gutted, and exact replacements for the old digestive system could not be found.

And so the Stitchery was allowed to fall out of fashion, then out of respectability, until it became a mote in an eyesore of a neighborhood, because Mariah had professed too much respect for her ancestors to fix a cockamamie shutter or tighten a baluster. This was the accretion of history that built up like dandruff or snow, and Mariah had always allowed it as one allows the sun to rise in the morning and set at night. Of course, her philosophy fit in nicely with her hatred of housework and her unwillingness to spend what little money the Van Rippers made on such a frivolous thing as a new doorbell. But whatever the root motivation, the result was that the Stitchery—regarded by some as the heart of Tappan Square, and regarded by others as the tumor—was ugly, dilapidated, and falling down.

As news of Mariah's death reached its tentacles into her neighborhood, a handful of Tarrytown transplants who had come from all corners of the world began to gather before the Stitchery's façade. The religious among the crowd crossed themselves and said their prayers, prayers that were not entirely altruistic, for Mariah's soul to be scooped up and deposited quickly in its final landing place, so long as it wasn't roaming the earth with the more well-mannered ghosts of Sleepy Hollow and Tarrytown. Women who were friendly toward the Van Rippers set colorful candles in tall glasses on the sidewalk and fixed carnations to the Stitchery's crooked gate. They did not need to speak a common language to share a common worry: What would happen to the Stitchery? And worse: With Mariah gone, what would happen to them all?

The Van Rippers were charlatans to some, saviors to others. Crooks or angels. Saints or thieves. But even if the gossip about the Stitchery was just and only that—if the strangeness of the Stitchery began and ended with the things that were said about it—uncertainty had never stopped many generations of Tarrytown women from dragging themselves in desperation to the Van Rippers' doorway, begging for help. *Make me a sweater, make me mittens, make my baby healthy, make my husband love me again.*

The magic of the Van Ripper family, they said, was in the knitting.

If it was magic at all.

2

"Make a Knot"

There were only a handful of places in the area of Tarrytown where Aubrey Van Ripper appeared with any regularity: the grocery store, the library, the pet store, the sushi house, and sometimes—when the evening was clear and cool—the park. And so when she made her appearance at the hospital on the day that Mariah died, locals looked on with curiosity, half fearful and half intrigued. She wore clunky white orthopedic shoes like an old lady—though she was only twenty-eight—a horrific polyester blouse dotted with tiny forget-me-nots, and thick black glasses with plastic frames. Her hair was a pretty blond that swept to her shoulders, but it was frizzy and kinked with knots.

As for Aubrey, she wasn't nearly as interested in the hospital as it was in her. To her mind, the hospital should have been lively, frenetic, caught in the teeth-gnashing clench between death and life. Instead, it was dull. Bored administrative types chewed gum and watched the game show channel on the TV in the waiting room, which played a rerun of *Wheel of Fortune*. The lobby would have looked just like this—sterile and sleepy—whether or not her aunt had just died.

"Sign, please." A woman behind the counter thrust a translucent purple clipboard toward her. "If you have any questions, don't hesitate to ask—anyone else but me."

Aubrey complied. There were so many words on every piece of paper, tiny words made of tiny letters, one running into the other. If she could unwind all the words out into a long, single thread, they would reach around the building and back again. She could knit them into a sweater. Or a heavy black shawl.

Out of the corner of her eye, Aubrey noticed a couple of the nurses standing together in a distant corner of the room, whispering softly with their heads bent low. They wore slouchy bright scrubs bedecked with cartoon flowers. One of them was Katrina Van der Donck, who liked to claim she was descended from the great seventeenth-century documentarian of Sleepy Hollow, Adriaen Van der Donck, who first recorded *Slapershaven* as name of the Hudson tributary that ran through the glen. The other woman was a stranger. They were trying not to glance Aubrey's way but were unable to avoid the temptation.

Aubrey bore their scrutiny as long as she could. Their whispers scratched at her eardrums like a dog at a door. Finally, she could not stand it. She glanced up, and both women winced. Aubrey spoke as loud as she dared. "You do realize I know what you're saying, right?"

"Oh my God. She's a mind reader, too?" the stranger said, loudly enough for Aubrey to hear. "You didn't say she was a mind reader."

"She's not a mind reader," Aubrey said.

"Oh no?" Katrina smirked. "What am I thinking now?" She crossed her arms and glared.

Aubrey lowered her eyes back to her paperwork. Her face was burning red; she could feel it. Her armpits were prickly with sweat. She did not know precisely why Katrina Van der Donck had come to hate her, but she guessed it had to do with the magic and that perhaps Katrina had paid for an ineffective spell. Aubrey hated confrontation more than she hated squishy white bread in long plastic bags, more than she hated laugh tracks in sitcoms, more than she hated Steve Halpern. Mariah would have known what to say.

The Stitchery—and the women in it—had always been touched by a vague darkness, a miasma of speculation. Aubrey's ancestors trailed all the way back to the first settlers who lived in ditches in New Netherland earth, and the more distant the modern world became from those starved and lice-ridden adventurers, the more mysterious and alluring they began to appear, so that the effect of time on the progenitors of the Stitchery was like the effect of atmosphere on the stars.

Unfortunately for Aubrey, the gossips of Tarrytown didn't think the village librarian's assistant, who shopped for beets in the grocery store and who carried a picture of her pet hedgehog in her wallet, was especially captivating. The lore of the Stitchery was mysterious. Mariah had been its peculiar but venerable old maven. Aubrey—poor Aubrey—she was just weird.

Her appearance didn't help her reputation. As the next in line to be the guardian of the Stitchery—the next in line after Mariah—she bore the Stitchery's Mark. In Mariah, the Mark had manifested itself discreetly: Even with no perfume on, even when it was a hundred degrees in August, Mariah's skin smelled strongly of flower petals. The scent glands that made other people stink like horses had literally made Mariah smell like a rose—granted, a cheap rose that sometimes put one in mind of an Old West hooker, but a rose nonetheless. The people of Tarrytown had assumed that Mariah was just another old lady who drowned her sorrows in drugstore perfume. And although there were always exceptions, people liked her as well as any Van Ripper could be liked.

But Aubrey's Mark—the thing that had established early on that *she* would be the Stitchery's next guardian—was not so inoffensive or so easily explained away. Her Mark made people uncomfortable. Her Mark couldn't be disguised. Although Aubrey herself could not see what was wrong with her when she looked into the mirror, she'd been told often enough what other people saw: Her eyeballs, far too big for her face, were such a bright, bright blue that they were very nearly nauseating. They were blue as a spring robin's egg, if that egg were dipped in blue food coloring, then rolled in metallic blue glitter. They were, in fact, aggressively blue, and a person could not stare at them for very long before he had to look away.

Now, Aubrey missed the act of eye-to-eye communication no more than an adult might miss a half-remembered imaginary friend—with one exception. His name was Vic; and once, just once, she wished she could look at him straight-on.

She felt a hand on her shoulder. And when she turned, Jeanette Judge was there, fresh off her shift at the library and still smelling vaguely of old books. Jeanette's eyes, wet black eyes that never cared to hide a feeling, were wild with concern.

"I just heard. Are you okay?"

"I'm actually doing fine."

"Don't you lie to me, Aubrey Van Ripper," Jeanette said. She wore a gray poncho that Aubrey had knit for her years ago, when Jeanette had been having some trouble getting a loan to buy a car, and the way she stood now, with her hands on her hips, her dark forearms poking out below gray woolen fringe, and her elbows jutting to the sides, it struck Aubrey that she looked a bit like a gray knight holding a diamond-shaped shield. "Come here." Jeanette wrapped her up in strong arms, and Aubrey hugged her back, languishing in the warm circle of her friend's strength, half tempted to see if she might lift her feet off the ground.

"What happened exactly?" Jeanette asked when at last she pulled away.

"Her heart blew out."

"Blew out? A heart isn't a spare tire."

Aubrey shrugged. She didn't want to say *heart attack*. A heart was not a thing that should have an *attack* mode. She might have explained herself, but Jeanette was glaring over her shoulder with murder in her eyes.

"Whatchoo looking at, Katrina Van der Donck?"

Aubrey turned slightly, saw the glint of wary pleasure in Katrina's eyes.

"Nothing much," Katrina said.

Jeanette's nostrils flared. "You like a good piece of gossip, huh? Well, I got one. It's about a certain person we both know who showed up on the Stitchery door looking for some of that Van Ripper voodoo."

"You wouldn't dare," Katrina said.

"I would, too," Jeanette said. "Now, why don't you go empty somebody's bedpan."

Katrina's upper lip lifted, showing her teeth. "Better than dealing with this crap." She grabbed her friend by the cotton elbow of her scrubs, and they disappeared into the labyrinth of hospital halls.

"You didn't have to do that," Aubrey said.

"Believe me. It's my pleasure."

Aubrey felt a smile crimping her lips despite the day's sorrow. *"Van Ripper voodoo?"*

"Bitch better not mess with me," Jeanette said.

Aubrey laughed. "I love your diction when you're angry."

"Just trying to do my college professors proud."

Behind the desk, the woman who had given Aubrey the

purple clipboard cleared her throat. Aubrey turned back to the paperwork with a sigh. She wondered how many times she would have to be reminded that Mariah was dead before she stopped needing reminding and before she stopped feeling surprised.

Years ago, Mariah had paid for her fortune to be told by a psychic—a chain-smoking single mother who had sworn that Mariah would be struck by lightning on her hundredth birthday. Instead—twenty years shy of a hundred—Mariah had dropped dead in the village hall on a day when there wasn't a cloud in the sky. Aubrey could imagine it: Mariah giving Steve Halpern a piece of her mind about the new shopping center that would replace Tappan Square, her fist raised dramatically in the air and her face as purple as an eggplant, when she'd collapsed on the floor never to get up again. If only there had been a curtain to drop, a crowd to throw roses and shout *brava!*—it would have been a more fitting ending.

Aubrey signed her name by yet another X.

"We're sure there was no foul play here, right?" Jeanette said.

"Of course not."

"I'm just saying. The guy might not have had a gun, but he killed her."

"Steve Halpern's a scumbag, not a murderer."

"He's a politician. And he killed her with stress."

"Well, he—"

"He did. He killed her. Over a damn shopping center. For God's sake, Mariah *died* fighting to keep him from demolishing her home!" Tears stained Jeanette's ocher-dark cheeks in giant rolling globules, the white of her irises shot through with red. "I don't understand how you're even here, Aubrey. Why aren't you home? Why aren't you crying into a cup of peppermint tea? This is *Mariah* we're talking about. The woman who brought you up. The only family you have left—"

"My sisters—"

"Don't count. Come on, Aub. You're telling me you don't have one tear? Not one?"

Aubrey thought for a moment. Sometimes, when people lost a loved one, they said they felt numb. They said things like *It just hasn't sunk in yet.* Aubrey understood full well what it meant that her aunt had died; already, there was a kind of off-ness to everything she did and saw. She could look at a tree—like the gnarly little dogwood in front of the high school that she'd seen a thousand times—and even though it was the same tree it had always been, she could feel that something was different about it. Different, but not changed.

Already the Stitchery was calling, pulling like a thousand little hooks under Aubrey's skin. She'd known since she was thirteen and her eyes had transmogrified into medical-miracle blue that she would one day be married to the Stitchery, just like her Aunt Mariah had been, and just like her grandmother had been before that, and her great-grandmother before that, and her great-great-grandmother's sister before that, and whoever else before that, going all the way back to Helen Praisegod Van Ripper who first had doomed them all. Aubrey was just the latest Van Ripper to be chosen by the Stitchery as the guardian of its secrets—her life no more or less important than the other guardians'. And she'd forced herself to reconcile with her fate at society's fringes—even embrace it—years ago. She lived daily with the understanding that, eventually, someday, when she was ready, years and years from now, she would assume her aunt's role in the Stitchery and the community. The women of Tarrytown would come to her and heap their secret woes and griefs and desires on her shoulders, and after a spell they would revile or revere Aubrey as they had reviled or revered Mariah, and Aubrey would grow old between the Stitchery's walls like a flower pressed between the pages of a book.

But all of that was supposed to have happened in the distant future—not the present, not while Aubrey was still so young. Mariah, who had shouldered Tarrytown's secrets with formidable resilience, was no longer around to help her. And her sisters, once as close to her as seeds in the heart of an apple, were gone.

"You want me to come home with you?" Jeanette asked, rubbing her back. "We'll order some pizza and stay up watching movies in our PJs?"

"It's okay," Aubrey said.

"I just don't think you should be alone right now."

"Thank you. But I want to," Aubrey said.

After she'd finished making arrangements for Mariah's body, and after she'd hugged Jeanette one last time, she dragged herself back to the Stitchery. She opened the door and realized she'd forgotten to lock it behind her when she'd left all those hours ago. She stood in the entryway. She stood still. The hallway stretched before her as it always had, with its brown shadows of water stains, its ghost lines where paintings once hung, its mottled blue wallpaper curling up along the seams. To her right was the parlor that no one used anymore. To her left, the knitting room, with its baskets and barrels, its profuse hanks and skeins and cakes of yarn. The house settled around her shoulders like a dusty pall.

She decided it was best not to think. She made an elaborate tofu sushi dinner—just for herself—then found she had no appetite. She took a long shower. She polished old silverware. She cleaned and cleaned. She gave her pet hedgehog,

Ichabod Van Ripper, a rinse in the bathroom sink, brushing his brown-flecked little quills with an old toothbrush as he snuffed in indignation. She attempted to read. But try as she might to keep her hands busy, she still felt her fingers moving of their own accord, stitching the air.

She wandered down the hall, her slippers shuffling because they felt too heavy to lift. Mariah had said, *I won't be gone long*, and her bedroom seemed to be expecting her any moment now. The splashy dahlia wallpaper. The vintage postcards tucked into the mirror's thick frame. Death had not come as some sinister shadow, some ponderous and brooding thing. It had taken Mariah as lightly and as absentmindedly as if the Grim Reaper himself had done no more than lift his hand to swat a gnat in the air.

Aubrey sat on Mariah's bed, her shoulders bent with sorrow but her eyes dry. On the bedside table, Mariah's last project, a Fair Isle beret, lay just as Mariah had left it when she'd had every intention of coming back to it again. The stitches were tiny and even, the pattern of burnt orange, navy, and buttermilk just starting to emerge. The beret was not a spell, Aubrey knew. Just a way to pass the hours. Aubrey picked up the unfinished project, which was more like a floppy Frisbee with a missing middle than a hat, and drew it onto her lap. How many times in her life had she heard her aunt say to no one in particular, "Where did my scissors go?" How many times had she seen her aunt tucking in loose threads from finished projects, hiding beginnings and ends?

Without Mariah, without her sisters, Aubrey's future in the Stitchery stretched out long and bleak as a winter shadow.

She thought: *Mari . . . I'm not ready.*

If there really were Fates, those ancient sisters who measured men's lives in yards of yarn or twine, Aubrey knew them intimately, knew them with a knowledge that ran as deep as her own DNA: women dyeing and spinning, women pulling fibers through their fingertips with educated scrutiny, women considering and cutting, talking things over, putting down their scissors, and then forgetting—just for a moment— where.

From the Great Book in the Hall: *We must never knit when we're feeling sad, or hopeless, or mean. Our stitches get filled up with our thoughts and emotions, and so we must be careful. Blessings are often made with trumpeting and pomp—our hearts cry out to God, to the Universe, and say "Blessed be!" Our blessings bless us because we feel so pleased to utter them.*

But curses do not always come from such places of drama, like King Lear rushing out into the storm, his fist raised to the heavens and damning words on his lips. No—curses can come easily. We mutter them every day: at drivers who cut us off, at long lines in the grocery store, at ourselves when we do something as frivolous as dropping a pen on the floor.

Curses can be carried around in our hearts with no more fanfare than a cocklebur catching a hiker's sock in the fall. They are as malevolent as a tiny new freckle, a contamination like a single black ant in the sugar jar. And so we must not knit if we feel negativity or sadness. Otherwise, a curse, even the smallest of bad wishes, may be passed on.

3

"Increase 4 Sts"

The second Friday of October brought rain to Tarrytown: The sky was gray, the Hudson River had hardened into pewter, the iron girders of the Tappan Zee Bridge were made melancholy by the clinging of raindrops, the trees were grisaille sketches of charcoal and lead.

It was pouring when Bitty woke her son and daughter. They were sleeping in the backseat of the minivan, Carson with his cheek flattened against the window, his breath making white flames dance on rain-flecked glass, and Nessa with her jacket bunched like a pillow, her bright red hair hanging around her shoulders. Neither child looked comfortable.

"Come on, guys," Bitty said. "Wake up. Grab your things."

She did not wait to see them come sleepily back to life. She flung open her door, a cold, heavy rain soaking her jeans even before her foot made contact with the ground. Water ran in little rivulets down the street, miniature rivers dragging sticks and fallen leaves. She looked through the telescoping alleyway between the Stitchery and the neighbor's house, but she couldn't see the Hudson River. Too much fog.

She lifted open the back hatch and stuck her head inside. "Guys. I said come on."

"God, Mom." Nessa's voice was tired and young. Bitty

could barely hear it over the pounding rain. "It's . . . what . . . like, seven o'clock in the morning?"

"Please just help me," Bitty said.

She grabbed all the bags she could—the duffels and back-packs, a grocery-store bag stuffed with Carson's sneakers, her brown leather luggage that she'd never used before. Her kids climbed out of the car.

Nessa complained. "I'm getting wet."

"We all are, stupid," Carson said.

Bitty shut the hatch. "Hurry! Come on."

She ran—galumphing along with all that she could carry—to the safety of the porch. For a second, she was trans-ported. She was racing her sisters to the top of the stairs. She was running, breathless, from the bullying kids who some-times chased her home before she learned to stand up to them. She was standing on the stoop in the darkness, secretly kissing the man who swore to love her forever.

When she turned around, she saw that her children hadn't followed. They were staring up at her from the ground, grassy brown puddles of mud rippling around them. The Stitchery lorded over its patch of soggy yard, its Depression-era porch drooping in a disapproving frown.

"Guys . . . come on. It's okay."

She saw them trade a glance—her two children who had already started to look to each other for comfort in the way that children did when they came from troubled homes—and then Carson hitched up his backpack and led the way. Nessa walked slowly, twelve years old and too cool to bother with a thing as trifling as rain.

"This place is a shit-hole," Nessa said.

"Language—"

"She meant to say *poop*-hole," Carson said.

Bitty looked around, thinking of some encouraging and motherly thing to say, like *It's not that bad*. But the house was crumbling, the yard was overgrown, and the neighborhood was on the brink. "Fine. It's a poop-hole," she said.

Aubrey had not yet dressed for the day when Bitty and her children arrived. She'd spent the entire night in Mariah's room. She'd picked up *Northanger Abbey* where it had been open at the foot of Mariah's bed, and she'd started reading where her aunt had left off. Sometime in the night she'd pulled on Mariah's fuzzy pink bathrobe for warmth against the autumn chill. And in the morning, she did not throw off the covers. She stayed in bed, fighting to stay asleep. She dreamed she was knitting a sweater for a tree and she couldn't figure out the proportions. When she heard her older sister calling up the stairs—*hello? hello?*—she wasn't startled. She'd called her sister and had been expecting Bitty to arrive. She tied Mariah's robe tighter around her middle and walked downstairs.

The last time Aubrey had seen her sister, Carson had been a toothless preemie, so small he might have fit in a shoe box, crying and wriggling in Aubrey's arms. And Nessa had been just two years old, dressed in pink and put out by all the attention that her new brother got just for being born.

In the weeks before Carson's birth, Aubrey had made a sweater—a simple top-down hand-knit in a cream-and-blue stockinette. As she knit, she'd cast her wish for him: She envisioned him discovering things that would brighten his childhood—books and bugs and mushrooms and games of tag among friends. She pictured him being handed a diploma, being offered his dream job. She imagined for him a partner, a perfect complementary heart, and she wished for him all the nerves and joy and anticipation of having children of his own. She knit all these visions as vividly as possible into the sweater she made for him, all these and more, and when it finally came time to bind off, she prayed that he one day would be received into heaven with perfect peace and ease, his great-grandchildren beside him, his cup running over for all he had lived, seen, and done.

The sweater had been beautiful—tiny stitches on size three needles, a neckline that opened with a birch button at the shoulder, nearly invisible seams. But when Bitty opened the brown paper package at the baby shower and took the sweater out right there in front of everyone—wealthy in-laws and fashionable playdate moms—her face fell.

"Oh, thanks," she'd said. And she'd gone on to the next gift as awkwardly as if Aubrey had given her some raunchy little nightie, or a subscription to a weight-loss magazine, or some other publicly embarrassing thing.

That day, Aubrey had no choice but to notice what she otherwise would have denied: Bitty had rejected the ways of their childhood, the ways of the Stitchery, once and for all. Soon her sister's trips home became phone calls, and her phone calls became greeting cards, and her cards became emails, her emails grew few and far between, until somehow all the long elisions of the years clouded over with fog, obscuring and isolating them one from the other—and the woman who stood in the Stitchery entryway, calling *Hello? Anyone home?* was no longer the same sister who used to braid Aubrey's hair, and tuck the covers around Aubrey's legs so she could feel like a mermaid, and make Aubrey peanut butter milk shakes when she scraped her elbow and cried.

Aubrey paused—a bit dramatically, as Mariah might have done—with her hand on the newel post. She looked at her sister standing in the front hall. "You're here."

"Yes," Bitty said. Water dripped from her hair into her coat collar. She had set down her bags—so many, many bags—but her children gripped theirs in clenched hands. "I got your voice mail. And I came as soon as I could." Bitty smiled tightly. "We tried to get a hotel but there's some kind of convention in town."

"The Descendants of Dutch Boerers Society," Aubrey said. "What about your husband. Is he . . . ?"

"We left a note for Craig. We didn't want to wake him." Bitty cleared her throat then turned to her children. "Anyway, guys, don't be rude. Say hello to your aunt Aubrey."

"Hello to your aunt Aubrey," Carson said.

Aubrey laughed.

Nessa murmured a hello.

"Nice to mee—*see*—you," Aubrey said.

She gripped the round ball atop the newel post. She was glad to see her niece and nephew; some of the emptiness in her heart eased. And yet there was some other feeling sloshing around inside her, too—one she couldn't perfectly name. Here were Nessa and Carson—Nessa with her lion's mane of red hair, Carson still boyish but becoming handsome—and already she loved them with all she had in her. But she hardly knew them at all.

"That's a great scarf," she said to Nessa.

Nessa reached up and touched the slouchy knit hanging around her neck. The scarf was the color of toasted oats, flecked by bits of hunter green and brown. Cables twined like snakes around one another, and dozens of little bobbles nestled among the braids. Nessa unwound it from her neck. "Thanks."

"Did you make it?"

"Mom got it for me."

"May I?" She reached out to touch the scarf. But no sooner

had she brushed it with her fingertips than she pulled her hand away, her suspicions confirmed. "Acrylic." She shot a glance at her sister. "You have her wearing *acrylic?*"

Bitty shrugged. "It was on sale."

"I'll knit her a new one while she's here. Or better yet—I'll teach her to make one herself."

"You can teach me?" Nessa's eyes lit up. "Really? You could, like, *make* this thing?"

In the space of a moment, Aubrey felt the room change, the air itself going lighter on her skin. When Aubrey was young, so young that she didn't know words like *expectation* and *estrangement*, her aunt Mariah had sat her down on a small footstool, then she'd sat behind her and pulled the stool backward until Aubrey's torso was nearly between her knees. A moment later, Mariah's arms were around Aubrey's shoulders and her hands were in front of Aubrey's face. A knitter's-eye view. To this day, Aubrey could think of no place that she'd felt safer, no place more loved. A thread of strong wool was wrapped around Mariah's left hand, her pointer finger extended and yarn dangling from the tip like twine from a fishing pole. Aubrey had held her breath.

Now, Mariah had said. *Watch this.*

Aubrey tightened Mariah's fluffy pink robe around her middle. Outside, the wind blew harder and faster, rattling the sidelight windows like loosened teeth. Nessa lifted a little on her toes while she waited for an answer.

Aubrey smiled. "Of course, Nessa. I'd love to teach you to knit. I'd be honored."

But Bitty put her arm around her daughter and tugged her close. "Sorry. No can do. We're just staying for the funeral. And then we're gone."

* * *

The three Van Ripper sisters may not have always seen eye-to-eye, and in their younger years they could often be heard by the neighbors bickering over the most peculiar things— their collection of pet worms, whose turn it was to cut Aunt Mariah's toenails, the right way to hold a frog. But there was one thing the Van Ripper girls had learned to do together without argument very early on, and that was knitting.

During the knitting hour, which usually took place after dinner and homework but just before bed, Aubrey and her sisters met with their aunt in what was once supposed to have been the Stitchery's front parlor for receiving guests. In the shop, yarns were just yarns. But when Mariah knit, they were transformed into sweaters, scarves, hats, first kisses, passing grades, newborn babies, and any number of desperately wished-for things.

In her brightly patterned dresses of the most god-awful colors, and with her gray hair hanging like seaweed around her face, Mariah would light a candle, say a prayer. Then the knitting would begin, each sister alone with the sound of her own breathing, with the stitches that dropped like pebbles into a quiet pool.

The trick, Aunt Mariah had said, *is to clear your mind*. To let your thoughts drain. At any given moment, a knitter was always knitting with at least two yarns: one that was the actual fiber, and another that was an invisible thread, the essence of the knitter, that accompanied every stitch. A wish held and sustained with clarity of mind while knitting would somehow wend its way into the fabric, and later when the fabric became a sweater or a hat, that wish would materialize. In this way, making magic was nothing more than intense, focused wishing. It all seemed very simple. It was not simple at all.

And so from a very young age, the girls learned to knit in

silence, to embrace the paradox of thinking of nothing as a mental preparation for the day when one of them, the chosen guardian, would actually knit spells.

Of all three Van Ripper sisters, Meggie, the youngest, had been the most restless each evening when Mariah had gathered them into the parlor for knitting hour. In kindergarten, other children were learning to tie their shoes, but Meggie was already an expert at both the knit and purl stitches— whether she liked it or not. She fidgeted and huffed, she curled her toes, she clamped her teeth. And it never failed that once she finally, *finally* began to give herself over to the knitting—to her, the rhythm sometimes felt like being lifted by ocean waves and 'set gently on her feet again—the session ended. The older she got, the more she understood: There was a beauty to be had by the simple working of her fingers, the stilling of her mind. But she'd never been able to do more than open the door to that peaceful place before it was shut again.

On some days she resented Aubrey, who seemed to knit so effortlessly, so *fast*. With her fingers working a pair of rosewood needles and a ball of soft gray yarn, Aubrey looked quite pretty, almost nun-ish, her eyelids drooping but her eyes glowing blue like the Chagall windows of Union Church on a dark night. Meggie, meanwhile, could not wrestle peace out of a brain that was always jammed up with other things: how her aunt had taken her out of school, how normal kids her age got to do plays in an actual auditorium as opposed to a living room, how normal kids had trophies from soccer, or ballet, or even math leagues, and how Meggie had only the knitting— the endless knitting—chains of stitch after stitch.

The older Meggie got, the more restless she became. When Meggie was twelve, Bitty, who had been out of high school for about eighteen months, ran away with the man who would become her husband. The evenings of knitting continued just like they always had, except without Bitty. Meggie wasn't surprised that her sister had flown the coop: Bitty had been skipping the knitting hour on and off for many of her later teen years, wiggling herself out of the Stitchery even as Meggie was wiggling out the last of her baby teeth, so that by the time Bitty's separation was complete, Meggie was prepared to bear it. She, like Bitty, was destined to leave the Stitchery. But she would not travel in her oldest sister's footsteps: She would cut and mow and bushwhack a path of her own. Aubrey and Mariah—they were the ones who would stay.

One day when Meggie was almost eighteen, Mariah found the old red backpack that Meggie had hidden in her closet in case of an emergency, stuffed with all the things she needed to run away. *You might go*, Mariah had said, *but you'll never really go. The Stitchery will call you back, and when it does, you'll need to drop everything. Whatever you're doing. And come home.*

It wasn't until Meggie was twenty-two, four years away from the stuffy strictures of the Stitchery, that she realized Mariah's warning had not been entirely metaphorical. She and her newest guy-friend were lying in his bed, pleasantly exhausted and sticky with sweat. They'd been at his place in Savannah for all of ten minutes. Meggie's shirt had landed on Phil's guitar case. Phil's boxers hung from a huge black amp.

Meggie plucked up a thread that had dislodged from the frayed black edge of her T-shirt, and she traced the loose end over the tattoos on Phil's chest—a dragon, a music note, a small black bat. He'd been talking for the last week about getting her name inked over his heart, but she warned him: *Don't.*

"What do you feel like for dinner?" he asked her.

"I don't know."

"Chinese? Italian?"

"Whatever," she said. "I'm not really that hungry." Conversations about food, especially ones that went on and on, were bad omens. Already, the heady rush she'd felt after she met Phil, the feeling of having held her breath for too long, was fading. She knew herself. She knew that once she got her feet under her again she usually started walking.

She sighed and traced the thread around his small pink nipple. She plucked up a few more threads and thought, *It's time to throw that shirt away.* She lifted the threads over his chest and then let them fall one by one. Slowly, they curled against Phil's sternum, forming loops and swags.

She lifted up on her elbow.

"What is it?" he asked.

She grasped all the threads at once, in one fist, raised them, and let them fall again. Still, the threads fell slowly, and slowly formed improbable scrolls. Her head felt simultaneously heavy and light.

"What are you doing?" he asked.

"Don't you see it?"

He ducked his head, his chin disappearing into his chest, to scowl at the threads that had settled on his breastbone. "See what?"

"Nothing," she said.

By midnight, she was on a bus north, the soft Georgia Low Country trailing like half a dream behind her, and a vision of the Palisades—five hundred feet of craggy Triassic diabase— before her like a battlement in her mind's eye. The man in the seat next to her was snoring and drooling on his suit.

Did it freak you out when you were a kid? the people she

met sometimes wanted to know when they found out she was from Tarrytown. *Growing up with all those stories about the Headless Horseman? Were you afraid?*

Meggie leaned her head against the bus's window.

Was I? she told them. *I still am.*

The message in the threads had been simple:

Go

From the Great Book in the Hall: *There is, of course, always a question—a question of the difference between what is real and what is true. A thing can be true without being real. You may not grasp this entirely, but don't worry. This is the nature of faith, of magic, of art, of a good life's work: If you ever understand perfectly what you're doing, you should stop right away.*

4

"Join Contrasting Color"

Nessa's thumbs worked fast: *Pls tell the cops I've been kidnapped by a woman who looks exactly like my mom and has sent me back in time to the 1700s.*

The reply from her friend Jayden Miller came swiftly: *Haha.*

Srsly, she texted him. *Save me. Pls!*

She watched her cell to see if he would text her again. She watched. And when he did not, she sighed and snapped her phone shut.

On a matching bed across the room, her brother—whom she sometimes called her "bother," since the only difference between a brother and a bother was a measly little *"arrgh!"*— was flopped on his stomach. While Carson got to lose himself in his graphic novels, she had nothing. Nothing but her bottomless, aching loneliness that never went away.

"Come on." She threw a pillow across the room; it missed him by a mile. "Get up."

"No."

"I said, get up."

"Why should I?"

"Because—*hello*. We're going somewhere?"

"Where?" he said.

"I don't know. Exploring?"

Carson looked at her. His face was round as a pumpkin, his hair blond and straight and to his chin. He should have been born in some California beach town instead of White Plains. "Mom said we're not allowed to go out alone because there's drug dealers."

"Not *outside* exploring. Inside."

Carson paused a moment—no doubt weighing the option of exploring against the lure of his comic book, with its wide-shouldered hero who was about to be tortured for information by his archenemy. But in the end, he did what he always did when Nessa wanted something. He got to his feet.

They went. The hallway of the second floor was long and straight as a hollow bone. A window at the far end let in weepy blue-ish light. Carson tapped his knuckles on the wall.

"Shhh," Nessa said.

He made a face but dropped his hand.

It was a game, of course, the idea that they were adventuring through the old house—as if they might find a room of spun gold or an enchanted rose or perhaps even a doorway through time. One by one they opened the many bedroom doors all along the long hall, and they found each room to be relatively the same. A dresser, a closet, a bed. Lace curtains. Sometimes a writing desk. No enchanted spinning wheels. No ghosts.

Carson sighed. "This is boring. I'm going back to my graphic novel."

"You mean your picture book."

"*Comic* book."

"Whatever." Nessa closed a door behind her. "What about the tower? Don't you want to find it?"

Carson shrugged.

"What? Are you a wimp?"

Carson frowned. "No."

"Dork? Are you a little dork?"

"I just don't care about a stupid tower."

Nessa gave as grand a huff as her slight shoulders would allow. Her mother had told her that the tower was part of an addition that had been put on the house sometime in the late 1800s. The base of the addition expanded the room they called the parlor, which apparently nobody used. But Nessa had no idea what might be in the upstairs rooms of the addition. From what she could tell there was no easy way of accessing the top of the tower, with its three gothic-arched windows and violently pointed roof. But she probably wouldn't have been interested in getting into the tower to begin with if someone had opened the door and said *Right this way.*

"Fine. I'll go without you," she said.

"Nice knowing you, Monster," Carson said.

"What did I tell you about calling me that?"

"Loch Ness Monster. Dumb-Ness. Ness-o-thelioma."

"Shut up!" She turned, not tiptoeing anymore, to show she didn't care. She got to the end of the hall, to the room that belonged to her aunt, to the shining cut-glass handle of the door.

Aubrey's room.

She turned the knob. Aubrey's bedroom was slightly bigger than the others, but it too was spare, neat, simple. There were signs of life: a book opened on the pillows, a few houseplants, a pretty goldfish in a glass bowl, some kind of hamster cage—she couldn't see the hamster—and even a small TV. But no Xbox. No hair dryer. No makeup. No perfume. (Her aunt obviously didn't have a boyfriend.) And no tower stairs.

Nessa thought of turning back. She thought of it. And yet, somehow, she couldn't go. Her brain was puppeting her body like a marionette, walking her across Aubrey's bedroom, shepherding her along. She wasn't afraid. She felt electric.

And so very *sure*. The feeling told her to open the creaky door at the back of Aubrey's room that looked like it was for a closet but was apparently not. It told her to climb into the musty, narrow staircase that folded in on itself sharply, all corners and right angles, told her to climb upward even though she felt like she was climbing down, deeper into darkness, deeper until the darkness began to dissipate like morning mist, and then, *then*, she'd found it. The top of the tower. Her breath was in her throat. She was standing in the middle of a fairy tale, gold here, silver there, a glinting and gleaming treasure trove that had been waiting for her to discover it, waiting, somehow, for *her*.

She only stayed a moment, but she stayed long enough. And when her brother asked her if she'd found the tower, she told him no, not because she was lying, but because she didn't quite understand what she'd found.

It wasn't until much later, after her mother had tucked them into their room for the night, when the darkness made her feel like the thing she wanted to say was slightly less crazy sounding, that she told Carson the truth. She tried to describe what she'd seen: *Like a cave in a pirate movie. A treasure trove.* In the top of the tower, which had three small windows in an alcove and a ceiling like the inside of a cone, she'd found a set of ivory combs and a ginormous gilt Bible, not in English. She found a bottle of wine dated 1887, the print so faded it was as blurry as a weather-worn headstone on a grave. There were oil paintings, porcelain figurines, crystal glasses, jewels spilling from jewel-encrusted boxes, a typewriter, a candelabra, more than she could take in.

"And the strange thing," Nessa said, "is that I got this— I don't know—feeling. Like I just *knew* how to get into the tower. Even though I'd never been there before."

"Well, you know why, don't you?"

"Why?"

"Brain damage. You got dropped on your head when you were a baby."

"Shut up, I did not," she said. She didn't have the will to fight with him, even though sometimes fighting made her feel better. "Don't you think that's weird?"

Carson's voice was heavy with sleep. "Maybe Aunt Aubrey sells antiques."

Nessa told him: "No."

Along with all the old tchotchkes that frothed and gathered and spilled into every crevice of the tower room, there were new things, too. Modern things. A Mickey Mouse lunch box. A wedding dress—slipping from its hanger. A bouquet of roses that had dried and darkened to reddish black. She saw a few books, a baby's car seat, a half-dressed Barbie, a pair of kitty-cat bookends, a red wagon, light-up sneakers, a crucifix, a vase . . .

Carson fell back to sleep listening to the catalog. But Nessa remained awake, staring at the ceiling. Her house in White Plains was on a quiet cul-de-sac, where the only noise she heard was the occasional bark of the golden retriever next door. But here in the Stitchery, the night seemed full of sound and menace. She heard the jungle of the streets—cars blaring heavy bass, people shouting to one another down cramped alleys, a baby crying, crying, left to cry. And she heard the house itself creaking, rumbling like the belly of a great beast with her trapped inside.

"Carson?" she whispered. "Are you still awake?"

He didn't answer. She knew he wouldn't.

There was something about the Stitchery that she did not trust. It seemed redundant in the darkness of the bedroom to close her eyes.

* * *

That night, hours later, Aubrey was startled out of a deep sleep, which was unusual. Thumps in the night never woke her. The hedgehog liked to rearrange his cage or run on his wheel at all hours, but she'd stopped hearing him years ago. Words spoken by strangers came in so clear and crisp that the speaker might have been sitting on the dimpled brown chaise in her bedroom instead of chatting on the sidewalk below. *You'd sleep through an earthquake*, Mariah had said with a glint of admiration in her eye.

But tonight, something wasn't right. A noise, a thump. Aubrey woke and didn't move. She strained to listen. *What is that?* Nessa getting a glass of water? Carson losing his way? The noises—a small shuffling, irregular thuds—were too self-conscious to be innocent: the sounds of someone trying not to make sounds.

For a moment, she thought: *This isn't real*. And yet she knew better.

The neighborhood of Tappan Square was full of good people—working parents, mothers who pushed their groceries home in shopping carts, men who sprawled in lawn chairs on the sidewalk, smoking cigars. But along with all the good people, there were people to be afraid of. Somebody's son gone haywire. Somebody who needed the money. Somebody's friend's friends.

The Stitchery had always been a hot mark for hopeful thieves; the rumors of treasure were a temptation to crooks big-time and small. But the same gossip that lured curious delinquents to the Stitchery also acted as a force field to turn them away. The last time the Stitchery had been robbed was in the early seventies, when a few stoned hippies snuck into the empty house and took only what they could carry in their macramé sacks. Shortly after the theft, which had left Mariah shaken but not cowed, the thieves had been found outside of Jersey City, floating on a powerboat-turned-ghost-ship down the Hudson, naked, blue, and dead, with their haul from the Stitchery spread out around them. Officially, the police said they'd overdosed. Unofficially, Tarrytown believed the devil had driven them mad. The rumors had been enough to keep most of Tarrytown's crooks at bay.

But now the neighborhood was changing, more each day. New people from all over the world flowed in and out like a tide, and they had increasingly little patience for the superstitions of old Tappan Square. Aubrey had talked about getting an alarm system installed, but Mariah had scoffed: *Whatever for?* She believed firmly that the Stitchery protected itself. Of course, she also believed that three starlings on the grass meant good luck and that there was no vegetable that couldn't be improved by a good long pickling. Now, with the shuffling and thumping getting louder, Aubrey wished she'd been more insistent about the alarm system. If the Stitchery was robbed tonight, her sister and children would never return.

She threw off the covers. She had no weapon, so she grabbed a metal knitting needle from her bedside, a size eight—just big enough to be firm, thin enough to be sharpish.

At the door at the end of the hall, she could hear noises. Someone was definitely inside. Shuffling. Knocking into things. She stood in the darkness, petrified.

She'd just begun to retreat, to rouse her sister and make a call to the cops, when the door flew open—a gust of inward-sucking air. Aubrey held up her needle and screamed.

"Wait! Wait!" The intruder grabbed her wrist. They were both screaming. "Wait!"

Aubrey twisted out of the figure's shadowed grip, insensible with fear.

"Aubrey. Stop. It's me!"

Aubrey stilled.

"Hey. It's *me*."

She drew back. "Meggie?"

Meggie flipped the switch on the wall, then squinted violently at the shock of light. When she'd left the Stitchery, her hair had been a warm brown-blond, falling to her waist in gentle waves. She'd loved wearing flowered dresses that skimmed the floor and going around Tarrytown with no shoes or bra.

Now her hair was short and raven black—moppish across her brows. Her face was fuller, more mature, though she still had the small features of a pixie. She wore skinny jeans and Converse sneakers, a silver-studded belt slung low around her hips.

Meggie had left the Stitchery four years ago. Four short years. Now Aubrey hardly recognized her. A lifetime might have passed since then.

"Well," Aubrey said.

Meggie held out her hands. "I can explain . . ."

The last time Aubrey saw her little sister, she'd been watching Meggie stuff jeans and shirts into an old suitcase without bothering to fold them. Her newly earned high school diploma—which had come in the mail only the day before—was open on the bed.

I saved up enough to go to Miami, Meggie had said with a grin. *To celebrate. After eleven years of homeschooling I think I earned a weekend off, don't you?*

Aubrey had sat on Meggie's bed, tying a braid of rainbow yarn to her sister's red backpack to repel pickpockets, mosquitoes, exchange-rate cons, transportation delays, and—just for the hell of it—untrustworthy men. Aubrey had wanted to say, *Can I come, too?* But she could not picture herself sipping sweet cocktails by a pool on an island, dancing all night in hot clubs and sleeping until noon. She could not even see herself getting on a plane. Meggie was free to go anywhere she pleased, to not only follow her whims but chase them down and tackle them in a headlock. Aubrey on the other hand was tethered by her belief in and her obligation to the Stitchery's crumbling walls.

Perhaps if she hadn't been thinking so much of herself, of her own lot in life, she would have noticed that the breadth of clothing Meggie was shoving into her suitcase was much more than was needed for a long weekend. Perhaps if she'd been paying closer attention, she would have pocketed her sister's plane ticket and demanded answers about where she really planned to go. But she hadn't been thinking—not of Meggie, anyway. And so when she dropped her sister off at JFK airport she had actually rushed Meggie out of the car with only the briefest hug because she hadn't wanted to hold up the taxis and rental vans behind her. She'd had no idea at the time that it would take Mariah's death, so many years later, to bring her younger sister home.

Aubrey felt dizzy. She pushed past Meggie and into the old bedroom. When Bitty rushed in she brought with her a wash of cold night air. Her eyes were puffy with sleep, and her highlights were disarrayed.

"Aubrey? Are you okay? What happen—?" Bitty stopped. Her gaze landed on Meggie. And then she straightened, surprised. "Oh. When did you get here?"

"Just now."

"Aubrey called you?" Bitty asked. "*She* knew where you were?"

Meggie's chin was tucked into her chest. "Um, no."

"Then . . . how did you find out?"

"How did I find out what?" Meggie asked.

Bitty blinked, confused. "How did you find out about Mariah . . . ?"

"What about Mariah?"

"Oh God." Aubrey's stomach bent into a sickening kink, and she clutched her middle as if she could stop the turning with her hands.

"Are you okay?" Bitty asked.

"I'm sorry. I have to sit." With her sisters watching, she put out a hand to steady herself, her fingertips sliding along Meggie's old collection of movie posters—*Creature from the Black Lagoon, The Abominable Snowman, The Blob.* Their jagged lines and bold colors made Aubrey want to keel over. She'd never felt so strange before in her life, but she recognized what this was: the prelude to fainting. It was too much, it was all too much, for one day.

"I'm sorry, Aub," Meggie said, her voice overly loud, her palms facing the ceiling. "I'm really sorry. I didn't mean to scare anybody. It's just that I got this message in some threads, you know? A totally new thing—never happened before. I thought I imagined it. And anyway I just knew that I had to get here ASAP but I didn't want to wake you up, so I thought I'd see if I could still sneak in, you know, like I used to, up between the walls in the alley . . ."

Aubrey leaned on the edge of the mustard-yellow love seat that Meggie had lugged up to the room when she was a teenager. Slowly, she sat down.

"What is it?" Bitty asked.

She held up her index finger because she could not speak. She closed her eyes. Once again, the Stitchery had returned to its usual quiet. The danger was gone. Now she trembled deeply—not a superficial shaking of her fingers or limbs, but a quivering so deep that it made her guts rock within her. When she opened her eyes, Nessa and Carson were there beside their mother, and Bitty had draped her arms over both their shoulders. Meggie stood near the doorway, her forearms folded and the promontory of her hip thrust to the side.

"Aubrey?" Meggie said.

Everyone was looking at her, waiting for her to make some pronouncement. All these people—her family—*here*—finally—but no Mariah among them.

She tried to speak, to say something that would fix things or at least put everyone at ease. But when she opened her mouth, it wasn't a word that came out. It was a gasp—and then an awful, primal lowing. She couldn't even apologize for the sound.

"Oh," Bitty said. "Oh, Aubrey."

The tears that had been dammed up since Mariah had died now fell grossly and heavily, until Aubrey's whole body was bent double with sobs. She felt her sisters sit down beside her, their hands on her—her shoulders, her back—the weight of their bodies pushing the old cushions down.

Meggie's voice was soft. "Is Mariah . . . is Mariah gone?"

Bitty must have nodded. Because then, all at once, Aubrey was no longer crying alone. Her sisters were crying with her, holding her even as she cinched bits of their clothes in her fists, even as their elbows and hip bones pressed into her sides.

Outside in the east, the first light—barely a light at all—blistered on the horizon.

5

"A Backward Loop"

The problem, as Ruth Ten Eckye put it to her knitting and reading club at the library and to anyone else who would listen, was that Mr. Scott—the new director of this year's Headless Horseman Extravaganza, who had been brought in from a college theater in Nyack—had no respect for tradition. In the dramatized reading of "The Legend of Sleepy Hollow," a Ten Eckye man had *always*, since as far back as anyone could remember, played the part of Brom Bones.

But this year, the upstart director had the audacity to give the part of Brom to Tony Pignatelli, who—even though he was "a burly, roaring, roystering blade" with a fair amount of "waggish good humor"—would never be able to pull off a convincing Brom. A Ten Eckye boy needed to be the hero of the country round. Not a Pignatelli. Who ever heard of a Dutch *Pignatelli?*

"My poor Todd deserves that part—and Tarrytown deserves for him to have it," Ruth explained to Aubrey on Saturday morning as they stood together in the yarn shop. The rain from yesterday had cleared and the sun was pumping out the last gold dredges of an Indian summer, but Aubrey's mood was gray. Although she'd been knitting in the Stitchery since before she could tie her shoes, she'd rarely had to deal directly with the clients. She sighed.

Ruth leaned an elbow on the counter and narrowed her eyes. "We Ten Eckyes have been in this town long enough to know what you Van Rippers are up to."

"All right," Aubrey said. "So what is it that you'd like?"

"What would I like?" Ruth said. She shook her head in annoyance. "What I would like is for you to knit something that will help my poor Todd!"

Aubrey crossed her arms, considering. Ruth Ten Eckye was the wife and partner of the late Charles Ten Eckye, of the Ten Eckye Center for Culture and Art. The Ten Eckyes owned buildings all over Tarrytown—mostly commercial properties and apartments that the family paid a management company to handle so they would not need to dirty their hands with a task as undignified as collecting rent.

Ruth was viciously judgmental—politically, socially, ecumenically. Ensuring that a Ten Eckye had the corner on Brom Bones probably meant something sacred to her; or at the very least, it bolstered the dominance and visibility of her old patroon bloodline. She had good friends where it mattered and enemies where it suited her. Aubrey had seen Ruth snap at the handicapped boy who bagged her groceries, and she knew that Ruth called the animal shelter the instant, the very instant, she spotted a cat that did not have a collar within fifteen feet of her garage.

And yet Aubrey could find things to like about her. Mariah had told her: *It's wrong to knit for a person you dislike.* Sure, Ruth had been on the board that forced the library to remove all vampire young adult novels from the shelves, but she'd also chaired the committee that kept wreaths on veterans' graves. She practically owned the community food pantry: Tarrytown's homeless ate like royals. She had backbone—and that was something. She cared about her family like a mother wolverine. Ruth, like anyone, had her strong points and weak points—and that, to Aubrey's mind, made her a good enough candidate for a spell.

"Have you talked to Mr. Scott, to tell him how you feel?" Aubrey asked.

"Obviously I tried that," Ruth said.

"What about someone at the school?"

"I talked to everyone. There is simply no other way. Believe me, Aubrey Van Ripper. The Stitchery is my last resort. My very, very last."

It always is, Aubrey thought.

Most people who came to the Stitchery arrived because they'd been following the faint scent of a rumor, the tail end of a last chance. Normally, clients approached timidly and with shy questions that weren't technically questions except for the tone they were spoken in: *Someone told me that these are, um, unique yarns? I heard that you offer a knitting service? I've been having this problem and I was told to see you?*

People came to the Stitchery for help because they had no choice left but to shuck their common sense and dignity to try something completely unbelievable. Aubrey imagined the feeling must have been similar, in terms of desperation, to an adult putting a tooth under her pillow in an effort to help pay her bills.

She pulled her cardigan tighter around her midsection. Light slanted through the window muntins, beams of squared silver bent to the wood floor. The furniture—two wooden stools, the counter, a low wicker coffee table—was dusty gray, the finest film covering all the bulbs of yarn in baskets and the thick hanks of yarn that hung from pegs on the walls. The look on Ruth's face gave the impression that she was counting the minutes until she could leave the Stitchery to go shower off, as if it might somehow contaminate or infect. Certainly Aubrey had every right to turn her out, to say—perhaps with a dose of Ruth's imperiousness thrown in for good measure— *How dare you come into this house while we mourn?* Mariah had not yet been dead for three whole days. The obituary had been published just this morning—probably Ruth would have been horrified to think of herself as intruding if she'd known Mariah had died. It would only take a word to send her away.

But then, Aubrey heard Bitty in the kitchen, rattling around in the cabinets to scrounge up lunch for her kids, asking what kind of house didn't even have ketchup, and she knew it wouldn't hurt if there was a little extra money on hand.

"I'll do it," Aubrey said. "What have you got for me?"

"What have I *got*?"

"What can you give me in exchange for the spell?"

Ruth laughed. "You mean there's not some pricing chart you can pull up?"

"Afraid not."

"What's customary for something like this?" Ruth asked.

"It's *customary* for you to make an offer."

"You do make this difficult, don't you?" Ruth adjusted her purse on her arm. "Two hundred. Cash."

Aubrey laughed. "You're better off trying to bribe Mr. Scott."

Ruth bit her lips, chagrined, and Aubrey resisted the feeling of guilt that flooded her. She'd never liked this part—the bargaining. The push and pull. For as much as Aubrey excelled at the knitting, she'd never been good at playing the role of negotiator. It was a hard role that cast her in a bad light. A little pushiness was always necessary for the success of a spell, and Aubrey had never been good at "pushy." Not like Mariah had been.

"Two hundred dollars," Aubrey said. "If you like. What else?"

"Two hundred dollars is a lot of money."

"Forgive me, but I suspect it's not a lot of money to *you*," Aubrey said, because she knew Ruth Ten Eckye had been squirreling away her family's fortune since the day she was born into it. "What else?"

Ruth blanched. "Five hundred?"

Yes please, Aubrey thought. With five hundred dollars, she could take everyone to dinner at the Tarrytown House. She could pay for the kids to take iPad-guided tours of the Old Dutch churchyard. She could restock the liquor cabinet. But for two hundred or even five hundred bucks, what she couldn't do was guarantee that Todd Ten Eckye would be strutting around Sleepy Hollow come this Halloween in knickers and a tricorn hat. She would need something more important than Ruth's money to ensure the spell would work.

People need to give up something they really and truly care about, Mariah liked to say. *They won't think magic is worth anything if they don't suffer a little for it. And if they don't think it's worth anything, they won't believe, and if they don't believe, the magic will just fester away.*

Aubrey looked over her client—Ruth's beauty-parlor curls, her gold glasses chain, her tiny pearl earrings—all very expensive and yet dated, as if she'd stepped out of 1952. On her long coat was a tin brooch in the shape of a jack-o'-lantern with a twisted grin. Aubrey pointed. "What's that?"

Ruth touched it. "What? This silly thing?"

Aubrey leaned forward. The pin was cheap, a stark contrast with Ruth's expensive pearls and pavé diamond rings. Ruth wouldn't wear such a tawdry thing unless it had some personal meaning. "Where did you get it?"

Ruth's gaze softened, the drooping white skin of her eyelids drooping farther still. "It was a gift from my late husband. He bought it for me at a street fair the week before he died. A year ago on All Saints' Eve." Ruth's eyes clouded over, and for a moment she was no longer in the yarn shop—Aubrey could tell. She was standing on a warm sidewalk in October, her husband still with her, still alive, handing his dollars to the man behind the card table, smiling, fastening a pin on Ruth's lapel.

The rules about sacrifices, about what could be sacrificed and what could not, were a bit perplexing in some ways. Keepsakes had emotional value, and it was generally accepted that meaningful objects were *real* sacrifices; they would stay in the Stitchery tower for as long as the Stitchery was around. Money, however, was a different story. Money was not, except in the rarest cases, considered a meaningful sacrifice; it could always be replaced. A guardian could never suggest to a client that he or she pay for a spell with money, but she could accept money if it was offered to her as a personal—non-magical—gift. This *Render unto Caesar* way of looking at sacrifices had first appeared in the Great Book back in the 1930s, when apparently the guardians needed a little green on hand for personal expenses, and they found that keeping their clients' Jacksons and Lincolns didn't damage their spells—as long as some *real* sacrifice had also been made.

Aubrey steeled herself. "Okay. Two hundred dollars."

Ruth started to open her purse.

"And I'll . . . Oh gosh. I'll also need the pin."

Ruth laughed in disbelief. She looked around as if she expected someone else might be watching. "What? Really?"

Aubrey nodded.

"You can't be serious."

"I'm sorry. I am."

"But . . . but it was a gift. To me. From my husband. I think he might have paid twenty dollars for it at the most!"

"Still," Aubrey said. "If you want the spell to work . . ."

Ruth frowned now, panic in her eyes. Her gloved fingers tightened around the strap of her leather handbag. "A thousand dollars. That's as high as I go. And I keep the pin."

Aubrey wished she could have said yes. She needed the money more than she needed Ruth's cheap pin. But she started to walk away.

"Wait!"

She stopped.

For a moment Ruth held her eye, which must have been uncomfortable. Then, slowly, with trembling fingers, she removed the pin from her lapel. She held it far enough away to see it without the glasses that hung around her neck, and she rubbed the front of it with her gloved thumb. Aubrey could hear the questions turning in Ruth's mind: Was her family's place in the community worth it? Would her husband be mad if somehow, from beyond the grave, he knew? Could she stand to part with the little pin—probably the last gift he gave her before he died?

Aubrey's heart went out to her. She, too, knew the value and pain of tradition. Of a place in the community that trumped personal will.

"I suppose if there's no other way . . ." Gingerly, Ruth set the pin down on the counter. A moment later Aubrey was counting out fifty-dollar bills.

"George would want me to do this," Ruth said under her breath. "It's a family tradition. Every family has its traditions."

"We sure do," Meggie said.

Aubrey jumped—shocked by the sense that she'd been caught doing something wrong. She looked up from the leafy stack of money. Her sister stood leaning one shoulder against the door frame, her short legs slung with bright teal pajama bottoms, her arms crossed and a shoulder raised. Aubrey had no idea how long Meggie had been watching.

"Oh how nice," Ruth said blandly. "Margaret. *You're* back."

"Just like the good old days," Meggie said.

Aubrey touched Ruth's arm. She needed to guide Ruth's focus away from Meggie, who had once, many years ago, pressed her naked butt against the window of a downtown café when Ruth and her husband were inside. "Mrs. Ten Eckye—" Aubrey said loudly. "I think what you need is a nice set of fingerless gloves. A gift for Mr. Scott to wear on chilly fall nights. I have just the thing."

She walked over to an old flour barrel that had been filled with yarn. She plucked one ball off the top—a soft, blue-black skein of wool—and brushed off the dust. The color had bleached in the light over the years, turning a dull slate gray one on side. She held it up for Ruth to see.

"Do *I* have to make them?" Ruth asked. "Because I can, you know."

"Drop by Wednesday morning. I'll have the gloves done by then. And of course, you can't tell anyone about this. If you do, it might break the spell."

Ruth nodded, and Aubrey tried to invoke the same gravitas that Mariah had so often conjured when Aubrey and her sisters were being warned not to play with the things in the tower or pretend the clothes hamper was a snake charmer's basket. She hoped she looked threatening.

"As if I would admit this to anyone," Ruth said.

What Ruth did not know, what she couldn't know, was that Mariah had completely fabricated the notion that telling someone about a spell would break it. *Crowd control*, she'd called it. *The people who are meant to find us will find us. The rest are on their own.*

Meggie spoke from the doorway. "Did you want to warn her about the other thing, too?"

"What other thing?"

"You know, the *other* thing?"

Aubrey blinked. She'd never been very good at dealing with people. She got flustered so easily. She'd thought she'd done an admirable job—until now, until her sister had gotten involved. "Oh, of course. I was getting to that."

"Getting to what?" Ruth asked.

Aubrey cleared her throat. "The magic . . . it might not work."

"Then what did I just pay you for?"

"Clients decide for themselves what they'd like to sacrifice—sometimes with a little, um, encouragement from me, of course. And if you set the price too low for yourself—well—nothing will happen."

Ruth laughed. "So I could have walked in here and offered you nothing but a box of tiddlywinks and you still would have knit the blasted things?"

"I've knit for less," Aubrey said, and she thought of those times that she had knit for trinkets—for a single plastic keychain, for a sun-faded photograph—and her heart had broken for how such great worth lived in small things.

Ruth scowled, a twist of her mouth that made Aubrey wonder if Ruth and her evil-grinning pumpkin pin shared some DNA. "I assume I get a refund if Todd doesn't get the part."

"You know what happens when you assume," Meggie said.

Aubrey shushed her. "No. I'm sorry. No refunds. If you knew you were going to get your payment back, there wouldn't be an emotional risk for you—and the risk is part of what makes a spell work. Magic's about taking a leap of faith."

"No leap, no magic," Meggie said. And Aubrey caught her eye, because that was something Mariah used to say.

Ruth held up a gnarled finger, the point of it poking the air. "You're creepy girls. The lot of you. It's a wonder your whole family hasn't been run out of town." She gathered the pinless lapels of her coat tighter to her neck, glared once more, and left. The Stitchery door whooshed open, letting in a gust of sweet fall air. Then Aubrey was alone with her sister. The room that had seemed small a moment ago now seemed even smaller.

"You know she's going to tell everyone you're a witch," Meggie said.

"Nothing they haven't heard before."

"Come on." Meggie smiled and canted her shoulders toward the kitchen. "Even witches need breakfast."

Aubrey didn't point out that it was lunchtime. She just went.

Excerpt from the *Tarrytown News* obituaries:

Mariah Van Ripper, of Tappan Square, died unexpectedly this Wednesday. She was known locally as a loud voice against the Horseman Woods Commons proposal. She served as president of the Tappan Watch, which recently attempted a campaign to stop the revitalization of Tarrytown's most depressed area. She was known for her love of yarns. Van Ripper is survived by her three nieces, whom she legally adopted, as well as a grandniece and grandnephew. No formal funeral is planned. However, residents are invited to gather at four PM on Monday at Kingsland Point Park to picnic and remember Van Ripper's contributions to the community. Police will be on hand.

The evening fell and Nessa was restless. Carson had abandoned her in favor of looking through his bug book: He was attempting to memorize it in a bid to impress his dorky friends, and so far he was up to *Latrodectus mactans*—and why he couldn't just say *black widow* like everybody else was beyond Nessa. Aubrey had disappeared into her room to knit. Meggie had gone outside, and when Nessa had peeked through the parlor window, she saw her aunt—her aunt who looked like she could have been hanging out with high schoolers—talking to some random guy. Her mother had a chat with her father on the phone in the downstairs hallway, and Nessa had heard enough of it to know that she would be in as good a mood as a hungry alligator for the rest of the night. It had sounded like this: *Of course I wanted you to come to the funeral. Why wouldn't I have wanted you to come to the funeral? Fine then—fine. Don't come.*

And so Nessa was alone. She felt a little like a princess trapped in a castle, except that no one seemed to notice or care what she did, and if she broke out of her confinement tomorrow it would take three days to sound the alarm that she was gone. She lay on Mariah's bed, her heart as heavy as a stone at the bottom of a cold lake. This was what it was like to lie on the bed of a dead woman.

She looked at the picture she'd found on Mariah's dresser, the gold frame gnarled with fruit and garlands and gaudy swags. The photograph within it was taken a long time ago; Nessa could tell by the hilarious 1990s shoulder pads that her mother was wearing. The three girls were standing with Mariah on some giant flat rocks in front of the river, which was so wide that it seemed more like a bay or lake. The picture had gone a little hazy because of the bright sun, faces shining out with unnatural brilliance. Everyone seemed happy enough: Aubrey's smile was cluttered with metal braces, her arms around her sisters, her shoulders so scrawny that her chest seemed concave. Meggie was just a little kid in a confection of pink frills, her head tipped, her grin verging on the ridiculous. Bitty, in her middle teens, was the only one who seemed like she was thinking about posing, about smiling prettily, looking happy instead of just being happy. And Mariah—this had to have been Mariah—was a heavyset woman with a wide, friendly face, wearing a floppy hat and holding some kind of tangle of yarns in her hands.

Nessa put the picture down, frustrated because there were no answers. There *never* were. Why had her mother and her sisters avoided one another for so long? As far as Nessa could tell, a person either belonged to her family, or she didn't. *Halfway* belonging to a family was just faking, which made things even worse for everyone. Her father had only halfway belonged to her mother for years.

She stood and made a lap around the room. At school, her friends—the friends that she'd played tree house with and that she'd chased up the slide—were starting to act different. Her friend Rachelle had smoked a cigarette last week. Her friends Eric and Tammy had made out and let everyone watch. She didn't hang out with Marcus McKerrick, but she heard that he got in trouble for stealing a magazine.

Nessa, on the other hand, was a good kid—maybe not as good as her brother, but still, she was good. She got okayish grades. She didn't talk back to her teachers unless they deserved it. If her mother said she wasn't allowed to watch a movie, she watched it anyway but covered her eyes at the parts with violence or sex. She longed, sometimes, to do something really terrible—even though she had no idea what terrible things she might do and even though she knew in her heart she would never actually do them. All the time, with her mother or alone, she felt like she was wearing a straitjacket, cinched up and tied.

But Mariah's room made her feel better for a little while. It was so *weird:* half bedroom, half museum. On her bookshelf Mariah had everything from poetry collections, to giant books filled with paintings by Monet and Van Gogh, to yellowed romance novels. She ran her hands over the old, odd books, wishing she could have known Mariah better.

She sighed, grew bored and restless again, and closed Mariah's bedroom door behind her. She stood looking out the hall window into the darkness, which seemed like it should have been some pastoral, moonlit hillside and distant river but was instead the close, tight-curtained face of the house next door. She was trying to imagine what she looked like standing at the window—a young maiden imprisoned behind castle walls?—when a sound caught her ear. An odd sound. An unearthly sound, hissy and poppy, a steady steaming. It was so faint she could barely hear it, but it was definitely *there.*

Her mind reached for explanations: Someone had left a TV on, and the cable had gone out, and all that was left was a static hissing. Or someone had forgotten a pot on the stove, the tinny and tinkling noise of a rolling boil with not much water there. The sound was distant and strange—a cross between a demonic whispering and the snap, crackle, and pop of a bowl of cereal. No earthly thing made that sound. No human thing.

Her heart turned to ice. The hair on the back of her neck stood on end. She was paralyzed with fear. Whatever it was, it was downstairs. And Nessa had to make a decision: Which way would she go? Toward the sound? Or away?

She swallowed. Her hands itched. Slowly, as slowly as she could bear, she put her foot on the first step of the long stairway. She leaned her weight forward little by little to muffle the stair's creak. If there was a ghost, she did not want to scare it off. She really wanted to get a picture of it on her cell phone to show her friends. Step by step, she made her way down the stairs. The night air was strange—oddly humid for autumn.

The darkness outside was falling; she could see it through the square windows around the paneled door. A mist had settled, so thick and awful that it seemed to be pressing its face against the front windows and looking in.

Her foot found the ground floor. The sound was coming from the yarn room. The whispering was louder now, the crackle of a soft fire. She lifted her cell phone in its pink rhinestone case, set it to record video. Then, with the same rush of bravery that had helped her jump off the high dive for the first time last summer, she stepped forward until she could peek into the yarn room. It was thick with darkness and whispers. Terrible whispers. The whispers of the dead. She could not focus into the darkness until she had stepped across the doorjamb. It took a moment for her eyes to see, and a moment longer for her brain to understand.

There was fog, the barest tracery of it, *in* the house. Mist clung to the yarns—the buckets and barrels and crates—like a demon guarding its hoard with sinewy arms. And the whispering—the yarn seemed to be whispering. Little consonants, T's, K's, P's, making soft pops. Nessa reached out a hand to grip the door frame, found it was not where she'd expected it to be, and nearly fell.

A voice behind her made her scream.

"What are you doing?" her mother said.

"Holy cheeses!" Nessa skittered around. Her mother was in the hallway, bathed in the yellow light from the bulbs in the ceiling. Her tracksuit was black with two parallel white lines that ran uninterrupted from ankle to armpit. "Mom! Mom! Listen!" Her whisper was hysterical.

Bitty stepped into the yarn room.

"Can you hear it?" Nessa asked. Her blood felt cold. The mist breathed around them.

Bitty put her hands on her hips, taking in the crackling yarns, the mist, with no more fear than a surveyor might exhibit looking over his terrain for the day. Nessa was struck by a bolt of annoyance that her mother could be so nonchalant. But then a deeper worry set in. What if her mother couldn't hear the yarns crackling or see the awful mist? What if only Nessa could? What if she was like one of those innocent kids in movies who gets targeted by the ghosts of angry murder victims?

Then her mother spoke. "Yeah. It's disturbing, right?"

And the whole awful wonderful terrible amazing spell was broken.

"It's a weird thing that happens," her mother said. She might have been talking about algebra or something she saw on TV. "If the atmosphere is just right. The temperature and the humidity and all of that. The fog condenses in the yarns."

"But what about the sounds?" Nessa asked.

"I'm not sure exactly. All the wool is a natural fiber. And it kind of holds moisture, like the ground. Or something. And the fibers flex or stretch and it makes that little noise. I'm not getting this right. Anyway, it's a scientific thing."

Nessa felt her heart sinking. She hadn't realized she would be so disappointed. "I thought it was a ghost."

"Nah." Her mother lifted a rope of Nessa's red hair and moved it behind her shoulder for no apparent reason. "No ghosts in this place."

"Are you sure?"

"Positive," her mother said. And her conviction was so strong, so unwavering, that Nessa immediately felt safer. But also a little sad.

"You should go get your brother," Bitty said. "He'd think this was neat."

"Okay," Nessa said. And she went to the bottom of the stairs, opened her mouth, and bellowed, yelling at the top of her lungs, yelling and yelling with her mother telling her to stop, but she couldn't, not even when Carson appeared, rumpled and perplexed, at the top of the stairs. In a few more minutes, the mist would be gone.

On a chair in her bedroom, Aubrey collapsed, utterly wrung out and spent, sometime in the muddled and forgotten hours that come after midnight but before dawn. Her muscles had cramped. Her head ached. Her eyeballs hurt as if someone had cradled each orb in a fist and squeezed. It was always like this. On her lap were two fingerless gloves. Done.

Ruth Ten Eckye's mitts had formed in her mind long before she'd started knitting them: ribbed two-by-two edging, the stockinette sheath rising up like a tall castle tower, stitch by stitch, brick by brick, the gusset of the thumb—born from an opening like a window—branching seamlessly outward, the tubular crenellations flowering where fingers would poke through to do their work—she'd seen all of it, so that by the time she readied a cable cast-on and had forty-four neat little stitches distributed on four needles squared, the pattern was already firmly entrenched in her subconscious mind, and all she'd needed to do in order to follow it was get out of her own way and let her fingers fly.

Aubrey loved knitting. When she knit for the sake of knitting—and not to make a spell—she enjoyed the work. It was pleasant, satisfying, and soothing. She loved watching her projects grow inch by slow inch, until she could look back on what she'd done and measure how much she'd accomplished. Even if she wasn't knitting a spell, she liked knowing that she'd done her best to keep a positive outlook while she was working and at least a few stitches bore within them her warmest wishes and blessings.

But when she knit a spell—a deliberate, concentrated, focused spell—she was not knitting for the sake of knitting. She was cinching up every last bit of focus and concentration in her mind; she was pouring herself out, wringing herself dry. And it wasn't that she didn't *enjoy* the process on some level. She liked the intensity, the sense that she was being driven forward by some crazed coachman whipping his horses— *faster, faster!*—into a demonic momentum. But when the mêlée ended, when the knitting was done and she felt so vacant that she could sometimes hear the sounds of air particles bumping into one another, she had nothing left. Nothing but the dog-tired optimism that the spell would "stick" as she'd intended.

Now the fingerless gloves were done. And with any luck, with the power of Ruth's sacrifice and Aubrey's concentration, it would work. Slowly, her knees creaking like brittle leather, she stood. She went to the dresser by the window, to the massive, clothbound tome that her family had used for record keeping since 1867. The Great Book in the Hall no longer occupied its original location, but the moniker had stuck—in part because it didn't sound as impressive to call the thing *the Great Book in the Spare Bedroom* or *the Great Book on Aubrey's Dresser*. Like the old Dutch Bibles of farmsteads past, the Stitchery's sacred book moved from room to room over the centuries, but it was never far from a window. If ever a fire were to break out within the Stitchery's dry timber frame, the Great Book could be tossed out to relative safety.

After recording Ruth's name, a description of her sacrifice, and her address—which Aubrey hadn't needed to ask for simply because *everyone* in Tarrytown knew where Ruth Ten

Eckye lived—she plucked up Ruth's pin from the table beside her and carried it reverently, cupped in two hands like a firefly, up the kinked tower stairs. The moment Mariah died, Aubrey had become the Stitchery's official guardian. It was hers now: her burden, her responsibility, her joy. All she could do was hope.

She placed Ruth's pumpkin pin among all the other relics. Then she went downstairs to her bed and fell on it belly-first, too exhausted to take off her clothes.

"Do you think she's happy?" Meggie asked. She and Bitty were stretched out side by side on Meggie's old quilt, their feet hanging off the end of the bed. It was sometime in the middle of the night, but Meggie wasn't tired. She was worried about Aubrey. There were troubling elements of Aubrey's lifestyle that she hadn't quite fully noticed when she'd left the Stitchery four years ago.

"I don't see how she could be happy," Bitty said. "She lives like a hermit."

"She's got a friend. Jeanette seemed cool."

"She's *knows* people," Bitty said. "But she doesn't have a social life. Nothing but her job at the library, and the Stitchery, and the hedgehog. She's cooped up in here all the time. And now that Mariah's gone, it's only going to get worse."

"So what do you think she wants?"

"I don't know." Bitty pulled the long end of her ponytail in front of her face and squinted at the ends. "Maybe she thinks it doesn't matter what she wants."

"I guess I can understand what that's like," Meggie said. And she paused, but her sister was lost in thought and didn't ask what she meant. "If she stays here . . ."

"I know," Bitty said. "It's dangerous."

They fell quiet, and Meggie knew they were both thinking of their mother.

"We have to respect her choices," Bitty said. "We can't save her if she doesn't want us to."

"Still," Meggie said. "We have to try."

From the Great Book in the Hall: *Where does the urge to create come from? Children will doodle a smiley face on a friend's shoe. Mothers will braid their daughters' hair. Fathers will teach their sons to use a jigsaw, or paintbrush, or awl. The impulse to create is a gift and a blessing. But take care that it does not become corrupted. There is a line between passion and obsession, between seeing and thinking you see.*

6

"Kitchener Stitch"

It was no stretch of imagination for the people of Tarrytown and Sleepy Hollow to believe in magic. From the beginning, they always had. Native people gathered around the big Hokohongus tree for decades, even centuries, during council meetings. The enslaved Kongolese men and women of Philipse Manor held that the mucky waters of the Pocantico were a boundary line between this world and the next. Even the old burgher Frederick Philipse, staunchly Dutch Reformed, had seen his share of the unbelievable.

As legend goes, he'd just started construction on the Old Dutch Church—his slaves quarrying rock and mixing mortar—when a freshet flooded his millpond. The dam crumbled and water sluiced through the vale. Philipse pulled the plug on the church's construction to stop up the pond, and when the water was behaving subserviently once again, the slaves returned to the church on the grassy mound—heaving its fieldstone walls higher and higher toward God and the big valley sky.

But once again, the millpond blew its dam. And once again, the church construction was halted. Repeatedly this happened. Rupture, pause. Rupture, pause. Until finally, one of Philipse's slaves pulled his master aside to tell him that God had sent him a dream. Until the Old Dutch Church—

which was of course the *new* Dutch church at the time—was overflowing with people and prayer, the dam would never hold. And sure enough, once the little chapel was up and running, the millpond did not burst again.

At least, that's how the old folks told it—a story unchanged since 1697, when wolves still howled by night in the wooded hillsides of Manhattan, when the Weckquaesgeck hunted beaver in exchange for teakettles and guns, and when mast-thick forests were still dotted with healthy American chestnuts.

But the story of the Stitchery was not so firmly fixed in people's minds as the story of the Old Dutch Church. Nor was it so cheery. Some people had heard that the Van Ripper house was haunted by a girl with yellow braids, a pointy white-winged hat, and little wooden *klompen* on her feet. But more than likely, the true story of the Stitchery—if such a thing existed—was the story that the Van Rippers told one another, a tale passed down from generation to generation, guarded like the treasure in the tower room. And like so many stories that are meant to explain things, that come sifting down through the ages like falling snow, the story of the Stitchery was a love story, a magical one.

On fall evenings when the river was a placid brown-gray and the Palisades were at stone-faced attention, Mariah bundled the girls into her bed—*my three little birds*, she called them—and told the story of the Stitchery's beginnings. It was important, she said, that they always remember where they came from. For the Van Rippers, the Stitchery was at the heart of every decision they would ever make, whether they liked it or not. A person's future could branch into infinite directions and redirections, but her past always had the same, reliable beginning point.

And so, the story started the way so many do: *Once upon a*

time. Back when the Stitchery was born, Mariah said, the Hudson Valley was a battleground. It echoed with the sounds of camp songs, drillmasters' orders, and gunfire. The summer of 1779 was hot, smelling of pond scum, boiled potatoes, and lightning. The Headless Hessian of Sleepy Hollow was scratching behind his ear and complaining about lice, with no notion of how he would go down in history. George Washington was stooping nightly over his maps and his Madeira and halfheartedly daydreaming about Sally Fairfax, who was perfect except for being a loyalist's wife. The women of the Revolution camped not far from their husbands, boiling the laundry, knitting stockings for men who could wear out a pair a day, and twirling their drop spindles to make strong flax thread.

Helen Van Ripper, whose maiden name had been buried by time, was among them. She lived in a tent near the army encampment so that she could be with the husband she had married only a few months before. Helen was young and strong; she had predictable blond hair beneath the flaps of her Dutch cap, but her fondness for a sweet *koekie* or two each evening lent her a bit of stylish plumpness beneath her chin. Every day she woke to the hot summer sun, the chirp of crickets and clatter of locusts, the cardinals whooping and blackbirds chirring in the trees, and she wondered if today she would be widowed.

One day a sentry rushed to General Washington's side with news that a line of lobsterbacks were marching on the camp. He saw them across the distant clearing, their bright red coats flapping in time to an inaudible fife and drum. Alarms were raised. Muskets and rifles were made ready. But when Washington himself laid his gray-blue eyes upon the line of advancing redcoats, he was said to have given the watchman a look of such steely disapproval that it momentarily turned the child to clay. The fearsome invading soldiers were nothing more than the women's knit red petticoats, hung across a line to dry. It had been a moment of mirth for Helen and her fellow wives.

So you see, Mariah told the girls, *this is what life felt like when the men were not fighting. But there was always the specter of tragedy looming over them all.*

The valley was dark with the shadow of death, and the soldiers ate and drank and slept with the weight of it pressing their chests. British forces had taken up residence not far away, at a rocky outcropping on the Hudson called Stony Point. Their intention was to push north up the river: If they took the Hudson, they took the Northeast.

Helen's husband came to her while the cicadas were giving their evening concert and the sky had softened to a pretty pink. He had red-brown locks that had been passed down to him from some northern bloodline, gray irises, and a mangled left ear from a childhood skirmish with a feral dog. That evening, there was a wild, dagger-sharp gleam in his eye. Helen listened, not looking up from her knitting, while he told her what he was not supposed to have told her—the plan. The daring, terrible, and completely mad plan to take Stony Point.

The fort, as everyone knew, was impregnable. To the west was a murky swamp that festered like a moat, and land that was marked by sharpened timbers, trenches, earthworks, and a squadron of cannons. Along the river were rocky cliffs, and in the waters below, the British sloop-of-war *Vulture* waited for easy pickings.

And yet, despite the probable failure of any plan of attack, General Anthony Wayne intended to attempt the impossible: to take Stony Point with 1,350 men. The strategy was deceiving: Two companies of Carolinians would stage a direct and distracting barrage, while the real attack would come in stealthily from the sides. To ensure perfect silence, the troops would not be permitted to load their muskets—they would advance with only their empty guns and their bayonets. Some of the men, brave soldiers specially chosen for the honor, would lead the midnight advances. The vanguard would wade through the muck of swamp and scale the steep and rocky slopes; then, once they penetrated the fort, they were to begin brandishing their empty weapons above their heads, yelling like bedlam, *The fort's our own! The fort's our own!* whether it was their own or not. The men had a nickname: the Forlorn Hope.

Helen's husband spoke of the advance with such pride and boyish excitement that her heart sank deeper and deeper with each glorious new description. Even before he told her, she knew: Her husband, who still had a boy's youthful grin and leggy build, had volunteered to be among them. *He* was the Forlorn Hope.

She pulled him into the semi-privacy of a copse of paper birches that cut white slashes against the dusk. With soft green leaves shimmering around them, she gave her husband a piece of her mind. It was the first time she had ever raised her voice to him.

What were you thinking? she told him. She did not need a husband who was a war hero. She needed a husband who was alive. Now more so than ever. Her heart felt as if a hundred little fissures were running through it, like the red clay rocks that washed up along the creek beds, and one small but precise tap would make the whole thing shatter. Why couldn't her husband have spoken with her first? She was a good Dutch woman, groomed to be the head of her home, not some Anglican church mouse too fearful to so much as whimper should her husband raise a fist. He was not to make such decisions without consulting her.

To his credit, her husband looked contrite, like a child who had expected praise but instead found censure. And the heart in Helen's chest that had been struggling to stay in one piece crumbled to bits. She began to cry. Her husband put his arms around her and rocked her, while a gentle breeze stirred the birch leaves to expose their undersides to the sky.

And there's more, Helen said, teary. She had not wanted to tell him. Not until she was sure. But her courses had not come in many weeks. And she suspected she was carrying their first child. Her husband gathered her tighter, and while on another occasion he might have whooped with joy and loaded his rifle to fire a few celebratory rounds, tonight he only whispered some prayerful words and kissed her ear beneath her cap.

So you see, Helen said. *You must come back to me. You must return alive.*

Her husband consoled her with assurances and brushed her tears from her face. He promised he would come to no harm. But Helen knew that while a man could make such promises, he had no say over whether he could keep them. Especially not if he was under orders to storm a fort full of trained soldiers without a single bullet to his name.

The night before the raid on Stony Point, Helen and the war-battered women she had come to call friends convened. Helen was not the only one who was afraid of slaughter. Many of the women who were with her had men—husbands, brothers, fathers—marching to their deaths at Stony Point. But only Helen's man was among the forlorn. Desperation drove her to panic. What could she do?

She told the women who were with her about an old folktale, and as she told it, she began to wonder if she might believe it. Her grandmother on her father's side had always knit one red thread into her husband's garments to protect him.

And she had liked to say that no one ever took her charms seriously until one day her husband went out with a June hunting party and was attacked by a band of angry Mohawks. Only he returned with his scalp affixed to his head.

Helen did not need to explain what she was proposing to the women of the camp—her own mad plan to match the general's. The women were not entirely convinced. But they were helpless enough to try.

In the hazy dark, fat-soaked cattails were touched to the cooking coals and coaxed into sputtering, stinky light. The women sat in a circle and they knit round after round, the smell of wool and smoke and sweet summer greenness in the air. Bored watchmen appeared in the quietest hours, prodded for conversation, and—finding none—went on their way. Red threads were pulled from petticoats and passed around. A woman suggested: *Perhaps we should make an offering. Just in case.* And each wife, sister, or daughter agreed to give up something important to her—just so God knew they weren't asking to get something for nothing. Helen wove a red thread into her husband's stocking and bowed her head, her prayers taking shape in the low Dutch of her parents and their parents before them: *Oh God in heaven. I'll do whatever you want. Just don't take him away from me so soon.* She knew she had to offer something more than prayers.

When it came time to head out to meet their destiny, some men went to Stony Point with new stockings on their feet— red fibers woven within—and some did not. Helen made her husband promise not to take his stockings off, not for anything. Then she kissed him good-bye as if they were in private, as if she might never kiss him again. With a crooked smile and a slouch that meant she should not worry, he turned his back and was gone. All of General Wayne's men were. The women stewed in the twilight of the valley, knitting and darning. Helen's worry was like the itch of the poison ivy pustules that sometimes ringed her ankles, and the more she scratched at it the worse it seemed to get. She lurked away from the fire, away from the other women, and sipped a bitter tisane of wild carrot. She worried that her sacrifice would not be accepted.

But—soon enough—promising news arrived. And then—even better—her husband returned. All the men who bore red-flecked stockings returned. Helen threw her arms around her husband and cried with relief. He smelled of river water and rifle oil and sweat, and she buried her face in the rasp of his homespun shirt. Her husband declared that the plan to take Stony Point had gone off in near perfection. Mad Anthony Wayne was a genius, the Forlorn Hope would go down in history, and best of all Helen and her husband were rich.

He held her by the shoulders, his eyes bright with reflections of fire and his own proud tears. There was a prize, he told her, for the first man to reach the fort—and he won it! He'd waded through the swamp with his rifle high and silent and empty over his head, and he'd pictured her—only her—and the life they would have if he could swallow his fear and win. He told her: Now they could buy that bit of land in Tarrytown. They could build a house on the ridge overlooking the river. He pressed his hands against the small of her back. They could raise their baby on land they themselves owned.

Helen hung her head. The sluggish dawn of guilt and dread was like a dark river swallowing its banks, a slow, thick flooding.

What is it? her husband asked.

She pulled herself up straight and told him: *I'm so sorry.*

His grip on her shoulders slackened.

She said: *Oh my love. There never was a child.* She explained with her palms facing the sky that she would have said anything—*anything*—to compel him to return to her safely, to fight to save his life. She hoped he could forgive her. She trembled, waiting, believing in the folklore, in her grandmother, in her prayers, in anything she could get her hands on to believe.

He blinked once, slow and dumb like an old cow, before breaking into laughter. The sound was a volley of cannon fire. So full of trickery was his little wife. They would just have to try again. He lifted her and kissed her and swung her around.

The end, Mariah said. And the spell of the Revolution encampment cleared like the last hiss of smoke from a doused fire. Then she tucked each girl into her own bed with her own kiss and a wish to sleep tight and don't let the bedbugs bite. Outside, the hills of the lower valley were bright with neon and traffic and the noise of human life, and it was a great comfort to the Van Ripper girls.

For in the silence, the terrible and threatening silence, was the rest of the story—the parts that Mariah had alluded to only in passing over the years. The end of the story, the real end, was told only in little dribs and drabs, like spots of paint laid at random on a canvas until with squinting and head-angling the full picture began to come into view.

With the money Helen's husband had won at Stony Point, the Stitchery was built on the edge of a grassy square in Tarrytown. Helen's husband became a trusted secretary to a lawyer who treated him less like an employee than a good friend. Her sons were born and raised, sent off into the world to marry, or sent off to sea or war. Her only daughter, who had a birthmark in the exact shape of a star on her cheek, was taught how to knit. One night when her children were grown and on their own, and Helen's hair had grayed, and people were whispering of a war between the North and South, her husband drifted out of life quietly and with no warning, falling into sleep within sleep. Helen donned her widow's weeds, sad but grateful for everything she'd had. She watched herself grow old in the family's black-spotted mirror, which had come down to her from two generations past.

With no husband and no children who needed her, she threw her life's focus into her knitting, so that eventually the people of Tarrytown began to refer to her home as the Stitchery. Women came to her door, women who had dirt under their fingernails and women who had never washed so much as a teacup in their lives. They heard rumors; they heard she could help. She asked them: *What are you willing to give up?* and she hid their treasures away. She continued to thrive—until one chilly day in October, when the winds blew down from the north so hard that the candle she had placed on the windowsill was snuffed out.

Helen's daughter, who had been taught her mother's secret of knitting, was in the kitchen boiling soup at their newfangled iron stove when she heard her mother shriek. The sound was unnatural. She hurried to the parlor. And she found Helen staring in mortal terror at nothing more than the wall. Her hands were motionless on her needles. Her eyes, milky with cataracts, were unseeing.

What is it? her daughter asked. But Helen would not speak. There were devils in the wallpaper, in the bread box, under the doors. Sometimes they were soldiers; sometimes, babies. She cried out against them; she threw the furniture to keep them away. Her daughter gently coaxed her back into the world of the living with cups of strong black coffee. But day by day, Helen became increasingly confused, increasingly tormented, as if demons were reaching their claws up from hell itself to drag her soul down through the Stitchery floorboards. People began to whisper. Her daughter fought to keep her mother out of the madhouse and in her prayers asked the Lord for the mercy of a swift and quiet death.

For the women of the Stitchery, this was the beginning of the end.

7

"K3tog"

Aubrey had not been expecting Vic Oliveira at her door on the morning of Mariah's funeral, although it was not all that unusual for him to appear there. He and Mariah had become good friends since he'd first moved to Tarrytown a few months ago, and he'd fallen into the role of being the Stitchery's go-to handyman. He often stopped by to caulk, nail, screw, grease, lift, wedge, and jury-rig as needed. When Aubrey saw him standing on the porch, in nice pants and a black dress shirt, gripping a handful of late-blooming sunflowers, a little fissure of longing opened along a seam in her heart.

"How are you holding up?" Vic asked.

"Great!" she said, so belligerently cheerful that it took them both aback. Then, because she realized that niceties weren't called for at a time like this, she told him the truth: "Actually, you know how a piece of celery gets when it's been in the fridge too long?"

"Yes?"

"I feel like that."

"I wish I could fix this for you," Vic said. "But even duct tape has its limits."

He held out the flowers and she took them. Sunflowers were perfect for Mariah, who had always hated "funeral flow-

ers" like carnations and lilies and roses that were too serious
for their own good. Vic must have known.

"I've been thinking of you," he said. "If there's anything I
can do to help . . ."

"That's kind." She risked a quick glance at his face; she
knew her eyes were awful to look at—alien and strange. But
she wanted to see him, just for a second, before she looked
away.

"I mean it," he said. "Whatever you need." Peals of laughter
rang from inside the Stitchery, filling it up like sound caught
in a bell. Vic glanced over Aubrey's shoulder. "Am I interrupting?"

"No. Not really."

"May I come in?"

In the living room, which might have been a dining room
for an earlier generation, Bitty had fired up her laptop because
Mariah's old TV set didn't play DVDs. She had put on a
movie for her children—something light and fun because
they all knew it was going to be a difficult day. Meggie was
holed up somewhere in the house by herself, doing whatever
it was she did when she was alone. Aubrey looked at Vic—his
long arms, his wide, high chest—and she felt suddenly, deeply
selfish. She told him: "Let's just sit on the porch swing awhile."

She closed the front door behind her. They sat together on
the weathered gray wood of the swing, Aubrey with the sunflowers sideways across her black skirt, Vic with a manila
folder ominously resting on his thighs. Aubrey's palms were
sweaty; her heart was fluttering—actually fluttering, beating
itself against her rib cage like a bug flying into a window again
and again. She took a deep breath to steady herself. Vic always did this to her, even though he was not actually doing
anything at all.

"I'm sorry to bring this up before the funeral," Vic said. "I wish it could have waited."

"Bring what up?"

"Your sisters are here?"

"Yes."

"Mariah said they might show up—you know—if something ever happened to her. I wanted to catch you while they're around."

Aubrey nodded toward his folder. "What is that?"

"Mariah's Last Will and Testament."

"Oh. I have a copy, too, in my bedroom."

"No, you don't." She was surprised when he put an arm around her shoulders. "This is a new will. She asked me to hold on to it. Actually . . . she made me the executor."

"You?" Aubrey asked. She didn't think Vic was lying to her—he didn't seem the type who would lie—and yet, she couldn't believe him. She was having trouble not thinking about the crook of his elbow, bare against the back of her neck. "Why you?"

"It's about the property. Mariah's got some things in her will that are a little—I don't know—a little *Mariah*." He was looking at the house across the street, with its hemorrhaging old sofa and broken baby crib left out by the curb. When his gaze turned to Aubrey's face, his look was grave. "We need to call your sisters together," he said.

Aubrey had first met Vic when she was on her lunch break at the library, listening to Jeanette chronicle the latest books that she'd mis-shelved, dooming them to literary purgatory because they were sexist or racist. Aubrey was mid-swallow when Mariah had marched unannounced into the privacy of the librarian break room with Vic on her arm and a grin the size of a half-moon on her face. Vic was a good foot taller than

Mariah and half her width and age. She had her elbow linked with his as if he were in a tux and she, a ball gown.

"Aubrey, I want you to meet our new neighbor," she said. "He bought a house in Tappan Square. He's Brazilian."

"Actually, I'm from Queens."

"But Brazil is in your blood! Oh, you *must* say your name for them, Victor. You pronounce it so much more beautifully than I. The way you say it is like a song."

With impressive showmanship, Vic complied. His full name was *Victor José Carlos Oliveira*. Aubrey put down her PB&J.

"I found him on the library lawn just now," Mariah said, her voice touched with giddiness. "He wants to pick out some children's books to read with his niece. Isn't that sweet? And I told him: Nobody could take better care of him than you, Aubrey. I'm sure of it."

Aubrey thought she may have blushed—not because of Mariah's compliment, but because the message of her chronic singleness could not have been declared more clearly than if Mariah had trumpeted it through the speakers at the ball field.

During her early twenties, when she'd still been making attempts at dating and romance, Aubrey had tried to cultivate her own brand of "library sexy." After all, what man didn't have a fantasy about a hot young librarian? In glossy magazines— the kind on the newsstands and the kind that came in opaque plastic sleeves—librarians were pure desire. Something about bare, glistening bodies clashing with the dusty sterility of old books. Something about erudite women spending cloistered hours in rigid lucubration—only to let down their hair and inadvertently pop a button between their breasts.

But alas, Aubrey was shy, awkward, and practical to a fault.

Her hair was a non-event, and her eyes were a natural disaster. Her feet hurt her from standing so she wore orthopedic shoes because they were more comfortable. She shopped at the thrift store because she saw no reason to pay full price for things and because, to a certain extent, she didn't mind when people looked through her. In the library break room, with Vic standing there so tall and built, she'd never felt more librarian-y in her life—as sexy as a set of recently outdated encyclopedias.

But Jeanette apparently shared none of her misgivings.

"I saw him first," she said.

From that day forward, Vic had started showing up regularly. Sometimes, Aubrey arrived for her afternoon shift to find him sitting on a bright beanbag chair in the children's section, his knees up to his ears and books splayed at his feet. With her hip bones pressing against the circulation desk and Vic standing on the other side, they talked about what books his niece might like, what books *he* might like—he preferred biographies and memoirs—and to her surprise, he even asked what books she liked.

"Oh, I read all kinds of books," she'd told him. "But I guess I like the soft kind the best. The ones that, when you close them, leave your heart feeling like your stomach if you just ate a big meal." And then she'd felt embarrassed, because Vic looked at her as if she'd sprouted a third eye, because good readers were supposed to like much different kinds of books, and because she could never say or do anything right when it came to men, especially ones who weren't afraid of looking at her face when she spoke and who were tall and narrow like a Popsicle on a hot day.

Still, despite her heightened awkwardness and self-consciousness when Vic appeared, she anticipated his visits—to the library or the house. Sometimes, she *lived* for them.

Once, she broke the clothes bar in the hall closet just so Mariah would call him to come fix it. But inevitably, when he got to the Stitchery, his tool belt slung around his hips, Aubrey said the wrong thing, did the wrong thing, and rather than embarrass herself by hanging around him like a lovesick puppy, she usually just excused herself to her bedroom once his work began.

She had considered knitting for him. It would be so easy. She would use a hand-painted alpaca yarn, something variegated with colors that shifted subtly and smoothly, and she would knit him a scarf, horizontally, in linen stitch. It would be a project that would take a good amount of time, one that she could saturate and stuff full of all her most wicked fantasies. Then, *I thought you could use this*, she might say.

But she knew better than to try it. The repercussions of her hand-knit on Vic's body—whether the spell worked or whether it didn't—were too complicated to bear. Plus, Mariah had always discouraged her from knitting spells that were solely for her own benefit; such spells were notoriously unreliable, clogged up by personal baggage. There was an unwritten rule that guardians did not knit for themselves.

Now Aubrey was leading Vic into the Stitchery to hear whatever it was he needed to say. She'd always known that Mariah had a certain fondness for Vic and that she'd never given up her stubborn hope that someday he and Aubrey might, well, *might*. But Aubrey was shocked to learn that Vic had been given some kind of instructions in the event of Mariah's death. Mariah had never mentioned a change to her will.

At her back, Aubrey could sense Vic's tallness, his slimness, the different way that he and she each moved through space. Meggie was tromping down the long stairs in the hallway, still in her pajamas, and her fairy's face lit with curiosity.

"Oh, hello. I didn't know we were expecting company," Meggie said.

Aubrey told Meggie to follow her and for once Meggie did not offer even the slightest back talk or smart-ass reply. Meggie gestured for Vic to go before her, and he did—with some awkwardness—so that Aubrey worried about whether or not Meggie was checking out his butt. She trailed them into the living room, where the computer speakers were blaring cartoon mayhem and Bitty was busy trying to keep her son and daughter from bickering by joining in the bickering herself.

"Guys?" Aubrey said. She set the flowers on the table. "Hello? Guys?" Her family quieted, not because of her call for their attention but because the Stitchery was not historically known for visitations from young, handsome men. "This is Vic. He lives a few blocks over. Vic—" She began to point. "This is Meggie, Bitty, and her kids, Nessa and Carson."

"Pleased to meet you," Vic said. "Mariah talked about you all so much."

Bitty told Carson to turn down the speakers. Then she stood up from the couch and gracefully held out her hand. Her rings flashed white and gold. From the way she smiled—so smoothly, with just a touch of exquisite mourning—Aubrey half wondered if she didn't expect Vic to kiss her hand. "You were close with Mariah?"

"She was a good friend," Vic said.

Meggie laughed and dropped into an armchair. "Something tells me you weren't a member of her Red Hat Ladies or whatever."

"I have to draw the line somewhere."

"Shame. I bet you look delicious in red," Meggie said.

"So, when did you and Mariah first become *good friends*?" Bitty said.

"Hey—" Aubrey choked on her spit. Vic made a little noise

of surprise and patted her back. She could feel her face turning bright with embarrassment, partly from the saliva, and partly because she knew what her sisters were thinking. It was far more reasonable that Vic hung around the Stitchery because he was interested in Mariah than because of Aubrey. Even though Mariah was older and a bit overweight, nobody would have been surprised if she had nabbed herself a younger man.

"Vic's been helping us out with repairs. He's been great to Mariah. And me. He's also been great to—um—me."

Vic gave a nervous noise like a laugh.

"So you're coming to the funeral picnic this afternoon?" Meggie asked.

"Wouldn't miss it."

Aubrey stepped forward for no reason except that she thought she should. She was sure Vic was counting the moments before he could get out of the Stitchery, and she wanted to rescue him. "Mariah made Vic his executor. He has a copy of the will he wants to show us."

"He can show it to us if he wants to," Bitty said. "But we already know everything goes to Aubrey. That's been obvious ever since—" She stopped herself.

"Since we were kids," Meggie said.

Aubrey could feel Vic looking at her, and so she looked away. When she was thirteen, adolescence had brought pimples, blood, breasts, and the deepening and sharpening of her eyes until they were a freakish, pricking blue. And now, with Vic beside her and her sisters scrutinizing her for clues, she felt thirteen again.

"I should probably read this," Vic said, and from the folder he drew a purple envelope that had been sealed with a fat red blot of old-fashioned wax. "Aloud. So you can all hear it at once."

"Of course," Aubrey said. "Go ahead."

He turned to her more fully now, and she couldn't help but look back for as long as she dared. She loved his face—his olive skin, the two little bumps of his cheekbones, his long nose, his thick brow bone that crossed between his temples like an old summer beam, and his eyes, the color of an almond's papery skin. He put his hand on her shoulder, gave a small squeeze. "I think it would be best if you sat down."

Dear Girls,

I don't really believe I'm seventy-nine. I thought being seventy-nine would have a seventy-nine-ish feeling—like old age would settle into my bones and make me feel as different as I look, what with all these new sags and folds and lumps that I didn't have twenty years ago. But even though I'm not feeling seventy-nine, it turns out I am.

Of course, if you're reading this, there's been a death in the family (mine) and I'm sorry for your loss. I can only hope I went out like a Roman candle on the Fourth of July— that death was fast and not very long and drawn out. I always did like the idea of death by lightning—Beam me up, God!

But if it dragged out, if it inconvenienced you much, I'm sorry. I shudder to think of the things I might say, the things I might do, if the Madness took hold.

I've spoken to Vic—there's a formal version of all this— legal and notarized and not worth the fortune it cost me to have it drawn up. But I thought you all deserved an explanation about the changes I've made—instead of hearing it from some old pinhead lawyer. Better it comes from the Old Mare's mouth (and yes, Meggie, I did know you called me that—hilarious, really, I didn't mind).

Here's what it is:

I'm not leaving the Stitchery to Aubrey. (Quick! Everyone gasp!)

Nope. I'm not leaving it to her. I'm leaving it to all of you, share and share alike. But there are conditions.

Your interest in the property, the house, and all my goods and chattel (isn't that a funny word?) is nontransferable within the family. You can't sell or transfer your individual shares to each other or to anyone else. If you want to sell this property, you must all agree to sell it to a third party. If one of you holds out, no sale.

And if you don't sell it, then you all must not sell it together—if that makes sense. Bitty and Meggie, you're good people, good sisters. Aubrey will need seeing to now that I'm gone. She's a menace in the kitchen—ask her about the time she put the microwave dinner tray in the oven—and if you don't watch her she'll eat spicy dragon rolls for three meals a day. She must not be allowed to listen to so many of those gloomy singer-songwriter records; that's a nervous breakdown waiting to happen. And the coffee! Dear God, the coffee! A woman can only drink so much coffee a day before her face starts looking like a bean!

I know. I know. I'm being a goof. But when a person dies, a smidge of silliness about it is absolutely necessary. You know—a little nonsense now and then.

In all seriousness, Bit and Meg, Aubrey will need your support in her new role as the guardian of the Stitchery. If there's such a thing as worry in the afterlife, she'll be what I'm worrying about most. She needs you. And if I know anything about anything, you need her, too.

This is my Last Will: that you girls come together again and be like you used to be, here—in the Stitchery—which is not so bad a place for a family to be.

And here is my Last Testament: I loved you—all and each—so much. I loved you, Meggie, for your mouthing off and for your ability to fully embrace and become all the many people that one person can be over the course of a life.

I loved you, Bitty, for the strength of your will and your uncompromising commitment to what you feel is right—even for the fact that you kept your kids away from the Stitchery, because you meant well, though it's not really the Stitchery that's dangerous when all's said and done.

And I loved you, Aubrey, for your sense of duty and your good, good heart. You were my role model—I know, funny to say that. But you were. Don't worry too much about the Stitchery. You already know everything you need to know; you'll do fine. The Great Book in the Hall will answer your questions if there's something I haven't told you already. And your core intuition, if you heed it without judgment, will never be wrong.

I want what's best for you, darling, whatever that may be. You and your sisters will discover what that is. And if happiness means giving up the Stitchery, then so be it. But I'm betting the farm that it won't come to that. I hope that you'll fight for the Stitchery and for Tappan Square as I have fought for it. I caution you to never be complacent about your battles. You are the music makers, you are the dreamers of dreams.

Be nice to one another. Build one another up. Hold one another's yarn.

How much do I love you?

Your Aunt Mariah

There is a sign among knitters, among women in a house of knitters: palms facing, fingers flattened, hands apart. This is a position familiar to anyone who has ever sat for hours on end, patient, still, holding a loose hank of yarn suspended between two hands while another person winds it tight. Of course, these days a hank can be turned into a practical little ball with an umbrella swift and ball winder in no time, so that the fibers won't knot while they're knit. But the old way—to ask *Will you hold this for me?*—is a rite of passage. Daughters still sit for mothers, mothers for grandmothers, committed to the fraught place where a mind can be both simultaneously drifting and pinched down, until their arms begin to ache and the circle of yarn begins to feel as heavy as a barrel hoop, until the tail end slips away and the task is done.

Once, in the days before Aubrey and her sisters were taken out of school, Aubrey had belly-flopped on stage during the third-grade production of *Rip Van Winkle*—tripped on the inflamed strata of her tulle skirts as she walked up the stairs—and the audience had laughed. The sting of shame was much worse than that of her purpling shin. She scanned the shadows of audience until she saw Mariah, who was looking at her, smiling—and holding her hands apart just so. *How much do I love you?* Mariah had said that God made all things possible, and that when she made the sign, palms apart, extended as if to say *This big,* she held the whole world there, just *there*—in the space between her hands.

Aubrey could not hold back her tears. Vic handed her a tissue that he'd pulled from the mantel. He leaned over her where she sat on the couch. "You okay?"

She dabbed at her cheeks. "I'm . . . surprised," she said. She didn't mention that she also felt a little hurt that Mariah had kept secrets from her. She figured that was a given.

Bitty stood and snapped her arm toward Vic, palm up. When she spoke, it merely sounded like she was asking a question. "Can I see that?"

"Sure."

She stood reading in silence, her brow furrowed. Meggie moved to peer over Bitty's shoulder. In black from head to toe, she might have been her sister's shadow.

"I don't get it," Nessa said. "What's it mean?"

Carson sighed with the gravitas of a fifty-year-old man. "It means they have to *all* sell the house to somebody else, or they *all* have to keep it and live in it together."

"No it doesn't," Nessa said. "Aunt Aubrey can stay here even if Mom and Aunt Meggie don't want to sell. Right? Right, Mom?"

"She could," Vic said. "But that's not what Mariah wanted."

"So—what? She expects us to all stay here? Like she can micromanage our lives even from beyond the grave?" Meggie said.

Bitty shook Mariah's letter in the air. "I can't believe this. This is ridiculous."

Aubrey pulled herself together—tamping down all her hurt, her wondering if she perhaps didn't *deserve* the Stitchery, if she'd done something to offend her aunt, if she just wasn't worthy. From the time she was a teenager, she'd been told that the Stitchery had *chosen* her and that she would one day own it. Mariah's muddling of the laws of the outside world with the laws inside the Stitchery seemed sacrilegious. Aubrey felt as if she'd had the floor pulled out from under her—as opposed to just the rug.

But she got herself together.

"Nessa's right," she said to her sisters. "Really, this doesn't change anything. After the funeral you guys can head back to your respective homes, and I'll stay on. Just like always. Then, when I die, the three of us can will it to the next"—she glanced at Vic, she didn't know how much Mariah had told him—"person. Easy as that."

For a moment, the room was quiet.

"Maybe it's not *easy as that*," Meggie said.

Bitty put the letter down on the coffee table.

Aubrey saw her sisters exchange looks, and her heart in her chest beat so loudly that she thought Vic might have heard. She steeled herself. "Are you guys saying you might actually want to *sell* the Stitchery?"

Her sisters didn't answer.

Aubrey got to her feet. "That's not what Mariah wanted."

"Mariah wanted you to be happy," Meggie said softly. "She told us to take care of you. She said so herself."

"And that's what we want, too," Bitty said.

Vic cleared his throat. "Excuse me. But—I'm thinking maybe I should go."

"Don't go," Aubrey said, and much to her embarrassment, her hand shot out to him. She drew back. "I mean, you don't have to stay. But you can if you want."

His gaze firmed. "As long as you need me, I'll stay."

Meggie pulled her attention away. "Aubrey, we're not attacking you. We don't mean it to sound like we're ganging up. But you can't stay here. It was marginally okay that you lived here while Mariah was around. But now it's totally un-okay."

"Says who?"

"It's not healthy," Meggie said. "Your being alone all the time. The Stitchery's holding you back."

"And besides," Bitty said, "isn't the place supposed to be bulldozed anyway?"

"Our whole neighborhood is," Vic said. "To make room for the shopping mall."

Bitty's tone softened. "I'm sorry for that. I really am. But the point *for Aubrey* is that even if she does cling to the Stitchery, she might lose it anyway."

"No!" Aubrey said. "Mariah hasn't been gone a week, and

already you guys want to sell off everything she owns." She pushed her hair from her face and tried to tamp her anger. "Is this . . . is this a money thing? I mean—if it is, we'll talk about it. We'll figure it out."

"I am *not* desperate for money," Bitty said stiffly.

"I am," Meggie said, snorting a little. "And the junk in the tower alone could pay my bills for years."

"You shouldn't call it *junk,*" Aubrey said.

She balled her hands into fists at her sides. Part of the particular torture of living in the Stitchery was knowing that life would never really be comfortable on the income of a part-time librarian and part-time knitter. The Stitchery did not do a big business. It never had. Many times, Aubrey had seen Mariah knit difficult projects that required days of concentration to pull off big, important spells—in exchange for nothing more than a pack of beat-up trading cards. It was the equivalent of swapping the wondrous magic beans for a dried-up old cow, as opposed to the other way around. Although family rumor held that the early Van Rippers had been well off, the recent Van Rippers were forced to water down their hand soap and orange juice, had more bread crumbs than beef in their meat loaf, and had to turn off the water mid-shower to lather up or shave.

And yet the tower—old miser that it was—could make Ali Baba's cave look like a roadside flea market. Who knew how much money all those treasures might sell for? On the wall inside the tower, some ancestor had written a verse: FOR WHERE YOUR TREASURE IS, THERE YOUR HEART WILL BE ALSO. When Aubrey was sleepless over her high property taxes and the Stitchery's leaking roof, the treasure tormented her. She was a miner on a mountain of silver—without a shovel or pick to her name.

"Listen, we don't have to decide about this right now,"

Bitty said. "Let's not fight. Okay? Let's just table the whole conversation until after the funeral."

"Plus, there's the Madness," Meggie blurted. "Could we talk about that for a second? Aubrey, you know what will happen if you stay here. Your brain will turn into oatmeal inside your skull! And what are we supposed to do? Just sit back and let that happen?"

"It will be better to talk about this later," Bitty said, her voice tight with false patience.

"I don't see how *waiting* is going to help," Meggie said.

Bitty glared at her.

"Seriously. We all know she can't stay here alone."

"I will stay," Aubrey said. "I *have* to stay."

"Majority rules," Meggie said. "We'll take a vote. It's legal that way."

"No it's not. You need my signature—"

"Not if we outnumber you."

"That's *enough*!" Bitty said. Loud. The children were sitting on the couch with their feet together and their eyes down as if they were trying to make their small bodies even smaller. Vic, too, was unnaturally still.

Aubrey felt some of the heat go out of her. "You're right. Let's not fight. That's the last thing Mariah would have wanted."

The room was quiet. Aubrey went to the window.

Although the property around the Stitchery had changed over the decades, the building itself hadn't been updated in years. Since the late 1700s, the Van Rippers had been in the Stitchery. The scuffs and dents in the baseboards, the slight crookedness of the back door, the long arcing scrapes along the hallway floors—all marks of the people who came before.

True, Aubrey was tempted from time to time to throw it all away. To pawn the treasures in the tower and start over somewhere, anywhere, else. How could she not be tempted? The work was draining, the hours long and lonely, the rewards dubious. But if *she* did not continue the traditions of her family, there would be no traditions at all. And what would Tarrytown do without the Stitchery? Long before she'd been born, her job had begun.

She looked at Vic, whose face was grave with worry. "Come on," she said. "I'll walk you to the front gate."

Outside, they traipsed across the Stitchery's yard, over its blue slate walk that was slowly being swallowed by moss and crabgrass. The unseasonably warm sun glazed Vic's hair in gold. The day had brightened slightly, smelling of charcoal and burning leaves. In the distance the river was cobalt blue.

"I'm sorry you saw all of that," Aubrey told him. "My sisters and I . . . it's complicated."

"Family's complicated. Don't apologize."

"Are you walking home?" she asked. He lived a few blocks away in a small two-family that he owned and also rented to his sister. She knew this, but she'd never been to his house.

"Yes. Could you use a walk?"

He held out his arm and she took it. He made it so easy.

They went down the old, blocky street, the sounds of seagulls and car tires, the smells of fresh air and fabric softener. To other people in Tarrytown, those old families who lived high on the ridge and high on the income spectrum, Tappan Square was one strong gust of wind away from being rubble. But Aubrey knew that just because a block was a bit rough around the edges, that didn't mean it was *bad*.

All the people of Tappan Square were pariahs in one way or another: They were artists and students and vagabonds who lived to push the envelope. They were people who had emotional or mental disabilities—or some harmless quirk that made them "not quite the same." They were immigrants who came from many countries, some scrimping by and living under the radar, others with empire-sized dreams. They were all on the fringes, caught in an eddy that churned far from the mainstream.

Horseman Woods Commons—Steve Halpern and his buddies said—would be a "great improvement" over Tappan Square. Whereas Tappan Square was a patchwork of mismatched houses from hand-me-down decades, Horseman Woods Commons would be an über-sleek, brick-and-glass complex that offered the occasional neoclassical column or fanlight window as a nod to the past. The lower levels of The Commons would offer upscale salons, boutiques, a café, and even a few novelties for the tourists, including the Headless Horseman Museum of Oddities and Legends. The three upper stories of the plaza would be luxury housing for the fifty-five-and-up crowd. Retired people—everyone said—would be a great addition to Tarrytown. They were as low-maintenance in condos as hamsters in cages. They brought in a lot of disposable income and little aggravation (the current Tappan Square residents offered the exact reverse).

Aubrey had been active in the effort to stop Horseman Woods Commons—writing letters and managing campaigns from the shadows. But she'd never been visible or outspoken. It wasn't her nature to call attention to herself. It was Mariah who would have leapt in front of the bulldozers and cried, *Over my dead body!* Mariah had been the one with the semaphore and bullhorn, and Aubrey was the one who held them for her when she needed to free up her hands.

"What are you thinking about?" Vic asked.

"This place." She kicked a soda can that had been smashed against the sidewalk. "What it means."

"Your sisters can't make you leave if you don't want to. You can stay."

"But for how long? Until Steve Halpern decides I have to go? That we all do? If we don't sell our property to them they'll take it anyway."

"But we're fighting it. We're going to win."

Vic walked slowly, as if they were having a gentle amble along the river rather than a stroll in the paved heat of Tappan Square. His arm was bent at a gentlemanly angle, and it held the weight of her hand. It occurred to her: Why had she ever been so tongue-tied around him? When her sisters had practically attacked her just now, Vic had stood by her. In light of Mariah's death and the change to her will, the idea of being nervous around Vic seemed almost petty—proof that worry was relative, that the fears of last week were the fears of a different woman at a different time.

"You know," she said, laughing a little, "I think I have a better shot at convincing the town to let me keep the Stitchery than convincing my sisters."

He was quiet for the space of a few steps. "I'm sure they mean well."

"There's a lot you don't know," Aubrey said.

"So why not tell me?" His pace slowed until he was stopped on a street corner. She didn't know what direction to head in, so she stopped, too. They stood: together, but not quite facing. "I am a good listener, you know."

"All right." She focused on his chin and spoke. "I don't really have a choice but to stay in the Stitchery. Our family has these . . . um . . . traditions. And it's up to me to keep them going."

He was quiet, waiting.

"Mariah didn't tell you anything?"

He faced her. He squinted hard in the sunlight, his face crinkling, his upper lip drawn. "I know about the yarns."

"You do?"

"I'm not saying I know everything. But—yeah. The spells, all of that. Mariah told me." He glanced down at her.

"And, what do you think of it? Did it freak you out?"

She felt his muscle tighten under her hand. "I guess I have to tell you a story," he said, but he did not begin it right away. They walked a few more paces, and she looked up at him with the sense that something was caught in the balance—though what it was she couldn't say. "When I was fifteen, my father was working illegally, you know, under the table, at a construction site. The crane operator apparently had too much whiskey in his coffee one morning, and the jib smacked into a neighboring building." He paused, and Aubrey held his arm a little tighter. "They said my father didn't even know what hit him. Stone and glass from the building fell four stories. Nobody but my father was hurt."

"Hurt? As in . . . he recovered, right?"

"No."

"Oh, Vic," Aubrey said. "I'm so sorry."

"It was a long time ago. I still miss him every day. But I'm not telling you this story to make you feel bad for me. I'm telling you because it has to do with the Stitchery."

"How?"

Vic sighed, a full exhalation through his nostrils. "He was a quiet man, never the life of the party, but always the guy you'd want to talk to one-on-one. When you needed him, he was right there—but not really noticeable until you looked over your shoulder and realized he'd always had your back, but was letting you lead the way."

"He sounds like an amazing person," Aubrey said. "I would have liked to have known him."

Vic looked down and smiled warmly. "Three days after he died, I was at the park. I didn't have any friends with me; I'd gone by myself because I didn't want to be in the house. I felt—well—I felt like hell. I was sitting on top of this metal dome when I saw the jaguar."

"Did you say—*jaguar?*"

Vic nodded solemnly.

"Like, the car?"

"Like the cat."

"Was it . . . on a leash?" Aubrey said.

"It was lazing on the top of the slide. It must have been there for a while. It was all black, and it was blinking at me like it was sleepy. The weird thing was that I didn't feel scared—well, not too scared. It didn't seem like it wanted to eat me or anything. It was just . . . hanging out."

Aubrey caught a glimpse of the river between the houses; it was bold today—blue and sparkling. "How does that connect to your father?"

"He collected jaguar pictures. He didn't have a huge collection. But there were a few jaguar figurines and stuff around the house here and there, and I always knew they came from him. He felt, I don't know, some kind of understanding with them."

"You think your father appeared to you—as a jaguar?" she said, and though the question felt strange on her tongue, she'd hoped it came through without even a trace of judgment.

Vic sighed again. "I don't know. I don't know if it was anything that literal."

"What did your family say?"

"I never told them. I knew they'd think I was crazy, that I was imagining things because of grief. But a few days later I found out that a jaguar had actually escaped from a man's house—he was keeping it as a pet, if you can believe that."

"I believe it," she said. "You don't live this close to New York City and not hear about those kinds of things."

"So, there's an explanation for me seeing the jaguar—I accept that. But there's not an explanation for the *timing*. That's what's tricky. Think of the odds. Not only did I see a jaguar in Queens, which must be a million to one—but I saw it just after my father passed. When you beat those kinds of odds—" He shook his head, his eyes lowered in thought. "—I don't know what it is, but I can't think it's coincidence."

"I don't either," Aubrey said.

"That's how I feel about your magic," he said. "It's more than coincidence. It's something."

Aubrey's heart was flooded with warmth for him. And she thought of what a more-than-coincidence it was that she was standing here, and he was standing here, that they'd met each other, and were talking, and now their lives were, at least for this moment, intertwined. Even if she never got to know him any better than she did right now, she would think fondly of this moment for the rest of her life. "Thank you for telling me this story. I'm glad you did."

He nodded, suddenly bashful, and he was charming and boyish all over again. "Can I ask you a question?"

"Sure."

"Why didn't Mariah just knit something for Steve Halpern? For everybody on the town council? It seems like that would have been the easy way out."

"Oh. Well. She did. I mean, she knit for them. But Jackie Halpern's family has been in Tarrytown a really long time. So she knows things about us—she thinks she does anyway. And she told everybody not to accept gifts from Mariah."

"And they don't?"

"They're not really interested in hand-knit neck warmers. More like . . . Yankees tickets or nice watches."

"Fair point." He resumed walking. "Anyway, to go back to

the Stitchery, what I'm saying is, you shouldn't give it up if you don't want to. But it seems to me like your sisters mean well."

"Yes. I guess they do."

She fell into thought, lost. She'd hoped that her sisters' return would mean a change: Maybe Meggie would come back and be her normal old self again. Maybe Bitty wouldn't be so standoffish. But Mariah's will—which was meant to tie them together—had them thrashing even harder than usual at their common bonds.

"You've had a hard week," Vic said.

She looked up at him, his brown eyes that—to her amazement—never shied away from hers even though Meggie had once described them as "bug-zapper blue."

In the overly warm sun, in her long black skirt and her unseasonable black turtleneck that was the only black shirt she owned, she must have looked awfully dire. Because after a moment Vic said, "Come here," and he closed the distance between them and put his arms around her. She felt the hardness of his chest, the press of his cheek against her temple. He smelled of deodorant. His body was warm.

"Better?" he asked.

She pressed her nose into his chest and slid her arms around him. "Better," she said. But she sniffled a little—then a little more—just in case he was thinking of letting her go.

8

"Drop a Stitch"

A funny thing happens in the Hudson Valley in the autumn.
At first the twilight seems peaceful, the electric blue of day
fading and the heavens softening to a pinkish white. The gar-
ish red and orange trees mellow like a cat gentling beneath its
owner's hand. And yet the serenity is deceptive. The mood of
a Hudson twilight is so uniformly peaceful—a blank canvas—
that it routinely invites nightmares.

Beneath the wide-open sky, Bitty could feel the dark possibilities of the coming evening. Because she didn't want to
answer questions about her absent husband, and because she
wanted a moment to herself, she had taken her children to
the park an hour before Mariah's funeral picnic was set to
begin. The riverbank was low and flat. Canada geese were
snoozing like lumped gray stones at the water's edge. Rocky
hills shouldered the sky on all sides, and the metal girders of
the Tappan Zee Bridge spanned the river. The old white lighthouse where Bitty and her husband used to meet in secret
jutted beyond the trees.

"Mom?"

Nessa leaned her head on Bitty's shoulder as they walked.
Her skin was pale and freckled, her long cinnamon hair pulled
into a high bun. Her scarf, the one she'd absolutely had to

have last week or else she'd die on the spot, had been left
behind.

"Mom? I was thinking . . ."

"Uh-oh. Don't hurt yourself."

Nessa laughed. "No, seriously. I was thinking that we
should maybe, like, stay here a little while. Not go back right
away."

"How come?"

"Aunt Aubrey needs us. No, really. I can tell. This is her
time of need. And it's not like Carson and I can't afford to miss
a few days of school. We both get good grades . . ."

Bitty glanced down.

"Fine. *He* gets good grades. But mine have been okay."

"We're not staying," Bitty said.

"But . . . why?"

She swung her arm around her daughter's waist. Nessa
hadn't asked if her father would be coming to the funeral.
Neither had Carson. "Because we just can't."

"Why do you hate this place so much?"

"I don't hate it. I have a lot of good memories here."

"And a lot of bad ones?"

"Some," Bitty admitted. "Your aunt and I didn't always see
eye-to-eye."

"About what?"

"Typical things," Bitty said, though in fact their disagree-
ment wasn't typical at all. The issue—the chronic, divisive
issue—was the magic. It *always* came down to the magic. At
first, when she was too young to know better, Bitty had
bought into the hype—just like she'd once believed that Saint
Nicholas came down the chimney at Christmastime and left
candies in her shoes. But as her capacity for logic grew, she
realized that a man could not travel the world in a sled in the
sky. And eventually, after years of prodding and poking her

own doubt about magic as she prodded and poked the holes where she'd lost her baby teeth, she realized that people could not fix their problems with scarves and hats—no matter what Mariah or the Great Book in the Hall claimed. The magic of the Stitchery was no more than smoke and mirrors. If spells worked, it was only because the power of belief was so very persuasive, like a placebo that cures cancer or shortens colds.

And while she didn't claim to know much about science, she had an understanding that it only took one instance—one single deviation from the predicted outcome—to prove a theory to be fully and completely wrong. Magic was a way for people to try to control the uncontrollable; and if it had worked with regularity, Bitty would have been happy to believe it was real. She would have been the first person to say "Sign me up!" But in the end, magic was a false security, a grasping at power that humans didn't have but desperately wished for, and Bitty found that there were better, more reliable ways to control her own destiny than knitting a sock.

The Stitchery had been the Great Embarrassment of her youth—and even now as an adult, she still caught the faint whiff of it lingering about her like a smell that would not wash out. And when Bitty was in a dark mood, she conceded that it was not just the Stitchery that embarrassed her, but *Mariah*—a woman who had made herself a laughingstock in her clichéd broomstick "witch skirts" and her corset-tops and her moon-and-stars jewelry. A woman who believed the unprovable and the unbelievable—and who couldn't understand why Bitty didn't do the same.

"Are you okay?" Nessa asked.

"Of course. Why wouldn't I be?"

"It looks like you're chewing on your teeth," Nessa said.

Bitty looked off into the distance. At the south end of the park, Carson was calling and waving his arms over his head.

He wanted them to come see the lighthouse. It was just beyond the trees, white metal pocked by bolts and smeared by rust. Just like always.

Bitty gave her daughter's bottom a little whack.

"Ma!"

"Go ahead. I'm right behind you."

Nessa ran. Bitty kept walking. She had been back in Tarrytown for only a few nights. And as she stood under the wide sky, a longing that she could not quite put a name to was growing within her. Perhaps it was nostalgia, coming up through her bones like a cold draft through floorboards. Or perhaps it was a longing for the new life she'd built for herself—or at least, for the life that she'd tried to build but that still seemed to elude her. Whatever the cause, she felt she was growing heavyhearted, more with each minute she stayed in Tarrytown. She was sleeping under the same roof as her sisters, and yet she missed them. They had chatted a little, made the necessary conversations, but they had yet to talk, to *really* talk—except to argue about selling the Stitchery. They tiptoed around one another, didn't ask questions, gave a wide berth. Bitty thought she would have appreciated the effort. But she didn't.

Before her, the lighthouse reared up, unlit and rugged in the quiet sky.

For a few shared years, the Van Ripper girls were said to have been inseparable, an isolated little unit that never let an outsider in. At playgrounds and basketball courts, delis and pet-store windows, the three girls appeared to the better families of Tarrytown to be street rabble left over from another century—one with newsboys and orphanages and men who lit lamps. Even before Mariah had taken them out of public school, the girls had been derelicts. They wore clothes that didn't quite fit, smeared with grass and ketchup, and their hair was stringy and wild. Bitty was a knobby young teen fighting her way into womanhood; Meggie was a child, jelly-smeared and dirty and always wanting to hold one of her big sisters' hands; and Aubrey was bookish and distracted and a little bit flakey, but always by her siblings' sides.

In the afternoons, when good children were at home doing their schoolwork, the Van Ripper girls could be found in the park between Tarrytown and Sleepy Hollow. It was there that Benedict Arnold's traitorous plot against George Washington, the plot that might have changed the outcome of the Revolutionary War, had been discovered when his sidekick and scapegoat John André was captured.

Bitty would climb on the edge of the monument and lean off it with one hand. "You guys be the militiamen and I'll be John André."

Sometimes, they'd play it straight: John André, smuggling Benedict Arnold's papers in a stinky boot, assumes that because one of the bumpkins he meets is wearing a Hessian coat the man must be a loyalist—as opposed to a patriot in a stolen coat—and he spills his plans only to realize he's just signed his own death warrant. Other times, they played it so John André gave chase through Tarrytown—leading the girls to run shrieking and crashing into people and generally making a nuisance of themselves.

But the John André game was the least of Tarrytown's worries when it came to the Van Rippers. As children with magic at their fingertips, they raised a special kind of hell.

Although she was the youngest by far, Meggie was the troupe's lead instigator. She wanted the baker to give them free pastries. She wanted Tommy Matsumoto to let them use his bike. She wanted Heather Noble to be knocked off her high horse, and she thought that casting a spell to make Heather get a crush on Lance "Hot Pants" Weemly would do the trick.

With each new spell, Meggie made a sacrifice. And with each new spell, it seemed to get a little easier for her to do it: She gave up her favorite stuffed dinosaur, her book about poisonous snakes, her collection of river stones. Sometimes her sacrifices made for successful spells; other times, they were wasted. But failure had never stopped her from coming up with new ideas to put the Stitchery's magic to good use.

Unfortunately, she had to rely on her older sisters to turn her ideas into spells; she was not a very good knitter of magic. She could not do it alone. *Aubrey* was the one whose spells turned out the best. *Aubrey* was the most reliable. But Aubrey was also the most scrupulous and serious of the three of them—*chickenshit*, Meggie said—and convincing her to knit a spell just for fun was always a terrible chore.

This, of course, was where Bitty came in. She was glib and smart. She was persistent, stubborn, and always the voice of reason, even when what she was arguing for was technically unreasonable. She liked getting people to do what she wanted. So when Meggie pitched an idea for a new spell, Bitty set about convincing Aubrey to knit it—if only because knitting spells was a good way of testing out the truth, and because she had nothing better to do with her time than antagonize the people of Tarrytown.

As for Aubrey, she tried to resist her sisters' pleadings but almost always gave in. She knit old Mr. Piotrowski a set of wrist warmers, and for a whole year they played free rounds of the King Kong arcade game that he kept in the back of his pizza shop. She knit a lace headband for Sue Hormack's mother, and from then on the girls had a standing invitation to come to dinner whenever they pleased—which was important because Mariah was a terrible cook and Sue's mother made amazing chicken potpie.

Eventually Mariah caught on. They were grounded for an entire summer, not even allowed to leave the Stitchery's front yard. Magic was not a toy; it was a responsibility, and no sister felt Mariah's disapproval and disappointment more keenly than Aubrey. She began to realize that her duty to the Stitchery made her different from her sisters. They could not keep going forward as they had been, as three parallel lines. The summer that Mariah had grounded them was the summer they began to go their separate ways.

Aubrey became increasingly awkward and withdrawn; she was a child of the Stitchery, and certain women did not say very nice things about her—she was that weird Van Ripper girl with the witchy eyes. As Meggie got older, she broke every rule she came across with a kind of good-natured detachment—smoking marijuana right in the middle of the park if it suited her, openly dating both boys and girls, and refusing to wear a bra—much to the consternation of every woman who walked with her husband into the air-conditioned movie theater where Meggie worked. Bitty, known as the angriest of the three sisters, was also bad: It was not the fact that she was "fast" that rankled matronly nerves—if anything, people half expected one if not all of the Van Ripper girls to end up pregnant by the time they were eighteen. The trouble was, Bitty's fastness was directed at the wrong kind of boys; instead of motorcycle-riding drug dealers or sons of plumbers and cabinetmakers, she went after the quiet college-bound boys with soft hands who lived up on the hill. The old dames of Tarrytown trembled to hear a beloved son mention her name.

Each generation had a story to tell about the Van Rippers— some stories friendlier than others. There were pockets in which the sisters were welcome, mostly in Tappan Square. But even in their own neighborhood, certain people avoided them. For all their unabashed poverty and strangeness, the Van Rippers were to be feared.

There had been no witch hunt, no torches or battering rams, no inquisitions with fire irons, but two of the three Van Rippers had—by the insidious and awful pressure of observation, conjecture, and gossip—been driven out of town. It was a wonder that Aubrey, the shiest and most nervous of the three sisters, had found the strength to stay.

Aubrey had brought her knitting to Mariah's funeral picnic. She sat with Bitty and Meggie on an old Navajo-style blanket, the urn that held Mariah's ashes resting beside her. The evening had turned chilly. Aubrey had done little more than notify the local paper of Mariah's passing and of their plans for a "funeral." And now the people of Tappan Square—those who had good feelings toward Mariah and toward the Stitchery—had gathered to remember. Adults lined up their lawn chairs or spread out blankets. Children horsed around on a slide shaped like an oversized macaroni noodle. It was part picnic, part memorial, and Mariah would have loved it. She'd always thought that life was a thing to celebrate, and the ending of life was no less astonishing a transition than the beginning of it. Aubrey had cried, on and off, through the course of the evening. Her knitting was a twist of buttery yellow in her lap.

She shivered.

"You okay?" Meggie whispered.

She stopped knitting and glanced around. She felt like she was being watched. But she pulled her denim jacket more tightly around her neck and said, "I'm just chilly."

"You should have brought a warmer jacket," Meggie said.

Aubrey did not immediately resume knitting. She was certain that if she looked behind her she would catch someone's eye. But whose?

One by one, Mariah's friends climbed up onto the stump of an old oak to say a few words. Although no one spoke the word *magic*, the fact of it hung in the air like dew settling into the trees. Aubrey recognized most of the speakers as people who had come to the Stitchery at one time or another in their lives.

"Mariah had a big heart," one woman said. "She helped me reconcile with my father whom I hadn't seen in twenty years. I'll never be grateful enough for that."

"Because of Mariah, I got over my fear of flying—and that allowed me one last trip out to Arizona to see my best friend before she died," another woman said.

"Mariah taught us all to pass along goodness, to be a good listener, to be generous. Plus, she never turned down an opportunity to help somebody. I know there are people in this town who say unkind things about her, but that's only because they never got to know her like we did," another woman said.

Aubrey had known that Mariah had a good number of supporters, a few of whom were even friends, but she hadn't quite understood until now just how many. The park was full of families, of men or women standing in groups or alone. And although Aubrey knew she shouldn't, she found she was thinking of herself, of her own place in the community. Where Mariah was boisterous and outgoing, Aubrey was reticent and self-conscious. Where Mariah was larger-than-life, Aubrey willed herself to shrink. Where Mariah had stood up against the Halperns with all the gumption and balls and loudmouthed rabble-rousing that a single woman could muster, Aubrey was withdrawing. Her heart felt heavy. She wished she could be more like Mariah—more like her without losing the fundamental things that made Aubrey *herself*.

"Mariah was irreplaceable," a woman said.

Aubrey was wiping the tears from her cheeks when she saw Jeanette Judge crossing the park, jouncing heel over heel as she cut through the crowd. She was tall and beautiful, dark skin offset by a peacock-green scarf that Aubrey had made for her last year—not a spell, just a gift. As Jeanette hurried and tried not to look like she was hurrying, heads turned.

"Hey." Jeanette sat down on the blanket beside Aubrey. Her breathing was shallow. There was panic in her eyes.

"What is it? What's wrong?"

"I got stuck at the library. Some old guy fed spiral notebook paper into the printer. It made me late."

Aubrey relaxed. "Don't worry. It's no big deal."

"Oh, and the Halperns are here."

"What?"

"They just climbed out of their town car."

"Where?"

"There."

Aubrey followed Jeanette's gaze. The Halperns stood at the north end of the park behind the seated crowd. Steve Halpern was dressed in a black slash of a suit—far too severe for a picnic. Jackie was elegiac in a gray chiffon dress and dark furs. On a good day, the Halperns were disliked in Tappan Square. On a bad day, they were hated. Today—Mariah's funeral—was a bad day.

Aubrey felt a shift in the air, and she wasn't surprised when Vic bent down beside her. He'd been sitting with his sister on a blanket about ten feet away, the closest available patch of grass that had been open when he'd arrived. Now his starched shirt whispered and popped as he rested his elbows on his knees where he crouched.

"You saw them, too?" she said.

He nodded. "I'll ask them to leave for you."

"Leave?"

"Believe me, nothing would make me happier than to go over there and send them on their way."

She laughed, though nothing was funny.

"I'm serious. Do you want me to tell them to go?"

"I . . . I just don't know."

She looked out over the park. The sky was darkening. One police officer leaned against a tree, cross-armed and scowling. Another picked her way among the picnic tables, hands behind her back. The police had been sent by the village to "keep the peace" among the uncontrollable heathens of Tappan Square. And now that Aubrey was paying attention, she noticed that the peacefulness of evening was starting to fray. Tribes of young men who had not been there earlier in the evening had coalesced in deepening shadows. They laughed loudly and took long swigs from what looked like bottles of iced tea but could have been anything. They eyed the cops, who eyed them back. Somewhere a firework went off—rude and wailing. The air buzzed like a snapped rubber band.

Vic touched her arm. "Aubrey?"

From across the park, the Halperns were looking at her. No doubt there were some people in Tappan Square who would blame the Halperns for Mariah's passing. The Halperns stood for everything Mariah did not—the marginalization of the poor, tax breaks for the wealthy, legislation favoring the 1 percent. It had been the Halperns who first put forward the proposal to demolish Tappan Square. And now, everyone was waiting for Aubrey to decide if the Halperns should be allowed to stay among them, all her neighbors, all the volatile young men sitting on the hoods of their cars and loitering near the park's periphery, all the police who walked heel–toe, heel–toe, and scanned the crowds.

She rubbed her forehead. She looked down at the stitches in her lap. "I guess they can stay. I mean, what's the worst that could happen?"

"Famous last words," Meggie said.

"You doing okay?" Vic shifted his weight.

Aubrey nodded. She loved the warm concern in Vic's eyes. "Can I join you for a minute?"

"Of course," Aubrey said, and she scooted over to make room. She could not focus on her stitches, could not focus on the speeches being given about Mariah, could not focus on the Halperns. She felt terrible for being so distracted by the nearness of Vic's person, his hand that was so close she might reach out and cover it with her own. But Mariah's voice was there in her mind at once to chastise her for her unnecessary guilt complex: *Are you kidding me? I want you to be distracted*, Mariah said.

They watched as another speaker climbed onto the stump in front of the lighthouse to talk about Mariah. He was a tall, lean young man with a face like an actor—all eyes and mouth—and he introduced himself as Mason Boss. He had neat, espresso-dark hair, brown skin, and leather shoes that were so shiny a person could pick broccoli out of her teeth if she happened to be standing near him and she looked down.

"Does anybody know this guy?" Aubrey whispered.

Jeanette didn't look away from him. He was standing solidly on the old tree trunk, speaking more softly than the other eulogizers, so that people who wanted to hear him—and everyone did—shushed their children and leaned in.

"No," Jeanette said. "Not yet."

"Is it just me, or does he sound . . . what is that? A little bit British?"

"How could you be a little bit British?"

"He sounds really *proper*," Aubrey said.

"He has good diction," Jeanette said.

His soft, shy words gradually became louder. Aubrey was sure she'd never met him. He said he was new to Tappan Square. But he spoke of Mariah. Her morality. Her guts. He talked about how she saw beauty in Tappan Square's diversity and its grit—even if lawmakers couldn't. It wasn't fair, he said, that any one person or group of persons should have the right to take away the property or properties of any other persons. Wasn't it John Locke who said that people had a fundamental right to life, liberty, and *prop-er-ty*? Wasn't that the *point* of the *Constitution*? The people needed to rise up and remind Tarrytown that a government by the people was by the *whole* people—not by a privileged few.

Aubrey had goose bumps. She hadn't realized that she'd stopped knitting.

Out of the murmuring crowds, someone called out: *Hey! The Halperns are here! It's Steve Halpern!* Around the park, people began to boo, low and weird, and over the drone of booing, shouts and jeers began to burst like bottle rockets. Aubrey saw Steve Halpern put his hand on his wife's back and begin to guide her toward the parking lot, away from the increasingly loud crowd.

But the young men at the park's edge saw an opportunity and were not about to let their lawmakers leave without speaking their minds. All at once, on the heels of Mason Boss's blood-rousing speech, it was as if Mariah's death had come not on a hand-knotted rug on Steve Halpern's floor, but at the end of a rope at Steve Halpern's hand. The police, who had been at the edges of the park, began to tighten. A crowd—

thirty people? Fifty?—surged toward the Halperns, men and women chanting *Save Tappan Square! Save Tappan Square!* Aubrey felt her guts clench, partly with worry, partly with excitement. She was thrilled to see her neighbors taking such a passionate, political stand.

And then, fast as lightning, it all changed.

Another firework went off, this time in the middle of the crowd. People yelled and pushed and screamed to get away. Aubrey cried out, worried. Was anyone hurt? Near the Halperns, the chanting went on. *Save Tappan Square! Save Tappan Square!* Shouts of protest turned to shouts of fury and rage. Aubrey got to her feet. Everyone got to their feet. Chairs tipped. Parents snatched up their children. Dogs barked and strained at their leashes. The geese at the park's edge lifted into the sky. Another firework exploded. A bottle shattered against a tree. Aubrey felt the great swell of danger.

She felt Vic pull her arm. "We should probably get out of here," he said.

Ten minutes later, it was over. The Tappan Square riot, as it would go down in history among the locals, was, as far as riots went, not much to speak of. Compared with anticommunist violence in nearby Peekskill in 1949, the Tappan Square riot was the work of halfhearted amateurs. There were no rubber bullets, no clouds of tear gas, not even so much as a single car turned upside down. The police had easily cleared out the park; most people went willingly, not interested in being a part of a mob scene. And then there was only the quiet of the dark river, sucking at the thick bulkheads that kept the land from slipping down into the water, and the twinkle of lights like stars on the distant shore.

Only the lighthouse was left standing its ground, as it had

since 1883. It had seen the river filled with steamboats so thick it was said a person could walk from one side of the river to the other without getting wet. It had seen the dirigible *Hindenburg* make its gaseous, big-bellied salute to the people of Tarrytown. It had seen the eastern shoreline, once half a mile away, creep within a few feet of its casings when an automobile factory had dumped so much landfill that it changed the shape of the mighty Tappan Zee—and it felt rather resentful of the change. But it did not have much of an opinion on the riots of Tappan Square. Nor did it have special feelings for the Van Ripper sisters, who had crept from the safety of their old manse back to the park as soon as the coast was clear, and were now sneaking around the bushes with flashlights in hand.

"I think I left it around here," Aubrey said.

It was well after midnight and the beams of their flashlights lit the grass in bright circles. Colorful leaves, paper plates, napkins, and bendy straws littered the ground.

"I don't see anything," Bitty said.

"It's here," Aubrey said, trying to sound confident. "Nobody would have taken it."

Meggie sniggered. "Yeah. They probably think it's cursed."

"We'll find it." Aubrey squinted into the darkness. The river was glinting black and silver. During the mêlée—the mad rush and enforced evacuation from the park—Aubrey had left Mariah on the picnic blanket. Her knitting was still there, too. At least, she hoped it was.

"There it is!" Meggie shouted.

Bitty shushed her.

Aubrey hurried in the direction of Meggie's beam. "Oh thank God." She righted the urn and hugged it close. It was cosmic blue, swirled with purple and flecked with white clusters like musical notes or stars. Mariah had grown portly in her later years. Now she weighed no more than a baby in Aubrey's arms. "See? It's fine. I told you it would be fine."

Bitty started to walk away. "Great. Let's get out of here."

Aubrey stood.

Meggie was wandering off.

"Hey." Bitty shined her flashlight between Meggie's shoulder blades. She spoke as if she were whispering on stage. "Where you going?"

"It's a nice night. I want to see the river."

"Do you want to get arrested? The cops are *everywhere*," Bitty said.

Meggie called over her shoulder. "Don't be a chicken."

"We have to get back to the kids," Bitty said.

"They'll be fine," Meggie said, turning around to walk backward for a moment. "They've got a movie and enough popcorn to feed a small country."

Bitty glanced at Aubrey.

Aubrey shrugged with Mariah in her arms.

Bitty's shoulders sank with resignation. "Well, at least let's turn off our flashlights. I don't want to explain to my husband why he needs to come spring me out of jail."

Aubrey laughed.

Together, they followed Meggie to the edge of the water, where the rocks were bunched and jutting. The lighthouse rose up before them, dark where a light should have been. The Tappan Zee Bridge was strung with pearly green lights on their chain.

Meggie kicked off her basketball sneakers.

"Ugh. What *now*?" Bitty asked.

"What's it look like?" Meggie rolled up her pants, then sat and plunked her feet into the water. The moonlight braceleted her calves. "Just for a sec. Nobody's gonna bother us."

Aubrey pulled off her socks and shoes—which required a

lot of unlacing, hopping, and prying—and then she sat beside her sister.

Reluctantly, Bitty joined them. "It's cold."

"Freezing," Aubrey said.

"You get used to it," Meggie said.

They sat together, and yet not together, in silence. Aubrey gritted her teeth against the icy water. The bones of her ankles were cold to the core, as if she could feel the marrow turning purple and blue. For two nights her sisters had been with her again, in the Stitchery. And except for that first night, when Meggie had appeared and they'd cried together with Mariah on their minds, Aubrey felt as if they were *together* in physical proximity only. Bitty busied herself with her children. Meggie holed away. They exchanged only as much information as one might exchange with a friendly stranger on a bus or plane. Now, sitting at the water's edge on the night-cold rocks, this was the first time that the three of them had been alone without the walls of the Stitchery listening in on their conversation and without Bitty's children nearby. The nighttime obscured Aubrey from her sisters just enough to give her a sense that she was free from them even as they sat close by.

Meggie must have shared some of Aubrey's feeling. She broke the silence. "I just keep thinking Mariah would have loved this."

"Yes, she always loved the lighthouse," Aubrey said.

"No—I mean the riot. She would have loved it! God! If only she could have seen it. She *lived* to stir up trouble."

"No, she didn't," Aubrey said, rankled. "She lived to put an end to trouble."

"Same difference," Meggie said.

"Hard to believe the Halperns showed up like that," Bitty said. "I can't imagine what they were thinking."

"Maybe they meant well," Aubrey said. "Maybe they were just trying to say that even if they disagreed with Mariah, they still respected her."

"Um, that didn't really transmit," Meggie said.

"Just because they're rich doesn't mean they're *bad*," Bitty said. "I mean—look at it from their angle. They're making tough decisions for the greater good."

"Fine, fine," Meggie said.

Bitty lifted her legs out of the river by straightening her knees. The water dripped off her feet in silver droplets. "Who was that guy? The one with the face. You know him?"

"Mason Boss," Aubrey said. "I don't know him."

Bitty dropped her feet back in the river. The water softly adjusted to the move. "Don't take this the wrong way," she said. "But—given how crazy it was that Aunt Mari didn't leave the Stitchery to Aubrey, do you think she was going mad?"

"No way," Aubrey said.

"Still," Bitty said. "She *was* starting to lose it."

"No she wasn't," Aubrey said. "There's no such thing as the Madness."

Bitty laughed. "Seriously? Really, Aub?"

"What?"

"You believe that you can change somebody's future with a fisherman's rib pattern but you don't believe that dementia runs in our family?"

The nerves of Aubrey's spine prickled. "Mariah must have known what she was doing. She wasn't going mad."

Bitty leaned forward on her knees. "I'm not saying there was some magical thing that made her go crazy—the curse of Helen Van Ripper. I'm saying that there was something getting funny with her brain."

"But at least she had you to take care of her." Meggie

squeezed Aubrey's shoulder. "It would have been much worse if she was alone."

Aubrey knew what her sister was getting at, and she moved her shoulder just slightly, so that Meggie's hand fell away. Aubrey tried to picture herself as an old woman—shuffling through the halls of the Stitchery, yarn twisted around her fingers, and the big, empty house around her like a force field, keeping the world out. The thought depressed her. And yet it was an image of herself that she'd grown accustomed to. Her particular future had been going forward before her like a shadow since the day she was born.

"Do *you* believe in the Madness?" Aubrey asked Meggie.

She shrugged. "I never know what to believe."

Aubrey traced her fingers along the surface of the cold water. That Mariah was quirky had never been in question. She was known to pick the flowers in other people's gardens—at midday—and arrange them on the counter in the yarn room (*because it's not stealing if they'll grow back*). At village meetings she never raised her hand or waited for permission to speak—she just launched into whatever new tirade struck her fancy. Sometimes they were logical tirades (*We must have a traffic light at the end of the road; it's impossible to make a left!*), but sometimes her tirades verged on nutty (*People should be allowed to enter their dogs in the Halloween parade, dammit! If there's not enough parking at the diner, why not park the cars on the roof?*). In the quiet of her mind, Aubrey was beginning to wonder if Mariah wasn't starting to push the boundaries of quirkiness. And that scared her. Because if the Madness was real, then the sacrifice of being a guardian of the Stitchery was a bigger, scarier thing than any single sacrifice made in the name of a single spell.

"Let's not talk about madness." Aubrey dipped her hands into the water; it was cool and slicked with moonlight. "That's not what Mariah wanted. She wanted us to remember her in a happy way."

Meggie chuckled to herself. "Remember how Mariah used to feed all the cats in the neighborhood in the backyard?"

"Yeah—until she saw that *Batman* movie about Catwoman," Bitty said.

Aubrey laughed.

"Oh, Meggie." Bitty leaned forward now, taking up the momentum. "Remember that time when you and Mari snuck out to the Horsemen's practice field—"

"And turned the stallion into a unicorn," Aubrey said, laughing. "I remember."

Meggie grinned. "You can't prove anything."

"You would have had to go to summer school for that," Aubrey said.

"Yeah, except the vice principal really *loved* those argyle socks Mariah made him."

They laughed together, and the sound traveled out over the water.

"We really were a bunch of street urchins, weren't we?" Bitty said.

Meggie huffed. "Maybe we still are." She picked up Mariah and turned the urn in her hands. "I think we should leave her here."

Aubrey flinched. "What? No."

"She doesn't want to sit on the mantel in the knitting room. Let's just . . . let's just cut her loose. Right now."

"That's illegal," Bitty said, though the tone of her voice suggested she wasn't entirely against it.

"Everything's illegal," Meggie said.

"I don't know about this." Aubrey rubbed the back of her neck. "Mariah didn't ask for a burial at sea—or at . . . river. Wouldn't she have asked for that if it was what she wanted?"

"Maybe she didn't care what happened to her body," Bitty said. "Maybe she wanted to leave it up to you."

"Right." Meggie circled her ankle on the water's surface. "Maybe she figured we need her body more than she does at this point."

"I guess."

Aubrey held out her hands for the urn. Meggie handed it over. When she and her sisters had been young, the Stitchery had been the thread that held them together. Everything that was good about it and everything that was bad was their common point of reference, the center of their world. But as they got older, the thing that should have bound them together in unity drove them apart. Bitty became embarrassed by the Stitchery, by magic, and she'd fled Tarrytown with the first rich guy who had offered her a ticket out. Meggie seemed ambivalent about magic but she, too, had left, bent on playing by her own rules and probably even breaking them just to prove she could. No one in the family had any idea what Meggie had actually been doing with herself for the past four years.

Aubrey shored up her courage, took in a deep breath of the cold river air. Her sisters were correct about one thing at least. Mariah did not want to spend the rest of eternity as a bibelot on the Stitchery mantel. "Okay," Aubrey said. "You're right."

"I am?" Meggie said.

"Mariah wouldn't like the idea of being a human tchotchke."

"But she always loved the river," Bitty said.

Aubrey pulled her feet from the water and stood on a smooth boulder. If she had to let Mariah go, she would at least do it with her sisters by her side. She walked carefully, stone by stone, as far as the rocky shoreline would take her. Her sisters followed.

Aubrey lifted the lid. Somewhere in the darkness of the

river, a fish jumped skyward and splashed down. She felt something passing among them, an energy, buzzing like electricity down a line. She knew there were rough waters ahead: fights that they were going to have about selling the Stitchery. Accusations. Maybe blame. And then, God help her, the inevitable loneliness that would descend once her sisters went back to their old, regular lives.

But right now, for a moment, all of that was put on hold. She could have sworn—but she didn't mention it—that she saw the old dead bulb in the top of the lighthouse, the bulb that had been out for decades, glowing a faint yellow-green, like a firefly just before it dies.

"Ready?" Aubrey asked.

Her sisters didn't answer. Meggie let go of her hand. Aubrey squatted down. Gentle waves petted the rocks. A meteor scraped across the dark sky. A frost was coming—she could feel it in the chill, could nearly see the shimmer of it crackling along the surface of the water. She tipped the urn; the heaviness sifted from her hands. Mariah was gone.

From the Great Book in the Hall: *There's something perfect about the knit stitch: the crescent swing of it in Continental-style knitting, the lassoed swoop of it in English-style. The knit stitch satisfies because it has a clear beginning and a clear end, but it's also fully dependent on and balanced against what comes before it and what comes after. Knitting soothes because it steadies.*

Buddhists have mantras and mandalas. Nuns have prayer beads. Native Americans have the beat of drums. Repetition makes space for the infinite. Our stitches are systematically knotted lemniscates, opening the mind.

9

"Slip 1 with Yarn in Front"

Tarrytown Gazette police blotter:

Police responded to a call that a woman saw a giant yellow snake in the top of a tree on Castle Heights Ave. The animal had been reported missing two days prior by its owner, who had a license for it. It was returned without incident.

The owner of the popular Tappan Square hangout El Palacio was issued a summons for noise violations due to excessively loud music. He had received a warning in weeks past.

Three cars were broken into on Storm Street. GPS systems were stolen. Owners admitted that they may have left their doors unlocked.

In Tappan Square, unknown vandals absconded with a sign that read "Vote Yes On Horseman Woods Commons."

Extra staff were on hand at Kingsland Point Park for the funeral service of Mariah Van Ripper. Councilman Halpern and his wife were attacked. Jackie Halpern was treated for minor injuries at Phelps Memorial Hospital. There have been no arrests.

On Wednesday morning, Ruth Ten Eckye stopped by to pick up the fingerless gloves Aubrey had made for her. The cold streamed in a rush behind Ruth as she entered. In the yarn room, she seized the fingerless gloves that Aubrey had made, holding them in the light this way and that to inspect them. Aubrey lifted her chin; she was not confident about many things, but she was certain she was a good knitter. Her stitches were even, her ends expertly woven in. Ruth folded the gloves, stuffed them in her handbag, then snapped it closed.

"How long will it take before I see results?" she asked.

"I can't say. It might be immediate. It might be a while. It might not happen at all. You'll have to let me know what happens."

Ruth lifted the pencil marks that were her eyebrows.

"Or don't," Aubrey said.

The little bell over the door rang when Ruth made her way outside, but no sooner had she left than Aubrey's next client came in. The Stitchery kept no consistent hours: Visitors had always relied on lucky timing to connect with Mariah, and if luck wasn't on their side—if Mariah happened to be out or sick or too overbooked—they were always welcome to stop back again.

Aubrey recognized the girl who stood before her now. She lived on the next block over in Tappan Square. Her name was Blanca and she wore a scarlet football jacket. She was a round girl—round face, round eyes, round cheeks—with large, low breasts that might have been more suited to a woman twice her age. Her brown hair was long and loose. If Aubrey had been in high school with her, she would not have wanted to get on the girl's bad side.

"Where's Mariah?" the girl asked.

"She's not available," Aubrey said. If she'd admitted Mariah was dead, then she and the girl both would have been sucked into a conversation about how and when and murmurs of sympathy and understanding. Aubrey had had enough of that over the past few days.

"Do you know when she'll be back?"

"It's probably best not to wait around. What do you need?"

The girl swore, not quite under her breath. "I have a problem. It's with this thing Mariah knit for me." She reached into her big purse and pulled out an entrelac scarf, the diamond checks alternating in red and black. "I need to return it."

"Oh? Why?"

"It's not working."

Aubrey sighed. This morning, before she'd lifted her head from her pillow, she knew without going to the window that it was going to be just the kind of fall day that she liked—the kind of day that starts off cold and dark but warms like a crackling fire in the afternoon. The kind of day to pick apples or knit with thick wool. She'd pulled on her favorite pair of jeans and a heavy Aran sweater that was big enough to get lost in. She thought now that she should have worn armor.

"Tell me the whole story," she said.

And Blanca did. Blanca was the oldest of six children. Her littlest brother was two and a half. Blanca desperately wanted to go away to college; she'd even figured out all by herself how to get her applications together, pay the application fees, and send them out. And she'd got an acceptance letter back, too, from a small school upstate. The trouble was, her mother had died last year and her father was not willing to let her go. He insisted she could make a perfectly good living without paying all that money for school.

"I did everything Mariah told me to do," Blanca said. "I gave the scarf to my father. But nothing's happening. Nothing's different. What am I doing wrong?"

Aubrey's heart was sinking. "Can I ask what you gave up in exchange for the spell?"

"My locket. My mother had given it to me. It had a picture of the two of us inside."

Aubrey nodded. She'd seen the locket in the tower. It was beautiful, dull yellow gold with a floral pattern. When she spoke, Aubrey tried to appear as if she dealt with broken spells all the time. "Well, get him to wear the scarf for a little while longer. Sometimes these things can take a while."

"But I don't have a while," the girl said. "I got a letter of acceptance and I have to send the deposit soon. Part of what I asked for in the spell was for him to change his mind *quickly*. You know? Quickly. But nothing's happening and it's already practically too late."

"I'm sorry," Aubrey said. "I have no control over when a spell will work. Just have him wear it a little while longer."

Blanca's tough face was no longer so immutable. "You and I both know that's not going to help."

Aubrey didn't know what to do. She turned away from the girl and fussed with a bit of yarn in order to compose herself. "Mariah explained it all to you?"

"Yes," Blanca said. "Maybe I didn't give up the right thing. Maybe the locket wasn't enough."

Aubrey said nothing.

"But it *seemed* like enough," she went on. "It really hurt to give it away like that. It hurt so much. It was like getting my heart ripped out. Like losing my mom all over again."

"I'm sorry," Aubrey said.

"The scarf's not going to work." Her voice sounded small. "So . . . can I have the locket?"

There were moments when Aubrey hated the Stitchery and wished it would burn to the ground. "I'm sorry," she said.

"Please?"

Aubrey turned to her. Blanca was holding the red-and-black scarf in her hands: She clasped it near her sternum like a child hiding behind a blanket. Aubrey shook her head.

Blanca's face went red. "Are you friggin' kidding me? First you tell me you can help me, then instead of helping me you take the one thing away from me that's most important in the world?"

"I don't know how to explain. I don't want to sound like I'm making excuses."

"There's no excuse for this," Blanca said. She lifted her spine, her large chest jutting forward, until she stood at her full height. Her eyes were red-rimmed now. Her body seemed to shake. "They told me not to come. But did I listen? No. No, I didn't." She balled up the scarf and threw it at Aubrey as hard as she could. Aubrey didn't catch it. She felt the soft bulk of it as it hit her in the face, heard the quiet thump as it landed on the floor.

"Fine," Blanca said. "I'll do it without anybody's help. Like I've done *everything*."

Aubrey said nothing. When Blanca left, a whiff of cold fall air came through the door. She was glad neither of her sisters was around.

Nessa had been sitting on the porch stairs, in a fraught struggle to detangle a sprawling knot of yarn, when a girl dashed out of the Stitchery. The screen door slammed behind her. Nessa could hear by the way her feet pounded the wooden porch stairs that the girl was upset. She gathered up the awful tangle on her lap and went into the yarn shop. The air inside the Stitchery was no less crisp and cool than the air outside.

Aubrey was alone. She was standing at the window looking

out. She wore loose cotton jeans that might have belonged to a man at one point, and a thick sweater that was shot through with cables. She was so very still that Nessa couldn't even tell if she was breathing, so still that she might have been part of the room itself—like the curtains, or the shelving, or the spindly wooden chair. Gently, Nessa cleared her throat. Her aunt jumped a mile, and Nessa couldn't help but laugh. "Sorry!"

Aubrey laughed, too. "It's okay. I was just . . . lost in thought."

"What did that girl want?"

"The one who just left? Oh, right. She just wanted to ask me a question."

Nessa took a few steps deeper into the room. Since she'd arrived at the Stitchery, she hadn't had much time alone with her aunt. But Nessa wasn't one to miss an opening. Her mother had once called her an *opportunist*, and she liked the sound of the word—so sharp, so dangerous. An hour ago, everyone else had gone out shopping. But not Aubrey. Nessa had decided to stay behind.

"How are you doing?" Aubrey asked.

"I'm okay. How are you?"

Aubrey tipped her head, gazing thoughtfully, and Nessa winced. Her mother had warned her that looking at her aunt's eyeballs would be a little uncomfortable. Her eyes were enormous and blue, but more eerie than pretty. They were hard to look at. Aubrey lowered her eyes to the floorboards. The motion seemed more automatic than polite.

"I'm adjusting. It's always hard when you lose someone you love," Aubrey said. "I thought you were going with your mom to the store?"

"No. But you don't have to *watch* me or anything. I stay home by myself all the time."

"That's not—I didn't . . ." Aubrey's face went a shade whiter. "What are you doing with that yarn?"

She'd thought she was holding the bunched yarn behind her back, but one long tentacle had wiggled out of the main knot, trailing behind her and to the floor. "Oops. Guess I'm caught!" She giggled nervously and brought the yarn out from behind her back.

It was a hideous tangle—twists and loops like a bird's nest and one silver knitting needle shoved down the middle like a stake in a vampire's heart. But when Nessa had first found it sitting on a shelf in the yarn room, it had been a neat little twist like a cruller or a loaf of challah. It had called to her in a way she couldn't begin to explain, almost as if a tiny firecracker had gone *pop* in her peripheral vision and made her turn her head. The strands were the color of grape bubblegum—more grapey than an actual grape could ever be. A person could pop a color like that in her mouth it would burst into juice. She'd *had* to have it.

"Are you mad?" Nessa asked.

"No, I'm not Mad, I'm perfectly fine—oh. You mean, am I angry?" Aubrey wrapped her arms around her middle, her sweater bunching in thick wrinkles. "I'm not angry. But your mom wouldn't want you to have it."

Nessa let out a breath she hadn't known she'd been holding. "I was watching you knit—when we were at the park last night. It doesn't look that hard."

"I thought somebody was watching me," Aubrey said.

"I want to learn," Nessa said. She glanced down at the storm of yarn in her hands. "I'm, like, ninety-nine-point-nine-nine-nine percent sure I can do a knit stitch or a purl stitch by myself. But I can't"—she held up the tangle; it made her want to weep with frustration—"I can't get started."

Aubrey uncrossed her arms. "Let me see."

Nessa handed it over. The needle fell to the floor with a clang, and she bent to pick it up. When she was standing again, she saw her aunt was smirking. The yarn in her hands was like an angry swarm of hornets frozen in time.

"It's okay," Nessa said. "You can laugh."

Aubrey smiled and thumbed a petal of bulging yarn. "Happens to the best of us. At one point or another, we all end up losing an hour or two to detangling."

"It just started doing that," Nessa said. "The more yarn I pulled out of the loop, the more it got tangled."

"That's because you have to wind it into a ball before you use it. Otherwise it just knots."

"Well—even if it wasn't all knotted, I still can't figure out how to get the stitches on the needle. I tried using a book. But it didn't make sense."

Nessa could feel herself scowling. The books she'd found in Mariah's room had been frustrating. The best they offered were line-drawn sketches that looked like spaghetti noodles and sticks. A book explained a cast-on the way a dictionary explained a word—but Nessa always needed to hear something in a sentence a few times before she got it. "I want to make a scarf. Just easy garter stitch, to start. If you can just cast on the first row for me and get the stitches on the needle, I'm pretty sure I can take it from there."

Aubrey's smile dimmed. She handed the yarn back to Nessa. "I have to think about it."

"But . . . *why*? It's just knitting."

"It's more complicated than that."

"'Cause my mom doesn't want me to learn?"

"Partly."

"Because of that girl who just went running out?"

"It's grown-up stuff."

"That girl wasn't a grown-up," Nessa said. "She was my age. Practically."

Aubrey sighed.

"I already know how to do a knit stitch. And—listen—I memorized the poem on Mariah's wall. You know? *In through the front door, out through the back. Peek through the window and—*"

"*Off jumps jack.* I know it. That's how I leaned to knit, too."

Nessa's hopes rose. "So? See? You don't have to teach me anything hardly. It's just that . . . I can't figure out this *casting-on* thing. I need you to do the first row."

Aubrey looked at the yarn.

"*Pleeease?*"

She glanced up.

"Pretty please?"

Aubrey was about to give in. Nessa could tell. She was *this close.*

But then, as per usual, her mother showed up at the wrong time.

They heard her voice at the same moment. She was climbing the porch stairs, telling Carson to get the door.

Quickly, Nessa shoved the yarn into a wooden barrel. She moved so fast she startled even herself. And then she knew—even before she looked up at her aunt again—that any chance she'd had of getting Aubrey to cast on for her was totally gone.

"Hi, ladies," Bitty said cheerfully. The autumn air had turned her cheeks into pink apples. Her hair was pulled back in a jaunty ponytail. "Hey Aubrey—Meggie and I were talking about the three of us going out to dinner tonight."

Her mom didn't wait for an answer. She made a beeline

down the Stitchery's center hall toward the back of the house, her arms loaded with groceries.

Nessa looked back to Aubrey. Already, her hands missed the weight of the bright purple yarn. She began to wonder if maybe she'd miscalculated, if her aunt was going to rat her out.

"I'll think about it," Aubrey said.

Bitty called her husband in the afternoon when she got back from the grocery store. Her cell phone had a full charge so she went to the top of the basement stairs and closed the door behind her. The smell of dust and cement and dry rot filled her nose. She dialed her husband at work. If anyone happened to hear one side of the conversation—his or hers—it would have sounded cordial enough.

Hi. How are you?

Good. Fine. The kids are fine, too. The funeral? Yes, it was . . . well . . . it was interesting.

Is work okay?

Good. The kids and I are thinking of spending a few extra days here. What do you think?

Well . . . I figured you would want to have a say in it.

Yes, I know it's almost Halloween. They can trick-or-treat here.

I don't know how long.

I'm asking you.

No.

Plus I thought maybe you and I could use some space.

Well, maybe I need space.

Okay. So since you don't have feelings about it either way, we're staying.

What about the will?
No, she didn't leave us anything.
Nothing.
That's a terrible thing to say!
It's different when I say it.
I have to go. We're going out to dinner tonight.
Yes, I'll have the kids call you tonight before bed.
Try not to miss me too much.
Uh-huh.
Right.
Bye.

Aubrey had forgotten what it was like to live in a house full
of people—messy, loud, energetic people who bumped up
against one another like heated atoms. There were things on
the floor to step around. There was barely enough space on
the hall coatrack, and inevitably one or two jackets ended up
slumping to the ground. The iced tea pitcher, which had been
full in the morning, had been put back in the fridge with no
more than a few swallows left in the bottom. The Stitchery,
which had been so very still and quiet for so many years, was
now a tornado.

Bitty had scheduled dinner for five o'clock, and Aubrey
had thought it funny to *schedule* a dinner among people who
lived in the same house—until five o'clock rolled around and
she was the only person who was ready to go. Meggie had
locked herself in the bathroom, just like the old days. Bitty
was in a motherly tizzy: Sandwiches had to be made for the
children and there was a question about whether or not the
ham was actually organic. Carson's handheld video game con-
sole went missing quite suddenly, as if it had materially vanished, and for some reason that Aubrey could not divine, this

stopped the entire process of leaving the house. Couch cushions were lifted, pillows thrown. The video game reappeared in a duffel bag that had been checked three times.

By the time Meggie sauntered down the hall stairs, the creak of old wood under her feet, Aubrey was starving, and she thought *Finally*. She'd skipped lunch and her tummy was growling. But the moment Meggie appeared in the living room, all preparation halted. Everyone looked at her, paused.

"*What?*" Meggie said.

She was standing with one hand on the door frame, dressed in a billowy fuchsia shirt that fell off one shoulder. Her leggings stopped at her shins. She was Meggie as usual. But it was her hair, her shocking new hair, that had rendered the family tongue-tied.

"Like you've never seen a person color her hair before," Meggie said.

"It's just so . . ." Bitty trailed off.

"Bleached!" Aubrey said.

Meggie's short black mop of hair was gone, replaced by even shorter white-blond spikes that pricked up not unlike Icky's quills when he was in a snit. Yesterday Meggie might have stepped out of a biker bar; "gothic fairy" she'd called it. Today she was showing her roots—literally and figuratively— as a child of the eighties.

Bitty lurched back into motion, tossing the video game controller to Carson and putting the couch pillows back in place. "Come on, guys. We have to get moving. We have— *had*—reservations."

But her children moved toward their aunt like cabbage moths to a lightbulb. "That's awesome," Carson said.

"Are we ready?" Bitty asked. "Is anyone forgetting anything?"

After a few more minutes, they finally left.

Aubrey was famished by the time they sat down at their table in the little tavern, so hungry that her napkin was beginning to look like it could be edible with a little ketchup and salt. But the waitress was busy, hustling from table to table, and so Aubrey waited in agony with her menu open before her. Each description of each dish (*mixed greens with dressing; burger and fries*) struck her as being on par with the most exquisite poetry ever penned.

Finally, the waitress arrived. After a long Q&A followed by humming and hawing, Meggie settled on a fruity, frozen concoction called the Vampire Barnabas. Bitty got a white wine spritzer. Aubrey ordered a microbrew pilsner. They'd been sitting so long that the waitress not only took their drink orders, but their dinner orders as well. She looked up from her notepad, her gaze skimming Aubrey's face.

"Hey—are you the girl who does all the knitting?"

"Oh. Yes."

"Huh. How 'bout that." The waitress tapped her pencil on her pad.

"How did you know?" Bitty asked.

She ducked her head in embarrassment. "Eyes like that. Even bluer than everybody says—but pretty, I mean. In a certain way."

Aubrey thanked her. But she knew her eyes weren't pretty so much as pretty awful.

"I was sorry to hear about Mariah," the waitress said.

"Thank you," Aubrey said. And she thought: *Now please, God in heaven have mercy, go get us some food.*

But the waitress just stood there, her face wrinkled as if she was having a debate with herself that only she could hear. "I should tell you. I went to the Stitchery last year, you know? I met Mariah. I was . . . there were some problems with my ex-husband."

Aubrey tensed. The waitress was getting emotional, her eyes dangerously red. When she spoke, she whispered. "If it wasn't for Mariah, I don't know what I would have done. He wasn't paying the child support. And I didn't know how I was gonna feed my kids. But Mariah . . . well, anyway. She knit me a beer koozie to give to him. Isn't that funny? Knitting a koozie? Anyway, it worked. And without that, I really don't know what I would have done."

Aubrey nodded, relieved that—this time anyway—she wasn't being held responsible for a spell gone wrong. Because the woman was on the brink of tears, Aubrey gave her a quick hug. By the time she left, Aubrey's sisters were looking at her as if they were seeing her for the first time.

Aubrey laced her fingers together on the table. "Okay. Let's have it."

Her sisters were quiet.

"Come on. Let's hear it. Tell me all about how I need to sell the Stitchery." She waited. They all had known—though it hadn't been spoken aloud—that tonight would be the night when they hashed things out, when the question of selling or keeping the Stitchery would be put to rest. The only thing holding Meggie and Bitty to Tarrytown was Mariah's rather vague last wishes. This last little hindrance had to be done away with; then they would be on their way.

Meggie spoke first. "About that . . . I might have reacted a little too strongly."

"Me, too," Bitty said. "We didn't mean to seem so harsh."

Aubrey sat back in her chair. It occurred to her that when her sisters had gone shopping this morning, they must have been talking about her—and laying out their plan of attack. "So . . . does that mean you're not going to give me a hard time about staying in the Stitchery?"

"We didn't say *that*," Meggie said. "We just want you to

know that we understand where you're coming from. We get why you want to stay."

"But we still think you should sell," Bitty said. "To a private individual or—if this eminent domain thing goes through—to the town."

"Not gonna happen," Aubrey said, trying to keep her voice light. In New York, legislatures liked to call the process of seizing property *appropriation*. In other countries, it had different names. But whatever the terminology, the idea was uniform: The government had the right to take a person's property for the greater good. Aubrey might have been able to accept that if Tarrytown needed to turn Tappan Square into an orphanage or a hospital or a park. But if Horseman Woods Commons passed, the land was going to be sold for a song to a private developer—as if strangers could take better care of the land than its current stewards. That just plain hurt. "We're having an emergency election of the Tappan Watch tomorrow night," Aubrey said.

"To replace Mariah?" Meggie asked.

"Nobody can replace Mariah," Aubrey said. "But, yeah. We have to figure out who's going to take the lead."

The waitress brought their drinks. She was smiling now, fully composed. "My name's Jess Nysen, just so you know. And the first round's on me."

"Thanks," Aubrey said. The waitress winked and went away. Aubrey sipped her beer; it was golden and smooth. She wiped at the foam on her lip and turned her focus back to her sisters. "You heard all of those people yesterday. At the funeral?"

"The people who got up and spoke?" Meggie asked.

"They weren't just talking about Mariah, how important she was. They were talking about the Stitchery. About what it means to Tarrytown. People *need* the Stitchery. It's important. Think of all the people who have been helped over the years. Like our waitress."

"Right. And like the girl who was there this morning?" Bitty asked.

Aubrey looked at her sister. "How do you know about her?"

"Nessa said she saw somebody leave. Crying."

"Oh." Aubrey stamped wet circles on her paper place mat with the bottom of her glass. "What did you tell her?"

"The truth: that I had no idea what she was talking about," Bitty said. "For the record, the Stitchery does *not* help everybody."

"But that's their own fault," Aubrey said. "The magic is perfectly reliable. It's just that if they don't give up something—"

"I know the rules," Bitty said.

Aubrey scooted her chair closer to the table. "The Van Rippers have been in the Stitchery since just after the Revolutionary War. There's a whole list of guardians in the Great Book in the Hall, back to when they started keeping track in 1867 and all the way through to my name. *I* can't be the one to leave. *I* can't be the one to break the tradition."

"But do you like the way things are?" Meggie asked.

"Sure," Aubrey said.

"Of course you don't," Bitty said.

Aubrey was quiet for a moment. Then she gave up. "It doesn't matter whether I like it. This is what I have to do. It's what I was born for. There's no other way."

"Sometimes that's true," Bitty said. "But *you* have choices. You could do something else."

"I just don't think you understand."

Bitty tapped the butt of her steak knife on the table. "I guess I don't. Why wouldn't you at least *think* about moving, making a better life for yourself? You could get a job in the city or go back to school. I mean—you don't want to reshelve books forever, right? And you can always knit on the side."

Aubrey laughed. "You can't do anything you're deeply passionate about *on the side.*"

Meggie jumped in. "Hey—how much money did the village offer you?"

"Two fifty."

Bitty frowned. "That does seem low."

"It's fair market value," Aubrey said.

"Why would the town put a decent value on properties that it obviously doesn't value to begin with?" Meggie said.

"Good question," Aubrey said.

"Even so, two fifty is still a big chunk of change," Bitty said. "We'd get eighty-three grand each, not counting taxes."

"Okay—that is a serious lot of money," Meggie said.

The waitress brought their food. Bitty had a cranberry walnut salad. Meggie had a plate of colorful nachos heaped with guacamole and sour cream. Aubrey had ordered a favorite: a margherita pizza, plain.

Bitty spoke with her fork in the air. "Finances aside, it's your decision, Aubrey. Whether the town takes the Stitchery or we sell it to someone else, it's entirely up to you."

"Neither of those things will happen." Aubrey put down her slice of pizza. It was too hot to eat. "And anyway, what about you two?"

"Us?" They spoke in unison, then laughed.

"What's the deal with Craig?" Aubrey asked her older sister. She tried to speak gently; she didn't want to accuse. "Why didn't he come to the funeral?"

"He had to work," Bitty said.

"Right. The woman who practically raised you dies and he has to work." Aubrey turned to Meggie. "And what about you? You haven't told us a thing about where you've been or what you've been doing."

"Maybe it's not your beeswax."

"For a while there it seemed like every time I got a post-card from you, it was from another state," Aubrey said.

"Right. Because I've been traveling around a lot."

"Are you working?"

"I have a website where I sell crafts and things. I don't really like to pay bills, so I don't have a car or an apartment. Nothing to hold me down."

"And you're not lonely? Traveling around all the time?"

Meggie laughed. "I meet a lot of people. Trust me. A lot."

"But not *friends*," Aubrey said. "Not people who know you—who really know you—inside and out. You have people you spend time with and then forget about when you move away. I wouldn't call those people *friends*."

"We're not here to talk about me," Meggie said. "We're talking about the Stitchery."

"And now you're being cagey," Aubrey said. "What are you not telling us?"

Bitty put down her fork. "Why are you doing this, Aub? We're trying to help you."

"I'm trying to make the point that while you're both so busy scrutinizing my life, you've got your own stuff to work out."

Her sisters were quiet. Outside, a car horn blared. People were walking up the sidewalk. The moon was a curled thread suspended in the sky.

"I guess that's fair," Bitty said.

Aubrey sighed. There was a time, she remembered, for a few years during their childhoods, that she and her sisters had been fully and completely on one another's sides. Suffering could pull a family together; pain could be like gravity, pressure that held a shape, drawing everyone in to a central point. Or it could scatter a family apart, centripetal forces slingshotting each person wildly away. Sometimes, suffering could do both—gather and scatter—given a long enough time line.

The pain that had pulled them together, apart from any discomforts that might have been inflicted by life in the Stitchery, had stemmed from their mother. Years had passed between the day Lila Van Ripper went missing and the day she was declared deceased. Mariah, who had insisted that her sister was dead from the very beginning, had a terrible time forcing the government to recognize Lila's passing. As the newly appointed guardian of three little girls, Mariah had hired a detective, had her sister's bank accounts monitored, and had notified the Social Security agency of her sister's "missing person" status—not because she wanted to prove that her sister was still living, but instead to prove she was thoroughly and properly kaput. In the uncertainty, the Van Rippers had pulled together—tight as a military unit of highly trained operatives, watching one another's backs, until gradually the pain of Lila's vanishing began to grow dull, and the ties between the girls began to loosen, and the Stitchery became like a slowly rising wedge, and they grew apart.

For the most part, the people of Tarrytown had never cared for Lila. She lived in the Stitchery with Mariah and her girls, and she had what the good people of Tarrytown called a *reputation*. In the sixties, she'd been an outspoken protester of everything—bombs, men, meat, the status quo. By the eighties, she'd mellowed out somewhat. She had her children (the first two by one man who had floated in and out of her life, then Meggie by someone else when her diaphragm had failed). By the late nineties, she was beginning to lose it. She was bumming cigarettes in front of the liquor store and bothering people at bus stops. She was known to take her shirt off at the slightest provocation—whether in a park or a bar—and the local boys had great fun with her antics. She disappeared for weeks at a time, months; the girls didn't know where she went. Sometimes, she came home tan and happy. Sometimes, pale and gaunt. She was not a guardian of the Stitchery, but she threatened people with magic; when the convenience-store clerk accidentally gave her the wrong change, she spat on the counter and vowed to curse his progeny. One day, she went away and never came back. Her death was the final nail in her coffin. Lila Van Ripper didn't even have the courtesy to leave her body behind.

By the time the government acknowledged her death and the funeral director gave his (rather short) eulogy, the Van Rippers' tears for their mother had dried up. They stood on the stone porch of the funeral home, shivering in the chill of late winter. There was no hint of spring in the air. Few people had come to the funeral because the roads were clotted with snow. Few people would have come anyway. Aubrey stood with her sisters looking out onto the river, which was frozen at the edges but still moving slushily in the center channel. Bitty was fifteen; Aubrey, eleven; Meggie just five. They stood huddled together in their buttoned wool coats and thick hand-knit scarves. Although it was toasty in the funeral parlor, they did not want to go back inside. Eventually Mariah came out and stood behind them. She put her arms around all three of them, scooping them up and hugging them close. In the cold and snow, her body blocked the wind, and her breath blew out of her nostrils like an ox snorting in winter. "Don't worry," she said. "We'll be all right. We have each other, don't we?"

Sitting in the tavern, her pizza cold on her plate, Aubrey remembered her aunt's words but didn't remind her sisters of them. They hurt too much to think of, let alone say aloud. Instead, she finished her food as quickly as she could, aware that her sisters were doing the same, and tried to make small talk because she knew they were not going to resolve the Stitchery issue tonight.

When they returned to the Stitchery, Aubrey felt sullen and lonely, and she knew her sisters did, too. Meggie went back out, though she did not say where she was going. Aubrey went up to her room to visit the hedgehog. He was merrily running and swinging on his wheel, but she scooped him into her hands anyway and brought him to her bed. After a huffy, halfhearted spiking, he relaxed and began to crawl around her lap. His nose twitched, his dark eyes gleamed like bright black beads. Aubrey liked to run her thumb along his brown-and-white quills like fanning the pages of a book, and—when he let her—she stroked the baby-soft white hair on his belly and chin. Normally, she would have told him all about her day. But the walls were thin and her sisters already thought she was crazy.

A soft knock on the door. Icky snuffed and pulled his visor of quills down over his face at the sound. "Come in."

Bitty pushed open the door just enough to fit her shoulders through. "Am I interrupting?"

"Well, me and the hedgie were just about to figure out the meaning of life."

"And that is . . . ?"

"He says it's 'eating mealworms.' I think it might be more like, trying to do some good in the world."

"Good thing we live in a country that tolerates differences." Bitty smiled. She moved into the room and the old door

creaked closed behind her. She was wearing her pajamas—
a sporty, matching set of ginger-colored terry. Her hair was
wet and her skin was shiny with scrubbing. She took a few
steps closer to the bed. Icky sniffed the air.

"He's cute," Bitty said. "Carson won't stop talking about
him. You know I'm never going to hear the end of it until I
buy them one."

"Want to hold him?"

"Can I?"

Aubrey sat up a little as Icky pawed along her sternum. She
picked him up, careful of his soft belly and matchstick legs.
But when Bitty reached for him, he snapped into a tight and
hissing ball. Bitty jumped back and Aubrey laughed. "Don't
be scared. It's not like he can shoot you with his quills."

"Maybe I'll just admire from afar," Bitty said. She sat down
gently on the bed. Icky uncurled and began to sniff again.
Bitty played with the zipper of her pajamas. "I came to ask a
favor."

"Okay?" Aubrey said.

"I was wondering if you would mind if the kids and I stayed
with you for a little while longer."

Icky poked his head into a fold of Aubrey's sweater, and
she thought of Nessa, standing in the yarn room, a tangle of
purple wool in her hands. She decided that she would keep
the visual to herself—for a little while at least. "Why do I get
the feeling that you're not thinking this will be a vacation?"

"I thought it would be good for us."

"And?"

"And . . . I need a break from Craig."

Aubrey nodded. She knew how hard it was for her sister to
ask for a favor. She also knew how hard it was to admit that
there was anything wrong. Bitty was a lot like Icky in that

way: He was a prey animal, and by nature he was programmed never to show a weakness. It was very hard to know if he was sick or hurting. Bitty had come to be that way as well.

"You can stay as long as you want," Aubrey said. "Nessa and Carson are really great kids—no, they're great *people*. You know that feeling of—like—when you first wake up in the morning and you stretch your arms and your legs and your back, and everything pops and creaks, and it feels so so good?"

"Yes?"

"That's what it's like having you guys back."

"Thanks. I think." She reached out to pet Icky's back, and he let her.

"And besides," Aubrey said. "Technically, now it's your house, too."

Bitty was quiet, her chin tipped down. When she was serene—in passing moments like this one—her face had a kind of aloof queenliness like an old painting of the Madonna. She brushed Icky's spikes, her eyes downcast. "Craig and I . . . things haven't been easy over the last year. Especially not for the kids."

Aubrey waited for her to say more. She was nearly holding her breath. She wanted, so much, to be able to talk to her sister again. To know her. She couldn't imagine what it had cost Bitty to walk in here and ask for help—retreating to the Stitchery even as she was asking Aubrey to condemn it. She must have been in a bad situation. Really bad.

But Bitty didn't elaborate. She just got to her feet and walked wearily across the room. "I'm going to tell the kids the good news. They'll be glad we're staying."

"For how long?"

"You haven't lived until you've done Halloween in Tarrytown. Right?" She grinned—and for the first time, her smile reached her eyes.

"Can they do that?" Aubrey asked. "Can the kids miss that much school?"

"They have regular tutors. I'll call the school tomorrow and double-check, but I think they'll be okay. And besides . . ." She paused at the door. "We need this. A little break from everything. I think it will be good for them. And I think it will be good for me."

Aubrey wanted to say *I'm glad you're staying*. But she guessed that wouldn't have been quite the right response. Bitty closed the door behind her with a soft click.

Aubrey thought of Nessa. She thought of Carson. Her heart ached for them—for Bitty's family, for whatever it was they were going through, and she wished that there was something she could do for them.

In the morning Nessa woke to see her grape yarn wound into a perfect ball on her nightstand, and a line of neat stitches perched on a needle like birds on a wire.

From the Great Book in the Hall: *The new knitter may have her doubts. A top-down cardigan starts with just a few flat rows, knit straight across. That's it. A Möbius scarf begins with a straight line. A little black sheep knit into the yoke of a sweater first appears to be a few deranged blobs. Celtic cables, slithering across a scarf, can boggle the mind.*

But we knitters—when we trust the patterns, we learn the tricks. We are the man behind the curtain. We built the secret panel in the floor. We're the ones who put the rabbit in the hat in the first place. But that doesn't make the process less of a revelation.

Even the most accomplished knitters can feel as if they're wandering through a fog with little more than a dim lantern. You look at three rows of garter stitch on a knitting needle and think, How on earth could this scrap of fabric become a sweater? *But little by little, you keep at it, and it does.*

10

"Purl"

The old firehouse where the Tappan Watch met had wooden paneling, fluorescent lights, and a weary pink kitchen that could be scrubbed with a toothbrush from top to bottom and yet *still* never look clean. On a good night, twenty or so people might show up to say the Pledge of Allegiance, circle their folding chairs, and pass around a petition. On a bad night—which was to say, a normal night—eight people might wander in late or leave early, mostly for the doughnuts and cider.

This particular Thursday, however, was not a normal night. It was—Aubrey thought as she sat with her knitting, waiting quietly for the meeting to begin—a tremendously good night. News of the "incident" at Mariah's funeral picnic had spread, and nearly all of Tappan Square had shown up at the Watch meeting. Something about Mariah's death coupled with the approaching deadline for the council's vote had galvanized the neighbors to fight—fight at long last. And yet the flourishing crowd left Aubrey with an empty spot in her heart. It seemed such a shame that the Watch had finally been able to muster the energy that Mariah had been hell-bent on mustering—but only after she'd died.

She gathered the heavy Peruvian wool of her poncho more tightly around her shoulders. A cold snap had stampeded across the valley with darkness and rain riding hard at its heels. The chill was the kind that knocked on the bones.

"Hey."

Vic dropped into a metal chair beside her, and the hard freeze that had wrapped like a fist around her midsection began to loosen. She finished a stitch and then lifted her eyelids to take him in. He wore a jacket the color of burnt cedar. He smelled of leather, rain, and some faint cologne. His hair was dark and dripping. "Doing okay?"

"Yep."

"Whatcha making? Can I see?" He motioned to her knitting. She had a new project—a beanie in pale pink with a black skull-and-crossbones motif. With such brutally short hair, Meggie would need a warm hat on nights like this. If she stayed in Tarrytown.

Aubrey moved the work a little closer to Vic, and he touched the stockinette with reverence, caressing the pattern with the pad of his thumb. Her mouth went dry and her poncho felt far too warm on her shoulders.

"Are you making, um, a spell?"

"No. This is just for fun."

"Is that a pirate symbol?"

She laughed. "Kind of."

"That's pretty badass. And to think my grandmother used to knit toilet paper covers."

"Ah yes. Cozies," she said. "Knitters make the weirdest things. If you see a woman walking around in a hat that looks like it came out of a Dr. Seuss book, chances are she's a knitter."

"Why?"

She shrugged. "Because we like to show off what we make. Even if it's not really practical . . . like a toilet paper roll cover."

"Hey, now." His eyebrows drew down in false seriousness.

"Don't hate the cozies. I have fond memories of using them to hold paintball pellets."

She smiled. "As if I haven't knit my share."

He pulled away from her a bit. "Jeanette coming tonight?"

"She'll be here later." She glanced at him. He wasn't just looking at her; he was staring. His wide shoulders were turned nearly perpendicular to the back of his chair. She squirmed in her seat, heating under his scrutiny. "What's wrong?"

"You do know that it's dark outside."

"Oh." She touched her face. She'd decided to wear her brown-tinted glasses tonight—just to take the edge off should she catch anyone's eye. Should she catch *his*. "I'm really sensitive to the light. And I put my eyeballs through hell—you know—with the knitting."

"Why don't you take a break?"

She glanced down at the beanie in her hands. She had told him a partial truth: Her eyes hurt. Also, her hands ached with what she suspected was early arthritis. And working the kinks out of her back was as futile as massaging the knots out of a pine tree. But she loved knitting far too much to stop. How could she explain that to be sitting still and *not* be knitting, *not* be creating something, made her feel like she was wasting time?

"I'll take a break," she told him. "Later."

"Right. When you're sleeping." He smiled. His teeth, which she hadn't been close enough to notice until now, were nice teeth—adequately white and with just enough crookedness to please her. He looked around as if checking for eavesdroppers, then leaned closer. He put his arm around the backrest of her chair. Something warm and glowy eased open within her.

"So," he whispered. "Are you going to run?"

She whispered back. "From what?"

He laughed. "*For* what. Are you going to run to be the new president?"

"Oh. No."

He tipped his head. "Why not? Aren't you the natural heir?"

She looked at him now without trying to hide her face. Was he crazy? The leader of the Tappan Watch had to be many things—things Aubrey was not. The leader had to be confident about public speaking; Aubrey had not even spoken at Mariah's funeral. The leader had to be outspoken and brassy; Aubrey's sauciest moment had been in the eighth grade, when a teacher had asked her for an answer and she'd said, "You're the teacher, you tell me." The leader also had to be popular in Tarrytown—because who except a popular person could mobilize the people of Tappan Square for victory? That Vic thought Aubrey could be the new leader was flattering, but also ridiculous. She wished she could see herself through his eyes.

"I can't run," she said.

"But you'll at least get up and say something, right? To set the tone? I think people would want to hear from you, given everything that's happening."

She looked down at her hands in her lap, a dark swell of guilt coming over her. She wanted to help. She did. She wished she were a different person—the kind who could get up in front of a crowd without breaking a sweat. But then she reminded herself: It was actually better for everyone if she did what she always did, played a supporting role instead of a lead one. A bad leader was extremely dangerous. And while she knew she would not be *bad*, she didn't imagine she could be good, either.

"I'm really awful at speaking in public," she said.

"Really? But you're so . . . oh . . . what's the word I'm looking for? You know—when you have a way of putting things, when you have a way of making a point . . . ?"

"Articulate?"

He snapped his fingers. "See? You're a natural."

"Cute." She laughed. "That's just the bookworm in me. When I talk in front of a group, I lose the feeling in my feet. Seriously."

"Good thing you talk with your mouth then," he said. And if Aubrey didn't imagine it, his gaze dropped for a moment to the mouth in question.

At the podium near the front of the room, someone was tapping on the microphone and saying, "Testing. Hello. Hello. If everyone could please take your seats?"

A flash of disappointment crossed Vic's face, and it was a moment before he turned away from her and faced front. Outside, the wind gave a long, low howl.

"Everyone? Please?" Dan Hatters, the Watch's treasurer and the closest thing to a leader they had left, was a small man, nearly bald, with a nice argyle sweater and cheap jeans. His voice was piercing. "Everyone? Hello? Take your seats?"

Aubrey lifted her knitting. The proceedings to replace Mariah began.

The Tappan Watch did not have an especially long or auspicious history in Tarrytown. It was formed some time ago—no one could quite remember when—as a way for Tappan Square to rally against a rising tide of crime. The Watch put up street signs that declared a zero-tolerance policy. It sponsored "go-cart night" for students who kept up their grades. It held an annual street fair. In short, it *tried*.

But in recent years, some of the steam had gone out of the Tappan Watch as residents became less concerned about crime and more concerned about feeding their families. The street fair shrank to a few card tables and an amateur clown.

Students realized that one night of go-carts didn't make up for an entire semester of studying math. The zero-tolerance street signs had been vandalized so that pairs of watchful eyes now looked like pairs of droopy boobs. Aubrey did not quite know how the Watch would be able to put itself together, especially now that Mariah was gone.

"And now we'll hear from our candidates for president." Dan Hatters leaned a little too close to the microphone, and it squealed. The crowd grumbled. "Sorry. So . . . who's ready?"

First to approach the podium was Redmond Kingly. Between two limp flags he spoke about preserving Tappan Square for the future and protecting their homes. He was so impassioned that his fist pummeled the air and his face got sweaty and scarlet—and if it wasn't for his state of perpetual drunkenness he might have stood a chance.

Next was Gretel Couenhoven, a math teacher who had a voice like an airplane gliding past on a summer's day—distant, droning, and of a nature to put a person instantly to sleep. In fact, when Gretel had finally finished her speech, a long moment of silence stretched out before someone finally came to attention and began to clap—because no one had heard a difference between when she was talking and when she was not.

Old Wouter Van Twiller gave a little speech, too—and it was quite a good speech. Passionate yet educated. Cerebral yet accessible. The problem was that Wouter, a member of the historical society who spent his retirement digitizing old books, smelled like hamburger and mothballs, and he had a habit of picking the dry skin off his face when he got nervous.

Aubrey slumped in her chair.

"We're doomed," Jeanette, who had snuck in late as usual, whispered beside her.

Vic leaned in and sighed. "I would nominate myself. But

I've got my sister living in the house. And it's not a *legal* two-family. I can't put myself up for scrutiny."

"Half of the people in this room are illegal one way or another," Aubrey said.

"I can't do it either," Jeanette said. "I don't think a Tarrytown citizens' group much wants a Sleepy Hollower leading the fight."

Aubrey twisted her hands in her lap. She knew that being a leader meant being a little singular and *apart;* one couldn't lead a crowd forward from the middle of the pack. But how could Shawn Prior, who was banging on the podium and hollering about Moses dying within sight of the Promised Land, lead Tappan Square to any kind of victory? The wrong leader could do more harm than good. And the stakes were too high to make a bad choice. There was a little over two weeks before the vote that would determine the fate of Tappan Square.

"Is there anyone else?" Dan Hatters asked. He gripped the podium. "Come on now, people. Anyone? Anyone at all?"

The room was quiet except for the snap of raindrops on the window. Aubrey's palms were sweating. She held her breath. Her heart in her chest was beating at her ribs like an angry mob. Her feet began to tingle. None of the candidates who had voiced their opinions so far had come close to Mariah's energy, passion, eloquence, and chutzpah. Anyone would be an improvement—even Aubrey. Even *her.*

Please, she thought. *Somebody, please.* She could not be the one.

"Well then." Dan looked out over the crowd. "I guess. I guess if there's no one—if we're sure—and there really isn't *anybody* else who wants to run . . . anybody at all . . ."

"Oh, *hell,*" Aubrey said.

And she stood up.

It was said that a great rush of wind blew into the Tappan Square firehouse, so strong that chairs were knocked over, flags were blown off their flagpoles, and hair was whipped into stinging eyes. In any case, just as Aubrey got to her feet—her guts rumbling around within her, her feet like blocks of ice—the doors to the firehouse flew open and if it wasn't a wind that rushed in it was a man, Mason Boss, who seemed to be not at all caught off guard when everyone in the room turned to face him.

"Hello, good people of Tappan Square," he said.

Chairs whined and creaked as people craned their necks for a better view. He wore pants that on another man would have been called *gray* but on him were definitely silver. He had on a black leather jacket over a white button-down shirt. He did not carry an umbrella, and yet it was as if the rain had politely refrained from falling on him because he did not appear even slightly wet. His beautiful face and gorgeous dark skin were bright with cold.

"Sorry I'm late. What'd I miss?"

Dan Hatters was not immune to Mason's charm. He fluttered like a preening bird at the podium. "We were just going to vote on the new president."

"Then I'm right on time. Can I—" here, he paused to take off an invisible hat and then flick it like a Frisbee, "—throw my hat into the ring?"

No one had noticed that Aubrey was half standing, with her knees still slightly bent and her mouth open and her butt sticking out over her chair. Slowly, so she didn't attract any attention, she sank down. She was surprised to find that she was slightly disappointed. Relieved—and yet disappointed. Vic patted her leg. She was sure he meant to be reassuring. He kept his hand there.

"We just heard the campaign speeches." Dan Hatters'

voice was charged with new excitement. "If you have one ready, it's not too late."

"Do I have one ready?" At the back of the room, Mason Boss lifted his hands palms-up as if he was about to break out into song. He smiled, his eyes twinkling. "Of course I do." He strode to the front of the room, taking the podium from Dan Hatters. He spoke with eloquence and passion and charisma. He made people think and made them laugh. He lifted his index finger to underscore good points and better ones. The people of Tarrytown were starstruck; only later would they consider that there were many questions they should have thought to ask. Only later would they wonder if Mason Boss had pulled the proverbial wool over their eyes.

"In conclusion," he said after a time, "I want to be the president of Tappan Watch. All in favor?"

The people of the Watch began to clap their hands.

Aubrey whispered to Vic. "I don't think this follows Robert's Rules of Order."

Vic nodded. "Maybe we need a little more disorder if we're going to make this work."

"Maybe," Aubrey said.

After the Tappan Watch meeting disbanded—people flocking merrily into the streets as if they were celebrating a coronation—Vic insisted on driving Aubrey back to the Stitchery. Shadows shrank the wide-open valley down to the constricted scope of headlights. The rain flew like flecks of ice in the wind.

In the dark of the pickup, Aubrey sat with her knitting bag on her lap. The small cab of the truck smelled like tools—metallic and dusty, but not entirely bad. As Vic steered, taking a roundabout route to avoid the plug of traffic near the firehouse, it occurred to Aubrey that despite the thick flux of feelings he stirred in her, she knew very little about him. They'd had so many issues and topics to discuss—Mariah's death, the Watch, Mason Boss, the future of Tappan Square. Everything was so important, so dire—it was as if they'd skipped basic training and had instead thrown themselves directly into the foxhole. Except for a few friendly details gleaned from chats over the circ desk, Aubrey had not yet developed a clear picture of the way Vic lived when he wasn't mucking through the imbroglio of her life.

"So," she said, aware of the nervousness in her voice but unable to make herself sound natural. "How long have you been in Tarrytown?"

"I've been in the area about eighteen months. But only a few have been in Tappan Square."

"Why did you move up here from the city?"

He laughed. "The truth?"

"Why not?"

"There was a girl. She'd lived up here and worked in Queens. I met her at a beer garden. One thing led to another, and next thing I know I'm living in Tarrytown. We had an apartment on the border with Sleepy Hollow."

Aubrey watched him drive, a slow maneuvering down two-way streets that were big enough only for one car. "Are you . . . is she . . . ?"

"It didn't work out. I was too boring for her—that's what she said. Boring."

"I don't think you're boring."

"No? How can you tell?"

"You don't check out boring books."

He laughed. "She thought *all* books were boring."

"Then she doesn't know what she's missing," Aubrey said. She was glad for the darkness because it made her feel a little

braver when she smiled at him. And because she wasn't talking about books at all.

He smiled back. He waited patiently while another car
squeezed down a narrow block. "Anyway, she left Tarrytown.
But I hung around. I realized I could work for myself because
Tappan Square needed a handyman—somebody discreet, you
know."

"You mean somebody who won't snitch when three families are living in one house. Or when people pay for their new
roofs entirely in cash."

"My family came to this country just before I was born,
so—yeah—someone who gets it. I just bought my house in
Tappan Square a few months ago."

"When you met Mariah at the library," she said.

"Yes. When she introduced me to you." His fingers curled
around the steering wheel as if he might twist it like rope. "I
can't lose the house. Not when I'm finally starting to feel like
it's *home*."

"I know what you mean." She leaned her spine hard into
the seat. "I really wish Mason Boss hadn't come to the meeting when he did. I don't know why people can't see through
him. He really likes to hear himself talk—even when he's not
really saying anything. He's obviously just doing it for the attention."

"You're really annoyed," he said, a bit of speculation in his
voice. "Are you mad that he was elected president, or are you
mad because you didn't make a bid."

She glanced across the dark cab. The wipers squeaked.
"I'm *glad* I didn't have to run. I was just going to do it because
there was nobody else."

"Uh-huh."

"No, really."

"Know what I think?" He eased the truck onto the Stitchery's street. He drove slowly though there were no cars in front of them. "I think you really love Tappan Square. Maybe more than anybody in that room tonight."

"But that doesn't mean I want to be president. Or—that I'd be good at it."

"You'd feel more comfortable speaking in public if you did it a few times."

"How do you know?"

"I was on the debate team in high school," he said.

"You?"

"Why do you seem so surprised?"

Aubrey floundered. "Because you're, well, you're so *cool*."

He laughed. "Cool? Oh no. I was debate team captain. Two years of sax before I quit because I didn't like the marching band hats. And my comic book collection is still stashed in my mom's attic—even though she tries every year to get me to throw it away."

Aubrey narrowed her eyes. "Magic: The Gathering?"

"Every Monday until I was twenty," he said.

"*Star Wars* collectibles?"

"They were my only hope."

She relaxed into her seat, laughing a little, and she saw that he was laughing, too. He pulled up in front of the Stitchery. In the headlights, the rain fell like a million little meteors streaking toward earth, flashing yellow-gold against the darkness.

"Thanks for the lift," she said.

"Any time."

She tried the door handle but it was locked. She fumbled to find the switch in the dark. "I'm sorry—I seem to be . . ." She laughed nervously. Her hands fluttered. Where was the lock? "Um, oh gosh, a little help?"

"Aubrey." She stopped fussing and turned to him. His fingers were wrapped tight around the wheel. He scowled hard at the dashboard. "I'd like to take you out."

She heard the raindrops falling. "Like . . . on a date?"

"I would have asked you weeks ago, but I had this feeling that you were avoiding me. I'm hoping I was wrong."

"Oh. Of course not," she mumbled.

He gave a shrug, a glance, and a wobbly smile. "Well, I figured it couldn't hurt to ask."

"No—I mean, of course I wasn't avoiding you. Sorry."

"Oh." He looked at her now. The glow from the streetlight was coming through the windshield, painting his skin with golden undertones, and his cheeks were freckled with shadows of raindrops. His eyes held a kind of wary hopefulness. "Well? Do you want to go out with me?"

"Yes," she said. "I would like that. Thank you."

"Tomorrow? At six thirty?"

"Sure. What should I . . . how should I dress? Is it, um, formal?"

"I don't know. Nice-ish?"

"Where are we going?"

He grinned. "It's a surprise."

"So we're going to wing it?"

He laughed. "I'm not really a wing-it type of guy when it comes to things that are important. I already bought tickets."

"What would you have done if I'd said no?"

"I hoped you wouldn't," he said.

He unlocked the doors; the click in the muffled dark nearly startled her. She glanced at him with a sense that something was incomplete between them. But what was left to do? A friendly hug? A handshake? A kiss on the cheek, or—she could hardly think it—the mouth? She knew what this was: She was stalling. She wanted one more second alone with him in the car, one more minute with the rain tinkling on the roof, and the wipers skidding their rubbery arms over the windshield, and the air growing warm and moist from two bodies in such close proximity to each other. She wanted one more minute here, in the safety and privacy of his car, before she made her way back into the field of land mines that was the Stitchery. She did not move, did not breathe—she would have stopped her heart from beating if she'd had the power. He was looking at her. He felt it, too. One more minute to see how far one more minute could go.

But—it was time. She opened the door, shifted to plant a shoe firmly on the pavement.

"Aubrey?"

She stopped. "What?"

"I would have voted for you."

She looked at him—his long and narrow face, his heavy brow bone, and his eyes that glinted under the streetlight like pennies in a well.

She smiled. And she stepped into the rain.

11

"Cut Steek"

"Tarrytown is *not* scary," Bitty told her children. She tucked them snugly into their beds. She got Nessa an extra blanket because the shivery old windows of the Stitchery let in every cold gust, and she got Carson a glass of water because he was always thirsty in the middle of the night. She sat on his bed. "Tarrytown's a regular old town like any other."

Carson shook his head. "It's different here. It *is* scary. Even the sunset is scary."

Bitty brushed back his fine blond hair. When the sun had set tonight as Aubrey left for her meeting, its colors were violent and awful—a hue like a fresh-squeezed blood orange as rain clouds rolled in. The trees blackened to grotesque silhouettes, as if they had been frozen in terrible agony, reaching skyward even as they were being dragged into hell. Bitty was sure that at least some of the local lore had been inspired by an overabundance of sunsets, time, and sky.

"Nothing can hurt you here," she told her son.

"But what if it does?"

"I won't let it."

"But what about the Horseman?"

Bitty tried to cover her moment of pause. "There is no Horseman."

"Yes there is."

"No—"

"Then why are there all those movies about him killing people and stuff?"

"They're just stories. Sometimes people like to sit around and scare themselves for fun."

"Like we do at Scouts?" Carson adjusted his pillow. "When we're camping?"

"Right," Bitty said.

"But the stories have to come from *somewhere*," Nessa said from her bed across the room.

Bitty shot her a silent warning. "When a whole bunch of people start talking about a thing, they get themselves all worked up about it. And it doesn't matter if it's true or not. Remember that story 'The Emperor's New Clothes'?"

"Sort of," Nessa said.

"Well, it's like if all the people who were watching the naked emperor parade down the street didn't just *pretend* they saw him strutting about in his fine clothes. It's like if they really *believed* he was. The same thing happens with ghost stories."

She could see that her son wasn't convinced. And she, too, could remember what it was like to be scared of the Horseman.

Bitty glanced at her watch. She dragged her palms along her thighs as she stood. "There is no Headless Horseman. And I'll prove it. Just give me a minute."

She left and went down the hallway to Mariah's room, then scanned the bookcase. When she returned to her children, she had the story of Irving's Headless Horseman in her hands. She had planned to summarize a bit and skip to the ending, but to her surprise, her children wanted to hear the whole thing.

"It's a long story," she warned them. "Not exactly short-attention-span reading."

"As if there's anything better going on," Nessa said.

"Please?" Carson said. "Come on, Mom. Please?"

"Okay," Bitty said. And she propped herself up in Carson's bed with her kids on either side. She could not remember the last time they had read a story together; it must have been years ago.

Little by little, they made their way through the old tale—which felt both familiar and somehow new. She read to them about Ichabod Crane, poor, pitiable Ichabod with his gangly arms and legs, his quivering and overactive imagination, his legendary vibrato. She read about Katrina Van Tassel, the pretty, ankle-flashing coquette whose family table was always heaped with apple, plum, or pigeon pie, sweet corn, ginger cakes, *olykoeks*, and crullers. She read about the braggart Brom Bones and his surreptitious war against Ichabod for Katrina's affection. And eventually, she read about the Headless Horseman—the ghoulish chase down through the haunted hollow and over the infamous wooden bridge, ending with the monster's wicked aim with a pumpkin. She paused as she read, talking her children through the landmarks in the story, some of which were still visible or at least commemorated in Tarrytown.

Over the years, especially during the last few decades, the charming, coy little folktale of love and mischief in Tarrytown had somehow morphed into full-fledged horror. In recent movies and retellings, the Horseman had taken on a life of his own, completely separate and apart from the Horseman of Irving's imagination. He was a monster, a serial killer, what Jack the Ripper would have been if he were a headless ghost on a stallion of apocalyptic proportions.

But in Irving's tale, the Horseman was something else entirely. When the story was over, Bitty asked her children: "Now, who do we think is the real Headless Horseman?"

And though it took a while for them to figure it out, it was Carson whose round face lit up like a bulb as he said "Brom Bones!"

"You see?" she said as she bent to tighten the covers around her son's shoulders. "There is no Headless Horseman. It was just a trick played on poor Ichabod to scare him away from Katrina. And there's nothing scary about Tarrytown."

"Technically it doesn't *say* that," Nessa said. "It doesn't say that Brom is the Horseman."

"It doesn't have to say it; it's implied," Bitty said. Then she kissed her children, told them to go to sleep, and managed to keep a smile on her face until she left the room.

What she did not tell them, as she closed the door behind her, was that people in the Hudson Valley had been whispering stories of a Headless Horseman long before Irving wrote down the tale. Nor did she tell them about the grave supposedly in the Old Dutch churchyard, where a nameless German soldier was buried—his head taken clear off by a cannonball.

She didn't want her children to know that even the smallest kernel of truth existed down beneath the fictional puffery of the story. Because if they knew there was a hint of legitimacy, like a drop of food coloring in a tall glass of water, they would fixate on it. And eventually that one little dollop of fact would dissolve and expand and discolor everything, making all the ridiculous fiction seem like it could be real. Like what happened with the "magic" of the Stitchery.

She leaned against the door of her children's temporary bedroom. There *was* something to be afraid of in Tarrytown. But Bitty had no way of explaining what it was. Nor would she want to—because it scared her far more than any made-up story.

She went down the hall to her bedroom, ignoring the goose bumps on her arms.

* * *

While Bitty had been settling in to read to her children, and Aubrey had been trying not to think of the way Vic's elbow touched her arm where they sat in the fire hall, Meggie had been splashing along in a half-empty bus to Yonkers, where her old roller derby team, the Flying Dutchesses, was having a bout. Whenever she got to a new city, the first thing she did was look up the local rollergirls. She couldn't always skate on their team, but she could take tickets at the door, set up and break down seating, or even referee in a pinch. She knew that where there were rollergirls, there were new friends.

She paid her twelve dollars at the door and ignored the butterflies in her belly as she shouldered her way inside. The great dark ribs of the barrel ceiling arched overhead, and beneath them, the rollergirls were warming up. The crowd was electric; Meggie's blood heated with its noise and its verve. People laughed and talked, their voices hollowed out by the massive enclosure. Hugs were exchanged. Children played tag, or some game like it, and squealed at the top of their lungs. And yet for all the happy clamor, Meggie moved through the arena in perfect and unnoticed silence, finding a place on the bleachers, adjusting her leggings, sitting down just far enough away from her neighbor to be acceptable, feeling invisible and small.

She strained to see her old team, where they were stretching their calves and cinching the laces of their skates tight. She knew a few of them, those who were still around. She knew that "Simone Says" had a bum knee, that "Whip in Time" hated being the pivot, that "Hard Block Life" had an autistic daughter who adored elephants. But her primary reason for paying a visit to her old stomping grounds was not only to see her former teammates in general, but to see one specific person on the team. One specific person who might or might not be interested in seeing her.

Before Meggie had left Tarrytown, Tori Westmore—"Winged VicTori" on the rink—had been Meggie's closest friend outside of the Stitchery. Tori was tough to get a handle on. She'd never been against coercing the guys outside the liquor store to buy her beer, but she also went to church on Sunday mornings, where she sat in the back pew and prayed. She loved pulpy noir detective fiction—the more backward and sexist, the more she liked to talk about it and laugh; but she also liked to spend her weekend afternoons wandering through art galleries in Lower Manhattan. She believed in the Stitchery's magic—even more than Meggie did at times. She'd even tried on occasion to knit her own (failed) spells. But she didn't believe in people at all: She was cynical and distrusting and she made the people she loved jump through hoops to stay close to her. She often needed to be forgiven, but she was also the friend who was quickest to forgive.

Meggie had loved her to pieces. But after her high school diploma had arrived at the Stitchery, Meggie had left Tori the way she'd left everyone in Tarrytown—without so much as a hint of her plans.

She shifted where she sat. She could not see through the crowd if Tori was among the players. Maybe she had given up roller derby. Perhaps Meggie might never see her again. And maybe it was better that way. Tori's willingness to forgive a derelict friend might have a statute of limitations—one that Meggie had years ago surpassed. Tori had every right to be mad.

The bout started and the teams were announced. Meggie felt a shift in the air—the expectation of speed and violence. The visiting team, the Hotlanta Howlers, lived up to their name and then some—so ridiculously sexy and gyrating on their wheels that it was more hilarious than erotic. But beneath all of their good humor lurked formidable opponents with ripped arms, muscled legs, and challenge in their eyes. The Dutchesses skated out in black and neon green, some with Tinker Toys farthingales assembled around their hips, others with formidable neon pompadours. Meggie used to have a fichu and a little green fan. They curtsied to the crowd and pursed their lips and stuck out their rear ends with their pinkie fingers poking the air—a farce of Knickerbocker gentility. In a matter of moments, they would give their opponents a smack-down with whips and hip checks and the occasional "accidental" foul.

Meggie sat, watching while the rollergirls made their laps around the rink. It was a terrible moment when she realized that while she'd been keeping an eye out for Tori, she'd actually been looking at her the whole time—without recognition. Tori's hair was in multicolored dreads now, and she was a little thinner than she had been when Meggie last saw her—but still, Meggie felt terrible not to have recognized her immediately. Her feet felt as heavy as if she were wearing lead skates.

After the bout was over—Hotlanta lost—Meggie stayed put. She was glad the other team had flopped; Hotlanta was a vicious rival. Once, ages ago in high school, Meggie had asked Aubrey to knit sweatbands for her entire team because Meggie had despised Hotlanta so much that she'd wanted their upcoming bout against the team to be a shutout. She'd traded in her three favorite sundresses, her poster of James Dean from *Rebel*, and—just to be certain—her pillow, the irreplaceable old pillow that was the *only* pillow that could give her a good night's sleep. Aubrey had protested that it wasn't fair, that Meggie was asking her to cheat. But as usual, Aubrey eventually caved. The Flying Dutchesses not only beat Hotlanta that year, they murdered them. Hotlanta girls went home with sprained wrists, broken fingers, and knees that would never again let a rainy day pass without aching. Meggie had actually felt a little bad.

Now she watched with jealousy as her old teammates congratulated one another, smacking helmets and rear ends. They'd beat Hotlanta with no magic, with no help from Meggie at all. And they still didn't know she was there. She supposed she wasn't surprised that no one recognized her; her appearance changed with the seasons. It was the most constant thing about her, how much and often she changed.

The bleachers cleared out. The crowd drifted through the open double doors. The man selling popcorn and soda packed up. Meggie told herself: *I'll give it a minute, then I'll walk over and say hi.*

But before Meggie raised herself off of the bleachers, Tori turned her head. She looked at Meggie for a long moment, her eyes dancing away, then looking back for a double take. Meggie got to her feet and gave a limp wave. Her friend, or at least, the girl who used to be her friend, skated toward her in long, smooth strides. She was not precisely smiling.

"Well, well, well." Tori towered over Meggie in her skates. Her ashy brown hair fell in clumpy dreadlocks to her shoulders, streaked in pink and aqua. Her nose ring glinted. She wore a Girl-Scout-green vest and frothy black puff of skirt.

Meggie gave a shy smile. "Hello there, Tori."

"If it isn't our missing blocker." She put her hands on her hips. "It's about time you came back."

"Yep. The Prodigal Daughter returns."

Tori considered her for a long moment, bouncing her helmet in her hand. Meggie felt shy, shy like she had not felt in a very long time, shy with this person whom she'd once known almost as well as she knew herself. She resisted the urge to fidget—to adjust the hem of her tunic or push back her hair—

while Tori weighed her decision about whether to forgive Meggie or tell her to go to hell.

A little smile lifted Tori's right cheek. "I knew you couldn't stay away forever," she said. Then she pulled Meggie into a fast hug. She was a jumble of softness and clunky plastic pads. When she pulled away, her eyes were bright with pleasure. She hit Meggie, hard, on the arm. "Why didn't you let us know you were coming back? We could have used you tonight."

"I didn't know I would be here. Mariah died."

"Oh. Wow. Hey—I'm really sorry."

"Thanks."

"Are you okay?"

Meggie nodded.

"So—where you been?" Tori shifted her weight onto one skate. "It was like you just fell off the edge of the map."

"I wanted to see if the world was round."

"Is it?"

"I'm standing here again, aren't I? I started walking in one direction and next thing I knew, I was back where I started again."

"You're such an ass." Tori smiled.

"You totally missed me," Meggie said.

"Yes," Tori said. "I totally did."

Meggie reached for her friend's hand. In the years since she'd been gone, she hadn't once felt homesick—not so much as a twinge. She never looked backward. She just moved forward and on. But when Tori squeezed her fingers, she felt like crying. *Strange to feel homesick now*, she thought, now that she was home.

They went to a bar—a favorite old place with dark wood and loud music and cheap beer. A band was playing top twenty covers in the next room. The roller derby team had arrived a few minutes after them with gusto and flair; they laughed loud, drank fast, and gestured wildly. Meggie had greeted her old teammates, saw interest and envy spark in their eyes when she said *Oh—just traveling. Seeing the world.* She heard their friendly invitations to come skate again, to strap on her wheels for the next practice. And she'd accepted their offers to buy her drinks.

But now, Meggie was alone—as alone as one could be in a crowded bar—with Tori. They sat in a dark and greasy wooden booth, the backrests towering straight over their heads, their drinks sweating between them. They leaned forward and had to yell over the music to be heard. The skin around Tori's right eye was slowly turning purple from an elbow that had flown a little too high during the bout. She'd pulled back her clumped hair into a high, messy snarl.

"So you're a vagrant," Tori said.

"I prefer to think I'm nomadic," Meggie said.

"How long are you staying in Tarrytown?"

"Dunno. Until I feel the urge to get on the move again."

"Where will you go?"

Meggie laughed. "What is this? Twenty questions?"

"I've been worried about you. What the heck made you leave like that? And without even saying good-bye. That was kind of a dick move."

"I know. I'm sorry."

"You could have warned us. And by *us*, I mean at least *me*."

"I sent postcards."

"After the fact."

"I didn't want anybody to try and stop me," Meggie said.

"I know." Tori took a pull of cheap beer. "I definitely would have tried."

Meggie smiled. The band in the other room announced a

fifteen-minute break, and the music quieted as the bartender switched on the radio.

"So tell me everything," Tori said. "Tell me where you've been."

Meggie turned her beer in a circle, and she began to tell Tori about bits and pieces of her travels—the good parts, anyway. She'd made it a point to find something to like in each new city. In Denver, she'd liked the jagged and blue-peaked mountains, so much more raucous than the stooped old hills of the Hudson Valley. In Texas she'd liked that men wore honest-to-God cowboy hats and huge belt buckles. In Tampa, she'd liked how everyone was transient—that people never needed to show up at a party because they brought the party with them wherever they went.

She did not mention to Tori that in Savannah, where she'd been playing house with Phil before the Stitchery had so rudely interrupted, she'd had trouble finding much to like. Yes, there was the Spanish moss, which had always looked to Meggie the way music might look if it were a tangible thing and could get caught in the branches of trees. And yes, there was the lovely old architecture, and the mini golf places for the tourists, and the hospitality. But all of the things she might have liked about Savannah, including Phil, were soured by the one giant annoying thing that she did not like about it: Her lead in Georgia had dried up more quickly than usual. She'd gotten a tip about an "Emerald Van Ripper" at a basement nightclub on Broughton Avenue, and she'd thought that perhaps her mother had decided to be a bit playful about taking on an alias. But when Meggie had tracked down Emerald, it wasn't her mother she found but a beautiful young man who did an uncanny impression of Judy Garland.

"But how do you decide where you're going?" Tori asked. "Do you just wing it?"

"I pretty much just follow my nose," Meggie said. "Sometimes I go to a particular place for a particular reason. But other times, I'm just following a hunch."

"A hunch? Are you some kind of secret vigilante crime fighter? One of those people who puts their underwear on the outside and gives hamburgers to homeless people?"

"No, I'm not a superhero," Meggie said. "I meant, I go somewhere new when I have a *hunch* that I'll like the place. For example, I had a hunch that I would like Portland."

"Did you?"

"Yes. Except for the vegetarians. And the rain."

Meggie took a swallow of her beer. She hoped her face wasn't reddening. She would need to be more careful about her choice of words around Tori. Tori was the kind of person who heard everything—everything that a person didn't actually say. And she'd never let insinuations, deliberate or not, pass by unexamined. Instead, Tori would grip the thin and slippery thread of a hint and haul it fist-over-fist to the surface of a conversation like bringing a thrashing sturgeon up from opaque depths.

The truth, what Meggie could not say to her friend, was that much of Meggie's sleuthing was based on hunches these days. In the beginning, there had been leads—clues to where her mother might have gone that seemed to Meggie's eye to be authentic and viable. She'd kept a journal, jotting down all traces of her mother: the collected memories of old boyfriends, reminiscences from temporary friends. But eventually the leads began to require more and more leaps of the imagination, suspensions of disbelief. When Meggie had no viable leads in a new city, she carried her mother's picture around and showed it to people when she bought a sandwich at a deli or climbed on a bus. She showed it to old ladies in churches and middle-aged men in bars. She showed it to cops and homeless people. She explained that the picture was from seventeen years ago and her mother probably didn't look like this anymore. Sometimes the strangers swore they recognized her. A few had actually told her stories about Lila—old stories that must have happened in the days before she'd gone totally missing. Mostly, they just said no.

For all her endless searching, Meggie saw her mother's face all the time. She saw it in women shopping for perfume. In women walking their dogs. She saw her mother in grocery stores, and bars, and in the privacy of her dreams. Sometimes, her mother was in a crate in the hull of a cargo ship. Sometimes she was in a misty woods tied to a tree. Sometimes she was in a jail cell or the trunk of a car. Sometimes she wasn't trapped in any external place at all, but instead appeared to be trapped within her own skull, her eyes looking out in terror, pleading for rescue. That was the worst dream of all.

It was never too long after the dream resurfaced that Meggie hit the road, pursuing leads, hunches, and whims. Every city had brought the same thing: the rising hope, the letdown, and then, the moving on.

"What are you thinking about?" Tori asked. "Are you off on a mental walkabout again already? Where are you? Mexico? The Everglades? Yosemite?"

Meggie shook her head. "I'm not anywhere. I'm right here with you."

Tori tipped her head, not quite believing.

Meggie knocked back the last of her beer and put it on the table with a thud. "Come on. Let's go dance," she said.

From the Great Book in the Hall: *Knitting is not always blissful abandon. Sometimes, it's painful and fraught. At some point, you will find yourself knitting a garment with fifteen stitches per row—perhaps it's some lacy thing with complicated holes and increases and decreases—and quite suddenly you'll find that you only have fourteen stitches.*

Where did the missing stitch go? And what's the right course of action? Make a new stitch and not worry about finding the old one—in which case, you run the risk of seeing your work come apart down the road? Or go back and find where the stitch disappeared from, in which case you will spend valuable time unknitting, undoing all your hard work, with no idea how long you've been missing the missing stitch?

Knitting is an exercise in learning. And like physical exercise, learning can be uncomfortable. It's the end result that makes the fretting worthwhile.

12

"Continue in Pattern"

The sky was dark, but the birds that had not yet flown south for the season were just beginning to sing. Aubrey lay in bed, her thoughts winging her in a thousand directions, none of them expected. When she'd looked out into the distance of her life the day before Mariah died, down the long, telescoping tunnel of her imagination, she was certain to see her destiny square and true as a boat on the far horizon. She had not factored romance into the story of her life; in fact, after her early, failed attempts at courtship rituals, she had very staunchly and vigorously factored love *out* of her forecast. But then, last night, in the sticky warmth of Vic's truck, the projected story line of her life that she'd been regularly attending to as if it were an overindulged houseplant began to sprout unexpected fruit. And Aubrey could not have been more breathless if Vic had pulled a ring box from his pocket and proposed.

She was drunk on optimism, giddy and stupid, over such a small thing as a date. Expectation had left her sleepless, grinning into her pillow like a schoolgirl, her whole body taut and silly as Cupid's bow. All night long, she grappled with her hope, trying to wrestle it into submission, to remind herself that her future was prescribed—a life of lonely but satisfying work within the Stitchery walls. And yet her hope could not be quashed.

When the dim glow of day came through the blinds, she was glad for the excuse to finally get out of bed. She made coffee and watched the sunrise tease the sky into lightness out over the valley. Then, although all the inhabitants of the house were asleep, she pulled on a thick brown sweater with a yoke of Norwegian snowflakes. She girded herself in a hat, scarf, and gloves, and made her way into the backyard.

The morning was nippy, the sun sparkling down on the valley as if through the hard clear glass of an icicle. The backyard—which was older and slightly bigger than many of the properties in Tappan Square—was slicked with maple leaves like a pelt of wet, ruddy animal fur, and the air smelled sweet with fermentation. The Hudson in the distance, below the prehistoric ridges of the opposite shore, was gray as slate.

She wrestled a rake out of the old, sealed outhouse and got to work. Her breath was white. Patches of sunlight felt deliciously warm on her skin. She was sweating slightly, her scarf and hat removed and hanging from a gangly rhododendron, when Carson bolted through the back door and into the yard.

"Oh!" he said. His little feet skidded on leaves, and he nearly fell.

She smiled. "Good morning! Whatcha doing?"

"Nothing." His lip curled and he glanced behind him. "My sister's a jerkwad."

"What happened?"

"She took my 3DS, and didn't charge the battery, and now I can't play Spy Hunter until it charges again, and that's going to take forever, and it's not fair, and she can't even say sorry." He huffed, exhausted by the effort of his story.

"That stinks," Aubrey said.

"You can say *sucks*." He eyed her warily now, as if he'd first thought she was a compatriot but now was second-guessing. "Mom says it's not a bad word."

"Is your mom awake?"

"She's in the shower."

"Aunt Meggie?"

"Guess."

"Right. Sleeping." She looked at him; he was still wearing his pajamas—sweatpants and a sweatshirt. She held up her rake like a marching band baton. "Do you want to help?"

"Me?"

"Of course you."

"I'm too little."

Aubrey laughed. "Who says?"

"Well . . ." He shifted nervously. "What would I have to do?"

"The sticks," she said. She pointed here and there in the small yard. "If you could put them in a pile for me, that would be a huge help."

He made one last glance behind him, perhaps to see if he was being followed. Then he said, "Okay, but can I get my coat?"

"Absolutely."

He hurried back into the house, and a moment later he was with her again, suited up in a puffy, evergreen-colored ski jacket and a blue fleece hat with a stitched-on New York Giants logo. He bent to pick up a naked, twisted branch on the grass, a remnant of the summer's rolling storms. "Like this?"

"Perfect," she said.

They worked for a while in silence, Carson picking up kinked branches and Aubrey stripping leaves from the lawn to reveal the dull green grass beneath. Carson seemed agitated, working a little too quickly, with a little more focus than a boy his age should have been able to muster for such a job.

"Everything okay?" Aubrey asked.

He shrugged.

"Homesick?"

He shrugged again.

She dragged the rake along the grass; metal tines whinnied over the earth. A layer of dry, crisp leaves hid a layer of wet ones, clumping thick and damp like the skins of ripe fruits. Aubrey tugged them into a pile, the rake scraping along the grass in satisfying little roars.

"Aunt Aubrey?"

"Yes?"

"What's all the stuff in the tower?"

Aubrey kept her pace with her rake. "Did you go in?"

"No," he said quickly. "Not me. Nessa said she found all this stuff in the tower. Like a museum."

"That's nothing," she said, as lightly as she could. Nessa hadn't said anything to her about finding the sacrifices. Her niece must have been snooping. "It's just some old things."

Carson stooped then stood, another twig in his hand. "Is she gonna get in trouble for going in your room?"

Aubrey tried not to laugh. Carson was gunning to get his big sister into trouble. She must have really ticked him off. "I'll take care of it."

He frowned, disappointed. "She snoops all the time, you know. All the time."

"She does, huh?"

"Yep," he said, almost cheerful now. "She even goes into Mom's room at home. That's how she found out about the divorce."

Aubrey couldn't help but go still, a quick hiccup in the pace of her raking, before she picked up the tempo again.

Bitty had not said anything to her about a divorce. Bitty had not said much about her marriage at all. Aubrey guessed there were problems, but she hadn't realized how serious they were.

"You should *tell*," he said. "You should tell my mom what Nessa did. She's not supposed to go in Mom's room. Or your room—right? She's not supposed to go into *your* room."

"No, I suppose she's not," Aubrey said, and she stopped raking, leaned as much of her weight on the handle as it would bear, and looked out to the river. Nessa should not have been rummaging around, not if Bitty wanted to keep the secrets of the Stitchery away from her daughter. That would have to be stopped.

But Nessa's snooping was a minor problem—a passing shower on a bright day. Bitty's divorce, if there was a divorce, was a storm. Unfortunately when it came to helping Bitty, questions could not be asked outright. There always had to be a kind of oblique approach, a gauche stumbling-into, or a falsely innocent, no-eye-contact advance like one might draw near a snarling dog. Bitty did not distinguish compassionate questioning from being forcibly and critically questioned.

"Where should I put these?" Carson punctured her thinking. He held a bundle of sticks in his arms. She gestured to the side of the yard. He went in the direction she'd pointed and dropped his load.

"There's no more sticks," he said. He stood on the glistening grass, foreshortened, asking for something that couldn't be said. Aubrey heard the screen door swing open, and Bitty was there—awake, dressed, showered, and looking quite put-together and refreshed in dark jeans and a baby pink fleece. "You guys want breakfast?"

"Pancakes!" Carson shouted. He ran to his mother and grabbed her two hands, tugging and jumping. "Pan-pan-pancakes!"

"I'll have what he's having," Aubrey said.

"Give me ten minutes." Bitty pulled Carson's hat more firmly over his ears, then went inside.

"Ten minutes?" Carson said. "We better hurry!"

Aubrey must have glanced away for a moment—just a second split in half—because when she regained her focus, Carson was running and shouting *"Geronimo!"* And then next thing she knew, he was waist-deep in leaves. He grabbed big armfuls and tossed them into the air; some leaves floated gently, dry as bits of paper in the sun. Others lifted, flopped, and stuck flat and wet to Carson's hat and coat.

Aubrey laughed.

"Leaf fight!" Carson threw a fistful of leaves that did not fly very far. Aubrey held up her hands anyway and squealed. If she'd hesitated—if she'd paused at all—it was a pause that occupied no more time than it took for the sun to inch imperceptibly forward in the sky, or for the earth to turn its face hundreds of miles deeper into autumn. She dropped her rake and launched herself forward, into the little pile of leaves, into her nephew's impish laughter, into whatever happiness the day was going to offer or not, without question.

Meggie stood in the yarn room, an afghan in a chevron pattern draped over her shoulders, her cup of coffee steaming white. The Stitchery's ancient coal-burning furnace had been worked over to burn oil, and though it strove mightily, pipes clanging at their joints, radiators hissing with effort, the old heating system was no match for the chill of an autumn morning. Most winters, they hadn't had enough money to heat more than one room at a time of the big, drafty house. Meggie could remember waking up in the morning, the house so cold she could nearly see her breath, the tip of her nose frozen where it peeped from her half-a-dozen covers. She would throw her blankets off fast, merciless, and run as quickly as she could to the kitchen, where Mariah would be sitting at the table reading or knitting. Old cotton quilts hung over doorways and windows, making the room look like a child's play fort. The four burners of the gas stove were four blue lotuses, each flame a petal of heat. And while her sisters went a little stir-crazy in such tight quarters, Meggie loved their enforced company, loved that if they wanted to be warm, they had to be together, talking, knitting, reading, passing time.

She hitched her afghan a little higher around her shoulders. She was slightly hung over. Bitty had made coffee, and Meggie probably should have stayed in the kitchen to keep her sister company while she cooked breakfast. But she'd needed to get out of earshot. The banging of pans, the clinking of silverware on porcelain . . . each sound slammed her skull like a mallet on a bell.

Last night, she and Tori had stayed out late, like they used to. They linked arms and walked down bright blocks in the East Village, they laughed with strangers and with each other, they drank until the concrete buckled and tipped under their feet. It was as if nothing had changed.

Now she held up her arm, the knitted afghan falling away from her skin. Tori's cell phone number was scrawled on her wrist in bold, blue ink. When Tori had said good-bye, she'd said it as if they would never see each other again. She fanned her fingers along Meggie's short, short hair, then she'd smiled sadly and left Meggie standing at the Stitchery door. She'd made Meggie swear to call her sometimes. Meggie had agreed; she could promise that much. But she didn't know how much longer she would be in Tarrytown.

She moved across the cold yarn room to a lengthened rectangle of light from the window. To stand in the yarn shop was to stand in a bubble where time had stopped. Yarns that had been piled in an old barrel ten years ago were still untouched. The rickety umbrella swift was still perched on the edge of the counter. The dust in the shop had grown thicker over the years, like a ring of an ancient tree.

Meggie picked up a skein of deep blue wool and a feeling of nostalgia, mournful as the call of a distant train on a rainy day, passed through her. Often she knit while she was traveling—not spells, but projects: gifts or items to sell online. She knit because knitting reminded her of her family, because it distracted her, because she didn't know why. The urge to knit came like a monster—a deranged Mr. Hyde with needles and sock yarn—and she had no control. No matter what city she was in, she sometimes found herself scrambling for supplies, shoving her crumpled bills at the cashier—it didn't even matter that the yarn felt like garden twine—and then she was hurrying to whatever place she was calling home at the time, where she did not feel relief until she was firing off stitches like shots of dopamine to her brain.

But then as quickly as the drive to knit had lurched into gear, it just as quickly puttered out. Weeks would slip by, and she had no more interest in her knitting needles than she had in filing her taxes. She could not conjure even the smallest amount of love for the craft.

The whiplash—indifference transmuted into love and back to indifference again—made her speculate if the power of the Stitchery over her was like the moon over the earth, tugging unevenly on the oceans, pulling unevenly on her, making her sometimes love knitting and sometimes hate it, making waves. Then, in the same breath, she wondered if the Stitchery was just a house like any other, and if it was her own temperament that was like the moon—waxing and waning and shifting from one phase to the next, with the Stitchery never changing so much as counting on her to change.

She put down the midnight-blue yarn and sipped her coffee.

Last night Tori had said, with the depth and profound meaning that can only come from drunkenness, *I don't know what you're running from. But running from something doesn't make it go away.*

Now, with the morning light as thin and cold as the glass it streamed through, Meggie knew she should get moving. She was not running—not at all. She was searching, and the search had to go on. Sometimes, when she felt like her search had been futile, she reread her journal, the one she'd been using to record every little shred of a clue about her mother. It was full of Polaroids and jotted notes and pasted-on maps. Meggie had looked over her journal so many times that she'd nearly memorized it. Some of her notes, however, no longer meant anything to her, as she couldn't remember why she'd written them.

Who is Lucy M in Piscataway?

Pleasant Acres, nursing home. Denver.

She liked cashews. Saratoga Raceway—waitressed at pub and grill? Gambling?

The clues she'd found—sometimes nothing more than a note scrawled on a bathroom stall that said LVR WAS HERE— reminded her that there was every possibility that her mother wasn't dead. Lila had been a wanderer; she might have simply wandered away. Perhaps she was on some world-conquering adventure. Or perhaps she'd simply forgotten who she was—if the Madness had taken hold—and needed someone to bring her home again.

Unfortunately, the trail had gone cold. On her way back up to the Stitchery, Meggie had hoped—as she watched the miles go by and the autumn leaves become brighter and brighter—that coming home might give her some new ideas, some new leads to follow. Or at the very least, she hoped that she might *feel* her mother in some way, get a little closer to her by being in the Stitchery again.

But none of those things had happened. She assured herself: It wouldn't be hard to leave Tarrytown. Her heart went where she went, always leaving a trail of bread crumbs, a path between one city and the next that she would never trace back. *Leaving* was something she was good at, something she could do. To remind herself, she only had to think of Tori, and the Stitchery, and every man she'd ever met who made her think, simultaneously, *Maybe* and *I should go.*

And yet, standing in the yarn room, her throat tight with memories, and the sound of Bitty in the kitchen talking to Nessa and cracking eggs on the counter's edge, Meggie knew that if she left now, she would miss something—and she hated to be left out. She'd spent the first few years of her life being told she was "too little" to do the things that Aubrey and Bitty were allowed to do, and she had not liked the thought of being excluded then any more than she liked it now.

She supposed that as long as Bitty was at the Stitchery, there could be no harm in hanging around. The search for her mother still burned hot in her veins, but the trail seemed to be cooling. She would stay for a while longer—and she would knit. Something for Tori. A gift for her friend—possibly her only friend, when she was honest with herself—to remember her by. And then, when the sign came that she needed to return to her searching, she would be on her way.

Aubrey and Carson made their way into the kitchen, their cheeks tinged pink from morning air. The rest of the family had already settled in for breakfast. Bitty stood at the stove, nudging pancakes in a frying pan with a silver spatula. Meggie slouched at the table, a blanket over her shoulders in chocolate brown, pumpkin, and cream.

"It smells amazing in here!" Aubrey said. The kitchen was warm and stuffy compared with the air outside. "Like I died and went to heaven and it's made of pancakes instead of clouds."

"Thanks," Bitty said.

Aubrey shuffled Carson to the sink to wash his hands, then got him seated next to his sister at the table. She kissed Meggie on the top of the head as she passed by her chair.

"Aren't we the little ingénue this morning," Meggie said. "What's got you so happy?"

"Oh, nothing," Aubrey said, fairly singing. "Well, nothing much. It's just that—" She felt pleasure tighten her belly; what a delicious thrill it was to have news, actual news, worth sharing. "I have a date tonight."

"You do?" Bitty asked.

"With who?" Meggie asked at the same time.

"I do," Aubrey said. "With Vic."

"Shut the front door!" Meggie's palm smacked the table. "I had no idea he was into you. I totally couldn't tell!"

Aubrey glanced at her and slid into a chair.

"That's great," Bitty said, though her voice was flat. She set down a high stack of spongy pancakes that wobbled on the plate. The table was an instant flurry of children's hands—fingers snatching this and that, scrabbling for syrup and butter and refills of milk. Bitty returned to the stove. "So who did they elect last night to take over the Tappan Watch?"

"Please tell me it was the hot black guy," Meggie said.

Aubrey smiled, only slightly disappointed that the conversation had so quickly shifted away from Vic. "It was."

Meggie wedged a hunk of pancake between her lips, then tucked it into her cheek and spoke. "Good. He'll do a good job."

"You . . . you're *for* Tappan Square?" Aubrey asked, surprised. She'd presumed that since Meggie had hightailed it out of town the moment she could, and since she wanted to sell the Stitchery rather than hold on to it, she would also be glad to see Tappan Square reduced to lumber.

"Of course I'm for Tappan Square," Meggie said, bristling. "Just because I think you—we—are better off selling the Stitchery doesn't mean I hate Tappan Square."

"Oh," Aubrey said—and it was a dumb answer because she was dumbstruck. Her sister wanted to protect their neighborhood, but not their home. "What about you, Bit?" Aubrey asked, more quietly than she'd intended.

"Me? What do I think of the shopping mall?" Bitty ferried another great tower of pancakes across the kitchen. She sat down at the table but did not fill her plate. "I think that Tappan Square, in its current form, is bad for Tarrytown."

"Oh, come on," Meggie said.

Bitty brushed a blond highlight from her face with the back of her hand. "For the record, I'm not *for* the shopping mall. But I'm not for Tappan Square, either—not unless the village does something to revitalize. I mean . . . you have to admit that the neighborhood's changed, Aub. It's falling apart."

"We're in a recession," Aubrey managed. "The whole country is falling apart."

"This is different. Did you know that there's gang graffiti on the side of Mr. Dooley's garage? And I'm pretty sure there are no fewer than fifteen people—fifteen—living in the house across the street—that or they're dealing something out of there. And do you know what I saw last night? A bunch of young guys in puffy jackets lighting garbage on fire. Tappan

Square is different now. It was a poor neighborhood when we were kids. But now it's poor and dangerous. And while redevelopment might not be the gentler and kinder way of revitalizing, it's the most efficient, the fastest, the safest, the most economical, and maybe the best."

The table fell silent when Bitty was done. She'd always had a way of speaking, a brick-hard certainty that Aubrey had never known how to confute. Given that Aubrey could not even hold up her end of a casual debate during a pancake breakfast, she supposed it was a good thing that Mason Boss had swept into the firehouse last night at just the right moment—and that she had not made the mistake of putting herself forward as the leader of Tappan Square.

She glanced carefully at Bitty, who apparently had no fondness whatsoever for the Stitchery or Tappan Square. Her mind was riddled with rebuttals and attacks, airtight arguments of moral outrage that would take her sister down a peg. And yet the only reply she could manage was, "But . . . the Stitchery . . . ?"

"People need jobs more than they need a yarn shop," Bitty said.

"It's not just a yarn shop," Aubrey said.

Meggie cut in, pointing the tines of her fork at Bitty. "People don't need jobs more than they need a roof over their heads to protect them from the elements."

"They'll have better roofs if they have better jobs," Bitty said. "Or don't you remember those years of setting buckets in the hallway every time it rained?"

Aubrey pushed away from the table. She couldn't speak. She felt like she'd swallowed a fist. She did not excuse herself, but she fled the kitchen, ignoring her sisters' confusion and calls to wait, stalking down the hall, pounding up the stairs, feeling as if she were fifteen years old and throwing a temper tantrum. But she could not stand to look at her sisters for another moment. In her bedroom, she locked the door behind her. She flung herself onto her bed, breathing hard, and pressed her fingers against her eyes.

This place is important, Mariah had said, her voice a soft music in Aubrey's memory. They had been sitting on the swing on the porch, drinking root beer floats. It had been two weeks since Meggie had gone, and they were just beginning to wonder if perhaps she would not be coming back. Mariah had known Aubrey was hurting; she'd known just what to say. *As long as the Stitchery is here, the three of you will always have a place you can come together. A place nobody needs to be invited to, where none of you will ever be a stranger. As long as it's here— whether you're all living inside it or in different parts of the world—the Stitchery will be your meeting point, your parachute, your home.*

At the time, Aubrey had taken great comfort in the words. She'd invested all her hope in the Stitchery, so that each brick and nail and floorboard was a hedge against the unthinkable. As long as she stayed in the Stitchery, her sisters would know where to find her. And at any moment, they might come back.

Of course that had been years ago. And her sisters hadn't returned—not until Mariah had died. And they'd come back to say that they wanted Aubrey to sell the Stitchery as quickly as possible. Mariah had thought the Stitchery was their family's star, a beacon to follow in the darkness. Aubrey saw now that her sisters did not think of the Stitchery as a place to call home, but possibly as the thing that kept them from making homes of their own. Not until the Stitchery was gone would they be able to truly move on.

She pressed her face into her pillow. Perhaps her sisters were right. There were too many memories here, each one just a spark away from conflagration. There were too many unknowns. There was the question of their mother, who had disappeared from the Stitchery one day and never come back. There was the question of the Madness, the shame and doom of it, Madness that perched like a gargoyle on a steep gable, grotesque and watching, looking down. And of course, there was the question of the magic. Aubrey believed; she would go to her grave believing. But sometimes, even she had doubts.

Tears welled up and Aubrey did not fight them.

Once the Stitchery was gone from their lives, whether smashed by a wrecking ball or sold at a loss, her sisters could move on. And as long as Aubrey was the holdout, fighting to hang on to the Stitchery even as her sisters begged her to let it go, she was being selfish.

Wasn't she?

She thought of everyone, all the people who were her neighbors, sitting in folding chairs in the firehouse last night and rallying around Tappan Square.

Aubrey screamed into her pillow.

She had wanted to spend the day celebrating with her sisters, fussing over what she would wear tonight, over where Vic might be taking her—indulging in silliness of the most meaningful variety. Instead, the Stitchery was between them: a wall, a trough, a mountain. Until the problem of the Stitchery, of Tappan Square, was resolved one way or another, there would be no girl talk, no intimacies exchanged with laughter and conspiring smiles. There was only the house. And the neighborhood. And the questions, leading ahead of them into the future, taking them toward the inevitable, a change that was unwelcome or more of the same.

When Bitty needed perspective, she jogged. She liked the phrase *pound the pavement* and she imagined the balls of her feet were fists. In Tarrytown, she jogged out of Tappan Square, over to Patriot's Park and through it, then up, and up, and up, until she was looking down on the slate rooftops of the historic houses on Grove Street, until she was veering along the curvy brown shoulder of the reservoir, until she'd gone full circle and the Hudson River was no longer at her back, but was cinematic and massive before her, blue-gray like the shimmer of fish scales against the triumphant oranges and reds of autumn.

She stopped. She breathed. She closed her eyes. And with them closed, she saw everything, the theater of her youth with the curtains open: the thick neck of a pond where she had learned to ice skate, the boutique that once displayed a red dress that she'd loved but couldn't afford—God, she could still remember every stitch—the street corner where she'd punched Rod Doherty because he'd mocked Aubrey's blue eyes, all of it, laid out before her with all its indifference to the passing of time and how much a person changed with the passing.

She'd been eighteen when she met Craig. He was older, studying engineering at Cornell and doing adult things like pledging a fraternity and tipping the maid who tidied his dorm. Bitty had weaseled her way into an exclusive frat party, and she'd met her husband when he was hulking over a cooler filled with ice and silver cans of beer.

She'd asked him: *Got one for me?*

She had not hooked him right away. It had taken some careful plotting, some toying and teasing, before he began to chase her in earnest. She'd wanted him because he was handsome, because everyone else wanted him, because he was the type of guy she wasn't supposed to have. She'd wanted him because she knew money mattered to him, and she'd damn well had enough of being poor. She'd wanted him because he was the kind of man who seemed like he might control his own future with firm dexterity—and not accept anything less than what he intended to have. She'd wanted him because he was practically an atheist. Sure, he went to church when his mother dragged him on Easter and Christmas Eve. But he didn't believe in anything that could not be measured—nothing but science, math, and his own inevitable ascendance.

It took over a year after Craig had graduated college for him to find work. And when he did, Bitty packed up her things—a drawstring bag that Mariah had knit, a picture of her sisters, the teddy bear she'd carried since the second grade—and fled like a refugee with Craig to an apartment in Verplanck, without the blessing of her family or his. Craig had taken a job at a power plant to put his degree to good use until he got something better, though they should have known at the time he would never leave. Bitty worked two jobs: at a deli and a lingerie outlet. She signed up for college classes. She wanted to show Craig that she deserved him. She was hell-bent on hoisting herself up—exhausted by the fact of being both the person who is hoisting and the thing being raised. It didn't occur to Bitty until years down the line that Craig might not have wanted her to deserve him—that the point, the whole point, of loving her was that he *could*, and that she owed him something for it.

A chilly updraft blew in from the valley floor and conjured goose bumps on Bitty's skin. She wondered what her husband was doing with himself while she was standing here, thinking of him. In recent years, and intermittently for more years than she could count, she had been fantasizing about leaving him. The allure of separation was nearly erotic, charged with desire like the rush of sex coming from a last, final breaking from it. But here she was. Still married. Still stuck. And the wind was getting colder, and the sky was getting more wintry by the day, and somewhere in Tappan Square, Aubrey was embarking on her own foray in love.

Bitty thought: *I'll have to make this one up to her.* She should have been friendlier this morning. She should have asked more questions about Aubrey's date. She wanted her sister to be happy; Aubrey's quality of life was one of the key tenets in her argument to sell the Stitchery. And yet, instead of offering optimism and encouragement, Bitty had felt the terrible, violent urge to take her sister by the shoulders and say *Save yourself while you can.* She supposed that wasn't fair.

She shivered. Clouds cast amorphous shadows on the river, the hills. Bitty had not thought of Tappan Square as home for a very long time; and yet standing here, alone, she could not think of the house where she lived with her husband as home, either.

She took a deep breath and headed with heavy heels back down the once sleepy mountainside into town.

Aubrey stared at the sinister dimness that was her small, cramped closet, mutely pondering how the door to it could be wide open and yet somehow no light ever got in. If she stepped foot into the abyss she might never be seen again.

She was considering what Vic would say if she showed up naked, when Bitty knocked and let herself into the room. Bitty's hair was wet and her face was scrubbed. Diamonds flashed at her ears and neck, and her rings were as much a part of her physiology as the fingers they were on. "Am I interrupting?"

"No," Aubrey said, because politeness got the better of her. "Good run?"

"Yes. Killer hills in this town."

Bitty sat on Aubrey's bed and toweled off her wet hair.

Aubrey glanced at her. She tried not to ask the question that was on the tip of her tongue, which was, *Do you want something?* Her sister was sitting across the room, but she was miles away.

"Listen," Bitty said.

But Aubrey had started to speak at the same time.

"Oh." Bitty's gaze slanted to the side. "You go ahead."

Aubrey did. She was feeling peevish and irked by her sisters' joint declaration that they no longer had any attachment to the Stitchery. And so rather than politely edging around a topic until the central shape of it became clear, which was her usual way of taking on a difficult conversation, Aubrey just blurted: "Nessa found the sacrifices." And the ramifications of the statement resounded in the room like a big, satisfying *gong.*

Bitty was quiet.

"But that's not all." Aubrey stood before Bitty at the foot of the bed. "She asked me to teach her to knit."

"Did you?"

"Yes." Aubrey said, lifting her chin. "I did. Because she deserves to know."

"She deserves to know what? Knitting? Or spells?"

"Both," Aubrey said.

Bitty glowered. And Aubrey's nerve, her momentary flirtation with antagonism, began to fade. She leaned against the closet frame. "Look. I know you're going through a lot right now. The knitting . . . I didn't mean anything by it. I just thought it might offer Nessa some comfort. So yes—I helped her get started. She would have made Mariah very proud."

Bitty wrung her hair inside the towel. "As long as she doesn't know about the spells, I suppose it's fine."

"I didn't expect you to be so open-minded."

"Why wouldn't I be?"

"Because we both know that in our family, knitting isn't just a craft."

Bitty continued to squeeze the droplets from her hair. Aubrey could almost hear what her sister was thinking: *Whatever you say.*

"I'm really not trying to tell you what to do, so please don't think I am—but you need to tell Nessa about the magic. No, wait. Hear me out. It's her heritage. It's our tradition. And besides, it's better that she hears it from you rather than letting her stumble into it by herself."

"Please," Bitty said. "I'd rather get through eight more renditions of the birds-and-bees talk with Nessa than try to explain the Stitchery."

"What about birds-and-bees?" Meggie had come through the door. She'd changed out of her pajamas and into a gray-and-black sweater and faded pink jeans.

"Nessa found the tower," Aubrey said.

Bitty smirked and shook her head. "She knows how to knit, too, apparently."

"But Bitty doesn't want her knowing about the spells," Aubrey said.

Meggie flopped on Aubrey's bed and lay back against the pillows. "What's the big deal?"

"The big deal is that I don't want my kids having false hope. I don't want them growing up thinking that if they want to change something, all they have to do is wish upon a star. God—that's a cruel thing to do to children. I won't do it to mine."

Aubrey could not miss the bitterness in her sister's voice. And she wondered what had happened that made Bitty so certain the lore of the Stitchery was false. She ventured: "When did you stop believing in the magic?"

Bitty snuffed. She got up from the edge of Aubrey's bed

and went to the vanity. Aubrey's hairbrush was there—an old thing with a pewter handle and white bristles. Bitty regarded herself in the mirror as she tugged it through her water-dark hair. "There was no *one* spell that convinced me. More like . . . a gradual questioning. Mr. Elazar was the final straw."

Aubrey remembered Joel Elazar—Mr. Elazar at the time. For years he had showed up in her dreams, with his thick silver hair and his houndstooth cabbie's hat, and his round, haunted eyes. Mr. Elazar had sought out Mariah because of his thirty-year-old daughter. She had been given only a few months to live. He came to the Stitchery with a heavy, cut-glass bowl that had been prized in the family since the Depression. His parents had stood in New York breadlines and begged for work; they ran a household that reused bathwater in age order, that rationed bread. But they'd always managed to hold on to the bowl, that one semi-luxurious item. Sacrificing the bowl for their daughter had been his wife's idea, and Mr. Elazar had pretended to concur. But he had ideas of his own. He was prepared to give up anything so that his daughter would live; he was prepared to give up his life. Once he commissioned the spell, he'd had every intention of jumping off the Tappan Zee Bridge.

Mariah had talked him down. She'd said the spell wouldn't work unless the person who requested it was alive—whether or not Mariah had been making this up, Aubrey had never known. And so the cut-glass bowl was relegated to the Stitchery tower, and Mr. Elazar eventually returned to pick up a blanket of black wool thickened by holding doubled strands. He'd brought the girls lollipops and made them laugh by pulling quarters from their ears, and when he left, his face had born the soft, tremulous look of a man who'd had a great weight taken from his shoulders, weight lifted gently by a swell of hope.

Two months later, the girls had signed their names to a card of condolences. Mr. Elazar had never returned to the Stitchery.

It was the first time Aubrey had seriously and fundamentally *doubted*, a niggling fear that she hadn't dared voice to her sisters. What if there was no magic, and they were just fooling themselves and everyone else in Tarrytown? What if the Van Rippers really were the swindlers people said they were— swindlers who had gotten so good at their game that they'd even swindled themselves? Worry was not like a pit in Aubrey's stomach; it was a trapdoor in the bottom of a pit, and it opened unknown into unknown. Because if there truly was magic in the world, then it *should* have worked for Mr. Elazar, who would have given his life for his daughter if Mariah had let him. Aubrey had no way to explain to herself or to anyone why the spell had failed. And Mariah didn't seem to have any answers, either. She'd sat with her arm around Aubrey, her face full of regret, and she'd said, *Sometimes, it isn't about the answers. Sometimes, it's about the questions—the questions are the answers.* But her advice hadn't helped. Aubrey's confidence in the Stitchery had been shaken; Bitty's had been smashed to smithereens.

"But you've seen magic work, too," Meggie said. "Remember? You've seen it with your own eyes."

Bitty did not turn from brushing her hair. And so Meggie recounted the stories she could remember: The girls had seen Elle Greenfeder offer a set of candlesticks in exchange for a hat that would help her son with his ADHD, and then the son rose to the top of his class. They'd seen a young woman sacrifice a signed copy of an old novel, and a week later the woman appeared in the Stitchery to say how joyful she was now that her brother had agreed to move back to Tarrytown.

They'd seen Teddy Carpenter's family offer up their heirloom jewelry to have the doctors pronounce with wonder that the blot they'd seen in her breast tissue was suddenly and miraculously gone.

"So there must be *something*," Meggie said. "Even if we can't quite control it. Even if we're not getting it right."

But Bitty was obstinate. "What I've seen is the power of suggestion at work. The placebo effect. What happens here isn't magic. It's just people talking themselves into things, and then—because they're talked into them—the things start to happen, and everybody says *Oh, it's magic*, when really it's just the power of a person changing her mind."

Aubrey was quiet. What could she say to defend herself against Bitty's charges? There was nothing rational—no proof. Just a big, consuming *Maybe* that, for Aubrey, had always been in and of itself enough to get her through the low points. She gathered her courage. And then she spoke. "Regardless of what you think about the magic, it's up to Nessa to make up her own mind."

"I second that," Meggie said. She sat up a little on the bed.

Aubrey dug a nail into her thumb.

Bitty put the hairbrush down on its pewter tray. Her gold heart necklace lifted on her chest with each inhalation. When she spoke, she did not look at herself in the mirror; her eyes were downcast. "Okay."

"Okay?" Aubrey said.

"Whoa." Meggie crossed her legs beneath her on the bed. "What just happened?"

Bitty looked up. "I'll talk to Nessa. I'll tell her the theory about the magic. You're right that she's old enough to know and make a decision of her own. And I'm perfectly confident that she'll make the right decision."

"That's great," Aubrey said, gratified for once in her life to have won a debate with her older sister. *Maybe*, she thought, *things do change.*

"She's not a guardian," Bitty said. "I'm sure of it."

"Nobody said she was," Meggie said.

Bitty seemed to be holding her breath, and she let it out in a long stream. She turned away from the mirror to look at Aubrey. "I should probably thank you."

"For what?"

"For not telling Nessa about the Stitchery before I had a chance to. For giving me the opportunity to tell her in my own way."

"Of course," Aubrey said.

Bitty turned back to the mirror and picked up the hairbrush again. "So what are you wearing on this date tonight?" she said.

13

"Check Gauge"

Aubrey's sisters made a fuss over her after all—a lovely, gloriously indulgent fuss. Aubrey said the expected things: *You don't have to do this*, and *It's okay.* But the truth was, she loved the way her sisters tittered and clucked and made sure she had eaten a snack so she wouldn't overeat at dinner. She liked that they deliberated about her clothes and hair, that they demanded to paint her toenails and would not let her wear her cotton granny panties even though they were much more comfortable than the one thong she owned. For the first time in a long time, they were a team. And Aubrey had milked her own romantic cluelessness for all it was worth, asking about shoes and coats and first-date rules until her face hurt from smiling, and until her sisters decided to give her a moment alone.

Now she regarded herself in her bedroom mirror. She wore dark leggings and a white sweater that slipped from one shoulder in an angelic halo of cashmere. It might have been the luckiest thrift-store purchase Aubrey had ever made. The earrings she'd borrowed from Meggie were slender silver threads that made her neck look pretty and long. There was only one problem with her appearance. The effect of mascara and eyeliner—Nessa's doing—wasn't quite enough to tamp the blue lightning of her irises. Aubrey could not see their awful blueness, which was one of the worst parts about them. But she knew they were shining like two blue flames set deep in her sockets. A horror show.

She sighed. Mariah had always said her eyes were something to be proud of: *God doesn't light a candle for you to hide it under a bowl.* And yet what choice was there but to put on her dark glasses? Aubrey knew how people saw her. She wanted Vic to look at her without being appalled.

She pulled the frames from her dresser, slipped their thick plastic arms on her ears.

"Okay," she coached herself aloud. "No need to be pessimistic. Vic already knows you're weird, and he likes you anyway. So, *relax.*" She shook her arms and legs, wiggling them like a boxer warming up for a fight. She was not like other twenty-eight-year-olds. Her life was complicated. And Vic would have expectations, specific expectations of a romantic nature that she might not be able to meet. She half wondered if she should warn him.

"Relax," she said.

The doorbell rang; it warbled like a sick wren.

"Aubrey!" Nessa sang up the stairs. "Your *love-uh* is here!"

For a moment, Aubrey did not move. She looked at herself, thought, *This isn't my life.* She had the strangest sense that for things to be so wonderful, so right, something in the fabric of the universe must have gone wrong.

But—there was the rumble of Vic's laughter at the foot of the hall stairs. There was the cotillion of female voices, Carson's tinkling little laugh. There was the Stitchery, so filled up with possibility it seemed to be a different place entirely from the unchanging building she and Mariah and dozens of other guardians had called home.

This is the end of something, the Stitchery seemed to whisper.

She heard Nessa call her name.

"Coming!" she said. And she headed downstairs.

Nessa had fallen in love with the Stitchery. Her mother's house was much more beautiful, with every wall exactly perpendicular to every floor, and with every countertop glinting black granite, and with every room connected with intercoms so that they could talk to one another even when they were apart. But the Stitchery . . . it was everything her house was not. It was a house that had secrets to tell. And it was telling them, Nessa realized, to her.

She was knitting in her bedroom, Carson across from her on his identical bed playing a video game, when her mother came in quickly and without warning. Or there might have been warning, but knitting did something in Nessa's brain, something that made it feel like water must feel when it turns into steam, and so she did not hear her mother come in. Too late she looked up from her scarf, which was trailing down off the bed like a purple waterfall.

"Sh—*oot*," Nessa said, choking off a curse word. She scrambled a little to hide her work, realized there was no use, then set her foggy brain into gear. "I was just looking at this scarf Aunt Aubrey was making. I just wanted to see if—"

"Save it," her mother said. "I already know."

Nessa scowled at her brother, who was watching her now from across the room. "You little rodent!" she yelled at him. His eyes went wide in feigned innocence.

"It wasn't your brother," Bitty said. "Aubrey told me. And she told me you went into the tower, too."

Nessa's anger came up swiftly, as it sometimes did, hot and gusty like a strong, sudden wind. Her eyes pricked with instant tears. Her heart knocked into overdrive. She threw the scarf down on the floor. The silver needles clanged against the wood and the last little ball of yarn rolled away. "You always do this! You always take away everything that makes me happy!"

She got to her feet, but her mother was there in a moment. She took Nessa's shoulders. Nessa would have wrenched away, but she saw that the look on her mother's face was not exactly angry so much as *scared*.

"Nessa," she said. And she held Nessa's hands.

Nessa quieted. Her mother's grip annoyed her. She pulled away.

"Sit down."

Nessa did. She watched as her mother bent and gathered the scarf, yarn ball, and needles. She stood with Nessa's handiwork, looking down at it with only the smallest wrinkle between her brows. Nessa was more nervous than if the yarn had been a report card.

"Pretty good," her mother said. "Your stitches are really even."

"But they're not perfect," Nessa said with caution. She wasn't sure if this was a test. "Some are looser or tighter."

"When you're all done, we'll block it. That will help even things out."

"Did you say *block it*?"

"Yes. Your great-aunt Mariah always said that blocking was how you got the stitches to share with each other. We wet it down, give the fabric a few careful tugs, and pin it into the shape we want it to be."

"And it stays like that?"

"If we do it right," Bitty said.

"So . . . does this mean, like, you're not mad?"

"Mad at what?" Bitty said.

Nessa was confused. She'd always assumed there was

something off limits about yarn and knitting, about anything having to do with the Stitchery, since the fact was that her mother came from a house of professional knitters but had never so much as picked up a skein of yarn in Walmart just to see how it felt in her hands. Nessa could not shake the sense that she was being tricked.

"May I?" Bitty asked, and she gestured to Nessa's bed to ask permission to sit. This, too, was new.

"I don't care," Nessa said.

Her mother sat. Old springs wheezed with the weight. "You know, I guess I haven't really told you guys much about the Stitchery."

Understatement of the year, Nessa thought.

"What's all the stuff hidden in the tower?" Carson asked. He came to the bed and sat down with them, snuggling babyishly against his mom.

"Oh that," Bitty said. "Well, you see . . ."

And then she began to hint at the thing that Nessa had been waiting for, the thing that she'd been fully expecting and counting on her mother to say, even if she had not known the words for it but had felt it glowing inside her. And there was some rambling, some excusing and eye rolling about the things people say, about how certain people got certain ideas in their heads, and how everybody had their own ideas but nobody knew for sure, and how it was just old wives' tales, family traditions, the stories that every family had, until the whole darn speech was going in circles, circles that her mother was trying to draw with her eyes closed, circles that opened into spirals, and Nessa was clenching her teeth and shouting in her mind, *Please please please just say it already!*

And then, her mother did say it. And no amount of hedging or couching or not-quite-apologizing could change the way it landed in the room like a fat black cannonball crashing through the ceiling and wedging in the floor. Because *it* was *magic*.

Nessa could have sworn she heard the Stitchery creak in reply.

Later that evening, after Bitty had said that she and Nessa would be going out to do a little shopping, Meggie did not need it clarified that she would be staying home with Carson. She was happy to see Bitty and her daughter getting along, and she liked Carson. She thought that of everyone who was in the Stitchery, it was Carson she understood best—maybe because they were both the youngest.

"Do you want to go out and do something?" she asked him. The Stitchery felt empty and oppressive without her sisters in it.

"Do we? Of course we do," Carson said, and Meggie laughed. Earlier in the day she'd found herself telling Carson about *the royal we*—she didn't know how it had come up— and he'd thought it was the most hilarious thing he'd ever heard. He'd been referring to himself, with charming pint-sized kingliness, as *we* ever since. "But how shall we go anywhere if you don't have a car?"

"Oh please. You've been stuck in suburbia for ten years too long," Meggie said. "Did you bring your Halloween costume with you?"

"I dunno." His little lip sprung out.

"What are you going to be?"

"A dalmatian. It's Mom's idea."

Meggie frowned in sympathy. "Yeah. That's kinda lame. Did she say you *have* to be a dalmatian?"

"Well—" He struggled, working out details. "Well, no. But

I can't make the costume; she has to make it. So I have to be what she says."

"Let's see what we can do about that."

She gathered the far-flung pieces of his outerwear, then stuffed, buttoned, and zipped until he was toasty. Then they were off into the streets of Tappan Square. Meggie was not nervous about walking around her neighborhood, but by force of habit, her eyes made quick assessments of passersby, watched shadowy alleyways, and took unconscious note of houses that had their lights on. It was not yet late, but the sun was going down earlier by the day and the sky was graying into darkness. As they walked toward the center of town, she held Carson's hand in hers and they talked over their options for Carson's costume for Halloween in Tarrytown.

Meggie was, she liked to brag, kind of an expert at Halloween. The awesomeness of Halloween was like the awesomeness of all the other holidays all rolled into one, except without the stress and drama. No matter what city she was in, she always found something to do and people to be with on Halloween. Her costumes were epic—no slutty vampire dresses or Renaissance princess corsets for her. A good Halloween costume was bigger than one person alone; it was zeitgeist. One year, when she was just a little kid, she was a Chia Pet. Another year, she was the gorilla from Donkey Kong. She'd once found herself a pretty empire-waist gown, which she'd embellished with enough blood and gore to tell people that she was Jane Austen's zombie, and she was sure that the rash of funny zombie books that followed were because some writer must have seen her in a bar. And—okay—*once* she was a slutty vampire. It seemed to be the thing to do at the time.

She took Carson to the bus stop, where they boarded a bus that took them to a shopping plaza. Meggie hoped for inspiration, maybe one of those Halloween stores that popped up in September and vanished six weeks later. But all she got was a drugstore, brightly lit and crawling with equally well-lit frat kids looking for energy drinks. She held Carson close to her as they found the Halloween aisle.

"What do you think?" she asked. "Let's get you some gear!"

He looked with professorial scrutiny over the rows of cheap polyester tunics made to look like superhero chests, flattened wigs in plastic pouches, and uncomfortable-looking rubber masks. She watched his optimism fade to dismay.

"Okay—so—" She tried to sound cheery; she wanted so badly for him to be happy. Not only later when they found his costume, but right now. "So here's an idea. What if you pick out *my* costume for Halloween?"

"Really?"

"Sure. Anything you pick, I'll wear it."

"Swear it, declare it?"

"Swear it, declare it," she said. And she ignored the completely juvenile little frisson of worry that Carson might pick out a costume that was beneath her standards. Carson made another, closer survey of the Halloween junk—because it was junk—that lined the store shelves. He touched a French maid costume and Meggie had to bite her tongue to keep from suggesting that she should be allowed one veto. "Keep an eye out for a getup for you, too," she suggested hopefully. "In case you see something you like."

Carson took an extraordinary amount of time. He went up the aisle, then down, then up again. He teased her: "What about this one for you?" and pointed to a girl in footie pajamas with pigtails and a pacifier. Meggie gave a histrionic groan. "Oh, I know," he said. "*This!*" And Meggie shrieked in true horror when he gripped the corner of a package to show her an old-lady costume, complete with muumuu and gray wig.

She didn't speak again until they were done laughing. "Look, it doesn't have to be a costume from this store. I mean, we could . . . like . . . think of something. And make it. I've made my own costumes plenty of times before. And I could make yours, too."

He came to stand beside her again. And though he'd been cheerful a moment ago, now his face was full of somber intention. "Aunt Meg? Maybe this year you could be yourself for Halloween. Because that would be the best costume of all."

Meggie was speechless. She would have sworn on her life that the floor tipped. *Be yourself* . . . She saw the long parade of her Halloweens past, costumed versions of herself walking down the street and waving. And more: There was her hippie phase, her punk-rock phase, her goth phase, her nerdy girl-in-pink-cardigan phase, her glam phase, and her current phase, which was an amalgamation of eighties chic and things she happened to have lying around. If she'd had a gun to her head and had to answer the question *Which are you?* she wouldn't have been able to say. She was all. She was none. She'd had more Halloweens than she had years. And here was Carson, who had taken her hand and was looking at her with his soulful, beatific eyes, telling her she was perfect just how she was.

"Are you serious?" she managed.

And to her further shock, Carson laughed—a big bellyful of laughing. Reluctantly, Meggie joined him, though she didn't yet see the joke.

"Fake out!" he cried. "You totally got *had*!" And he laughed for a while more, then gave her a stinging high five.

Gradually, Meggie got her feet back underneath her. She didn't know what to think, so she thought nothing. "Seriously, though. Do you see anything here that will work?"

His cheeks were bright from cold and laughing. But he sobered before he spoke. "I think we shall end up being ourselves for Halloween."

"Is that . . . the royal *we?*"

He nodded.

She rolled her eyes. "Okay, Your Majesty. We'll find something for you better than a dalmatian. We'll make something. We still have time."

Vic had not brought flowers. Instead, he'd brought exactly three paper roses, folded neatly from pages of a novel that he'd picked up at a thrift store. Aubrey had been incredulous. Lines of black text crisscrossed delicate paper petals. She brought them to her nose: they smelled like old books and rose oil.

"You made these?"

In the soft light of the front hall in the Stitchery, his eyes had glinted with pride. She didn't hide how much the gift had touched her, even though she suspected it might be gauche to gush over the flowers the way she did. The roses had no practical function—Bitty would probably call them dust collectors—but they had a purpose. They whispered a message that had no words.

Vic did not immediately tell her where they were going, but when they parked, she guessed. He'd circled the block a few times, passing the Tarrytown Music Hall repeatedly, before finally settling on a spot far from the old theater, where the road sloped down toward the lip of the river. They walked up the hill to the hall, beneath spotty streetlights that cast umbrellas of light beneath the darkening sky, passing a colorful candy shop and a bright ice cream parlor and a svelte, sexy bar.

"Is this okay?" Vic asked. "You said a few weeks ago when we were talking at the library that you'd never seen *House of Dark Shadows*, even though they filmed it right down the road."

"That's right!" She remembered talking to him about the vampire tours they'd started giving at Tarrytown's gothic mansion—which led to talk of the vampire movie. She'd thought he was just making mundane, forgettable small talk to be friendly; apparently, he'd been listening to everything she said. "I totally want to see it. But do you think it will be too scary for me?"

"The only thing that might scare you is the dialogue," he said. "Or the acting. Or the plotline. Actually, there's a lot to be scared of—in a so-funny-it's-scary kind of way."

"Sounds perfect for Halloween," she said.

They walked into the foyer, which had probably seen better days. The theater had opened in 1885 to a Gilbert and Sullivan show; now Aubrey and Vic settled into folding chairs in front of a movie screen just as the reels started to turn. The crowd was lively, reacting with exaggeration to each new plot twist or meaningful stare. All the clichés of vampire horror were unleashed: A platinum vampire seductress in a white nightgown thrashed at the men who held her down, while another approached her with miserable bravery and a wooden stake in hand. Aubrey laughed aloud.

After the movie, they drove out of Tarrytown, out to the voluptuous pastures and acres of sweet fields that silvered under a high, bright autumn moon. Aubrey couldn't get her fill of Vic. He told her he was the oldest child, and he talked about taking care of his younger brothers and sister after his father died—about his mother crying when certain songs came on the radio, and about his sister getting pregnant and then moving in with him. He talked about how much he loved cities—any cities—for the bonds that came of people living so close to one another, but he also confessed that he was not as interested in traveling as he was in getting his feet under him, strong and solid, to settle down. By the time they parked, Aubrey knew she was half in love.

Slowly, arms linked, they walked across a wide piazza surrounded by the fieldstone walls and steep roofs of a grand, Normandy-style farm, with buildings and walkways made of dark stone. Aubrey had been to the busy farm many times to watch the pigs rooting in and tilling up the dirt fields, to sit and have a rustic lunch on a picnic table, to watch the hooded beekeepers pump smoke at drowsy honeybees. Now the moonlight touched the hillsides, the looming silo, and steep slate roofs, and Aubrey's heart was in her throat.

"Too much?" he asked.

She shifted her eyes from the moon above the stone silo down to his face. "Do you want to sweep me off my feet?"

"Yes."

"Then it's not too much," she said.

Inside, the restaurant was beautiful, simple, dimly lit. Tiny orange pumpkins and green-and-yellow squash were laid out on sideboards. Real candles flickered. At their table, Vic folded his hands; they were hands that spoke of hard work, dirt and grease that had dug in so deep no amount of soap would get it out, and it was a shock to see them against the bleached white of the tablecloth. And yet he didn't seem uncomfortable, so neither was she.

They talked—not about Tappan Square, about eminent domain laws, about the possibility that they might lose their homes. Instead, they talked about the little things, childhood pets and favorite books and preferences for coffee or tea. And they ate. She got an egg that she swore was made of sunshine. Turnips that, if she closed her eyes, tasted of grass and rain. Vic had ordered a bottle of champagne: She drank until her thoughts began to effervesce and burst cheerily in her mind.

For the first time in her life, she was on a date that was going perfectly. Just a week ago, her understanding of Vic was incomplete and not fully formed—and yet it had been enough to make her heady with curiosity and wishes. But now, as each moment passed and her date with him become more romantic, more intimate, she saw that the promise being ful-filled in him was even better than she might have imagined. She did not allow dark thoughts to creep into her mind; she didn't think about the Stitchery—which had always had a way of making itself the exclusive and singular priority of guardians past. Nor did she think about her previous roman-tic failures. The evening felt enchanted, seamless, infinite, and full of a thousand possibilities—all of them good. She wondered if it was too soon to be thinking of what she'd been missing in her life before this evening with him.

Vic might have felt the same way. He leaned his cheek on his fist and gazed at her, a faint smile playing around his lips. "When are you going to knit something for me?"

"Oh," Aubrey said. "You need a spell?"

"I don't want a spell. I want something from you. You can knit things that don't have spells in them, right?"

"That's always a little bit of a question. A knitter always leaves something of herself in everything she makes."

"Nobody's ever knit me anything," he said.

"Never?"

"Not since I was a kid, and I didn't know enough to appre-ciate it."

"Aren't you worried that I'll knit some kind of spell into it without telling you? Maybe a spell that will make you have a sudden impulse to repaint the Stitchery? Or a love spell . . . ?" She blushed; apparently, she'd had too much champagne.

"I trust you," he said. "If you need the Stitchery painted, all you have to do is ask. And if you want to knit a love spell, then . . . I guess I'll just have to enjoy the ride."

She smiled to herself and looked down at her plate, emotions warring. She must have been quiet for too long, because when he spoke again, he was apologetic and embarrassed.

"You're right," he said. "I'm sorry. I guess it's a really personal thing to knit a gift for someone, and I shouldn't have asked."

"No, it's not that!" she said. "It's just that there's a rumor. Like, a curse. Well, not a real curse. Not one that's associated with the Stitchery. But there's this thing that happens; it's called 'the curse of the boyfriend sweater.' "

He laughed. "Sounds like a B horror movie."

"The theory is that as soon as you make a new, um, boyfriend, a sweater, or something, you get on the fast track to splitsville. It's like the Murphy's Law of knitting."

"So I should be glad you don't want to knit for me."

"I wouldn't mind if you stuck around."

"What a ringing endorsement." He chuckled. "How long will I have to wait?"

She felt her throat tighten. "I don't know. I've never knit a boyfriend sweater before."

"You haven't?" he said, and then he caught himself. "Oh—I'm sorry. I know you just said you haven't, obviously. I was just surprised."

"It's okay," she said, and she kept the rest of her thoughts to herself.

"Have you been with anyone, seriously?"

She let the waitress refill her glass of water. The ice tinkled. "I'm not sure what constitutes serious."

"Someone you loved," he said.

She forced a smile that she hoped looked mysterious and flirty. "Why would it matter?"

He edged away, leaning against the back of his seat. "Maybe I want to know what I have to contend with. If there's anybody I should be worried about."

"There isn't."

"No?"

"No." And she almost added, *How could there be? How could there be anyone but you?*

He was looking at her. She had taken off her sunglasses when they'd sat down—not because she'd wanted to, but because the layers of candlelight and shadow in the restaurant were so dim that she could not read the menu or see her glass of water if she kept her glasses on. And yet, across the table, Vic regarded her steadily, directly, and without the skin-tightening around his eyes that suggested he was uncomfortable looking at her.

Aubrey could see, in that moment, that whatever he felt for her was serious. He gave her a thing she had been missing for most of her life: He looked at her eye-to-eye, without judgment. He—of all the men she'd ever met—confirmed what she'd sometimes suspected about herself: that she was beautiful in her way, in spite of her eyes.

Her heart swelled with gratitude and, strangely enough, with a hope that she'd never dared claim: Was this even happening, this possibility of love? Could it be that her dire projections about her long, lonely future in the Stitchery were *wrong*?

She saw Vic's face change, his pupils darkening, his breath coming between open lips.

"God . . . this table," he said. His hands gripped the edges; the tablecloth bunched. "Do you think anyone would notice if I threw it over, got it out of the way?"

Aubrey felt like a thousand little butterflies had alighted on her skin. She wanted Vic's mouth, his hands. When she spoke, her voice rasped. "What's stopping you?"

It took a moment before she realized that the buzzing and chiming in the back of her mind was not her overwrought imagination but was her phone ringing in her purse beside her. She hadn't known she'd been clutching the stem of her champagne. She put it down. "Sorry." She shoved shaking fingers into her bag until she found her phone.

The Stitchery. She answered immediately. "What's wrong?"

It was Meggie's voice she heard. "I think we need you. Quick."

"What happened?"

"Craig happened. He's here."

"Why?"

Meggie was whispering. "He says he's not leaving without the kids."

"We're ten minutes away," Aubrey said. She snapped her phone shut. "I'm sorry," she told Vic, her heart sinking. She had the sense of something inevitable happening, of the Stitchery herding her violently back into the microcosm of her normal life. It had been nice, she thought, to get away for a while.

"What is it?" he asked.

"I'm so sorry. I need you to take me home."

From the Great Book in the Hall: *There are times when it will be critical to know how to knit quickly. Early knitters in the British Isles developed methods of knitting for an economy of movement; the smaller the motion, the quicker the stitch. They threaded their yarn in their left hands, to work fast by the light of a fire in a winter hearth. This was functional knitting to bring in money—knitting that fed children, paid doctors, patched fences. Human as machine.*

Some people have said that when factories began to erode the work done by cottagers, yarn-holding techniques shifted. The highborn lady did not knit for income. She knit for leisure. She knit at teatime in sun-bright parlors; she exchanged patterns with friends. And so she held her yarn in her right hand not her left, a choice that forced her hands to swoop and loop beautifully for each stitch, a choice that distinguished her from the callused and bone-sore farm women who knit so fast and crudely for their bread.

We women of the Stitchery today, we have always learned to knit with both hands, not because one hand is better than the other, but because each hand has its advantages. We knit for speed. We knit for gratification. We knit because we must, either way.

14

"Wrong Side"

Craig Fullen was a large man. In his youth he had been muscular and bulky, an ox of a boy with wide shoulders. But now, long past his high school years, his largeness was no longer quite so firm. He had neat black hair and a handsome face, with a good-sized nose. He was memorable, people said. Not because he said witty things or stood out in a crowd, but because of how perfectly he was just enough of everything: just enough handsomeness, just enough humor, just enough arrogance, just enough kindness—just enough and never too much. At least, this was how he appeared to good society.

Now he stood in the Stitchery's yard, with his capacious lungs bellowing out and in, and his arm raised in a fist like an upside-down exclamation mark. Bitty had suggested he come inside so they could have a quiet, private talk. But he had refused; in the rust- and pothole-scarred hovel that was Tappan Square, there was no reason to be on his best behavior. He thundered at his wife with a tenor's paunch and gusto, demanding that Bitty send his children outside with packed bags.

"I'm not giving you a choice here!" He raised up his cell phone in the darkness; it shone like a searchlight. "Send those kids outside to me right now or I'll call the police."

Bitty stood on the porch, looking down on the man she'd married. "Don't be an ass."

"Me—an ass? Me?"

"You're the only middle-aged man I see standing in the freezing dark and yelling like the sky's falling—so, *yes*, you."

"Elizabeth," Craig said. His voice was dark with warning. "You should think carefully before you talk."

"Why's that?"

"Because if you're thinking about trying to divorce me, if it ever comes down to that, then you've just handed me the winning hand."

"How do you figure?"

"Do you honestly think I would let you just take our children away from me? That I wouldn't come looking for them? What you've done here is kidnapping—no question about it. You took our kids away, in secret, without my permission. You *kidnapped* them. And I'm three seconds away from calling nine-one-one."

Bitty's stomach began to burn. *Oh God.* Had she kidnapped the children? She'd meant to antagonize Craig a little bit by disappearing and leaving only a note. But . . . kidnapping? Could what she'd done be misconstrued that way? She began to tremble.

"I didn't *abduct* them."

"No need to waste your time convincing *me* that you didn't take them," he said. "Save your breath for when the cops get here."

"You wouldn't put our kids through that," she said.

"Oh no?" He laughed. "Try me."

"I won't let you have them," she said between her teeth.

"I won't let *you* have them," Craig said. "Not now. And if you're going to be a bitch about it, not *ever*."

"Excuse me?"

"You know I won't go in that dump." He gestured toward the Stitchery, his lip curled in disgust. "So—fine. You've managed to keep them away from me for a few days. But if you're thinking you'll get the upper hand by divorcing me, think again. I'll have better lawyers than you. Much better. You'll have a state-assigned rube and a rap sheet for child abduction."

Bitty laughed as if he'd just told a joke over the fizz of champagne. But her fear was rising, rising from her belly to the middle of her chest and tightening, rising up to the base of her throat and clotting there. She reached out for a porch post and hoped the gesture looked more breezy than desperate.

"And what would you do with our children twenty-four hours a day while you're at the office, or going to cocktail parties, or going—wherever you go? I don't think you have any idea of what it's like to raise your own children; and I don't think that's something you'd even *want* to do alone."

"Who says I would be doing it alone?" Craig said.

Bitty wanted to double over—her stomach hurt so bad. Her fingernails dug into the wood. "What do you want?"

"This ridiculous power play of yours ends now. I'm taking the kids back. They're *my* kids. And if you know what's good for you, you'll send them out here. I'll give you five minutes. Why are you still standing there? Go!"

"Okay, I get the point. The whole neighborhood does," Bitty said. She could barely hear herself over the banging of her heart in her ears. "Just—hold on." She turned around. The front door gaped and the hallway enfolded her, and then she was inside and Craig was in the yard, and she actually felt a little relieved to be behind the Stitchery's walls.

Since her adult personality had first begun to take shape, Bitty had spent her time trying to take control of her circumstances. And she had succeeded admirably—without needing the unreliable and pathetic fallback of magic to help her succeed. She had taught herself how to make men love her; then she nabbed Craig. She had thrown in her lot with him because she knew he would give her a stable, respectable life; like her, he wanted an orderly existence, with everything just so. The problem, of course, began when Craig's idea of a good life began to conflict with—and even encroach upon—Bitty's idea of it. And now it had come to this.

She headed to the kitchen, where she knew her family had taken refuge. Aubrey was still dressed from her interrupted date, having slipped through the back door by way of a neighbor's yard. Meggie was beside her, her pixie's face rumpled with concern. Bitty's children were standing so close to each other that their shoulders were touching.

"Mom?" Carson said.

"Everything's okay," Bitty said. She went to him and kissed his head, his baby-fine hair. She did the same to her daughter, who smelled of strawberry shampoo.

"Let me guess," Nessa said. She mocked her mother's voice: *"This is between me and your father."*

"That doesn't help," Bitty said. The Stitchery had grown hot. She was sweating. "I need you to take your brother upstairs right now."

Nessa sighed. "Oh *brother*. Come on."

They went, Nessa holding her brother's hand. The kitchen was different without them in it, as if some of the air had gone out of the room with them. Bitty looked at her sisters, who were looking back at her. She was too overwrought to be embarrassed now that the truth about her life—the classless, coarse vulgarity of it—had come out. She was what she was, what she had always been at heart. She was Bitty who had never left the Stitchery. And her sisters, they knew.

"Is he drunk?" Meggie asked. "Is he a drinker?"

"No," Bitty said. She could feel a line of moisture at her hairline. "He just has temper tantrums sometimes. He bottles things up, then *boom*. An explosion. But this . . . this is epic."

"What should we do?" Meggie asked.

Bitty sighed. And then she spoke the question that had been haunting her since the day she realized her husband no longer loved her but wasn't willing to let her go. "What can I do?"

Her sisters said nothing. They seemed to have realized that telling Craig no was not an option; he wouldn't leave the Stitchery without his children. Even if Bitty could offer him a rationale, the kids had become a point of stubborn pride.

Bitty pinched the bridge of her nose and squeezed her eyes shut. "I'm not sending the kids home with him," Bitty said. "It's not safe. He isn't in a condition to drive himself around, let alone the children."

"Good," Meggie said.

"So I'll drive them myself."

"Bitty!" Aubrey's exclamation was so pointed Bitty nearly jumped. "No!"

"I have to. He's right. They're his kids, too. And I did just . . . take them."

"To a *funeral*," Meggie said. "You took them to a funeral that *he* should have been at, too, if he was half a man."

Bitty couldn't hide her disgust.

"Oh Jesus, Bit." Meggie held out her hands. "I'm not criticizing you. The guy turned out to be a total crapbag. It's not your fault."

"He's not a . . . crapbag. He works really hard. He makes more money in a year than some people see in their lifetimes. And regardless of how he feels about me, he loves those kids." Bitty pushed away from the wall. When she spoke again, she knew she was trying to convince herself, to firm up her resolve that she was doing the right thing. "Okay. Everything's okay. I was thinking that maybe we needed to leave anyway . . . with Nessa knitting and everything, I'm not sure we should stay."

"What if there was a way?" Aubrey said. "If you could stay at the Stitchery for a while more, would you *want* to?"

The kitchen grew quiet. The house was quiet, too, and Bitty thought it seemed the Stitchery itself was listening for the answer. Aubrey had asked the question that Bitty had not wanted to ask herself. She looked at Meggie—her silly hair, her creamy, child's skin. She looked at Aubrey—her makeup smudged under her eyes, her mouth bracketed with frown lines. Perhaps Bitty didn't want to stay in the Stitchery forever. But she was not yet ready to leave. She could see that her sisters were ready to fight for her, to do whatever it might take. And their loyalty, their dedication, moved her. She'd forgotten what it was like to love her sisters when love was a thing that was right in front of her and not projected from afar.

"Yes," she said. "I want to stay."

"Then it's done," Aubrey said, and she clapped her hands. The blue of her eyes was flashing and iridescent, the electric blue of damselfly wings. "What do you have to offer as a sacrifice?"

"Oh no. Hold up," Bitty said. Her hope plummeted: She should have known. "I didn't know you were talking about spells."

"It's worth a try," Aubrey said.

"Good Lord." Bitty shook her head, laughing in bitter disappointment. "Spells. I thought maybe you had a *real* plan. This is ridiculous."

Meggie took her arm. "What's ridiculous is you having a potential way to keep your kids here with you at the Stitchery so that if you go back to him you could do it in your own good time, but instead you're going to go outside, roll on your back, and say 'Okay you win.' *That's* ridiculous."

Bitty couldn't speak.

Meggie let her go. Her hair was clumped in hard, thick spikes like thorns. "Plus, what kind of example does it set for your kids if you pack them up and go home now? Nessa's a little girl, and she's looking to you to teach her how to be strong. I don't know what's going on with Craig, but I do know I wouldn't want my daughter learning a lesson like that."

Bitty was quiet. She felt—she hated to admit it—chastised. Especially since her sisters didn't yet know the half of it. She was not a good role model; sometimes she was intractable, sometimes she was a doormat. She'd hoped a retreat to the Stitchery for a while might offer some clarity or strength of mind.

"But . . . a spell?" she said, lamely.

"Look at it this way," Meggie said. "It couldn't hurt."

Bitty crossed her arms and raised her eyes to the water-spotted ceiling. "If you want to try, I guess I won't say no."

"Great." Aubrey's voice was unusually commanding. "Does Craig know about the magic and the knitting?"

"If he does, it's not because I told him. He'd think I was nuts."

"That should make our job easier," Aubrey said. "Now— Bit—this isn't the time to rationalize, okay? Quick—what would it be worth to you to keep your kids here with you a few more days? Don't think about it, just tell me. Quick. What's it worth?"

"I don't know. I guess . . ."

"What?"

Bitty heard something hard in her laugh. She fingered her wedding ring; it was buttery yellow and simple—the least expensive piece of jewelry she had.

"Really?" Meggie asked. "Are you sure?"

"Seems like poetic justice," Bitty said. She twisted it off her finger and dropped it onto the flat of Aubrey's palm.

Meggie's voice was soft. "But what will you tell him you did with it? What if you need it back?"

"You're assuming he'll notice it's gone," Bitty said. "And I can always tell Craig to buy me a new one. A really expensive one, with so many diamonds you can see it from Mars."

Aubrey's hand closed around the ring, and it was gone. Forever, Bitty realized. Gone. She had been making jokes; she should have been saying good-bye. The loss of it was real and heavy, and it made her realize that giving it up was perhaps not the easy and straightforward thing she'd wanted it to be.

"Here's the plan," Aubrey said. "Meggie, you go outside and stall Craig."

"On it," she said.

"Bitty, you go upstairs with the kids. We'll call you down when we're ready."

"Okay," Bitty said.

Meggie had hurried out the front door; Bitty took a step—one step—toward the stairs when Aubrey stopped her. She turned.

"I'm glad you're staying," Aubrey said.

"Let's hope so," Bitty said.

* * *

Aubrey skinned her knuckles on the rough side of a wooden barrel. She rummaged through thick, spongy balls of yarn. *Where is it?* Years ago, she'd started a scarf—an uninspired little thing of two-by-two ribbing. She'd given up on it when another, more promising project had come along, and she'd speared her live stitches with a silver stitch holder then shoved it away. Now it was exactly what she needed—nearly done, a blank slate, a fabric ready for an infusion of magic.

She found it at the bottom of the barrel, and she thought: *Yes, of course.* She snatched the half-done scarf, grabbed needles from the counter, and sat on a sealed wooden crate. There was no time for leisurely candle lighting, for a quiet prayer. She needed to clear her mind—fast—and make way.

And yet the channels of her thoughts were clogged. It was not that her focus was lacking; she was not distracted, exactly. But she doubted herself, her abilities. She did not even know if it was possible to graft a spell to a half-done work; possibly, the thing was too far along and magic would run off it like rainwater sliding down a road. It occurred to her how very little she knew about the family's craft, how hard she'd always leaned on Mariah, and how many questions she should have been asking when Mariah was alive. But she'd always thought she and Mariah would have more time later, more time later, until one day, later was gone.

Mari, she whispered in her mind. *If Bitty leaves, I don't know that she'll ever come back.*

She closed her eyes, needles in her hands, poised and still. She exhaled. And then she felt as if Mariah were with her, that somehow her aunt was around her, soothing her, assuring her, blessing her, telling her it would be okay. Her mind snapped to blankness. Her fingers started moving—no longer working a ribbed pattern, but instead taking the quickest route to work the stitches into place. There was only the knitting, the darkness, Mariah, power tucked like a seed in her heart, and the rapid-firing machinery of her hands.

"Bitty!"

Bitty heard the sound of her youngest sister trying to keep her voice normal as she called up the stairs. Nessa and Carson tensed beneath Bitty's arms. Fifteen minutes had passed since Aubrey had disappeared into the yarn room and Meggie had gone outside in an attempt to stall. And Bitty was having an existential meltdown.

She had no good way to tell her children what her sisters were doing, what she had authorized them to do. She wasn't sure she *should* tell, because she doubted that a good role model would attempt to hijack her husband's brain with magic that she purportedly did not believe in and that she'd all but told her children *they* should not believe in. All she'd been able to offer was a tepid excuse for her family's collective behavior: *Aunt Meg wanted to talk to Dad for a minute.* Her children believed her with the slow reluctance that comes with accepting a convenient lie.

Bitty felt sick to her stomach, more now than when Craig had shown up. More now than when he'd threatened to call the police. The questions cramped her up. Was she no better than an atheist who goes to a funeral and starts talking about angels and *a better place;* was she as much a hypocrite as someone who scoffs at prayer until the day their car is seesawing on the edge of a cliff?

It was quite possible, she realized, that crises brought out people's true nature—and that this crisis had brought out *her* true nature. But she also worried that this particular drama hadn't forced her to face the truth about herself so much as betray it. And that felt just plain wrong.

"Bitty? Bit!" Meggie's voice was pinched with panic.

Bitty pulled herself together. "Stay here," she told her kids. She rushed through the hallway and met Meggie halfway down the stairs. "What now?"

"Our pal Craigster called the cops. At least, he says he did. They're on the way."

"Crap," Bitty whispered. "What if he tells them I kidnapped the children? What if the cops take them away?" She was panicking now, fully panicking. The tears that she'd held back began to stream. "What am I going to do?"

"It's okay," Meggie said. "I promise. It's going to be okay."

Together they trampled down the stairs to the first floor. They stopped in the doorway of the yarn room, not a toe crossing over the threshold into the space Aubrey occupied. Light from the hall pushed forward into the yarn room but deferred to the shadows inside. Stillness, eerie and complete, had settled so deeply that not even the clock on the wall could be heard to tick. Perched on a crate, Aubrey might have been made of nothing more than dead stone, except for the fluttering of her hands and the ribbon of black yarn that trickled from its ball.

"Aubrey. We're outta time," Meggie said.

Bitty's heart was pounding. Her muscles were jumping around under her skin. She was shocked and horrified to realize that her hope—some of it anyway—was pinned to the scrap of fabric in Aubrey's hands.

Meggie looked at Bitty. Their sister hadn't moved. She tried again. "Hey Aub—"

Aubrey opened her eyes.

Bitty cried out, lifted her hands in instinctive self-defense. "Oh my God!" The yarn room had burst into hot blue strobe, blue fracking into the joints of beams, blue beating its fists on the walls, blue like a star burning on the brink of implosion.

From outside the window, Craig roared. "What the hell is going on?"

Bitty couldn't speak.

But then, Aubrey blinked. Once. And just like that, with a loud boom like the report of a gunshot, the light was gone. Darkness, cool and soothing, washed over the yarn room. Bitty realized that the power in the Stitchery had gone out. Light came only from the streetlight outside.

Aubrey wrenched her needle from her stitches like a soldier brandishing a sword. "Take it," she said. She held the scarf up for Bitty and gave it a shake. "Come on!"

Stunned, Bitty walked forward and took the scarf. She was only a few feet away when Aubrey doubled over and vomited.

Bitty stopped.

"Don't worry, I got her." Meggie rushed to Aubrey's side. "You go."

"Are you sure?"

"Did I mention that the cops will be here any second? Just go!"

She ran from the yarn room.

In the yard her husband stopped pacing and looked up at her, his torso as thick as a black bear's, teeth glinting white. Bitty felt as if someone had taken over her body, someone who wasn't her. She stepped off the porch and into the overgrown grass.

"You must be cold," she said.

From GovSpyDog.org:

Thanks to reader D.Avid, who reported hearing this call go out over his police monitor:

Residents of Tappan Square, a run-down neighborhood in the storied village of Tarrytown, New York, responded to a "domestic disturbance" but found something way more disturbing than that. Although there was no dispute to be seen, multiple agitated residents approached officers to report a "powerful blue light coming down from the sky." As far as we know, there's been no indication that law officers are taking the complaint seriously.

People, this is where you come in. I don't have to tell you about the Hudson Valley, about those unexplainable stone monoliths that are all over that region that scientists have not been able to figure out. I don't have to tell you that the Hudson River might be a giant landing strip for highly advanced spacecraft who first visited us during ancient times.

If you saw the blue light in Tarrytown, I want to hear about it. Otherwise, theories welcome.

Aubrey lay on the cold white tile of the bathroom floor, wedged beneath the protruding bowl of the porcelain sink and the militant bulwark of the tub. A few candles had been set out on the back of the toilet tank, and the air smelled like strawberries. The room was freezing, and despite the unforgiving angles at which she'd contorted her body, Aubrey felt as weightless as if she were floating in a cold salt sea. Her sisters were with her. Ribbons of their conversation sifted around her, and she grasped at the elusive threads, Bitty saying, *He didn't put the scarf on, but he held it.* Meggie saying, *Do you think she'll be okay?*

She tried to lift her head. In a moment, her sisters were there to help her. She opened her eyes and the blurry world went clearer. She sat up and leaned back against the tub.

"Easy, killer," Meggie said.

"Water?" Aubrey managed. A moment later, Bitty was pushing a mug into her hand. She drank; her throat cooled.

She looked up at her sisters. Meggie was hunched on the closed lid of the toilet. Bitty was perched on the lip of the tub. "Did it work?"

Bitty said, "He's gone."

"Does this, like, always happen?" Meggie asked. "The puking? The passing out?"

"No. It's never happened before."

"Why now?" Bitty asked.

Aubrey sipped her water. She felt as if she were being slowly poured back into her own body. She was shivering down to her bones. "I don't know. I guess because of the intensity of the spell." She'd never knit so quickly before; it shouldn't have worked. Normally, it took time to build the momentum of magic, like pushing on the bumper of a stalled car—that slow heave toward acceleration. But the spell Aubrey had just knit went from zero to sixty in no time flat. It should have been impossible. It wasn't. It made Aubrey afraid of the amount of magic that she now knew existed within her. Some part of her did not want it, did not want to know. For all the power she'd glimpsed, she knew she'd merely peeked through a keyhole and not stepped fully into the chamber. The question was, What did it mean?

Her sisters were talking again; apparently, she'd checked out. She heard the strain in Bitty's voice. She heard Meggie's replies: soft questions uttered with intensity and care.

Bitty's sigh was long. "I promise I'll tell you everything. But I'm exhausted. So can we talk about this in the morning?"

"Only 'cause Aubrey's conked out," Meggie said.

But Aubrey could no longer follow. She was falling asleep. Or she was already sleeping. Bitty and Meggie were talking, dressed up like Victorian vampires and having tea. There was a crowd in the yarn room, and they were knitting capes for stop signs and pondering how the capes would fit since stop signs did not have shoulders. Aubrey was trying to tell everyone that the moon had turned into a giant wrecking ball that was barreling toward Tappan Square.

"Come on." A voice came into her dream like a flashlight through fog. She did not know who spoke. "Let's get her to bed."

15

"Place Marker"

Saturday morning came to the Stitchery on the heels of a passing rain shower, and all of Tappan Square shimmered. Clusters of purple asters and pots of hardy mums trembled on the roadsides. Scarecrows in floppy hats smiled where they had been strapped to mailboxes. Gauze-fettered zombies, strung from porches, turned slow circles in a cheery breeze.

Most of Tappan Square was still sleeping and did not know that strangers were visiting their corner of town. A survey crew had arrived just after dawn, with their tripods and hard hats and cups of coffee steaming in bare hands. They worked quickly, fanning out, signaling, talking into their phones. They were measuring the outline of a neighborhood that soon would not be there, drawing invisible lines around buildings to be felled like so many acres of trees.

At one point in its history, Tappan Square had been an actual square, a small public park, and the Stitchery perched on its western lip. Each morning the people of Tarrytown walked their dogs or, if they were feeling spritely, spread out their picnic blankets over the dewy grass. To the children who sprinted and turned cartwheels on the great green lawn, it seemed that Tappan Square Park went on forever, that it would always go on. But eventually, when the first automobile factories opened along the waterfront and tens of thousands of employees needed housing, the park was filled in with as many identical two-story Colonials as could fit on the dirt, and a neighborhood was born.

Aubrey was sleeping while the surveyors were crossing the street in front of the Stitchery, looking up at the windows of the old, peeling house. She slept and slept. She was dreaming of Vic, dreaming of his thumb pressed into the hollow at her throat, dreaming she fit herself against him, skin-to-skin. Though her mind was sluggish her body was burning, awake and hot on the precipice, engulfed by the blur of sensation from a knee that was not there, pressed between hers, by the slick of shoulder blades that were not there, straining under her palms, by livid muscles, by the iron heat of hard weight, by a thousand live wires of electricity bowing and tangling and snapping under her skin until—bitter disappointment— the phone. Ringing. The power must have come back on in the night.

Slowly, she wandered downstairs. She was surprised to find Meggie in the kitchen, sitting cross-legged at the table and sipping coffee.

"You're up early," Aubrey said. "Who was that on the phone?"

"Vic."

"Why didn't you get me?"

Meggie looked up, grinning. "I took a message."

"Okay—what's the message?"

"He wanted to give you a lift to the Tappan Watch meeting tonight. So I told him, you'd love that."

"Oh," Aubrey said. She might have given Meggie a hard time for interfering, but in truth Meggie had done the same thing she would have done. "Well, thanks." She poured herself a mug of coffee. She needed it; she was still feeling weak from last night's exertions. "The Watch is meeting at six.

We're going to hash out a plan to really drum up some awareness for our situation. If we kick up a big enough fuss, maybe the council will have to vote it down."

"The public shaming approach. I like it. Mariah would be proud."

Aubrey looked at her. "Do you mean, of me?"

"Of course I mean you."

"Why?"

"Because you're fighting the good fight. Even though she's gone."

Aubrey glanced at her sister, who had deposited herself cross-legged in a kitchen chair. "You could come, you know. To the meeting tonight?"

Meggie scoffed. "And crash your hot sexy date at the fire hall?"

"You and a few dozen other people."

"I don't know," Meggie said, musing. "It's been a while since I raised hell in Tarrytown."

Aubrey smiled.

"I guess we'll get a lot more money for selling the Stitchery if we don't let city hall tear the whole neighborhood down."

Aubrey said nothing, saddened by the idea that Meggie still wanted to sell the Stitchery out from under her. She'd hoped that last night had changed something. If Meggie noticed her disappointment, she didn't let on.

"Hey. Here's a question," Meggie said. "Do you know where Bitty is?"

"She's not here?" Aubrey absentmindedly peered into her mug and considered dumping her coffee down the drain. It was a little strong for her taste, but she hated to waste it. "She didn't tell you where she was going?"

"I only just woke up," Meggie said.

"She probably went grocery shopping or something."

"Mmm," Aubrey said through another swallow. Tremors of last night's revelations were still echoing at the periphery of her brain. Craig's sultan-like bravado. Bitty's sad eyes. The great cavernous cistern of power Aubrey had discovered deep inside.

She noticed a packet of bundled papers on the counter, folded in thirds, with Bitty's perfect handwriting on the front. It said A & M.

"Meggie?"

"What?"

Aubrey reached for the bundle. She was afraid to open it. She didn't want to know if it was possible that, after everything, everything that had happened, Bitty was gone.

Dear sisters,

Last night after Craig took off, I promised I would come clean. But I'm not good at this whole opening-up thing. Writing's the easiest way to explain.

Let me start where I left off—where we left off from one another. Twelve years ago, after I moved out of the Stitchery, I called to tell Mariah that I was pregnant and that Craig and I would be getting married. I was happy. Or at least, I thought I was. I was going to have a husband. A family. A house of my own.

Mariah didn't take the news well. She begged me to come back. She said I was making a bad decision. I practically hung up on her. I was trying to make a better life for myself, but Mariah had never been able to see it that way.

Anyway, a week before we were slated to take our vows, Craig began to act odd. He avoided me. He fell asleep on the couch and didn't come to bed until morning. He started saying maybe we didn't have to get married right away. Maybe his parents would accept a long engagement instead.

For days this went on. And then I found a pair of thick charcoal-gray gloves hanging from a hook in the entryway. Handmade. Craig confirmed my suspicions: Mariah had mailed them to him as a wedding gift. He had no idea about the spells.

Now—to be clear, I don't believe it was the gloves that made him have second thoughts about marrying me. But it was the principle of the thing, that Mariah would attempt to meddle like that when Craig and I were already having a vulnerable moment. I called her and she didn't deny it. I threw the things away. I vowed I would never let myself get close to Mariah again; I would do little more than be polite.

After the wedding, Craig stopped acting so weird. At least for a while. But in recent years, things changed again. And it burns me to say it, but maybe Mariah was right after all.

The fundamental problem of our marriage can be summed up in four words: He has a mistress. I discovered her about eighteen months ago when a neighbor gave me a tip. At first I was upset, but then I thought about it a little more. I decided an affair might be good for him. I felt really . . . big. Like I was a big person to be able to understand why my husband was cheating and permit it to go on. And also, rich men do have affairs, just like they have Jaguars, expensive pens, and pretty wives. I knew what I signed up for when I married him. I figured the thing would run its course, and I would allow it.

But then, he began to get arrogant, flaunting. He pays her rent with our bank account (it's his money, of course, but I keep his books). He treats her to dinners and buys her jewelry and groceries. He takes care of her. She has become his life in the wings, the life when he's not on stage. And me? I'm the mother of his kids, his cook, his housekeeper, his interior decorator, his accountant, his live-in nanny.

He'll never willingly divorce me; divorce would be too crass, too lowbrow, for him. That's why I fell for him to begin with, knowing that once I married him, I would be married forever. But I didn't see the difference, then, between being married and being owned. He's made it clear that he'll use the children as leverage, if he has to, to keep me with him— just like he'd fight to keep his house, or his car, or any other thing.

It's my own fault, I suppose. I should have pitched a fit about the affair the moment I discovered it. Twice over the last year I tried to leave him. I took the kids and his credit card and got us a hotel. I tried to get away. But he's got me right where he wants me, and there's nothing to do but go back to him, again and again.

How can a woman leave her husband when she has nowhere to go? Craig had suggested I quit school when I got pregnant, and I very willingly agreed. Now I couldn't get a decent-paying job if my life depended on it. Maybe I could give up my highlights and waxing, my gym membership and my cell phone data plan. But even if I did all of those things, I still could not support my children.

Do you know what that feels like? I am the poorest rich woman in the world.

And here's one more confession. Probably my worst one.

Aubrey, when I learned that there was a potential that we might sell the Stitchery, I thought of myself. Selfishly and unfairly, I thought of myself.

The money from selling the Stitchery would have given me the resources I needed to leave Craig and take my

*children with me. I saw an escape route. Freedom. For my
kids, for me.*

I was sure that I could convince you to sell.

But after last night, I realize I don't want to anymore.

*I've missed you, both of you. I didn't realize how badly.
When I left the Stitchery, I thought that if I didn't uproot
myself quickly there was a danger I would chicken out and
not do it at all. Meggie, I imagine you know something about
what that feels like.*

*But for the first time in my life I'm actually glad that the
Stitchery exists, and that, Aubrey, you're still in it. I don't
want to go another year without you guys in my life. I don't
want to go another day. I want my children to know their
family. Mariah was right: We're stronger together than we
are apart. I'm only sorry it took so long for me to come
around.*

*Okay—there's just one more thing to say. Last night, I
watched Craig's face as I talked him down from the ledge, as
he held the scarf in his hands, and I saw his anger
mellowing, I saw him calming down. I thought it was magic.
For a second, I almost believed. That strange blue light had
convinced me.*

*As I write this in the middle of the night while you both
are sleeping, the power company has a truck parked outside
the Stitchery; I think a transformer blew. And now that I'm
thinking more clearly, it makes sense to believe that Craig's
change of heart came about because of the fact that I assured
him everything was fine, that he was overreacting, that the
kids and I would be home again shortly, and that he should
enjoy "his freedom" while he could. It was all very
explainable and normal, watching reason set in.*

If I ever saw proof that there's magic in the Stitchery, I

*would be the first to believe. But at this point, I'm thirty-two
and I haven't seen anything conclusive, so I'm not holding
my breath. I am, however, willing to admit that just because
there's something about the Stitchery that I personally don't
get, doesn't mean there isn't something to get at all. I'm not
saying it right. God, this is hard. The point is, maybe a Van
Ripper belongs in the Stitchery. And maybe the Stitchery
belongs in Tappan Square. And maybe Tappan Square
belongs in Tarrytown. Even if I don't.*

I think that's everything. I'm going out for a long run.

Your loving, imperfect, exhausted sister,

Bitty

After Meggie read her sister's letter, she didn't have time to
talk things over with Aubrey—which was a good thing because she didn't want to talk things over. Aubrey glanced up
at the clock and almost lost her coffee through her nostrils
because of how late she'd slept. Then she blustered around
the house like a tornado, getting ready for her shift at the library. Meggie hadn't bothered to point out that Aubrey left
the Stitchery with a backward sweater and mismatched socks.
She suspected it wasn't the first time.

Now, with Aubrey gone, Meggie was alone . . . alone with
Bitty's confessional. It made a gloomy moue at her from the
kitchen table. To keep herself from tearing the letter to bits,
Meggie threw on some clothes and took herself for a walk
around the block. She felt angry and pinched and ready to
burst. She did not know why.

Outside, she found she'd underdressed for the chilly afternoon, but she did not return to the Stitchery for her jacket.
The neighborhood was as cramped as it had ever been. Without a garage or driveway in sight, every person who had a car

in Tappan Square had to park on the too narrow street. If the choked thoroughfares were human arteries, as lined with cholesterol as the streets were with traffic, the village of Tarrytown would have stroked out by now.

She shoved her cold hands into her pockets and walked fast. Her breath went up in little puffs like gunpowder. She felt like there was a hard rope tied around her chest. What was making her so surly? She hadn't woken up this way. She supposed that it had to do with Bitty's unburdening; Bitty had heaved off all the heavy stones of her life's labors, and Meggie felt they had piled right on her own chest.

Bitty hardly ever talked about her problems—either because she wanted everybody to think her life was perfect, or because she didn't want to worry anyone. And so Meggie could not claim that her sister was whining, or moping, or wallowing in annoying self-pity. But even though Bitty had never complained aloud about her marriage until her sisters had demanded to know what was going on, the miasma of her personal dramas niggled into every crack and crevice, ballooned into corners, edged out air particles, blotted out the damn sun. And Meggie wished, just once, that she could confess to her sisters what *she* had been doing for the past four years. What *her* life had been like. She wished that her sisters would have given her the common courtesy of healthy suspicion, maybe with a hint of wholesome familial prying. But—they took her at her word.

When she'd been on the road, she'd wondered, sometimes, about her sisters. When she was in Nashville negotiating with the owner of a cheap motel for a room with a broken shower, was Bitty buying chocolate bars and popcorn for her kids at a movie theater concession stand? When Meggie was clutching her pepper spray and wondering if the man she'd just interviewed was now following her down a dark street in Detroit, was Aubrey curled up with *Jane Eyre* and a cup of tea? When she was trying to figure out how to tell Lance, in Dallas, that it didn't matter whether or not she loved him because she *had* to leave—were her sisters even giving a thought to where their mother might be?

She walked past the chain-link fence where Mr. Smith's drooly old Doberman used to snarl and bark with only half as much fury as its owner. She huffed up the hill to the east of the Stitchery and passed the house that used to have a concrete fountain of a woman pouring water from an amphora, but which now showed only a slight depression in the yard where the statue had been. The old neighborhood made her long for her aunt Mariah, who always had room for her littlest niece in the crook of her arm even when her older sisters wanted nothing to do with her.

Meggie kicked a mailbox post, and then she knew two things. First, she would not be going to the Tappan Watch meeting tonight with Aubrey. And second, what she'd felt after reading Bitty's letter was not annoyance. It was jealousy. The same jealousy she'd felt as a kid when her older sisters had shooed her away so they could talk about "big girl things"; the jealousy that festered because Bitty and Aubrey had actually known their mother and Meggie could hardly remember her at all; the jealousy of having sacrificed so many years searching for a woman she didn't know, while her sisters went on with their lives.

She had come full circle and found herself standing before the Stitchery again, but she did not step foot off the sidewalk. Rising up before her, dilapidated and yet still powerful, was the root of her problems. Her feelings toward the old building were as muddled as its architecture. Like Bitty, Meggie had ulterior motives: A sale would give her the funding she needed to live more comfortably as she searched for her mother, to leave hostels in favor of motels, to swap fast food for real food. But unlike Bitty, she had no intention of recanting her intention of selling the horrid old place. It was two against one now—but Meggie's one vote was bigger than both of her sisters' combined. *She* was the one on the moral high ground. *She* was the one who had been doing the right thing.

She stood at the old black iron gate.

If Meggie were ever to write a letter like Bitty's, left so cowardly on the table in the morning for her sisters to find, it would have only had one sentence on it:

Dear Sisters: Why haven't you *been out there looking for her, too?*

She pushed the gate open and headed inside.

Normally, Aubrey loved the library. From the street, it cultivated the image of a worldly schoolmaster, benevolent but stern. But inside, oh *inside*, the library's warm and curious nature could not be repressed by the grumpy neoclassicism of its façade. Technically, the rooms were quiet. But they were never *still*. Even during the sleepiest afternoon hours, the library had an air of restlessness like a child who kicks its legs, and hums under its breath, and generally does everything it can not to burst out a rain of questions, observations, or songs. Even the library's bespectacled and hoary patroness, who hung on the south wall in a gold frame and who could look a bit dyspeptic on a cloudy day, gazed down in pleasant approval when the Reading Room was full of sunshine and when Tarrytown's bookworms and students came to lounge in big, comfy chairs.

Today, however, Aubrey found her work to be painful. She was reshelving oversized art books in the nonfiction section—which never failed to give her a kink in her lower back—and she could not get her mind to focus. Several times a minute, she forgot what she was doing. Her brain grasped the tail end of a thought only for a moment before it slipped through her fingers or frayed.

She stared at the spine of a book, stared, but did not read. Even as she was wondered if it was possible that she was falling in love—to be asking herself the question seemed like a freak miracle in and of itself—her sister's love life was falling apart. Aubrey saw a simple solution to everyone's problems: Bitty and her children should move permanently, or at least semi-permanently, into the Stitchery. And yet, of all the things Bitty's letter had mentioned, an extended stay at the Stitchery was not among them.

Aubrey was standing near the crotchety old dumbwaiter, scowling at the book she held, when Jeanette appeared from behind a tall shelf as if from behind a wall in a garden maze. She wore a grapefruit-pink sweater with the edge of a white T-shirt peeking from the collar. Her hair had been twisted back in rope-thick rows.

"Oh, hi!" Aubrey said a little too loudly. She lowered her voice. "What are you doing here? I thought you worked the morning shift?"

"I did. I came to see you. I wanted to get the dirt on your date last night."

Aubrey smiled. "You know that feeling of, like, when you're standing over the river at the top of the rocks on Anthony's Nose, and the wind blows a little bit, and it feels like if you jumped the wind would catch you and you might just be okay?"

"Please tell me you are never going to test that theory."

"It was a really good date."

Jeanette asked a hundred questions about him, about their date: *Where did he take you? What did you eat? Did he kiss you? Did he get to first base?* And Aubrey replied in practiced whispers, not louder than what was necessary to be heard. She'd told Jeanette briefly of the incident with Craig. When at last it seemed Jeanette's line of questioning began to fade, her voice changed. She lowered her eyes and looked up through dark lashes, the very picture of humility. Aubrey was immediately on guard.

"So . . . speaking of romance, I wanted to ask a favor," Jeanette said. "I need you to knit me a love spell."

"For who?"

"For Mason Boss."

Aubrey laughed.

"Hey—I'm not playing. I *want* Mason Boss."

"Two months ago you wanted the guy who worked at the farmer's market."

Jeanette grinned. "And I had him, too. Thanks to you."

Aubrey felt discomfort worm along her spine. For as much as Aubrey's love life was dusty and on the shelf, Jeanette's was rampant. When it came to love, Jeanette didn't merely fall; she sought out cliffs and hurled herself from them. She dove without checking the water's depth. And each time, to her credit, she dusted herself off, had a good cry, and climbed back up to do it again.

Aubrey touched her friend's shoulder. "You don't need a spell to make this guy notice you. Look at you. You're six feet tall with cheekbones like a supermodel and muscles like Wonder Woman. What would be weird is if he *doesn't* notice you."

"But what if I'm not his type? You've gotta do this for me. Come on, Aub. Please? It's not fair, you know. It's not fair that all of a sudden you're like *Vic this and Vic that* and all I'm asking is for one tiny spell so I could be, like, a tenth as happy as you are right now. Are you seriously gonna tell me no?"

Aubrey picked up a heavy book. She thought of Vic, and it was enough to make her feel happy all over again.

"Please?" Jeanette half whispered. "Look! I even have my sacrifice with me." She reached into her camouflage handbag and pulled out a teacup. "I bought this for myself in the fourth grade with money from walking the neighbor's dog."

Aubrey didn't move to take the cup.

"Aubrey, I really *like* him," Jeanette said.

Almost without her mind's consent, with years of instinct and DNA and tradition propelling her on, Aubrey felt the strange out-of-bodyness that sometimes happened when she stepped into her role as the Stitchery's guardian. She looked down her nose at the cup in Jeanette's hand. "That's not going to be enough."

A second passed. "You're right. You know that? You're absolutely right." Jeanette secured the teacup in a palm, then stripped her purse strap from her shoulder, and thrust the whole bag at Aubrey's midsection.

"What are you—?"

"Take it. Take the whole thing."

Aubrey glanced down at the bag that jangled in her hands. "But what if there's something important in here? What about your license? Your credit cards?"

"I don't know what all's in there. But it's making me damn uncomfortable to give it to you. So I figure it ought to do the trick for a spell."

"Jeanette—"

"Please, Aub." Her eyes were wide. She was pleading and growing tired of it. "Please?"

"This is crazy," Aubrey said, but they both knew she'd already given in.

"You're the cherry on the sundae—you do know that,

right?" Jeanette said. She was already moving away down the aisle, smiling and walking backward foot over foot. "Oh, and would you mind giving me a lift to the meeting?"

"Why?"

"I lost my car keys," Jeanette said. And she pointed to the bag in Aubrey's hands.

If the congregation that had elected Mason Boss had been a big crowd, then the group that coalesced for his first official meeting was enormous. Fifteen minutes before the meeting had started, the last chair had been unfolded and occupied. People continued to crowd in, shoulder-to-shoulder, and Aubrey had to shuffle to keep from falling down. The close quarters—the unfamiliar smells of strangers' shampoo and armpits, the sounds of their breathing and the pressing of un-identifiable body parts—should have made her uncomfort-able. But instead, she felt buoyed up. People she'd never met were introducing themselves to one another, even *to her*. Aubrey's heart was in her throat. She told them: Nice to meet you. And if they knew she was the girl from the Stitchery, if they were startled by her awful eyes behind her sunglasses, they didn't mention it. Beside her, Jeanette worried her fin-gers and craned her long neck to see over the crowd.

"See him?" Aubrey asked.

"Not yet."

The crowd moved. Vic had been standing with his back to the wood paneling, and Aubrey suddenly found herself jos-tled against him. She'd worn her hair up high on her head, and she felt Vic's exhalation against her bare neck as she knocked against him. "Oh! Sorry!" she said. Vic's hands stead-ied her—her upper arm, her waist. And when he didn't let go, she felt more off balance than when she'd been jostled by the crowd.

Aubrey stood that way, pretending to watch for Mason Boss but conscious only of Vic's hands, until at last—after people began to grumble and their feet started to hurt—at last, Mason Boss swept in through the fire hall doors. Jeanette made eye contact with Aubrey just for a moment, her eyebrows high with hope and her lips drawn into a kind of wide rectangle, like the middle of the word *please*. In her hands, she held the wrist warmers that Aubrey had brought her. Aubrey ignored the pang in her gut and gave Jeanette an encouraging nod.

The crowd began to quiet without being told as Mason Boss strode to the front of the room. His oversized head was tipped down as he walked, his brow furrowed in presidential concentration. He shucked his coat and tossed it onto a table.

The moment that Mason Boss clapped his hands together and asked "So what have we got?" Aubrey felt a ripple of electricity move through the air. All at once, Tarrytown was energized. Mason Boss offered some interesting arguments—and his ideas were *arguments* in that they went against every organizational technique the Tappan Watch had believed in so far. Mason Boss wanted a media blackout; he wanted the website taken down; he thought the petition idea was a joke. He didn't care about the protest march that had been scheduled; he wanted something more dramatic, more spontaneous and spectacular—he wanted a *flash mob*.

"So, we're going to break out into a dance number in the park?" Dan Hatters asked.

"Picture this," Mason Boss said. "Without warning, we descend on village hall. All of us. All at once. We stop up traffic. We block the doors. We make things inconvenient for people. We're loud and we're not taking no for an answer."

"Shouldn't we at least issue a press release first?" Dan Hatters asked.

"Good God, man," Mason Boss said with stiff elocution. "What you do think would have happened at the Boston Tea Party if the patriots had put out a press release?"

Within ten minutes, everyone had agreed that a flash mob was the perfect idea. Forty-five minutes were spent on setting up a phone tree—*so we're totally under the radar before the flash mob*, Mason Boss had said. When the meeting was over, Aubrey half expected Mason Boss to take a bow. Chairs scraped on metal as people stood up. The sound of struck-up conversations swelled. Aubrey felt a tight grip on her right arm, and she realized that Vic had let go of her. It was Jeanette who held her tight. Her eyes were deep obsidian and glossy with brightness. She spoke in a hurried hush.

"He's brilliant, isn't he? The way he gets everyone so worked up. So eager to *do* something."

"Yeah," Aubrey said. And she realized that she'd warmed to Mason Boss; he was what they needed, perhaps.

"I'm going to go talk to him." Jeanette's voice was unusually tight with nerves. "Wait for me a sec?"

"Don't worry," Aubrey said. "You have the wrist warmers I made for him. You'll be fine."

Jeanette took in a deep breath. She tossed her dark cords of hair and strode across the room. Even in the dense crowd, her walk was brimming with liquid sex, and Mason Boss was not the only man who turned his head to see.

Aubrey stepped away from Vic to face him.

"What was that about?" he asked.

"Girl stuff," she said. "Do you mind waiting a few minutes? If Jeanette can't get Mason Boss on the hook, she might need a ride home."

"No problem," he said.

A few minutes later, Jeanette was walking away from Mason Boss, coming toward her. And Aubrey thought, *Oh no.* Jeanette's lips were angled into a frown and her shoulders slightly slumped. Aubrey hadn't thought it was possible: Mason Boss must have turned Jeanette down. She swallowed her guilty conscience.

"Jeanette," Aubrey said when her friend had reached her. "I'm so sorry. I'm so so sorry."

For a moment, Jeanette's eyes were dim and still. They regarded Aubrey with banked disappointment. Then, at once, a great smile came over her face like the sun coming through clouds. "Kidding!" she said. "I'm totally kidding. The spell worked *perfectly.* Mason and I are going out for drinks as soon as everyone leaves."

"Jeez, you scared me!" Aubrey laughed and put her palm on her heart. *Thank God.* She reached into her oversized bag and retrieved her friend's purse. "Here. You can take this back now."

"Take it back? But won't that ruin the spell?"

Aubrey waited.

"Aubrey . . . ?"

Aubrey couldn't help the small smile that curved her lips.

"Oh my God," Jeanette said. "You never knit a spell?"

Aubrey grinned.

"I did that all on my own?"

"All's fair in love and war."

Jeanette took her bag, then threw her head back laughing. "Aubrey Van Ripper. Everything everybody says about you is true."

"Uh-huh," Aubrey said.

"And anyway, I told you I didn't need a spell."

Aubrey laughed as Jeanette sauntered across the room,

back toward her quarry. Aubrey raised her eyes to find Vic watching her.

"What?" she said.

"I can't seem to get a handle on you," he said.

She smiled and was glad for once in her life to feel a little mysterious. "Let's get out of here," she said.

From the Great Book in the Hall: *There is no more pleasant way to spend a quiet afternoon than to knit a love spell, especially if there's a chill in the air. Spells that encourage affection may be born from lack—from people who are lonely, heartsick, overlooked, hopeless. But sad as it is to know a love spell is motivated by the absence of love, the act of knitting a love spell is a treat.*

Love spells are perfect for beginners. They are rowing along with the current or running downhill. They are white seedpods that lift into the air, effortless, carried by wind. Love is the natural, forward direction of life. It's our purpose, our reset, our bottom line. If there are barriers to love, it is only because we think there are barriers. The same can be said about all magic that resides in a knitter's hands.

16

"Wrap Stitch"

After the Tappan Watch meeting disbanded, Aubrey was thrilled when Vic asked if she wanted to get a cup of coffee at his favorite place in Sleepy Hollow. He parallel-parked between a Toyota and a Mercedes, the shine of headlights glaring in the truck's mirrors, and then they crossed the street to the café. Vic ordered two pumpkin lattes spiced with nutmeg and clove, and Aubrey breathed in the fragrant steam as he paid. She'd never had any luck with second dates—she'd never been on a third—but tonight, her heart in her chest was like a singing bird, and she breathed in the sweet smell of spiced espresso and believed that, for once in her life, she would go on a second date and nothing—*nothing*—would go wrong.

With one mitten curled around her cup, Aubrey followed Vic out into the bustling evening and across the street. They walked up the hill to the high school, where the football team was playing against a rival Aubrey had never heard of. They sipped their hot lattes and watched the field through a chain-link fence. Aubrey had never been to a football game; she didn't know how to follow the action. But she loved the noise of the crowd, the roil of snare drums and brassy-voiced cheerleaders, the screech of the referee's whistle and the salty smell of the hot dogs. Vic did such an admirable job of explaining what was happening, and seemed so knowledgeable about the Fighting Horsemen and their coaches, that she knew this was not his first time keeping an eye on the game.

"Do you do this a lot?" she asked.

He smiled, embarrassed. "In the fall, yes."

"Did you ever play football?"

"No. And I don't watch any of the professional teams, or even college. But I like *this*—" He gestured beyond the chain links. "All the people. Families. For me, this is sports at its best. Homegrown and commercial-free. I just—I thought you might have fun."

She stepped closer and he put his arm around her; even through the weave of her denim jacket, she could feel the warmth of his body and an answering warmth in hers. She might not ever learn to understand football, but she knew she could love this: the cold fall night, the exultations of the Tarrytowners in the stands, and Vic—giving her a safe little glimpse into a kind of life that she'd always wanted for herself but had always been afraid of wanting. She nestled in closer, dazzled by how natural it felt to touch him, as if they'd been standing just like this, with their arms around each other in casual closeness, all their lives.

"Come on," he said. "Let's go sit on the bleachers."

She stiffened. "Now?"

"Why not?"

"I can see pretty good from here."

He laughed. "You cannot."

"Fine. You're right." She settled her hat closer on her head. She was being ridiculous; there was no reason to be afraid of the crowd tonight. It had been a long time since witches were burned at the stake or stoned. The worst Aubrey might suffer would be a few dirty looks—and she could stand that, could stand anything, tonight. "Let's go sit down."

They crossed the field and shuffled into an open spot on the bleachers. The metal was cold on her rear end.

"Isn't this great?" Vic said.

"It's great," Aubrey said.

The game went on. Aubrey's coffee began to cool, and she finished it quickly. Vic answered football questions with patience and not even the faintest trace of condescension, and it wasn't long before Aubrey was jumping to her feet and cheering. Little by little, her worries began to wane. She noticed that some of the students from the high school—these must have been the thespians—had gathered, and when halftime came, they did a rowdy little skit inviting the audiences to the annual staged reading of "The Legend of Sleepy Hollow." Aubrey wondered if the boy playing Brom Bones was Ruth Ten Eckye's grandson. But she had never met him and couldn't see any resemblance from this far away.

When the game was over—the Horsemen won and the crowd was electric, strangers giving high fives—Aubrey's heart felt full and bright as the moon that hung above the tree line. No one had bothered them; no one had pointed or made the sign of the cross or the evil eye. Anxiety had siphoned away, and its absence felt weightless and fresh like the air after a summer storm. In the thick of the crowd, they shuffled away from the bleachers, people around them waddling side-to-side like penguins in a large clump. Vic took her hand, the connection secret and illicit, a low-voltage message passing between them. She felt the call of the autumn, the urge to run until she panted, to lie on her back between the grass and the stars, to spin in a circle until she fell down. But since the Van Rippers were already infamous enough, she only tipped

her face so Vic could see her, and she lifted the lid, just a little, on her smile.

"What?" he asked, but he smiled back as if he knew the
secret—and that made her smile even more.

"I don't know," she said. She forced her lips closed.

She was still glowing, still holding Vic's eye and his hand,
moving forward in the depth of the crowd, her overwrought
brain suddenly filled with different, more carnal, more primal ways of worshipping a wild fall night with a gorgeous
man—when she bumped into Ruth Ten Eckye. The crowd
had stopped, complete and unexpected, and Aubrey walked
right smack into the gray fur of Ruth's expensive raccoon
coat.

"Ruth!" Aubrey said cheerfully. "I'm sorry. You okay?"

Ruth turned slightly to see who had addressed her.

"Was that your grandson I saw in the halftime show?"

Ruth drew her shoulders back; her eyebrows lifted in
silent-movie drama. Understanding hit Aubrey like a stone
between the eyes: Ruth Ten Eckye did not want to be seen
talking to a guardian of the Stitchery. Of course.

Okay, Aubrey thought. *That's okay.* And yet, the question
she'd asked hung in the air between them and there was no
way to unask it, just as there was no way for Ruth to baldly
ignore Aubrey without forfeiting her manners. On another
night, Aubrey might have felt embarrassed—she'd forgotten
herself, her place, to think she could address Ruth in public.
But tonight, Aubrey decided she didn't care. She was having
a nice night, she was going to continue having a nice night,
and no one—certainly not an elitist old lady who had no com-
passion for people outside her income bracket or apparently
for raccoons—would get in her way.

She stepped a little bit closer to Vic. She expected Ruth to
flee without deigning to recognize that Aubrey had spoken;

instead, Ruth turned a little, saw Vic, and then—to Aubrey's bewilderment—her hard face lapsed into an involuntary smile.

"Oh, look who's here!" Ruth said. "Well, hello there, Victor."

"Mrs. Ten Eckye," Vic said. His mouth turned up at the corners. The crowd thinned enough to let them stop walking. "You're looking well this evening. Did you enjoy the game?"

"I don't care for football," Ruth said. "But my grandson was in the halftime show. He's got an important part in the reading this year."

"Great," Vic said. And he smiled again.

Aubrey stood still. She noticed, quite suddenly, that Vic had let go of her hand, that he had let go of it some time ago, though she could not say when it had happened. She lifted a mitten—a purple-and-white Latvian-style mitten decorated with owls sitting in a tree—and pretended to scrutinize the design.

"How's that new screen door treating you?" Vic asked.

"Like royalty," Ruth said. "I understand you did some work for my friend Gladys."

"Her window seat," Vic said. "Thanks for the referral."

"Oh, it was my pleasure," Ruth said.

They talked for minutes that might have been hours, and Aubrey listened in silence. She began to feel more and more outside—of herself, of Vic, of everything and everyone around them. The crowd that had been like a plush spring creek dwindled into a trickle, and Aubrey realized that without the heat of all those bodies the night had grown brittle with cold. She shivered beneath the layers of her sweater and coat. She hadn't expected Ruth to address her, and she tried to keep the surprise off her face when the old woman turned.

"Aubrey, dear," Ruth said. Aubrey knew she'd taken a risk:

Ruth could be seen talking to Vic but not to Aubrey—not if she wanted to avoid becoming an object of speculation among her friends. "Vic's been doing such wonderful work on my house. I do hope he'll be able to continue."

"Of course I'll be happy to," Vic said, laughing.

He did not hear what Aubrey heard: the veiled threat. The unspoken warning. Vic had been working for months to build up his business one client at a time. A venomous word from Ruth, carefully dropped before one or two of Tarrytown's nice families, would ruin Vic's chances of establishing himself with well-paying clientele.

Aubrey didn't reply, but her silence didn't seem to matter one way or another. Vic and Ruth said their pleasant good-byes, and once Ruth was gone, Vic started in the direction of the truck. He chatted pleasantly enough but did not take her hand again.

By the time Vic had parked in front of the Stitchery, with the engine idling and the hazard lights on, Aubrey had fallen into a deep silence, mired in the pit of her thoughts and searching for a way out of them. She looked out the window at the Stitchery and it struck her that while other people were decorating their houses with crooked shutters and cobwebs, the Stitchery already had them.

"Are you okay?" Vic asked.

"Oh—yes," she said.

"What's wrong?"

She sighed. The worrywart in her wondered: Had Vic let go of her hand because he realized that being with her in public could perhaps be a threat to his business—a consequence that Aubrey should have foreseen? Or had the withdrawal been nothing more than the need to scratch an itch or make some other use of the previously occupied fingers?

She leaned her head back on the seat. She didn't want friction between them, not so soon. She'd relished every moment with him: she'd never been courted before, never wooed. She felt as if he'd been leading her down a long, narrow hallway, pointing out beautiful things, tempting, rare, and desirable things, showing her what was his, and she had a sense that if she continued along with him, deeper and down, the narrow passageway would eventually open up into a wondrous and cavernous palace, whole and wholly dazzling, all for the two of them. But there was a chance, she saw now, a very real chance, that they might never finish that journey. And in fact, it might be a better choice for both of them to turn back now.

"Sometimes I just . . ."

"What?" he asked.

"I wish things were different," she said.

"You didn't have a good time?"

"Oh yes, I did. It was perfect. I was talking about the Stitchery. I wish things were different with the Stitchery."

"I'm sorry, Aubrey," Vic said, his voice slightly stiff. "I'm not following."

She rubbed her cheek with her mitten, taking comfort in the rough scratch of the wool. Mariah had told her that the only way to say a hard thing was to say it, and think about it later on. "Ruth Ten Eckye might not give you any more referrals or jobs."

"Why wouldn't she?" Vic asked. His brow was furrowed. "She likes the work I do. And I give her a bargain."

"She won't let you into her circle if you keep showing up in public with me."

Vic was quiet. He looked out the front windshield; Aubrey could tell that something she'd said clicked—that if he hadn't already been thinking consciously of what it meant to run into Ruth with Aubrey at his side, he was now. "What do my feelings for you have anything to do with installing a door on Ruth's back balcony?"

Feelings for you, she heard. *Feelings for you.*

She wrapped her arms around her middle. "I can't really go into the specifics; it wouldn't be right. All I can tell you is that the women of Tarrytown have been handing over their secrets to us Van Rippers since the Stitchery began. We know a lot about people, more than we should know. So we're kept out of the inner workings of Tarrytown—at least on the surface. They don't really want us around."

"I doubt you're missing anything," Vic said.

"No—Vic. I want to be sure you understand. If you hang around with me, it's only a matter of time before you'll be kept out, too."

"Hmm," Vic said.

Aubrey felt tears in her eyes, but she blinked them back. "Plus, there's the Madness."

"What?"

She couldn't look at him. She stared out the window. "My family . . . something happens, sometimes. My sister Bitty says it's just run-of-the-mill dementia, the kind of thing that could happen to anybody, you know? And she says that being alone in the Stitchery for a whole lifetime just makes it worse. But Mariah and the other guardians always said it was the curse of Helen Van Ripper. There's no telling who'll get it or who won't. But some of us Van Rippers lose our minds."

Vic looked at her for a long moment. "Aubrey . . . What are you really trying to tell me?"

She wished he would touch her again, touch her in that easy, familiar new way, an arm around her shoulders, a pressing and promising heat. But he only sat with his palms flat on his jeans and did not reach for her.

"I worry that this isn't a good idea," she said. She felt oddly disconnected from the words, probably because she did not fully believe them. "You and me—I mean."

He looked out the driver's-side window and exhaled hard enough to fog it. She could say no more. She trusted him to put the other pieces together: to understand that it was not merely his *business* that he put at risk by being with her, but his place in the community, and his future children's place, and his life's happiness as a person who wanted to be a part of the core, beating heart of Tarrytown. He deserved to be happy, long into his old age.

"Are you saying *you* want to call it off?" he asked at last.

No! she cried in her mind. *I'm saying I've never felt like this with anyone before, and that I don't know if I'll ever feel this way again, and I'd pitch my knitting needles into the river tomorrow if I wasn't already promised to Tarrytown, and if I thought it would mean you could be with me without risking the life you want for yourself.*

Her throat knotted, the words she couldn't speak choking her. Did she want to call it off? Of course not. But she said: "Maybe that's what's best."

He was silent.

"This has been really . . . fun," she said. Her voice cracked on the lie. *Fun* was not what this was. Trampolines were fun. Ball pits were fun. This feeling of her heart being ripped out of her chest every time Vic looked at her—this was *not* fun.

She knew what was happening: She was falling in love. And a falling heart was no different from any falling object, so that the more time it spent plummeting, the faster it went, faster and faster, speed doubling, quadrupling, building on itself. And she knew that perhaps it was best to put a stop to this—the gravity-defying sensation that comes with falling—

because the longer she waited, the harder and faster she would tumble, and the greater the impact when at last, inevitably, she—and he—hit ground.

"I'll always want you in my life," she said, doing her best to keep from crying. When she closed her eyes, she saw his future: his kids, his wife, all of them happy, at a football game in the autumn, all their many friends and neighbors gathering around. Her throat ached. "But maybe it's better if we just be friends. We've got really different futures ahead of us, you know? We're headed different ways."

She heard him sigh. The sound was a gentle letting down.

"You can think about it. You don't have to decide right now," she said.

"How generous that I don't have a deadline," he said.

She waited. The moment drew out long. It occurred to her that optimism could be a kind of self-inflicted torture, because what she'd wanted was for him to say *There's no decision to make* or *I don't need to think about it*, and then kiss her so hard and deep that they both would forget this whole awkward conversation ever happened.

But instead he said, "Maybe we both need to think."

She nodded and blinked back tears. She tried to flash him a friendly smile; she suspected it failed. With a deep breath, she threw open the door and launched herself from the truck. Vic didn't wait to see her safely inside. The engine roared as he drove away, and then there was only the cold, the smell of charcoal and frost, and the Stitchery, rising like a dark and craggy mountain at her back while she watched Vic's brake lights burn.

Aubrey wiped the tears from her cheeks with her mittens. She looked up at the Stitchery. She gave it her best wet-eyed, acid-blue glare.

"I hope you're happy," she tried to say. But the words broke up like ice on the river, and then there was nothing left to do but drag herself inside.

In the late evening, just as the sun had been going down, Meggie had climbed up to the roof of the Stitchery to lounge as she had not done in many years. She'd heaved open the window of the room that used to be her mother's, then scrambled carefully up the steep, gritty slopes. She lay back on her elbows and crossed her ankles and looked out over the wide sweep of the river, shining and black. In the distance to the south, she could make out the jutting skyline of Manhattan, glittering and bright under the sky.

She used to come up here with her sisters. They would sit and talk and watch the sun go down—and then inevitably get in trouble with Mariah when they were caught. But now it was Tori who was by Meggie's side, drinking a black cherry wine cooler. A variegated, Möbius scarf was draped around her neck. Tori did not yet realize that Meggie had made it for her as a parting gift. A Möbius, a shape that had only one single edge, one line that curved infinitely around itself, seemed like the right gesture: Meggie was leaving, but she wanted their friendship to always go on.

"I was thinking," Tori said. "Maybe when you leave, I should go with you."

Meggie turned her head; the wind blew softly behind her ear. "Why would you want to do that?"

Tori shrugged. "Same reason as you. To see the world. To get out of Tarrytown. There's only so many reenactments of colonial America that a person can take."

"I hear you. You can't go into a convenience store this time of year without getting in line behind somebody in pinafore and petticoats."

"Or a semi-retired guy wearing breeches who's texting on his iPhone and smells like barn," Tori said.

"Or zombies banging on the windows of your car in the parking lot of Dunkin' Donuts at seven A.M. before you had your coffee, waving around fliers to promote a haunted house."

"Okay, you win," Tori said.

Meggie laughed.

"Seriously," Tori said. "Let me go with you. We'll have fun."

Meggie felt a warm glow rise behind her breastbone. She thought of what it would be like to have Tori with her, with her for all the sleepy no-name towns, with her for all the long car rides, with her for all the adventures in sleazy city neighborhoods. But Tori had a romantic idea of life on the open road, and Meggie knew the truth: that it was dirty and difficult and so lonely a person could go nuts. And if Tori agreed to follow Meggie from town to town, state to state, it would only be a matter of time before they had a fight—and Meggie would rather Tori was here in Tarrytown having good thoughts about her than by her side and hating her guts for dragging her from Coxsackie to Kalamazoo.

Plus, she didn't know how she could tell Tori about her mother. She didn't know how to tell anyone.

"I don't think it would work," Meggie said.

"Why not?"

"I just don't."

"Such a damn rebel." She turned away and tipped back her glass bottle. It caught the streetlight gleam. "You should have been born a cowboy. Or maybe a peddler. Or a—what are those people who join the circus called? A carney."

"I didn't like working the circus," Meggie said. "Those monkeys look cute but they're nasty sons of bitches."

Tori looked at her.

"I'm kidding," Meggie said.

Tori offered a halfhearted laugh.

"The monkeys are very nice," Meggie said contritely.

Tori rolled her eyes.

Somewhere above the jutting shins of the Palisades, a militia of Canada geese drove hard down the dark sky. Meggie couldn't see the birds, but she could hear them—the strident honking alarm. Mariah, who would buy anything from anybody when it came to things like smudge sticks and sacred stones, said that if you saw a Canada goose, it meant that you had come full circle—that you were at a new beginning in an old cycle. Meggie had never been quite as gullible as Mariah, nor quite as ready to believe without question. But Meggie did believe in signs—not the dregs of tea leaves in porcelain cups, not pennies that landed heads up, or the fortune-telling properties of dandelions. But she believed in signs as focal points, manifestations that were noticed only because an already existing desire caused them to be noticed. A person might encounter a million telling moments a day; the mind would choose the ones that would be *signs*.

Now, as the sound of the geese disappeared, her heart felt the slow sad drift that meant it was time for her to start moving on.

"Oh no you don't," Tori said.

"What?"

Tori sat up and crossed her legs beneath her. "Dammit, Meggie. Sometimes a bird is just a bird and a tree is just a tree—because whether you like it or not, God isn't reconfiguring the whole universe just so *you* get on the road again."

Meggie sighed. The geese had forced Meggie to give a name to the feeling that was in her heart—the feeling that it was time to go. And that seemed to her to be the very point and character of a sign. "I don't want to argue with you," Meggie said.

"And I don't want you to leave."

Meggie tipped her wine cooler upside down and watched the last purple droplet run down to the lip and land on the roof.

"Did something happen?" Tori asked. "Did you have a fight with the sisters?"

She thought of Bitty's letter. She would have to leave tomorrow; she could not stand another day. "No. We didn't have a fight."

"Then what?"

"It's just time for me to get moving again," she said. And to her misery, she felt her throat fill with tears. She was tired of traveling, exhausted down to her bones. She was weary of having to learn new neighborhoods and new streets every few weeks or months. She was tired of waking up and not remembering which direction to head in to find the bathroom in the darkness. On voyages and trips in the movies, people found themselves. But she sometimes felt she was nothing more than one giant question mark, a placeholder for the person that she might someday, with any luck, become.

But it didn't matter. What mattered was finding her mother, if there was even the slightest possibility that her mother could be found.

"I'm sorry," she told Tori. "But I'll make you a promise. This time, when I go, I'll call you more. I'll come back again. Often. To see you. I won't lose touch with you again."

Tori downed the last of her wine cooler. "Whatever you say."

* * *

Bitty stood outside her children's room in the Stitchery, at war with herself. Nessa and Carson were connected to their father by the speakers of Bitty's cell. They were wishing him good night, as they had almost every night since they'd arrived in Tarrytown. She did not feel comfortable eavesdropping, and yet she wanted to know what Craig was saying about her, if he was saying anything at all. She worried that he would try to turn the kids against her. Through the door she could make out a word here or there, nothing more. She paced the long corridor with its night-blackened window at the far end. She dragged her fingertips along the wall that was the color of sun-bleached sand.

Do you love him? Aubrey had asked her those many years ago when they'd still lived together under the same roof and the idea of a wedding was half a dream.

Oh yes, she'd said.

From the bedroom, her children laughed.

This morning, she'd written out her confession and she knew it had been read. She hadn't been able to talk with her sisters about it—because Aubrey was at work and then at her meeting, and because Meggie had been in a standoffish mood. But nevertheless, she felt unburdened. The weight she'd been carrying was suddenly put down. And for the first time in a long time, her head felt clear and she could think. She flattened her hands above her tailbone and leaned on the wall beside the children's door.

Once, a long time ago, she and Craig and their teething daughter had gone to visit his parents at their house on the hill in Tarrytown. The Fullens' house was a lot like the Stitchery: a little old and crabby, a little imposing on its lot. But unlike the Stitchery, the floorboards in the Fullens' house did not creak, not even in hallways. The walls were not mottled with leaf-brown stains. The Fullen house was what the Stitchery might have been, if the Stitchery had not been in Tappan Square.

Sitting in her in-laws' living room, she'd hated to think of the terrible and falling-down old house she'd grown up in, how her family had so willingly accepted their own poverty and their suffering in the name of a thing that did not exist. And yet, every time they'd gone to visit Craig's parents—which was not often—Bitty sat straight-spined on the Fullens' tasteful armchair in their pristine old manse, and she longed for Mariah and Aubrey and Meggie.

Do you want to stop by and see them? Craig used to ask, back when he'd done such things. And Bitty had told him no. She couldn't bear it.

All these years, she'd believed she was alone. Her sisters had seemed to be as irrecoverable as time. But last night, they had helped her even when she hadn't wanted to be helped. They had held her like splints latched to a weakened bone. With a suddenness that inflated her whole heart, she knew: *She could do anything.* Or at least, she could do what needed to be done—because she was not, and had never been, alone.

She heard her husband's voice carrying over the speakers of her cell phone, squeezing like smoke through the seams around the bedroom door. And she pushed herself off of the wall and walked to the kitchen, where she opened herself a bottle of wine.

There was something about the darkness, Aubrey thought, that changed sounds, made them sharper, harder, more crystalline. The old radiators of the Stitchery hissed and gurgled; the glass in the window shook with the passing of trucks or breeze. She grasped her pillow, tucked it up under her rib cage, and curled around it. She'd told herself that losing Vic wouldn't hurt that bad. She'd told herself she was prepared. But she was standing in a storm with nothing to protect her but an umbrella. Vic—as it turned out—was not her unconditional defender. He would not stand at her side through thick and thin.

It was entirely unfair. For years she'd kept her hopes under lock and key, locked them away in the back of a closet and never let them see the light of day. Then, with a curious sleight of hand, Vic popped the lid—and now Aubrey could see no way of forcing them back into docile imprisonment ever again.

The night wore at her, wore on. Every time she told herself not to think of Vic, she thought of him. Every time she promised herself that she would not waste another second pining over what could not be, she pined over it anyway. There were moments in the darkness when she wished she might have taken it all back—taken the whole night and done it again. In her revised second date, she would put her foot down and say, *No, I won't go sit on the bleachers.* She would lure him with the promise of a different kind of entertainment, slowly sipping her latte, looking at him over the lid, licking her lips and inviting him to watch it happen. She would take him back to— *Where? The Stitchery? Would they go to his house?*—and push his jacket from his shoulders and pull his arms from his shirt, and she would take him into her, and surround him, and *have* him, bind him, as if sex could be a spell that might entrap him into loving her blindly and forever.

But reality was not fantasy: She did not want Vic to love her if he did not love *all* of her, if he could not love her for what she really was. Before tonight, Vic had seemed to be the only man in Tarrytown who might be able to handle being with a guardian of the Stitchery. He was open-minded, and yet he knew where he stood. He loved books the way that Aubrey loved them, and he was content to listen to her babble on and on about whatever she was reading and what she planned to read. He was not—Aubrey had realized with relief—afraid of the Van Ripper magic, not afraid of knitting, not afraid of being with a woman who was powerful, and as if all of that were not enough to make Aubrey fall ass-over-teakettle for him, he was the only person in Tarrytown with enough self-control to keep himself from frowning when he looked into her fright-blue eyes. Vic had seemed, in almost every way, to be Aubrey's match, her destiny, even. But it would have been wrong of her to have let him go on thinking that a life with her in Tarrytown would be easy and without great risk. She would not have been able to live with herself if—sometime down the line—it dawned on Vic that a good portion of Tarrytown had turned against him because of his choices, that he had given up his particular idea of happiness in order to be with her, and that a sacrifice, once made, could not be undone.

When he'd driven away from the Stitchery, he might as well have tied a chain to the bumper of his truck and dragged her heart behind.

She willed herself to sleep, worked at her despair with crowbar and rolling pin, attempting to forge it into a better shape. At first, she did not recognize the noise that was coming through the window as her name. She heard only the vowels, the tail end of an *eee*. But gradually, the sound became a searchlight reaching into her dark thoughts, a beam in the haze, and she followed it out, followed it, until she understood that the sound was someone calling to her from outside. She drew back the curtains and opened the blinds. She knew he was there even before her eyes adjusted to the uneven light outside, even before she saw the faint outline of him in the front yard, half washed in streetlight gold.

"Vic?"

He gestured toward her, wild movements she couldn't decipher. She held up her index finger to him: *One sec.*

She dropped the venetian blinds and rushed around. She wrapped a wool shawl around her shoulders over her long nightdress, grabbed socks, and shoved her feet into boots. Excitement made her chest tight, made her dizzy with anticipation. Had he come to explain to her why he did not see a future for them, to make her feel better that he was letting her down? Or—she hardly dared hope—for something else?

She went down the stairs as quickly as she could, out into the night. She met him on the lawn. The air was icy and smelled like river. All around her, there was motion she couldn't quite make sense of—and she realized it was snow, the first snow of the year, nearly invisible, flurrying down.

She gathered her wrap around her throat. "What are you doing here?"

"I needed to see you. In person." His eyes gleamed in the streetlight. He was so beautiful it broke her heart. And it occurred to her that perhaps she should have looked in the mirror before going outside. Her hair was probably a rat's nest of frizzy blond. Her eyes were probably swollen red. But if Vic noticed, he didn't seem to care. "I'm sorry I didn't call first. I thought you'd tell me not to come."

"Okay," she said.

"You're freezing."

She didn't deny it.

"And you're . . . crying?"

She wrapped her arms around herself and looked away.

"Oh, God—Aub." He lifted his hands to touch her but cut the movement short. "I'm such an ass."

She pulled herself up straighter. She realized, with some surprise, that as badly as her heart ached for him, she was not prepared to throw herself at his feet in gratitude or brush the hard realities aside. Her heart could not take another letdown.

"I want you to know," he said, "I'm not afraid of Ruth Ten Eckye. And if anyone in Tarrytown has something bad to say about you or your family, I don't care."

"You say that now." She glanced at him. "But what about in the winter, and you need to heat the house and buy groceries, and there aren't enough clients to let you do those things."

"It doesn't matter."

"It *does*. Trust me. I know what it's like not to have enough, to have to decide between buying vegetables or fuel oil. And I wouldn't wish that on anyone."

"Listen to me, Aubrey," he said. He took her hands. He was not wearing gloves, and his skin was icy. "I want to see where this goes with you. If I let you get away now, I might regret it for the rest of my life. I don't know if I'd be able to live with that."

"The rest of your life . . . What about the Madness?"

"What about it?"

She shifted in her boots. They looked ridiculous under the hem of her nightgown. "It seems to run in the family. At least, it shows up now and again. Let's say, hypothetically speaking, let's say, we—we get old together. Then what? What will you do if I go Mad?"

His gaze was strong. "And what will you do if I ever get cancer? Or heart disease? Or anything else like that?"

"I guess when you put it that way—" Aubrey saw a light come on in the house across the street; her eyes flicked toward it. She thought to suggest they might go inside. But Vic reached up to touch her cheek and asked without words for her to focus on him once again.

"I should have done things differently," he said. "I'll admit it: Ruth scares me. Okay? I wanted to get on her good side for lots of reasons. And yes—it didn't occur to me until tonight just how . . . complicated . . . it is to be associated with the Stitchery."

"You mean, to be associated with *me*," Aubrey said.

"No." His thumb traced the corner of her jawbone. "Not with you."

"No?"

His smile fluttered and was gone. "It's not complicated with you. How I feel about you—it might be the simplest thing I've ever known."

"Vic . . ."

"When you started talking that way tonight, telling me about how I could lose clients, and even friends, I should have just—stopped you. I should have kissed you and not let you get another word out. Hell, I should have made love to you on the damn seat of the truck if that's what it took to—"

"Hey! Aubrey? You okay?"

Aubrey's face flamed—the visual of getting naked in Vic's truck instantly obliterated. Bitty had opened a window on the second floor of the Stitchery; Meggie was just behind her. They were looking down into the yard.

"I'm fine!" Aubrey called with too much vigor. She could see movement now in the homes around them, the stirring of her neighbors at three AM. She turned to Vic and whispered, "We're waking up the neighborhood."

He stepped back from her and spoke loudly. "What was that? We're waking up the neighborhood?"

She tried to shush him.

"GOOD!" he said. "I WANT to wake up the neighborhood. That way, everybody in Tappan Square will know HOW I FEEL ABOUT AUBREY VAN RIPPER." He spun away from her, cupped his hands around his mouth, and shouted into the dark. "Hear that? I'M COMPLETELY INFATUATED AND CRAZY ABOUT AUBREY VAN RIPPER."

"So get a room and shut up!" a neighbor called from some hidden place.

"Woo-hoo!" Meggie shouted from above. "You tell 'em, Vic!"

Despite herself, Aubrey began to laugh. The snow fell softly, disappearing into the dark. In the streetlight, Vic's skin had a gold-brown glow. "You're crazy!" she told him.

"Oh yes," he said. He came back to her, breathing hard, and looked into her eyes without blinking. When he spoke again, his voice was intimate, private, *hers*. "Did you think you were the only one who could cause trouble in Tarrytown?"

She smiled. The night was cold but she felt superheated, deeply warm in a way she'd never felt before. Vic was so close, so very close. She searched his face, dizzy with the need to touch him. He glanced up to the window, where Bitty and Meggie were making no effort to hide their interest or eavesdropping.

"Don't mind us," Meggie said.

"Sorry, ladies. Show's over." Vic put his arm around Aubrey's shoulders and whispered to her; she felt his breath, warm against her skin. "Come on."

She let him lead her up the Stitchery's crooked stairs and into the deep shadows of the porch. When she turned to him, he smoothed his hands along her hair.

"I hope you know what you're doing," she said.

"I have no idea what I'm doing," he said. "I only know that I'm not ready to stop seeing you. You're unlike anyone I've ever met. God, that sounds like a line. But it's true. You're fascinating. Unpredictable. You're interesting to talk to. You've got a heart the size of the Tappan Zee. It's like the world you live in is a different one than the rest of us live in, and God help me I want to get in there with you." He settled his hands on her hips, and the only thing between his palms and her body was the thin white cotton of her nightgown. "I want you to know that I'm not afraid. I'm not afraid of Ruth Ten Eckye, and I'm not afraid to see where this goes. If you still want to. If I haven't blown everything."

Aubrey hardly trusted herself to speak. "I was worried."

"About what?"

"I was worried I might never get to kiss you."

If he had moved toward her, she hadn't seen the movement. But suddenly he was closer, the cool wall of the Stitchery at her back, and the heat of him, shadowing over her, his thumb grazing her lip. "Don't worry about that," he said.

She lifted her face, and when his mouth came down, the sensation was nothing like what she'd felt during the few fleeting kisses she'd experienced in the past, when desire had played delicately as chimes in some distant corner of her mind. No—this was a carillon booming down the valley on a clear day, a bolt of lightning snapping to incinerate a tree on the ground. He tipped his head and hers, asking for something hotter, deeper, and she parted her lips and felt the crush and scald and knotted-up frustration of his body as he pushed for more. She could no longer feel the cold. Her shawl fell to the ground. His hands were careless, were everywhere, seeking every point of contact, every inch of skin, and if he'd asked to shuck her nightgown from her body even in the night chill she would have helped him do it, because there was nothing in the world she wanted more at that moment than the collision of cold air with the heat of his body, moving against hers. But, finally, with a painstaking withdrawal, he pulled away.

His breathing was hard; her hands made tight fists in his jacket. She fit herself into the curve of his chest, and the noise he made was somewhere between pain and relief.

"I won't do this to you again," he said. "From here out, whatever happens between us, happens between *only* us. I promise."

Aubrey smiled against his coat and held him tighter. It did not occur to her until later, much later, that she might have promised him the same.

17

"Slip Slip Knit"

Carson had fallen under the spell of Tarrytown. He had—Meggie realized—become obsessed with Internet videos of ghost hunters, spiritual pioneers who arrived with their microphones and heat guns and Geiger counters to prove the existence to Tarrytown's living-impaired. The ghosts of Tarrytown were as merry and popular a party as one could expect of dead people: the insane monk who killed the five virgins; Major John André, the gentleman soldier whose execution stirred the sympathies of even the most dogged revolutionaries; sweet Matilda Hoffman, just seventeen when she died on the brink of her wedding, and the fiancé who never married after he lost her, Washington Irving; Hulda the Witch, the Bohemian pariah who was a deadeye for a redcoat until her mortal wound; and occasionally, the Hudson River's own Flying Dutchman, the *Half Moon*, with its mutinous crew watching the dangerous shores and biding their time.

The armies of Halloween had arrived in full strength to take up their posts all over Tarrytown and Sleepy Hollow; long-nosed witches grinned in shop windows, faceless ghosts hung on fishing line, dismembered hands crawled up from dying lawns. And that, coupled with Carson's ghostlore infatuation, meant Meggie was not surprised when her nephew announced what he wanted to be for Halloween. Meggie had borrowed Aubrey's car and spent the morning gathering the necessary things: the three-cornered hat, the dusty old black jacket, the rickety wooden cane, the gray wig, the scuffed black boots. And now Carson stood admiring himself in the mirror of Meggie's room, hunching his shoulders and pointing his feet to the sides. Meggie smiled to see that he was happy; she could not leave Tarrytown until her obligation to him was fulfilled.

"Think anybody's gonna know who I am?" he asked.

"Around here? You bet." She stood up from her bed and handed him a book. "Plus, you'll be carrying this. This is the kicker."

He posed with *The History of New York* tucked with scholarly jauntiness against his ribs. Then he turned to Meggie and tipped his hat. "Why . . . hello there. Diedrich Knickerbocker, at your service."

"How do you do," she said, laughing a little.

He turned to the mirror and took off his hat and gray hair. "The wig itches me."

"You can always take it off and just wear that hat."

He considered it, then put the wig back on. She did not tell him how adorable he looked; she struggled to keep from launching herself from the bed and pinching his cheeks. He asked her: "Why didn't Washington Irving just put his own name on the book? Why did he have to write it as Diedrich Knickerbocker?"

Meggie thought. "It was like a different persona. Like acting and trying on a new voice. I guess, anyway."

"Or maybe he was shy," Carson said.

"Maybe," Meggie said.

"Hey, guess what."

"What?"

"I decided what you're going to be when we go trick-or-treating."

Meggie said nothing.

"Don't you wanna know? It's *really* good."

"Carson." Meggie pinched the crocheted afghan on her bed. "Come sit down."

He did not move immediately. She saw his face slam shut, and she knew the look—that he was already steeling himself for disappointment. She did the same. He walked toward her, his boots clomping until he climbed onto the bed beside her. She put her arm loosely around his slight shoulders. Already, she missed him.

"I'm not staying for Halloween," she said.

"But I thought you said I could pick out your costume?"

Meggie faltered. She'd broken many hearts before, but never a child's. It was more painful than she could stand. She thought for a moment about agreeing to stay after Halloween—but that would only prolong the misery. "I'm sorry," she told him.

"But . . . why?"

"I just can't."

He didn't speak.

"I know it seems like a surprise," she said. "But I have responsibilities. Grown-up stuff."

"I understand," he said, and though his voice was a thin thread he did not cry. "When are you going?"

She pulled him a little closer. "Today."

"Today?"

"Yes."

"How come you didn't tell me before?"

"Nobody knows," she said. "And I need you to keep this a secret just between us. You can't go telling your mom or sister or Aunt Aubrey."

"Will they yell at you?"

"Yes. And I don't really want to be yelled at. So, can you promise? Can you promise me you won't tell?"

He gave a sigh, deep and long, and his small body in his old man's clothes was so replete with pathos that Meggie might have laughed if she wasn't so sad.

"Hey, don't worry," she said. "We'll see each other again soon. You have my absolute word that I'll be back again, and I'll find you, wherever you are."

He blinked up at her; she saw his eyes were swimming, though tears did not fall. "But I won't get to pick out your costume."

"Still. *You* have a great costume, and that's the important thing. You're going to have a fantastic Halloween."

He seemed to grow smaller inside his cravat.

"Now let's get you back into your regular clothes so your costume can be a surprise for everyone on Halloween," Meggie said with all the false cheer she could drum up.

"Okay," Carson said.

Nessa lay on the scuffed and scarred floor near the stairs at the top of the tower. She knew for certain she was going to get in trouble for what she was about to do; the question was, How much? She'd read deeply into the night from the giant beast of a book that she'd found in Aubrey's room, and she knew now that it was only a matter of time before she attempted to conquer the unconquerable with her own magic spell. But because she did not yet know how to do magic and because she did not have much time, she was stuck with her usual, non-magical methods for fixing things that went wrong.

She adjusted her leg so it jutted more vulnerably. She pulled a blue plastic jar from her sweatshirt pocket and smeared its contents under her eyes. She heard her mother pounding heavy and fast up the tower stairs, followed closely by Aubrey and Meggie. She drew in a breath just as her mother appeared around the sharp corner of the stairs below her.

"Are you okay?" Bitty asked. "What happened?"

"I'm sorry," she said. "I know I'm not supposed to be up here. I just—"

"Tell me what happened," Bitty said. "What's hurt?"

Nessa sniffled and rubbed at the tear that slid down her cheek. She'd learned the trick about smearing vapor rub under her eyes from a TV show, and she was surprised at how well it worked. She was perched at an awkward angle, her left shoulder against the wall joint at the top of the tower stairs, her right leg stuck out and her knee bent inward. The outside of her ankle bone was a hard white knob where she'd taken off her sock.

"I was only going to be up here for a second," she sniveled. It sounded very convincing to her own ears. "I swear, Mom. I'm really sorry."

"Is it your ankle?" Meggie asked, crouching beside her.

Nessa nodded. "I know Mom told me not to, but I had to come, and then when I started to go back down the stairs I just stepped on my foot the wrong way." As she spoke, she began to imagine the scene exactly as she'd described it, and the vision of herself tumbling, gasping in surprise and pain, made her eyes sprout fresh tears—real tears, having nothing to do with vapor rub—even though her fall hadn't actually happened. She squeaked: "Is it . . . do you think it's broken?"

"Can you move it?" Aubrey asked.

"I don't know." Nessa feigned experimentation, the slightest flex of her toes. She sucked air hard between her teeth, then gave a little cry.

"Shoot." Bitty raised herself up to stand and Aubrey did the same. "I guess we have to go to the emergency room."

"No! No emergency room. I'm fine. I'll be okay. I just need a minute." Nessa lifted her eyes to her mother with what she hoped looked like suffering bravery. This next line she was about to speak was the most important line of all. If anything was going to make or break the charade, it would be this. She let a tear fall. "Could you guys, like, give me a little air? I just—I can stand up. I just need everybody to give me a little room."

"Let me help you," Bitty said. "Here, take my hand."

Nessa shot her an angry look.

"Okay, okay," Bitty said. And she took a few steps back with her ten fingers lifted as if Nessa had pointed a gun. Aubrey backed up with her. The tower room was not especially large and was packed with stuff, and so there wasn't a lot of space between Nessa and her mother—just a few feet. Hopefully it would be enough.

Only Meggie hesitated where she was squatting beside Nessa. Meggie's eyes were sharp and suspicious. Nessa felt a little watery snot dripping from the tip of her nose, and rather than wipe it off, she let it be. She hoped it was the finishing touch.

Wordless, Meggie pushed her body up with her hands on her knees, then stepped away.

Here we go, Nessa coached herself. Tentatively, she wiggled her foot. Her mother and sisters were watching her like hawks: Bitty's arms crossed in disapproval, Aubrey's face contorted with worry, Meggie's hands on her hips and a wary glint in her eye. Slowly, Nessa got to her feet without touching her sore foot to the floor. Her mother started toward her.

"No!" Nessa shouted. "Stay back."

She pivoted on one foot until she was facing the hard darkness of the stairs. The smell was familiar, musty and old; she'd smelled it once before when she'd stuck her face against the bars of a mausoleum.

"Okay?" Aubrey asked.

"I think . . ." Nessa put her foot on the first stair that led down into the dark. Then, after only the slightest pause—which stretched to eternity—she began to run. She took the stairs two at a time, her footfalls booming. She registered the sounds behind her, shouts of disbelief, dismay. She counted on shock to give her the few seconds she needed to get ahead of them. She reached the open door at the bottom of the stairs and turned around as fast as she could to throw her weight against it.

"Go go go!" she shouted to Carson, who was waiting for her. He stared at her stupidly for a second that was nearly a second too long. "Come on!"

Jolted, he dragged a solid wooden chair up against the door. They wedged it under the old glass knob just a fraction of a second before it turned. She heard her mother, drumming the flat of her hands on the wood.

"Nessa! Nessa, you let us out of here right this instant! Nessa—you're in a lot of trouble for this!"

"No!" she shouted at the closed door. "You're in time-out."

She heard her mother pause. "Nessa—I'm not joking. You better unlock this door right this second!"

"Or else you'll do what?"

Her mother growled, a sound Nessa hadn't known she could make. "Let us out! I said, right now!"

Nessa walked herself closer to the door so that she could talk through it without yelling. "Okay. I'll let you out. No problem. But first, you guys have a lot of talking to do. And we're not opening this door until it's done."

"What are you talking about?" Bitty said.

"You're not coming out until you're not fighting anymore."

"What fighting?" Bitty said. "Nobody's fighting."

"But you're not getting along all the way," Nessa said.

"Sure we are."

Nessa rolled her eyes "Okay. So then I'm sure you know that Meggie is planning to sneak out later today? Like, leaving and not even telling you?"

There was no reply.

"That's what I thought," Nessa said.

"You are so grounded," Bitty said. She banged the door. "You're grounded until you're eighteen. No—until you're old enough to be tormented by kids of your own! Nessa? Nessa!"

Nessa took in a shaky breath. There was nothing more that needed to be said. She looked at her brother, whose big eyes were wide and mousy. *Okay?* she mouthed. He stuck up his thumb. She knew she was going to get in trouble—this had been *her* plan, after all. But it was worth it. Carson had come to her an hour ago, blubbering and snotting on his sleeves because Aunt Meggie was planning to run away. Nessa sometimes wondered if she was the only grown-up she knew.

"How long do we leave them in there?" Carson whispered.

"You're asking me?" she scoffed. "I have no idea."

Her brother's eyes were beginning to water again.

"It's fine," she told him sharply. "If anybody's going to get in trouble here, it's me." She heard her mother yelling behind the door, making pathetic threats about Nessa's cell phone and mall privileges and driver's license and college and whatever other things she could think to name. Nessa pulled herself up straight, looked at her brother, and spoke loudly. "It's getting a little noisy. Let's go downstairs."

* * *

By the time Bitty emerged from the thicket of shadow in the tower stairwell, Aubrey knew that something was wrong— something more than a child playing a prank. Bitty's eyes were full of apology; her mouth was drawn.

"Let me guess," Meggie said. "We're locked in."

"What? Why?" Aubrey scowled in worry. "Are the kids okay?"

"Oh, they're fine," Bitty said. "They're perfect little angels."

Meggie snorted.

"I don't understand this," Aubrey murmured.

"I'll explain it," Bitty said. "Our friend Meggie here decided that she would take off without telling anyone. And it ticked off my kids."

"It's not my fault you can't control your monsters," Meggie said. She was leaning against the Stitchery wall, her posture slumping, her arms crossed.

"And it's not their fault or mine that *you* don't give a thought to anyone but yourself!" Bitty said. "Those kids love you, Meggie. You can't just take off out of the blue. I mean, what was I supposed to tell them when you were gone?"

Evening was falling, and a hard chill came through the Stitchery's rattling boards. The air was freezing cold, as cold as if they were standing directly outside in the twilight without so much as a light jacket to warm them. Aubrey began to shiver. When she spoke, her breath was faintly white. "Let's back up a sec," she said. "Meggie—is that true? Were you going to leave today without telling us?"

Meggie glowered.

"Again," Bitty said. "She's leaving *again*."

"Knock it off, Bit," Meggie said. "Like you're some kind of saint or something. Like you didn't leave the Stitchery, too."

"I at least had the decency to say good-bye. To say where I was going."

"So you have better manners than me," Meggie said. "Big deal. You deserve a medal, and I should go to hell."

"Let's give Meggie a little credit," Aubrey said. "I'm sure if she was going to leave without telling us, she must have had a really good reason. Right, Meggie? I'm sure you had a reason."

"Yeah—" Bitty said. "Just like you had a good reason for leaving the first time."

"I do what I have to do," Meggie said through clenched teeth.

Bitty laughed. "By screwing over your family? Sorry if I don't think that's high on the list of honorable intentions."

"*Me* screwing over the family?"

"Stop it," Aubrey said. "Just stop!"

She looked at her sisters, who—although they stood on opposite sides of the little room—seemed to be ready for a prizefight. Bitty was taut as a bow, practically on her toes, her hands clenched. Her muscles trembled faintly with cold. Meggie was deceptively still beneath the heavy hood of her sweatshirt, her eyes narrowed, her body bent into the dangerous slouch of a person about to explode.

"Everybody just calm down!" Aubrey said. She stood in the room between them. "Bitty—I'm sure Meggie didn't realize the position she put you in with the children by leaving. And Meggie—I'm sure Bitty doesn't mean to sound so . . . insensitive. Right, Bit?"

Bitty exhaled loudly. "I don't need to accuse anybody of anything. Meggie knows what she did—and she knew damn well how much it was going to hurt my kids, how much it was going to hurt *us*, if she just took off again. This was flat-out punishment for something—her punishing us. The question, obviously, is *what* is she trying to punish us for?"

"Is that true?" Aubrey asked.

Meggie was hunched deep in her hoodie. "I think a better question is, How the hell are we going to get out of here? Apparently Bit's kids don't know the word *hypothermia* yet."

"At least you have a sweatshirt," Bitty said. Her nose was beginning to redden, and her eyes had glazed.

Aubrey glanced around. She opened a trunk and dug in it until she found a blanket. It was old and smelled like mothballs, but it was relatively un-dusty. "Here," she told Bitty.

Bitty moved closer, and Aubrey draped the blanket around both of their shoulders. Together they sat down on the floor, draped in a quilt of fire trucks, and rubber duckies, and green dinosaurs.

"Are you coming?" Aubrey said.

Meggie just scowled.

"Suit yourself," Bitty said. "You always do anyway."

"Get over it," Meggie said. And she walked herself to a corner and plopped down.

"Stop it, guys. This isn't helping. Meggie—" Aubrey's teeth chattered. "I don't believe for one second that you would do something that might intentionally hurt Nessa and Carson. There must have been a reason you had to leave so abruptly. A very good reason. Whatever it is you're not saying, I bet it will feel really good to get it out in the open, once and for all."

Meggie shook her head. Maybe she wanted to yell. Maybe she wanted to cry. Instead she sat there with her knees drawn to her chest, her lips pressed tight, and her face turning hot red under her translucent spikes.

"Aubrey's right," Bitty said. "What's going on? Why didn't you clue us in?"

"Because. I've been looking for someone," she said, each word carefully measured out and dispensed.

"Who?" Bitty asked.

Meggie was silent.

"They're not going to let us out of here until we know the whole story," Bitty said.

"Well—who do you *think* I was looking for?" Meggie said. "Hello? *Mom.*"

"Our mom?" Aubrey said.

Meggie rolled her eyes.

"I don't understand," Bitty said. "Mom's been dead for a long time."

Meggie shook her head. "I don't believe that. That's a story that Mariah made up and that everybody else started to believe because it was convenient."

"Why do you think she's not dead?" Aubrey asked. "Do you know something we don't?"

"I know a lot of things you don't. You might have known Mom better than me, but I know things, too. Things I found out about her when I was out there."

"What things?" Bitty asked.

"She's alive?" Aubrey said.

"I found hints. Proof of her. In places she'd been."

Her sisters looked at her as if she'd lost her mind.

"People don't just go missing. Not these days." Meggie crossed her legs in front of her, sitting upright despite the damp, raw cold. "I've been everywhere. A hundred cities you can think of and a thousand towns you can't."

"How did you know where to look?" Bitty asked.

"When I first started, I had leads to track down. But these days, I mostly just have to follow my heart," Meggie said. "It's a shot in the dark, but once in a while something turns up."

"Why didn't you tell us what you were doing?" Aubrey asked.

"Because I knew you would try to stop me. And I

thought—I thought you'd make fun of me. Or tell me I was wasting my time."

"I would never do that," Aubrey said. "Your heart was in the right place. And Mom would have been honored, and proud of you."

"Would have been?" Meggie scoffed. "Would have? She *will* be proud—when I find her. For all we know, she forgot who she is or where she comes from, and she needs us to bring her back."

Aubrey glanced up at Bitty—a look that made Meggie feel horribly, miserably left out. She rubbed at her nose with her knuckles; the tip was cold. "It's not that I didn't *want* to tell you. It's not that I didn't *want* to come back. A thousand times a day I thought, maybe I'll just go to the Stitchery for a visit. Maybe I'll just stop by. But I knew that if I stayed for a second, it would be really, really hard to leave again."

"But you were going to leave today," Bitty pointed out.

"Not because it was going to be easy."

"Then why?" Aubrey asked.

"There was no choice. Somebody's got to be out there looking for her. Somebody owes her that."

Aubrey stared at the spot on the floor. She adjusted the quilt around her shoulders. "I wish I knew this before. I would have tried to help."

"You couldn't," Meggie said. "You had to stay here, right? That's your thing. To hide out like a nun in the Stitchery for your whole life?"

Aubrey didn't answer.

Bitty let out a long breath. "Meggie, you were really young when Lila vanished. You might not remember everything. Maybe, in your head, you made Lila out to be some kind of better mother than she actually was."

"I know what she was," Meggie said. "For the most part."

"But do you remember how she was in the end? Do you remember the time she threw away every left shoe in the house—every one she could find? Do you remember the time she got arrested trying to carry a lawn chair out of a store without bothering to pay for it? Not something she could fit in her pocket, but a lawn chair?"

"Why would she do those things?"

"My theory is that she was a meth-head," Bitty said.

"If that's true, you guys should have told me years ago."

"It hurt too much to talk about," Bitty said. "We all loved her, you know. Not just you."

"Then why weren't you out there looking for her, too?"

"Because she's *gone*, Meggie," Bitty said. "Gone as in dead."

"How do you know? They never proved it."

"There's things you don't know," Bitty said, irritation in her voice.

"Oh yeah? What?"

"Things . . ." Bitty looked like she might throw up.

"Bullshit," Meggie said.

Aubrey spoke, words rushed as fast as the air would carry them. "Mariah said Lila jumped off the bridge."

"I know. But I don't accept that," Meggie said.

Meggie pulled her frozen fingers into the sleeves of her oversized hoodie. The bridge—the Tappan Zee—she knew it well. As a little girl, she could press her face against her bedroom window at a certain angle and see the beautiful, graceful suspension of the Tap's east end, and the miles of flat roadway supported by beams going off to the west. There had always been something so dangerous in all that beauty, like the allure of a poisonous snake. Every year, people went to the Tappan Zee to jump to their deaths. Meggie would have been an idiot if she hadn't at least considered the possibility that her mother had jumped. But try as she might, she could not imagine her vibrant, passionate, insatiable mother on the bridge, hefting one leg over the rail, then the other, and making the decision to let go.

Aubrey spoke softly. "You were really young when it happened. Five years old. There were things Mariah didn't want to tell you."

"Like what?"

"Mariah told me that on the night before Mom died, she confessed that she worried she was going crazy. That the Stitchery was making her crazy. She said she would rather be dead than watch the Madness take over. Mariah thinks . . ."

"What?" Meggie prodded.

Aubrey pulled her knees closer to her chest. "There was a Jane Doe. The police found her a few weeks after Mom disappeared. The body was caught under a dock or something in Bayonne."

"Was it Mom?" Meggie asked.

"We don't know," Aubrey said.

"Why not?"

Bitty jumped in. "Would *you* have wanted to identify the body?"

Meggie considered if she would have done as much. *The body*. Such an awful thing to say. She remembered a man from Canada who had told her a story about human feet in sneakers regularly washing up on the beaches near his house. The man had been in the RCMP, and he'd said they'd believed for a time that they were chasing a serial killer because the pattern of feet in sneakers was so very specific. But after a time a new theory emerged: Fish and sharks and tides could do a number on a human body—but they didn't know how to untie shoes. The bodies of Vancouver bridge jumpers did not wash up on shores. But their feet in their sneakers did.

Meggie steered her brain away from visions of her mother's body floating all the way downriver to Bayonne. She did not let herself wonder whether her mother had taken off her shoes before she jumped. If Meggie hadn't been so young when her mother vanished, she would have been the only person in the family with the backbone to march down to the morgue and say *Show me Jane Doe*. Now it was too late. Mariah could have saved their family a lot of heartache; instead she'd been a coward. Meggie was pissed. She threw back her hood to rough her hair; the gelled spikes were brittle, and they crackled under her fingers. "Wouldn't it have been a lot easier to have gone and identified the body? So we wouldn't have had to wait so long for Mariah to adopt us? So we would have *known?*"

Aubrey's breathing was visible. "I can't blame Mariah for not wanting to do it. She thought there would be a different way to prove she was gone."

"I suspect that by the time she realized there was no better way, they'd already disposed of the body," Bitty said.

"I would have done it." Meggie lifted her chin. "I would have done it for *you guys* and for me and for Mom."

"I have no doubt of that," Bitty said. And Meggie felt a spike of pride and gladness that she didn't quite know what to do with, so she pushed it away.

"Meggie—what did you mean when you said, you know things we don't?" Aubrey asked.

Meggie hesitated. It had been so long since she shared her secrets, she didn't know how to share them now. But she forced herself. "I have a notebook. It's full of clues, hints. Some of the places I went—I think Mom had been there. At some point, anyway."

"How do you know?" Bitty asked.

Meggie told them about the picture that she'd carried of

her mother all over the States. Lila had often disappeared when they were young, sometimes for days, sometimes weeks or months. No one knew where she went. Meggie knew she must have gone *somewhere*. She'd started by looking for clues in Lila's bedroom, and she'd found them. Crushed plane tickets in old coat pockets, receipts wadded like dirty tissues, torn maps, phone numbers with area codes, business cards, a flyer that had probably been shoved under a windshield wiper at one point in its life.

There had been traces of Lila in Albany—a bartender near the State Museum had seen Lila decades ago. He'd told Meggie a story that Lila had told him, about the time she rode a mechanical bull for eight minutes straight. Meggie had jotted the story in her notebook. She also wrote down what her mother had been wearing (a belly shirt and cutoffs, to the bartender's recollection) and what she liked to drink (Bud Light). In a Queens dive bar, Meggie discovered that Lila once had a boyfriend named Clutch, and he'd told her that Lila had talked about going to California because she wanted to stand at the corner of Haight and Ashbury to see if anything from its golden age was left. When Meggie arrived in San Francisco, she found a ragged, cabled merino band wrapped around a lamppost in the neighborhood—and she was sure, sure with a full, complete, intense knowing, that her mother had been there. After a tip led her to Washington, DC, she found her mother's initials—they had to have been hers—carved into a tree near the Vietnam Veterans Memorial. The story had been that Lila had made the trip to the capital to give an earful to a senator about an oil pipeline.

Meggie had followed the trail that Lila had left in the years before she'd disappeared, which was as messy and meandering as a tornado cutting through a countryside of trees. And even after the trail had gone cold, she kept looking, because there was a hollow, empty place in her heart where her mother had been and perhaps, if she was lucky, could be again. The sense of loss drove her and drove her and drove her, sometimes with mindless sadness, sometimes with frantic optimism—and Meggie often felt she'd been doomed to chase the horizon line.

When she stopped talking, her sisters pounced.

"She left something she knit?" Aubrey asked.

"She told off a senator?" Bitty said.

Meggie nodded. "As far as I can tell." She glanced at one sister's face, then the other. She could see Lila's eyes in Bitty's; could see Lila's chin beneath Aubrey's mouth. Her sisters looked bereft. Aubrey's electric-blue eyes flickered like a live wire touched to a puddle. Bitty did not cry, but Meggie could see from the look on her face that she was pained. For the first time Meggie understood: All her lonely years had been spent searching for Lila because Lila was missing. But maybe, just maybe, Meggie had *found* her—as much as she could be found. And maybe there was a way she could give her mother back to her sisters, too. Slowly, she unfolded her legs and made her way across the tower.

"It's really cold out here," she said.

Her sisters scooted and shuffled and lifted the corner of the blanket. Aubrey said: "Always room for one more." And when Meggie lowered herself and wrapped the edge of the quilt tight around herself, she was surrounded by the pocket of warmth that her sisters had made, and she felt raw and weepy, and so very, very glad that she had not left.

"I have my notebook," she said. "I can show you the things I found."

"That would be wonderful," Bitty said. "We'd like that."

"Are you sorry?" Aubrey asked. "That you spent so much time looking?"

"No," Meggie said with certainty. "Not at all." And she knew that it would not be a betrayal of Lila to finally cease her searching. Because even though she didn't yet know much about herself, she knew her life was here, with her sisters. Maybe the thin possibility of doing right by her mother's memory paled in comparison with the absolute certainty of doing right by her sisters, who were here, who had not left her, who loved her, and who were unquestionably alive.

Meggie hitched the blanket a little higher. "I shouldn't have left without telling you; and . . . I shouldn't have tried to do it again."

"It's okay," Aubrey said.

"Let's not do this anymore," Bitty said. "No more fighting—or not talking to each other. No more arguing about the Stitchery or magic or anything else."

"Agreed," Aubrey said.

"Aubrey, I know you want to stay here," Meggie said. She squeezed her sister's hand. "In the Stitchery I mean. And if you want to, then I'm okay with that. I won't pressure you to sell the place anymore. It's your place. It's our family's place. I don't want it to go away."

"Thanks," Aubrey said. But Meggie wondered if there was a glint of something uncertain in her sister's eye. "And you're welcome to stay here as long as you like, you know. Both of you."

"Thanks," Meggie said. "I'll think about it."

"What about you?" Aubrey asked Bitty. "We still have to talk about your . . . situation. And I think staying at the Stitchery might be a good idea."

"I'll think about it, too," Bitty said.

"Can we finish this elsewhere?" Meggie said. "Because I'm seriously going to die of hypothermia. And it's not helping at all that I have to pee."

"It's always worse in the cold." Bitty laughed. "I think if we bang on the door loud enough they'll let us out."

"Is Nessa going to get in trouble?" Meggie asked.

"Well . . . a little," Bitty said. "A lot if she doesn't actually let us out."

"It's okay," Aubrey said, standing. "I know a way."

"You do?" Bitty said.

"What—the window?" Meggie asked.

Aubrey shook her head. She got to her feet and picked her way across the room. She moved a tall painting, and Meggie saw that there was a crude, narrow door behind it.

"Are you kidding me?" Meggie said.

"Is that a secret passage?" Bitty asked. They both stood and went to Aubrey.

"Yep. It goes out to the attic."

"You knew there was a way out all this time and didn't tell us?" Bitty asked.

Aubrey smiled. "The Stitchery has its secrets yet."

18

"Join"

If Tappan Square had still been an actual square, Vic's house would have been right across the green from the Stitchery. But thanks to the intrusion of new roads and the crop of mid-century houses, it was now a few blocks away. He had called it a fixer-upper. Another person might have called it a dump. Aubrey thought it was perfect; she loved the house's hardscrabble bone structure, its husk of blotchy and sun-faded paint. Vic ushered her from room to room, upstairs and down, and she could see how excited he was to be showing off his new cabinets, his newly upgraded wiring, his refinished floors. He even took her into his sister's side of the two-family house, though she was out for the evening. Owning a home had been a dream for him, one that his immigrant parents had not accomplished. *All this hard work*, she'd thought. They could not lose Tappan Square.

Now, on a Wednesday night in the third week of October, she stood in Vic's little bathroom-in-progress. The light was green and filmy and the walls were stenciled with faded, melon-orange flowers—relics of some prior owner. She took stock of herself in the medicine cabinet mirror. Her hair was pinned up in funky little twists and swags of Nessa's creation. Her brown-lensed sunglasses perched on the bridge of her nose. Her clothing was her best attempt at sexy: a navy cotton sundress embellished with tiny white camellias. Unfortunately, the dress was meant for summer sun, not damp October evenings, and she'd had to cloak its fitted bodice and spaghetti straps under a slouchy black cardigan. She slipped the sweater from her shoulders, the friction of cotton on her skin making her shiver with something other than the cold.

Days had passed since Vic had kissed her on the porch, and since then, desire had been with her constantly. It was with her when she woke in the morning, when she stretched beneath her blankets and her body felt sore and coiled with need. It was with her when she reached for her shampoo in the shower, when she pulled on her clothes, when her mind wandered away from her tasks at the library and she found herself wrapped up in a daydream of Vic's mouth, his skin. And it was with her now; it had been all evening. Each laugh, each casual brushing of hands, each glance was like a shot of oxygen that flared hot coals. Aubrey didn't know how much more she could stand.

She pulled the chain on the bathroom light and turned it off. Then she flung open the door. Vic was waiting for her in the tiny living room, standing as if he didn't quite know what to do with himself. She lifted her chin, her sweater draped over her forearm, her breasts sitting high in the cups of her dress. His eyes went wide.

"Hi," she said.

There were two mismatched glasses of iced tea on the scuffed coffee table, but he did not offer her one. His face was grave. "Aubrey . . ."

She put her sweater down.

His hands skimmed up her arms. He tipped his head. She expected him to kiss her, she wanted him to kiss her—she thought she would combust. But he didn't move. "Do you need these to see with?"

"My glasses? Oh. Not really."

"It's not very bright in here," he said. With two hands, he slid the glasses from behind her ears. She closed her eyes rather than look at him. She worried that the proximity of his face to hers, with her eyes hot as sparks from a welder's blowtorch, would quash any possibility that he thought she was sexy. In her self-contained darkness, she thought: *He'll kiss me now.* But still, she waited. And still he did not.

When at last she lifted her eyelids, she found he was looking at her, straight-on. "I like you without the glasses. You have a nice face."

"But my eyes . . ."

He chuckled. "Fishing for compliments?"

She searched his face. "I just don't want to make you uncomfortable."

"Why would it make me uncomfortable to look at you?"

His gaze was focused and intent. In the back of her mind, a little bell had begun to ring. "You haven't heard what people say about me? About my—my eyes?"

"No," he said. He smiled, amused. "What do people say about your beautiful eyes?"

Her heart misfired. "You . . . you think they're beautiful?"

"Now you *are* fishing," he teased.

She laughed. She touched Vic's cheek and looked at his face, indulged in looking. She felt as if she were being filled up, filled right up to the brim, filled right up to overflowing. Was he meant for her—this man? Was there any other way to interpret the miracle between them except to say that they were made for each other, that this was fated to be? She drew him down to her, kissed one of his eyelids, then the other. She took her glasses from his hand and put them on the coffee table beside the iced tea. "Are you thirsty?" she asked.

"Parched," he said, and he touched her lower lip with his thumb.

If there was a thing she'd meant to tell him, she had only the barest memory of it. She lifted herself on tiptoe and brought her mouth to his. His hands gripped her dress, smoothed along her waist, into her hair. Her breath came fast and sharp, her body ached, her hands sought Vic's skin under his clothes. They danced across his floor, shuffling and frantic. She tugged his shirt from his jeans, pushed her nose against his chest to smell him. She felt a tightness around her loosen, and she realized Vic had found the zipper at the back of her dress and slid it down. Taut straps went slack. Cool air touched her spine between her shoulder blades. Vic made a sound in the back of his throat, and she pulled away from him in a panic.

"Shoot," she said, more breath than sound. "Wait."

Vic still held her waist. His own eyes were wild, searching. She knew what she must have looked like: her kiss-battered mouth, her clutched dress, her tousled hair. It was a moment before his disappointment set in. "Oh. Okay. Sorry."

She collected herself and took a step away. "I just . . . I . . . ."

"It's okay," Vic said, adjusting his shirt on his shoulders. "I'm sorry. We don't have to . . . we don't . . . ."

"No—I want to," Aubrey said. She saw a flare in his eyes. "I do . . . it's just . . ."

"What?"

"Can we sit down?"

He gestured and she sat, holding her dress against her to keep it from falling.

"What's wrong?" he said. "Too fast?"

"God, no. I've been waiting forever."

He grinned and sat beside her, not touching. She glanced around his living room: no posters or framed pictures, just blank walls, necessary and mismatched furniture, a laptop, a few books. His things—simple as they were—gave her some courage.

"There's something you might want to know." She paused; he was quiet. His face was different now, more hard and strained. She squeezed her eyes tight. "I'm a virgin."

He laughed.

She opened her eyes. Her face burned. "No. I mean, really."

"Jeez." He was still laughing, though it was more of a chuckle now. "I thought you were going to tell me you had a communicable disease."

"I'm pretty sure what I have isn't catching."

His hands reappeared in front of him. He ran his palms down his thighs. "I'm not sure what this means. Are you . . . waiting for marriage?"

"God no," she said.

"Then . . . why?"

She shrugged.

"And now you want to . . . with me?"

She nodded again and hitched her dress higher on her chest. She knew asking Vic to be her first was not a small request—not at her age. There would be too much meaning attached to the thing. "It's finally happened, hasn't it?" She stood and crossed the room; she needed air. "You've finally realized the extent of just how weird I am and now you're having second thoughts."

He got to his feet and went to her. His hands brushed down her back, which was bare where her dress had fallen open. Goose bumps rose under the pads of his fingers. Her legs were weak. "Text your sisters. Tell them you're not coming home tonight."

She began to move away from him to get her purse, but he caught her wrist. "Not right now," he managed. Her dress fell around her ankles to the floor.

Later—which might have been minutes later or might have been days—Aubrey looked out into the cottony darkness of Vic's bedroom, the simple writing desk limned in orange streetlight, the walls that smelled of fresh spackle, the dark rug in the center of the floor. Vic had wrapped his body around hers. His breath was quiet in her ear, his hand curled around her breast while he slept. She felt so light in both body and mind that if his arm hadn't been thrown over her she might have floated straight up and out of the bed.

Sometimes, Mariah had said, *life will surprise you.* The long expanse of it, of the expected and ordinary going along day in and day out, can be rocked by bursts of the unbelievable. Rainbows appear like massive girders across the sky—or like tiny pinpricks of color caught in a single drop of rain. In the evening dusk over the valley, the moon appears fearsomely monumental, but so small as to fit under a person's thumb. *And yet*—Mariah said—*all of that surprising beauty is just ordinary magic*—like life that first formed from stardust, like the miracle of a baby drawing breath, like time that is space that sways and bends. The best kind of Mysteries, Mariah said, were sometimes not Mysteries at all.

Aubrey felt Vic's breathing, and with it, a thing passing between them, a nourishment, an exchange. She was glad she had waited. There was not another man on earth she would have wanted to give this particular moment to. It was Vic's and it was hers. She knew that in the morning he would wake and make love to her again. But now, she slept, gently and dreamless and trusting, as the hours wore on.

* * *

At midnight the Old Baltus Family Restaurant, which everyone knew was just a diner with a fancy name, was nearly empty. Meggie sat in a red Naugahyde booth by the large windows, looking out to the shops of Broadway in Sleepy Hollow. She pulled a cheesy french fry off her plate and listened to the orchestral version of a show tune that she couldn't quite remember.

"Good news!" Tori slid into the booth across from her. Today she wore the mandatory white polo shirt that was her waitressing uniform, complete with an embroidered cartoon of a plump, jovial farmer near the shoulder. Her dreads were gathered up into a large, wild knot at the back of her head. "I talked to the other waitress; she says she doesn't care if I leave a little early."

"Great," Meggie said. "What's it gonna cost you?"

"A night of free babysitting for her two-year-old terror child. But that's okay."

"Thanks," Meggie said.

"I just have a few more things to do, and then we can go," Tori said.

Meggie finished her disco fries as Tori went back to work. For some reason, her heart felt heavy. She'd thought that unburdening herself to her sisters should have lifted her spirits. But instead, she felt a vague, lingering sadness. She did not know why.

Within ten minutes, she'd finished her fries and Tori had appeared by her side, her apron gone and her coat buttoned to her chin. "Ready?"

Meggie reached for her wallet in her pocket.

"Don't worry about that," Tori said.

They went into the parking lot, and Tori unlocked the door for Meggie to climb inside. The car was old and rusted, but it had been Tori's trusted chariot since high school and seemed to be in no hurry to pass over into its next automotive life. The windshield was dirty and the dashboard was covered with stickers of Tori's favorite bands.

"Where do you want to go?" Tori asked.

"I don't know," Meggie said. "I really just wanted to talk."

Tori turned up the heat, but the fans blew cold air. "I thought you might. I mean—what are you still doing here? Not that I'm not happy you came and rescued me from the rest of my shift. But you said you'd be gone by now."

Meggie leaned back against the wide bench seat. "I guess there's something I have to tell you."

"About . . . ?"

"About where I've really been."

Tori turned toward her. "I knew you were hiding something. I totally knew. You're a spy, right? Are you a spy?"

"No," Meggie said, and she laughed despite herself. "Not a spy." She looked down at her mittens. And, amazingly, when she started to talk, saying the words that had been so hard to say to her sisters, she found it was not difficult to tell the truth at all. Once the story started coming, it came easily, pouring out. Tori listened without speaking. And when Meggie was done, Tori took her hand.

"I'm sorry you had to do that, carry that burden all by yourself for all those years," she said.

"It's okay. I don't feel bad for myself or anything. It was a choice." She adjusted the heat vent; the car was slowly beginning to warm up. "What I don't get . . . what I can't understand . . ." Somehow, she couldn't finish. Her throat tightened around the words.

"What?" Tori said gently.

"What I don't get—is—is why I don't feel *better*?" She rubbed her face before her tears could fall. "I mean, I'm *not* carrying things by myself anymore. So why do I have this weight on my heart even more now than before?"

"Do you have a lot of memories of your mother?" Tori asked.

"Some," Meggie said. But in fact, she recalled very little. She remembered Lila's red lipstick that was always such a shock against her skin. She remembered her mother smoking cigarettes on the porch in her pajamas while Meggie played with a puzzle. But the memories were just fragments.

"You must miss her," Tori said.

Meggie's throat closed further. "I do. I do miss her. But how do you miss somebody you barely even knew?"

"It doesn't matter how," Tori said. "You just do." She slid across the bench seat of her old car and pulled Meggie to her.

Meggie didn't resist. She dropped her face into the puffy down of Tori's coat and cried. "Sorry," she said.

"Don't be," Tori said.

"It's just . . . I was looking for her for so long, and now that I'm not looking anymore, I just—I just—"

"You'll have to let her go."

Meggie wasn't normally a crier. She almost never cried. But now, she wept openly, pathetically, and she couldn't not. She cried for her mother, for losing her again. She cried for the strange feeling of relief she felt at no longer having to search. She cried for her years spent in loneliness. And she cried with gratitude, to be back, to be here, to have come full circle again.

The bells of the nearby Korean church struck one—a long, singular tone ringing out over the valley. When Meggie pulled away, she saw she'd left a wet splotch on Tori's coat. "Sorry. I'll pay for dry cleaning."

"A few tears are the least of what this coat's been through," Tori said. "It's the least of what we've been through, I guess."

She fished in the glove box and found a handful of brown rumpled napkins. She handed them to Meggie.

"Is this for me or the coat?" Meggie asked, laughing.

"For you, goofball," Tori said.

"Thanks," Meggie said. And blew her nose.

"So, what does this mean? Are you going to stick around for a while?"

Outside, through the speckled windshield, the night was quiet. Meggie could follow the trail of streetlights down toward the hollow where Ichabod Crane and the Horseman had their legendary chase. She could see Aubrey's favorite sushi place across the street, dim inside. Meggie had spent so many years looking for her mother. So many years of searching and not finding, searching and looking and scouring and scrutinizing and pushing on. She blotted her face. Maybe it was time to see if she could uncover what there was to uncover when she wasn't looking for anything at all. "Yeah. Looks like I'm going to stay."

"Thank God," Tori said.

"Why's that?"

"I already told the captain we'd have a new blocker," Tori said.

From the Great Book in the Hall: *To take up knitting is to take up problems, and the business of solving them. There are knots to puzzle out. There is the difficulty of translation—of reading directions, of visualizing, of putting into effect.*

When problems arise, there are options. There are always options. One can tweak the pattern to accommodate the problem and forge ahead (this is a dangerous path that can lead to more problems . . . or to brilliant innovations). One can go back and start over (the grueling, but safe, perfectionist's way). One can fudge things a bit (accepting that lumps and bumps are inherent in a hand-knit). Or one can give up and put the project aside indefinitely—for an hour, a lifetime, a day. Problems are patient things; they are in no hurry and will always be right where you left them, as if you'd never gone away.

19

"Bobble"

Days passed, and Aubrey waited. Each morning she woke, sometimes in Vic's bed, sometimes to the sounds of her family banging cabinets and doors, and she had the oddest sense that she should not move, should not so much as take a breath that lifted the blankets on her bed, lest she break whatever enchantment had taken hold. She lived like a person having a deeply happy, unbelievably satisfying dream that she did not want to wake up from.

There was reason to be happy—blissfully, unexpectedly, indulgently happy. Bitty had talked to Craig, told him she was done. He was not going to make things easy for her—everyone knew that. But they knew it *together*, and they would tackle whatever was ahead together. Bitty was already looking through the newspaper for apartments in the vicinity of Tarrytown or Sleepy Hollow. Meggie, in the meantime, had hung up her red backpack on a hook in the hallway and she'd talked about letting her hair grow out again. *In my natural color*, she told them, though she hardly remembered what it might be.

In the evenings, Aubrey and her family amused themselves. They went to see the thousands of pumpkins carved and illuminated at Van Cortlandt Manor, jack-o'-lanterns arranged into scarecrows, and dinosaurs, and a graveyard, and skeletons, and endlessly dazzling bright shapes against a pitch-dark night. They sipped hot cider and stood around a campfire at the old Philipse millhouse, where a tall man with long sandy hair told ghost stories in his waistcoat and ostrich-plumed hat. Aubrey had not participated in local Halloween activities in years—and to enjoy them now, with her family, made her feel like a kid again.

And Vic, *Vic*, he was exquisite. To watch him get dressed and brush his teeth, to listen to him tell stories about his family, to see the spark in his eye when he talked about his plans to resurface floorboards and knock down walls—it was too much joy to stand. She felt as if she'd been starved of him for a lifetime, and now needed to make up for lost time by touching him whenever touching was possible. She loved to stand beside him as he cooked, looking down into the frying pan while her hand rested just above his sacrum. She loved the way he sought her out even at the library, to tug her into the dark corners of tall shelving and kiss her until her whole body was like a music note suspended in the air.

Aubrey felt, for the first time, that her life was about as perfect as a person could expect a life to be. Each day, her heart was squeezed in disbelieving gratitude. Each night, she fell asleep as if carried on a sigh. Her spells had never worked more beautifully; three people had come to the Stitchery in the last week and Aubrey had knit for them: Alyssa Carter wanted to lose ten pounds and so Aubrey had knit her a sweatband for her forehead; Leena Helsinki needed to have her windows replaced but didn't have the money, so Aubrey knit her a chunky green neck warmer with big bright buttons; Susan Bjorn, who was trying to build up her salon's clientele, got socks—delicate violet socks with scalloped picot edging at the top, lace that trickled down to the toe. Amazingly, all of the spells worked—and in record time.

And yet, despite her joy, Aubrey knew the foundation of

her happiness was unsteady, that she had built her hopes on a fault line. Halloween was marching inevitably closer; and the day after Halloween would bring the vote on Tappan Square. If they lost, her sisters might scatter like the October leaves tossed on the wind. Vic, in all likelihood, would have to move out of the Sleepy Hollow area if he wanted to buy another house; affordable neighborhoods were few and far between. The Stitchery, and its long, long memory of centuries past, would gradually be forgotten and would gradually forget that it ever was.

Aubrey had never considered herself an optimist or a pessimist, but rather a things-are-what-you-make-of-them-ist. And yet the great swell of optimism that had buoyed her up in recent weeks had made room for erratic, abysmal trenches of pessimism that left her shaken and fearful to go on.

During the last week of October, Aubrey waited expectantly for some news of the impending flash mob that would save Tappan Square, but the leaves of the phone tree remained unstirred. Tarrytown made its final preparations for the parade on Halloween morning: Pickup trucks were hitched with floats for the high school senior class. The marching band's trumpeters lubed up their instruments with valve oil and the woodwind players polished their descants to a high shine. Companies of young dancers donned their ghostly white robes and their ballet flats. The veterans polished and buffed their shoes, and the Masons ironed their white aprons, and the firemen gave their big red trucks a hardy wet-down and shine. Halloween edged closer. But still, the Tappan Watch waited. And still, no instructions for the flash mob arrived.

On Friday morning, two days before Halloween, Aubrey had been on her way to the pet store to pick up some worms for Icky when she saw that a few of the Tappan Watch members had gotten tired of waiting for the signal. Half a dozen people were walking in a slow circle in Patriot's Park with poster boards hoisted like slack sails. They looked—even Aubrey had to admit it—kind of sad.

"Well, maybe Mason Boss has a plan," Meggie assured her when Aubrey returned to the Stitchery with news of the rogue protesters. "Maybe he's going to rally the flash mob for tomorrow, on Devil's Night. I mean, wouldn't that be poetic?"

"Maybe," Aubrey said. But she was only half listening. She began to wonder how she might get in touch with Mason Boss to find out when he would activate the phone tree. She thought: *I'm the guardian of the Stitchery, aren't I?* She'd been in Tarrytown a lot longer than Mason Boss ever had. She had a right to know what he planned.

She thought of Jeanette, who as far as Aubrey knew was still seeing the leader of the Tappan Watch and who might have insight into plans that Aubrey did not. Aubrey had seen neither hide nor hair of her friend in several days.

Jeanette lived in an old brick building above a Laundromat in Sleepy Hollow, and her apartment often smelled of fabric softener and french fries. One end of her street banked hard to the left, sloping down toward the river with breathtaking yet dime-a-dozen views of the river. The other end of the street was pegged by an old iron clock with elaborate black hands that pointed to Roman numerals. Pumpkins and hay bales and stalks of dried corn sat at the clock's black base.

When Jeanette didn't answer her cell phone, Aubrey showed up unannounced. She stood before the dingy wooden door, waiting for Jeanette to greet her. It occurred to her that perhaps Mason Boss might be visiting Jeanette right at this moment, that Aubrey might be interrupting, and that— awkward as it would be—the situation might work to her advantage. But when at last Jeanette worked open the multiple locks of her apartment door and peered from behind it, she seemed to be alone.

"Where have you been?" Aubrey asked. "I haven't heard from you in days."

Jeanette's face, usually so cheery, did not lighten. Aubrey realized that the glint in her friend's eye was not happiness to have a visitor, but the slow gathering of tears.

"Jeanette . . ."

"Oh, Aub!" Jeanette dragged Aubrey with the fullness of all her muscle into the apartment. She closed the door behind them. Her face was a twist of agony. "Oh, Aub. I wanted to call you. Thank God you're here."

Aubrey escorted herself to the little dining area in Jeanette's apartment. Outside the window were more windows that belonged to the people across the street. Aubrey sat down in one of the plastic dinette chairs, her usual spot. She and Jeanette had been through many breakups over the years, with Jeanette outraged or defeated or confused or celebrating, and Aubrey listening and nodding and acting as if she could offer some kind of sage relationship advice, even though she'd had no real romantic relationships of her own.

"Tell me what happened," Aubrey said.

"The guy turned out to be a loser. A total loser."

Aubrey nodded, her heart full of sympathy. Even though Jeanette went through breakups every other month, her pain was no less real.

"Did he have a girlfriend?" Aubrey asked. "A wife?"

"Worse." Jeanette went to her sofa to get her laptop. She put it on the dinette table. The computer was old and slow, and they waited for it to load. "I found this when I Googled him. I wanted to scope him out, you know? See what I was getting into."

"After you were into it," Aubrey said.

"Naturally." She turned the computer more fully toward Aubrey. "Here."

Aubrey watched as the video began to play. A man was singing a song about lovebirds and he was tap dancing. He was holding a white-tipped cane.

"It's silly," Aubrey said. "But it's not offensive."

"It's totally offensive," Jeanette said. She muted the video. "Did you know Mason Boss isn't his real name?"

"No?"

"It's Richard Mumford. He's an out-of-work actor."

"Is there any other kind?"

"Aubrey." Jeanette closed her laptop with a *thunk*. "You're not listening to me. He's an *actor*."

"So?"

Jeanette sighed. Her eyes were tearing up again. She looked terrible. She wore a boxy gray sweatshirt that bore an image of a kitten and an unidentifiable stain. "I started to get suspicious when I realized he wasn't telling me the truth about his name. Then we were at his apartment in Tappan Square— which isn't even an apartment, by the way. It's just a room in some guy's house. There weren't any clothes in his closet or pictures on the walls or anything. I asked him what the deal was, and he told me he traveled light."

The darkening suspicion that had been growing in Aubrey's mind began to take a definite shape. "Tell me."

"I checked his cell phone when he was in the shower. Don't look at me like that. If he didn't want me to look at his phone he shouldn't have left it out. And anyway, I saw a text. It was from Jackie Halpern."

"What did it say?"

"She said she was just checking in and wanted to get the four-one-one. That's what she said. The four-one-one. Aubrey—"

"Don't," she said. "I already know. I should have *always* known."

She shook her head, furious with herself. Mason Boss—of course he was a Halpern plant. The signs had been there the whole time, signs that would have been obvious to her if she'd been thinking clearly, if she hadn't been—she hated to admit it—more focused on Vic than on Tappan Square. How easy it had been, she thought, to see what she'd wanted to see, to give herself a reason to let someone else be in charge.

"When did you find this out?" she asked.

"Very late last night."

"What did you tell Mason Boss?"

"Oh, I called his ass out. I asked him straight up if he was working for the Halperns. And he didn't deny it. He just kept saying, *it's complicated.*"

"So he knows you know."

"Yes."

"Then he probably knows that I know, too. That we all will, in a matter of time."

"I'm pretty sure he skipped town," Jeanette said.

Aubrey stood. She walked across the gray carpet to the other side of the room, then back again. Tomorrow was Devil's Night. The next day was Halloween, when all of Tarrytown would be distracted and not thinking of politics. And the day after that, bright and early on Monday morning, the Halperns would be voting on Tappan Square.

Aubrey went to the door.

"Where are you going?"

"I don't know," she said.

She left Jeanette's apartment, and because she did not know what else to do, she went to the lighthouse in Tarrytown to sit by the water and think. She took a bit of knitting with her, and she parked herself on the bulkhead not far from Kidd's Rock, a huge gray bunion of stone at the river's edge where the old slave trader Frederick Philipse was rumored to have had illicit meetings with the Hudson's most famous pirate. The air was light on her skin, the wind blowing gently, the water dancing. Behind her, children played on monkey bars and slides.

Since the day the Van Ripper family had first planted their heels on the Tarrytown earth that would become their property, the Stitchery had seen its share of hardship. In the early 1800s, the Stitchery had been attacked by an angry mob intent on running the Van Ripper "witches" out of town. In the 1920s, someone had tried to light the old manse on fire. By the time the Great Depression reached Tarrytown, the Van Ripper fortune had run out, and the family had nearly lost the property for an inability to pay their taxes. Aubrey was not the first guardian to have been charged with saving the Stitchery. But she was the first, as far as she knew, who had to save the Stitchery and all of Tappan Square.

She looked down at the project in her hands: She'd decided in a fit of hope and bravery two days ago to knit something for Vic—boyfriend curse be damned. She'd designed a brioche cap for him in taupe and deep brown; it was thick and sturdy and would look perfect with his eyes. She wanted to knit for him because she wanted something she made to be close to his body. She wanted to knit for him because she wanted to keep him warm on cold days. She wanted to knit for him because she wanted to tell him that she loved him, even though she worried it was too soon to say the words.

But try as she might to pick up the rhythm of the stitches, she could not bring herself to work. Her needles were still. Her fingers were still. The wind picked up a strand of hair and blew it across her eyes.

She didn't know what to do. No one from Tappan Square yet knew what Aubrey knew: that they had been duped—or they had *allowed* themselves to be, which was not quite the same thing. The danger of losing Tappan Square had never been more real than it was right now. Someone had to step up and take charge.

But Aubrey could not be the one to lead a protest. She wouldn't know how to cause a scene if she tried. And now that she was thinking more clearly, she was not entirely convinced that a protest alone would make the council vote down Horseman Woods Commons—not this late in the game. All over the country, cities and towns were seizing property for the common good. Front yards were sheared so roads could be widened. City blocks were knocked down. Tarrytown's property dispute was not newsworthy. It was regular, everyday life. If the Tappan Watch did manage to get a protest together at such late notice, the demonstration would hardly merit regional coverage, let alone national. The Tappan Watch was a small group of social outcasts whose squeak of disapproval had come too little too late.

A cat's-paw wind kicked up and tickled the surface of the water. Aubrey could not remember a time she had felt so hopeless. If Aubrey had stepped into Mariah's position right away, if she hadn't been so afraid of being the center of attention, and afraid of everything that being a decision maker entailed, the Halperns might not have hired Mason Boss. If Aubrey had swallowed her pride—because coarse, crude pride and a great fear of embarrassing herself had always been at the root of her public reticence—perhaps the Tappan Watch might have come up with a petition, a march, a website, a movement. They would have had *something* by now.

Instead, Aubrey had been as complacent as anyone, always happy to let someone else stand at the front lines. And now they had nothing. A figurehead leader who had sabotaged them. Just over sixty hours before a group of strangers decided their homes were worth less than a new shopping mall.

The sun was slanting through grayish clouds over the wide Tappan Zee. She admitted to herself: *This is my fault.* And yet, the thought didn't make her miserable. Instead, it gave her clarity. The kind of clarity that was so absolute, so purposeful and peaceful, that a person feels such precise and singular resolve only a handful of times in the long haze of a life.

They would lose Tappan Square. That was certain—unless Aubrey did something about it. Something dramatic. Something that would turn all of Tarrytown on its head. In recent weeks, the Stitchery had been teaching her new things about her own power. Yes, there was the knitting: Her capacity for strong, swift spells had taken her breath away on the night Craig had showed up at the Stitchery door—even if the spell's success had come with a terrible physical price. She had opened a thing in herself that was enormous; her idea of magic was limited only by the boundaries that she herself set.

She knew what she was capable of. Spells that were bigger than the ordinary wishes of a single person's life. Spells that could change a town, a world. She felt a strong white light shining within her, so bright she wondered if the families at the playground behind her could see the glowing beneath her coat and her sweater and her skin.

And yet . . .

And yet . . .

She put her hands over her eyes. Logistically, how could a person go about knitting a spell not just for a single person, but for an entire town?

And—more—what *thing* could she possibly give up that would be a sufficient sacrifice to make the magic work? What thing would hurt to lose as much as if she lost the Stitchery, as if she lost her neighbors, her life's work, her family's long history in Tarrytown? Was there anything she loved and wanted for herself as much as she wanted those things?

Her heart in her chest, which had been pumping so vigorously, sputtered.

Oh God, she thought.

She lowered her hands. And the future, which had stretched before her like a sunlit path only one day ago, was drowned in shadow.

She stood at Vic's door, trembling. She had not expected him to be home. She had not *wanted* him to be home. But she heard a loud noise, a harsh mechanical keen coming from his tiny backyard. And when she walked down the alleyway that took her into the cluttered little space behind his house, she saw he was there. His jeans were worn white in patches, his sleeves were rolled, and he wore clear safety glasses. He was severing a long two-by-four with a loud circular saw, chips flying at his feet. There was no sense in calling to him because he could not hear her, so she waited for him to finish, too aware of the set of his shoulders, his confident movements and intense focus on his work.

She wished he was not so handsome. Or so passionate. Or so kind. She wished they'd gone their separate ways weeks ago, after the incident at the football game, because then maybe her heart wouldn't feel so swollen in her chest, and then maybe she wouldn't feel like such an awful person for trying to do the right thing.

She felt tears in her eyes and called up her deepest resolve. But her brain played tricks on her, an imaginary devil whispering in her ear: *You don't have to do this. There's got to be another way. You can give up something else. You can try to fix it without a spell. You can wait and see what happens if you don't interfere, because it might turn out fine. You can just say* Forget it *and let everybody else in Tappan Square worry about it without you. Why should you have to give up your own happiness for a neighborhood where half the people don't even like you and will never appreciate what you've done?*

She willed the voices in her head to shut up. There were other possibilities for saving Tappan Square—that was true. But only the magic of the Stitchery was close to a guarantee. And she knew her spell to save the neighborhood would succeed. It had to. A sacrifice as big as the one she was about to make couldn't *not* end in magic.

She watched Vic turn off his saw, lift his safety glasses onto his head. Her belly ached and she worried she might be sick. How would she ever get through this?

"Hey! Look who it is!" He brushed off his jeans and walked toward her. Her heart sank. His eyes lit up, and his mouth, his mouth that had become such a revelation to her over the last week, pulled into a smile. If anyone else was about to hurt him like she was about to hurt him, she would have called out *Run!*

"What are you doing here?" he asked. But he did not wait for her to answer. He stepped forward and kissed her right out in the open where any of his neighbors might see. She held his face when he tried to pull away. She kissed him long and hard. She wound her arms around his neck and clutched. She pressed her body as close to his as was possible, felt his vital response. Vic did not pull away until his palm came against her cheek; he must have felt tears there. He drew back and peered into her eyes. "Hey. What's this? What's going on?"

She leaned her forehead against his collarbone for a moment, then painfully pulled away. "Can we go inside?" she heard herself say.

"What is it? Aubrey, is everything okay?"

"Let's—let's just go inside where it's more private."

He nodded solemnly, then they walked the few steps that led into his kitchen. He did not offer her a drink or a chair. "What's wrong?"

She looked up at the ceiling. Where to start? Should she tell him that the Stitchery was the reason she was giving him up, because she saw an opportunity to help Tarrytown in a way that was bigger and more important than the two of them? Or would the truth—knowing that she'd chosen *him* to be her sacrifice—only make it worse?

"Here." Vic pulled out a chair at the little kitchen table. "Sit down."

She did. She folded her hands in her lap. If she told him that she was giving him up for a greater good, it might make his heart ache less to know she was not rejecting him. But she also knew she was dangerously close to wavering. If she told him the truth, he would try to reason with her, convince her of another path. And in her weakness and her love she might decide to agree with him. No—she could not tell him everything. When she spoke at last, her voice cracked. "I don't— I don't know how to say this."

"When I can't figure out how to say something, I just try to spit it out."

She looked down at her lap. "Oh, God, Vic. I never meant for this to happen. I don't want to hurt you. I just . . . I don't see another way."

Even without looking up at him, she could feel the change in his demeanor, the tension in his body that readied him for pain, for a fight. "What are you talking about?"

She began to cry; she couldn't help it. She could see his

future and hers splitting off: Hers was full of the loneliness of life as a guardian. His was full of love—a wife, children, friends. "I just can't do this anymore," she said, her head bowed. "It's wrong. It's not going to work out between us. And we're just kidding ourselves to think it will."

He did not go to her, but his voice was soft. "Aubrey . . . It's already working out between us. Everything's been fine."

"No." She grabbed a paper napkin from the holder on the table, blew her nose. "It seems fine. But the Stitchery— I swear I hate it sometimes. It always finds a way to ruin things, to rope me back in."

"I'm not sure I understand," Vic said.

"I'm not allowed to have *anything* but the Stitchery in my life. It's the same with all the guardians. The Stitchery just . . . finds a way to always take away anything that might distract us from doing our jobs."

"You're breaking up with me . . . because of the Stitchery?"

She looked up at him. His mouth was slack with shock, his eyebrows high. "I guess so."

He gave a little laugh, then turned away and ran his hands through his hair. "This is ridiculous."

"Don't say that," she said. "It was probably inevitable."

"You really believe that?"

"I'm sorry."

"No. No, I don't accept this. The Stitchery is not a *real* reason to break up with someone. Something else is going on. Tell me what."

She shook her head. She didn't trust herself to say any more. She didn't want to give Vic up: She wanted to marry him, and bring him bread and broth when he got sick, and rock his babies to sleep. Aubrey would have cursed the Stitchery with everything in her, would have burned it to the ground, if it wasn't going to be the salvation of Tappan Square.

She had to focus on what was important. Not her, not him: *Tarrytown*.

She got to her feet. Vic was there in a moment, standing in front of her and blocking her way to the back door. "Last night you were in my bed. Right upstairs. And I didn't get the sense that you were unhappy in the least."

She couldn't reply.

"Tell me," he said. He took her shoulders. "What happened between last night and today? What changed?"

Her eyes brimmed over.

"You still want me. I can see it. Aubrey—tell me what's going on."

She dropped her head on his shoulder and cried. She couldn't lie to him. She owed him that much, at least. She wished she had never known what it was like to rest her cheek against his chest and listen to the rumble of his laughter, or to watch while he sang into the end of a spatula while making dinner. She wished she'd never known the wondrous feeling that filled her up when he gripped her hips, and pressed her hard, and, finally, collapsed his weight against her. Because if she hadn't known those things, or if she'd fallen in love with him a year from now instead of right at this moment when Tappan Square needed her most, her future would have looked a lot less desolate and barren.

He cradled her chin and looked into her eyes. "Don't do this."

"Vic—"

"You're not alone here. We're a team. If there's a problem, we'll work it out together. Aubrey . . ."

"Please stop. Please *don't*," she said.

"But—I love you," he said.

She felt the words like a deep thud in her heart, the firing of a cannon or the explosion of an underwater mine. The noise and pressure of it was so forceful, she swore it boomed out over Tarrytown, over the rolling hills and down to the mirror-flat river, which must have rippled a little with the sound. He loved her. Vic loved her. She wanted to crumple to the floor.

She pulled away from him. She knew her face was red and blotchy. Tears fell.

She wanted to say more, but she did not trust herself. Vic, she realized, had done something for her that no other person—not her mother, not her sisters, not Mariah, and not any other man—had been able to do. Because of him, she'd started to think of herself as more than just a guardian of the Stitchery. She was a woman, complete with a women's talents and interests, a women's needs, a woman's quirks—Stitchery aside. She was just beginning to see glimmers of the person she might have been if she hadn't been chained to the Stitchery from birth. She wished there was some way she could thank Vic for that—that gift—even while he stood looking at her, his eyes wet because she'd just broken his heart.

She leaned her body against his and put her arms around him. She felt the heartbreaking rightness of being in his arms. She pressed her nose against him and breathed in smells of sawdust and skin.

The temptation to scrap the idea of using magic returned, stronger now than before. Maybe . . . maybe there was a different way. Maybe she could give up something else, anything else. Maybe she could find a way to save Tappan Square without using magic at all. "Oh, Vic. I . . ."

Over his shoulder and through the haze of his screen door, she could see his equipment, his red toolbox of screwdrivers and hammers and wrenches, lumber leaning on a chain-link fence. He loved this house so much. He'd worked so hard on it already. He'd staked his future on Tappan Square. She squeezed her eyes closed as tight as she could, not wanting to see any more. If she gave up her future with him, she would—in many ways—save his. He would be able to go on with his life, with the life he'd dreamed of building before he'd met her, here in Tappan Square.

She pulled away from him and looked into his eyes, knowing it was the last time. "I'm so sorry. I hope—I just hope that someday . . . I hope you'll be happy."

His face was like stone; all the softness, the kindness he'd given her, was gone. She rose on tiptoe and kissed him. His lips felt lifeless under hers and she wished she hadn't done it. She felt the sting of new tears forming, and she turned away so he could not see them. *It sucks sometimes*, Mariah had told her, *to be a guardian.*

Vic did not stop her when she headed again for the door.

Back at the Stitchery, Aubrey gathered her sisters in the kitchen. She had to put Vic behind her for the moment: There was no choice. She had to not think of him. She mentally boxed up her feelings for him—all her love and regret—and she caught her sisters up to speed as if her heart hadn't been crushed to pieces. She told them the parts she could bear telling—about Jeanette and Mason Boss and the Halperns. She did not tell them about her sacrifice. She knew with perfect certainty what she needed to do, what she had already done, and she did not want anyone else to complicate her doing it or make her second-guess.

"So what are we supposed to do now?" Meggie asked.

They were in the kitchen, none of them sitting, and Aubrey thought of how many strategies had been thought up and how many family battles had been planned right here next to the cutting board, and the oven, and the fridge that Mariah had called an icebox until the day she died. Aubrey was never more grateful to have her sisters on her team than she was now. She would need them before this was over—and also after it was done.

"Do we have any proof of what the Halperns did? Can we get the vote delayed because of fraud or something?" Meggie asked.

"I doubt the Halperns left proof. And if there is any, I don't know how we can get it by Monday morning. Plus, we *elected* Mason Boss. Willingly. Happily. We have to take responsibility for that," Aubrey said.

"So that's it?" Bitty said. "We lose Tappan Square?"

Aubrey could hear what her sister was thinking: Finally they were back. After so many years. They were all where they were supposed to be . . . And soon the Stitchery would be gone.

"No. We don't lose anything," Aubrey said.

"What do we do?" Meggie asked.

"We do what the Van Rippers have always done," Aubrey said.

20

"Seam"

On Devil's Night, all of the lights were on in the Stitchery, hard golden windows floating against the soft purple gloam. Jack-o'-lanterns sneered from their perches on porch stairs. Bats launched from crumbling chimneys to wing around the purpling dusk. Aubrey stood at the phone in the hallway, Mariah's lace-edged address book open in her hands. The front door of the Stitchery was held open by an old brass doorstop in the shape of an angry hare, and Aubrey could see out through the screen door. She could distinguish the police cars from the civilians' by the way the cops drove slowly, so excruciatingly slowly, down the streets, cruising for kids with projectiles like toilet paper or eggs. Normally Aubrey liked to see law enforcement at work on the night before Halloween. But for the first time in her life, she wished they would go away.

She picked up the phone's fat white receiver. Her palms were sweaty. Her stomach was like twisted dough. *One call,* she told herself. She only needed to make one call to get the phone tree started. And then, once she made that one call, she would make another—just in case some of the branches in the phone tree broke down. Her palms were sweating as she dialed.

"Hello? Is this Mrs. Lippman?"

"Yes. And if this is a solicitor, I'm not interested."

"No-no. Mrs. Lippman. This is Aubrey Van Ripper." She waited a moment, and when there was no reply, she pressed on. "I'm Mariah Van Ripper's niece. From the Stitchery. We live in Tap—"

"I know who you are," Mrs. Lippman said.

"Yes, well." She cleared her throat. "You know how people have always said things about my family and knitting and magic spells?"

Mrs. Lippman was quiet.

"Depending on what people told you, it's probably true."

"Oh, I know it's true," Mrs. Lippman said viciously. "I know it's true for a fact. Your aunt tried to knit me a spell once to get my daughter off this toad of a fellow she was seeing."

"Oh. Well . . . what happened?"

"She married him!" Mrs. Lippman said.

"I'm sorry to hear that. But here's the thing, Mrs. Lippman. We have an emergency on our hands." She proceeded to share what she'd learned about Mason Boss. And then, she offered her plan. Her risky, preposterous, shot-in-the-dark plan. "Call everyone you can think of. Everyone who can knit or crochet or who cares to learn. Tell them to come here, to the Stitchery, right away."

She heard Mrs. Lippman sigh. "I don't know about all that."

"Please," Aubrey said. "There's no other way. It's worth a try."

The woman grumbled something Aubrey couldn't quite make out.

"And one more thing," she said. "If you could, it might be helpful to bring something with you. Something meaningful. Something that you're willing to part with—to help Tappan Square."

"Ah ha! I knew there was a catch. I knew you were just trying to get your hands on my money."

"No. Mrs. Lippman, no—it's not for me. It's for Tappan Square."

"Nonsense. You Van Rippers are nothing but schemers."

Aubrey heard the soft click in her ear of Mrs. Lippman hanging up the phone. She stared at the receiver a moment. She'd never been hung up on before.

"That didn't sound good," Meggie said from the kitchen.

"I think I need a different script," Aubrey said. She searched her heart. She'd never been comfortable with Tarrytown's dislike of her—or at least, its misunderstanding of her—which was why she'd spent so much of her adult life secreted among library shelves or balls of yarn. A month ago, Mrs. Lippman's disrespect might have made her want to slink away to her bedroom to unload her sorrows into a bowl of ice cream and a good book. But today, the woman's disdain felt almost entirely inconsequential. On her skin, she still had the imprint of paths Vic's hands had shaped. In her ears, she still had his words—*I love you*—like the long ringing of a bell in her mind. She would not give him up for nothing. She checked the next number on the list and dialed.

She was surprised when Bitty appeared at her side. "I can help with that."

Aubrey just looked at her a moment, the phone ringing in her ear.

"I'm good at talking people into things," she said. "I don't know that I'll be much good for anything else. Especially not the knitting. But I can make phone calls. And I can get people here, if that's what you need."

A woman on the other end of the phone picked up. "Hello?"

Aubrey didn't answer. She was holding the phone slightly away from her ear. Bitty was holding out her hand.

"If you're sure," Aubrey said.

Bitty took the phone. When she spoke, she had such confidence and authority it was as if the person on the other end of the line had called *her* instead of the other way around. "Hello, who am I speaking with please? Oh—Mrs. Lambert. Hi. Yes, this is Elizabeth Van Ripper. I'm calling to ask for your help."

As she spoke, Bitty winked in Aubrey's direction. Aubrey thought of the old days. She handed Bitty the phone book and went to prepare the yarns.

The sun set behind the Palisades on the far side of the river, and the neighborhood of Tappan Square fell dark and quiet. The police continued to circle. Bitty and her sisters had spent most of the day planning and preparing. The phone calls had been made and the Stitchery was ready for visitors. Chairs had been set out, colorful veggies arranged on platters, plastic cups stacked beside bottles of warm soda that would have to do. Bitty was arranging her hair in the mirror that hung in the parlor. Meggie, her friend Tori, and Carson were somewhere in the house, conspiring. Nessa lounged on the couch. Aubrey stood at the door, looking out into the frosty dark. The sky was clear and hard, only a few stars poking through the haze of suburban lights.

"What if no one comes?" Aubrey said.

"They'll come," Bitty said. And though she was sure to make her voice sound perfectly confident, inside she was wavering. She did not believe Tappan Square could be saved with a yarn spell. But Aubrey believed it, fully and doubtlessly. Aubrey believed it with such blind confidence that Bitty half wondered if the magnitude of Aubrey's actions alone would be enough to make the council vote down the plan—magic or no.

For the first time in her life, Bitty was rooting for the Stitchery. She had just called half the women in town and told them the story that Mariah had always told her nieces, the story about the magic. She'd said: *Yeah, you could say we're witches.* And she hadn't felt even the slightest bit of shame. If the women of Tappan Square or the good ladies of Tarrytown didn't like her family or her family's magical lore, they could go scratch.

At the door, Aubrey sighed. She was wearing white jeans and a white sweater. A yoke of pale blue snowflakes ringed her shoulders. Bitty knew why her sister was worried: There was a very real possibility that no one in Tappan Square would heed their call to arms, that the town would turn its back—or worse, would turn against them.

"Even if they don't come, it'll be okay." Aubrey's voice was soft and flat. "I'll knit the spell myself."

"No you won't," Nessa said. "I'll help." She moved to stand beside Aubrey at the door. "Is that okay, Mom? When they start knitting, can I help, too?"

Bitty's stomach gave a twinge. Her daughter was asking her for permission to knit a spell. This—*this* moment—was the reason Bitty had kept her daughter, her family, away from the Stitchery for all of these years. This was what she'd been afraid of: her daughter making the painful, doomed choice to try to control her circumstances through wishes, daydreams, and hocus-pocus. She wanted to cry out: *No!* Didn't her daughter see how heartbreaking it was to put faith in a thing that would—sometimes and inevitably—fail you?

But then, when she crawled out of the deep well of her

own thoughts on the matter, Nessa came into focus once again: her girl's body that was beginning to change, her big eyes that looked like her father's, pleading but hopeful. Impulsively, Bitty held out her arms, and Nessa walked into them, all awkward, skinny angles. Soon, Nessa would be taller than she was, and what a strange and dizzying day that would be. She held tighter. Her daughter, and her son, were going to grow up; she could not stop it from happening. She could not make all of their choices for them, and she could not protect them forever. But she supposed that her efforts to protect them from magic over the years might have been a bit of an overreaction. The world might fail her children in a thousand ways a day—or it might not. Nothing, she supposed, magic or otherwise, was a sure thing.

Bitty kissed her hair and let her go. "It's your choice."

"Really?"

"Don't give me the opportunity to change my mind."

Nessa laughed, and her eyes were sparkling. Bitty hadn't seen her daughter light up in quite that way in some time, and it made her glad. "Oh thanks, Mom!"

"What are you going to give up?" Bitty asked.

"I was thinking about that." Nessa reached into her pocket and pulled out her cell phone. Bitty recognized it as what it was: Nessa's tie to her school, her friends, her life back at home.

"Are you sure?" Bitty said. "You do realize that if you want a replacement, you're going to have to buy it with your allowance money."

"Don't give me the opportunity to change my mind," Nessa said. And she dropped her cell into her mother's hand. "Aunt Aub, I'm ready when you are."

Aubrey looked at her family, gave them a sad smile, then turned once more toward the door. Bitty followed her gaze, hoping to see someone—anyone—there, some friendly neighbor with a ball of yarn and her needles wagging from a handbag at her side. But there was no one, only the wooden door open on its hinges, and the night wind scented with sweet burning coal, and the darkness made uneven by the streetlights outside.

"Well, I guess let's get started," Aubrey said.

What Aubrey did not know, what she could not know, was that all over Tarrytown and Sleepy Hollow, women were on the hunt. They were looking for the knitting needles that had been stashed in attic trunks, shoved under beds, lost beneath couch cushions. They were scouring their rooms for remnant balls of yarn and for a fitting sacrifice—a little offering that they might be willing to part with.

And after the sun had set, they told their husbands and sons not to wait up, locked their doors behind them, and off they went—a marching, emerging, makeshift army, needles jutting like musket barrels, market bags loaded with ammunition that spilled over and trailed ribbons behind them in the streets. As they made their way through Tappan Square, converging on the Stitchery, cops in their cop cars did little more than nod. Because what could a bunch of women walking down the sidewalk on Devil's Night mean except that someone was having a Jane Austen moviethon, or that somebody was hosting a knitting club? How much harm could a motley group of women knitters do?

One by one neighbors clomped up the Stitchery's stairs, and Aubrey bumbled her way through greetings both uneasy and grateful. Women she knew and women she did not pushed things into her hands: bookends and cross-stitch samplers, favorite sweaters and music boxes and porcelain figurines. They made themselves at home, chattering and gossiping and asking questions about the Stitchery that would have been rude if they weren't so ridiculous.

Is this place out of a TV show or what? Is there a monster living under the stairs? Isn't it nice that you don't have to decorate for Halloween—oh I'm sorry, did you?

Blanca, who had thrown Mariah's scarf in Aubrey's face not many days ago, arrived with hot-pink needles and finger-thick roving. Aubrey overheard her telling Nessa that she would soon be taking night classes at the local community college, and Aubrey wondered in her heart whether Blanca had felt the touch of the Stitchery's magic or if, in its absence, she was making magic of her own.

Ruth Ten Eckye followed on the heels of her good friend Gladys Carlyle. "Oh, Ruth!" Aubrey didn't mean to sound so surprised—but she was. She did her best to recover. "It's— I'm glad to see you."

Ruth gave a smile that was nearly a sneer. "I'm sure you are."

"We're setting up in the parlor," Aubrey said, gesturing to what Ruth could obviously see for herself.

Ruth frowned. "You should know that I don't give a fig about saving Tappan Square. The only reason I'm participating in this . . . whatever this is . . . is because it would be very inconvenient for me if the Stitchery were to disappear. And also, I happen to be exceptionally good at crochet."

"Thank you," Aubrey said.

"I'm not doing it for you," Ruth said. She took Gladys by the arm and led her into the Stitchery's busy front room.

Aubrey looked around her in amazement. Extra chairs were brought out, then filled. Knitting projects were produced and compared. People discovered one another, surprised to find themselves together in—of all places—the Van

Rippers' front parlor. Meggie's friend Tori had been particularly supportive, excited to finally be taught the secret of knitting spells and seriously devoted to the task even before the others had arrived. Aubrey knew that not everyone had come to the Stitchery to save it; some came out of curiosity, some were toted along with a friend, some came because they did not want to be left out. But they were there, that was the important thing. And maybe Tappan Square had a chance.

Bitty nudged Aubrey's ribs. "I think they're waiting for you."

Aubrey felt her feet begin to tingle. Her throat was suddenly dry.

She took a step forward. "Excuse me," she said. Then, a little louder, "Excuse me, please."

"Hey, yo! Everybody!" Nessa yelled at the top of her lungs with surprising force. Aubrey was impressed. A dozen women looked up with wide, disbelieving eyes. "Go ahead," Nessa told Aubrey.

Aubrey's toes had gone as numb as if they'd been soaked in ice water.

"Go on," Meggie whispered.

"Okay, I'm going," Aubrey whispered back—as if everyone in the room weren't looking at her and couldn't hear. But still she could not speak. She closed her eyes and thought, *What is it people say about public speaking? Imagine the audience naked?* She did not know how she was going to get through it—the explanations, the confession, and all with the awful glare of her distracting blue eyes.

There was only one way she could do this: She thought of Mariah. She imagined Mariah was standing in the back of the room, her lavender cotton skirts hitched up in a faux polonaise, her gauzy Indian cotton shirt with its wide sleeves belled like angel wings, her gray hair waving down her shoulders, and her smile—her good, kind, complete, generous smile that had always said to Aubrey so absolutely: *I love you, you're perfect, just as you are.* And when Aubrey opened her eyes again to speak to the crowd that had gathered in the Stitchery, she swore she saw Mariah standing there, in the back of the room, nodding encouragingly as she had so many times before, and she thought, *I am okay*, before she opened her mouth and spoke to more people than she'd ever spoken to at once in her life.

"Some of you may wonder why we've called you all here this evening. You know the old saying about desperate times? Well, for tonight I'm going to ask you to put aside everything that you've heard about the Stitchery and everything you think about how the world works, and just—for now— consider everything that I'm going to say on its own terms. Tomorrow you can worry about what's what. But for just this once, suspend disbelief. Try to. And maybe we can make something unbelievable happen."

Little by little, Aubrey's nerves began to quiet. She realized that she could actually feel her feet, her two feet that were holding her up, solid as tree trunks. She talked about the spells, about how Mariah had taught her to knit them. She gave instructions for new knitters to pair with veterans, but she also told them that it did not matter what they knit or if they knit at all. Tying knots, braiding, crocheting—anything would work, Aubrey said. The important thing was the essence of the spell, the vision or energy or imagination that was soaked up by the thing being made.

Of course, she was improvising. Nothing like this—no spell this large and complex—had been attempted since her ancestral guardians had first started keeping records in the Great Book in the Hall. But magic seemed to have certain principles—the sacrifice, the balance, the vision sustained—

and she guessed that as long as she basically adhered to those principles, any spell would work regardless of the size. As she spoke, she realized what a simple thing magic was when you got down to it. She wondered in the privacy of her thoughts for a moment if perhaps they'd been doing it all wrong, if they'd made it too complicated, too exclusive, by limiting spell-casting to the Stitchery's guardians, by giving magic such a ponderous lore. She looked into the back of the room, hoping to see Mariah's face again just for the joy of it, but her aunt seemed to have served her purpose, and now she was gone.

"I can't promise this will work," Aubrey said in a voice that sounded stronger and braver and better than her own. "Magic is never a sure bet. But what is a sure bet is that if we don't try *something*, there won't be a Stitchery—or a Tappan Square— this time next year. Are we ready?"

The women of Tarrytown answered with steely and knowing nods.

"Then let's hurry," she said.

The idea—as Aubrey had explained it to Meggie earlier in the day—was to wrap Tarrytown in a yarn spell the same way Mariah wrapped a person up in a sweater or a scarf or a shawl. If they were lucky, the spell would work on the town the same way it worked on a person—with a quiet but persistent influence. And so while it fell to Bitty to convince Tarrytown's matrons to show up at the Stitchery via the phone tree, and Aubrey to lead the knitting of the yarns, it fell to Meggie to take up the last portion of the spell—which she liked to think of as benevolent vandalism. It was right up her alley.

With Carson, Bitty, and some of the other younger women who had come for the festivities, Meggie stood in the Stitchery's backyard, out of the sight of police cars. The night was crystalline with cold air blowing down from the North; the sky was clear black. With razor-sharp efficiency, Meggie split everyone up into small, nimble teams of two and three. They weren't exactly Navy SEALs, in their black gloves and black watch caps and black sweatpants pulled on over jeans. They were lumpy and out of shape, and their stealthiest silence was punctuated by uncontrollable giggling. But they would have to do.

"You two, hit the urns in front of the library. You guys, the music hall. You three, head over to Patriot's Park. And you, try for the swing set at Washington Irving Intermediate. When you've finished, return here and await further orders. We'll head out in shifts, project by project, until we've got our yarns all over town."

"But what if we get caught?" one of the women asked.

Meggie took in a deep breath. "That's the risk we all take, soldier. The important thing is, if you get caught, you don't breathe a word about this to the police. Not even if they threaten you with a night in jail. Not even if they threaten you with the bastinado."

"What's the bastinado?" Carson asked.

"Something that you wouldn't like," Meggie said. "If you get caught, you're on your own. Nobody's coming to your rescue. Understand?"

The little troop nodded.

"Good. Then everyone take my cell phone number—but be sure you put your phones on silent. *Silent.* Got it?"

After a whisper of agreement, Meggie sent everyone into the darkness. They went with all the giddy excitement that Meggie could remember from nights of playing manhunt with her sisters in the shadows of Tarrytown. Bitty and Carson remained by her side.

"What about us?" Carson asked.

Meggie looked down at him. "We stick together, Knicker-bocker."

Bitty shook her head. "I can't believe I'm doing this."

"We don't have time for second-guessing," Meggie said. "We have to move."

They climbed into Bitty's minivan. As they drove through Tarrytown, three cop cars glided past in the dark, their spot-lights peering into shadowed corners and up into trees. Tarrytown's Halloween decorations glared at them as they passed: wolfmen with bloodied claws, zombie butlers with trays of worms and severed heads, six-foot spiders with blink-ing red eyes, and of course headless horsemen, dark and pow-erful on enormous steeds. Their timing for this adventure was awful, Meggie thought to herself. Any other night of the year and they would have had no trouble stringing up the yarns all over Tarrytown. But because tomorrow was Hallow-een, and Tarrytown's finest were charged with the task of pre-venting Devil's Night mischief, they would have to be extra cautious.

"Should I drive to the park?" Bitty asked.

"No. Just find a parking spot up here and we'll walk down. We'll be much less obvious if we don't have a car in the lot."

Bitty took in a breath that would have been a sigh if she hadn't bottled it up at the last moment. She parallel-parked with ease, and then they climbed swiftly out of the car. Bitty started toward the little paved road that kinked and wound down to the river's edge.

"No, not that way," Meggie said. "We can't take the main roads. We have to go through the woods."

"But there's fences and stuff," Bitty said.

"And snakes," Carson said.

Meggie gave them both a look. She hitched her bag of yarn

higher on her shoulder. "Don't wimp out on me now, you guys. You got my back or don't you?"

Carson glanced at his mother. "We got your back."

"Then let's go."

Meggie began to lead them through the underbrush. Everyone had agreed—the lighthouse at the park was a key target for the spell. It had stood in the Hudson's waters off the shore of Tarrytown for over a hundred years. Meggie felt, in the illogical part of her mind, that if they could make the spell "take" to the lighthouse they might have a chance with all of Tarrytown.

The problem was that they weren't the only people in the village interested in the lighthouse on mischief night. Something about the lighthouse's round white walls begged for intrepid young vandals to graffiti it with giant penises. Meggie knew full well that the police would be making regular patrols through the park in an effort to keep miscreants away. But police or no police, the lighthouse had to be yarn-bombed before the night was through.

Quietly, Meggie, Bitty, and Carson made their way through the brush and over the fences that led down the long overgrown hill to the lighthouse. When they arrived from the east, it stood before them, monumental and glowing like a steeple against the black waters of the Hudson. They crouched in the bushes.

"Look," Bitty whispered.

Meggie followed her sister's gaze. A policeman was wandering around the park, his flashlight turned off, his arm swinging back and forth, back and forth, so that in the rippling dark by the river he looked like a figure in a story told around a campfire. She wasn't sure, but he might have been whistling.

"New plan," Meggie said. "Only one of us goes. It's too

risky for all of us to climb up to the lighthouse and wrap the yarn. And since I'm the leader of this outfit, I'll do it."

"No way," Bitty said. "If anyone goes, it's me."

"Why you?"

"Because like you said. You're the one in charge of these shenanigans. The yarn brigade can't afford for you to get arrested."

She reached for Meggie's bag of yarn. Meggie jerked it back.

"No—I'll go," Carson said.

Meggie shushed him to keep his voice down. His eyes were bright with excitement.

"Let me go," he said. "I'm the smallest. I'm quick. I'm not as big as you guys so the policeman won't see me."

"Try again," Bitty said.

"No, really." Carson pointed. "Look. There's a chain across the walkway that leads up to the lighthouse. If one of you guys goes, you'll have to go over it or under it. And that might make noise, right? But I can fit right under it in a flash."

"He's got a point," Meggie said.

Bitty was quiet.

"Look," Meggie said. "If it looks like he's going to get caught, I'll—I don't know—make a distraction."

Carson put an arm on Bitty's shoulder. "Mom. Are you worried you're setting a bad example?"

"I'm worried it's already set," Bitty said.

"Don't be. These are extenuating circumstances," he said.

"Nice vocabulary," Meggie said.

"This is the most insane thing I've ever done," Bitty said. "Ten years of good parenting and it's all flushed down the drain in one night." She turned to Carson and looked at him with pleading eyes. "You know what to do, right? You're just going to tiptoe up there, make a loop around the base of the lighthouse, then tie a quick knot and get out of there. It shouldn't take more than a minute."

"Ma," Carson said flatly. He took the bag from Meggie's shoulder. "I got this. All right? I got this."

He hitched the bag on his shoulder and waited. Meggie was impressed by his calm. She wondered if reading all those comic books had paid off. When the patrolman started away from them toward the north end of the park, Carson made his move. There was some noise as he pushed from the bushes and into the field, but then, when he made a dash for the lighthouse, he was soundless.

"You should be really proud," Meggie whispered.

"Proud that I'm teaching my son how to sneak around and avoid cops?"

"Your kids are awesome," Meggie said. "They're fun and smart and nice. I didn't actually think I liked kids until I starting hanging out with those two. And it all goes back to you, Bit. To the kind of mom you are. So—all right—I'm just saying, I think you should be proud."

Bitty said nothing.

"Are you . . . Is that . . ." Meggie thought she saw a slight flash of silver in Bitty's eyes.

Bitty wiped at her face. "I'm not crying."

Meggie laughed softly. "Right."

"It's just—" Bitty's voice hitched. "It's just . . . Being a good mom is important to me. And this past year, it's been hard to know what's right anymore. So it means a lot to me that you said that."

"No problem," Meggie said.

They watched Carson sprint up the gangway that led over a patch of murky water, stretching from the shore to the lighthouse. He set down the bag and began to pull out the long, thick cord of yarn that had been cobbled together in the

Stitchery an hour ago. It was part tubular knitting, part crochet, and part hand weaving that one of the older ladies had done using nothing but the fingers on her right hand. Like a firefighter tugging a hose, Carson pulled the long strand out of the market bag, his arms working fast. He started to run with the free end, but the whole blob slid along on the metal lattice behind him.

"He's got to tie the other end down," Meggie whispered. He seemed to have heard her. He ran back and fixed the free end to the steel scaffold. And as he began to run again, the patrolman at the far end of the park turned and began to amble his way back toward the lighthouse.

"He's going to make it," Meggie said. "He has time. At least, he'll make it around to the other side. Where the cop can't see him."

"Oh my God," Bitty said. "We're all going to jail."

"No, we're not. We're fine. We're—" Meggie's assurances died her in throat. Something unthinkable happened. The yarn—which had been ruthlessly shoved in the bag—tangled into a thick, ragged knot. Carson tugged it once. Twice. He looked up at the patrolman, who was getting closer to the lighthouse, swinging his hands as he walked like a bored child.

"*Distraction*," Bitty said. "Meggie—make the distraction. He's going to get caught."

"No, wait," Meggie said.

"If you won't do it, I will."

Bitty started to get to her feet, but Meggie grabbed her. "Wait," she hissed. "Wait!"

Bitty tried to shake her away. But then she saw that Carson had managed to tug the knot tighter, giving himself more cord to run with. And he was making his way around the lighthouse, gaining on the far side. He disappeared behind the thick white curve, and the wobble of the yarn as he moved was the only sign that a person was up on the walkway.

The patrolman had reached the base of the lighthouse. He was a young man—Meggie could tell from the way he carried himself, with his shoulders flexed and his arms bowed like he was carrying two five-gallon buckets—and he was looking up into the blackness where Carson had stood only a moment ago. He turned on his flashlight and ran its yellow-white oculus over the caisson and high white tower.

Bitty started to call out. "Hey—"

But Meggie pressed a hand to her mouth. Carson was a smart boy. She had every faith in him. *Come on*, she thought. *Come on.*

They watched in frozen dismay as the policeman ascended the gangway leading up to the lighthouse. He bent down and plucked at the trail of yarn. On the opposite wall, Carson poked his head around the curve of the lighthouse. He was looking into the bushes, but Meggie knew he couldn't see them. Gesturing to him was futile, but Meggie did it anyway, pointing frantically to let him know the policeman was just on the other side of the lighthouse's trunk, only a few steps away.

The patrolman, who wore heavy leather shoes, began to follow the chain of yarn around, stooped like Sherlock Holmes with his magnifying glass, running the fiber through his fingers as he traced the trail Carson had just laid out. His footfalls were loud and eerie on the steel.

Meggie realized that she and Bitty were clutching each other. The policeman circled, his shoes going *ping, ping, ping.* And as the sound moved, so did Carson. He shuffled to stay on the opposite side of the lighthouse from the officer, so they were circling each other, circling, Carson skittering back and forth, forward and backward, depending on the sound of the man's boots, always just a few feet away.

"He's brilliant," Meggie whispered, so softly she hardly spoke the words at all.

The patrolman stopped and so did Carson. The water lapped the base of the lighthouse, the rocks on the shore. The man stood slowly, listening with a hunter's attention. He'd heard something. He swept the beam of his flashlight across the bushes where Meggie and Bitty hid.

Meggie was sure they were done for—they were headed for the clink. But then a terrible wail split the darkness. The man jumped. It was a noise like a laughing hyena—the man's cell phone ring. He snorted to himself and answered it with good cheer.

"Hey, sexy," he said, loud enough that even Bitty and Meggie could hear him. "I was hoping you'd call."

Distracted, he made his way down the gangway, his boots *ping-ping*ing him over the mucky waters and back down to the grassy field. But Meggie did not breathe a sigh of relief until the man was once again at the far end of the park, until Carson had finished tying up the string of yarn around the great concrete trunk of the lighthouse, until he had hurried back toward the bushes.

"Did you see that?" he whispered. "Did you see that? I could be in the CIA!"

Bitty kissed him. "Don't get any ideas."

"You're total CIA material," Meggie said. "Great job, Cars." She held up a hand for a high five.

And Carson, in all his exuberance and pride, gave it the hardest, loudest, lightning-striking-in-the-middle-of-a-field smack he could muster.

At the far end of the park, the flashlight came back on. The patrolman's voice called out over the pine-dotted grass, his voice like a gunshot. "Who's out there?"

"Crapballs," Meggie said.

She grabbed Carson's hand, and like a herd of clumsy trampling deer, they began to run.

21

"Beg. Last Row"

On Halloween morning, Tarrytown woke to a spectacular day. The sky was crystal blue, the hills splashed with oranges and reds and the last lingering green of fertilized yards. Children lined up anxiously for the morning's parade, dressed as princesses and ninjas and gorillas and spiders and their favorite Saturday-morning cartoons. The Boy Scouts hitched their "Legend of Sleepy Hollow" tableaux to the back of the pack master's pickup truck. The high school band warmed up. The mayor's assistant ran his boss's cherry-red convertible through the carwash one last time.

But even before the parade began, perceptive people began to notice strange things. Joggers who rose early saw that a stoplight was covered with a cardigan sweater, and the red, yellow, and green were like three oversized buttons running down. Weekend commuters saw that the black receiver of Tarrytown's last remaining phone booth had been wrapped in a rainbow of garter stitch. The tree trunk in front of the mayor's office was encapsulated snugly in a tuber of stockinette. And lacy white sheets were draped like monster cobwebs on the decorative shrubbery in front of the bank.

One by one, the people of Tarrytown pointed to the odd vandalism that didn't quite seem to be typical of Halloween, to the big peace sign of yarn that had been woven into the chain-link fence at the high school, to the curls of yarn that hung like streamers from the awning of the pet store. But few people knew what to make of what they saw. Some smiled to see such a funny thing as a NO PARKING sign made to look like a pumpkin. Others, who had other things to worry about, hardly noticed at all.

Mischief night, they said. *Every year, it's always something.*

In his house high on the hill, Steve Halpern was going out to get the paper off the front lawn in his bathrobe. His wife was inside, spinning his tie rack in an effort to find the flaming Horseman tie that he wore every Halloween. He bent to reach for the paper on the dewy grass and saw that the old cement horse tie-up at the curb had been covered in some kind of crazy, mismatched yarn. It seemed to him to sparkle for a moment, a Technicolor obelisk, and his first instinct was to laugh with delight. But then he thought of the Stitchery and everything his mother had told him about it. He thought of Tappan Square.

He yanked the yarn sock—or whatever it was—off the concrete tether with some difficulty, and then he tossed it into the bottom of the neighbor's recycling bin. When he went inside, he did not mention what he'd found to his wife. He knew she would have tried to assure him. Instead he thanked her for the tie.

Little by little, theories about the yarn began to spread among people who did not know about the Stitchery. Bloggers took pictures of the hats that had been fit over the pumpkins in front of the day care. The local online news magazine reported on the mysterious displays, teasing out the fine line between vandalism and art. It seemed an excellent omen, many people along the parade route agreed. Good-natured high jinks. A friendly rib.

But Tarrytown's old burghers—who did not want to credit

the displays with even the barest acknowledgment, and who had always thought the Van Rippers would be Tarrytown's downfall—stood in the Halloween sunshine at the parade they had organized, clutched their steaming cups of spiced cider, and smiled so fiercely that passing children had to squint at the shine off their teeth—all the while wishing for the end of Tappan Square.

"I can't believe we didn't get caught," Meggie said.

Bitty looked up from her cereal—delicious sugary cereal that she hadn't eaten in uncountable years of calorie counting. Although she had every reason to be exhausted, she could not sleep. She had tucked her children into bed when the sun had started to rise an hour ago. Carson seemed to be unconscious before his head hit the pillow. Nessa had mumbled something about shadow knitting before passing out. Aubrey had vanished in the wee hours before dawn, at about the same time that the yarns had vanished—presumably recovering from her spells. In the yarn room, every last strand of yarn, every skein and hank and cake in the Stitchery, was gone.

"Maybe I should go into town and look around," Meggie said. "To see what's happening."

Bitty poured herself a second bowl of cereal. "We decided that we would let it go, remember?"

"Don't you want to know what people are saying?"

"Of course I do," Bitty said. "But at this point, it'll be what it'll be, whether we're out there listening or not."

"Fine." Meggie sighed. "You're right."

"You know, I think it's going to work," Bitty said.

"You do?"

"Absolutely."

"You don't believe in magic."

"That's true," Bitty said. "But I believe in the power of symbolism. Wholeheartedly. And I think what we did last night, all over town, was a powerful symbol of protest and a strong showing of how Tappan Square is fundamental to the fabric of Tarrytown."

"Fundamental to the fabric? Was that a deliberate pun?"

Bitty smiled. "I always thought I'd make a good lawyer."

"Seriously," Meggie said.

Bitty laughed.

"No, I mean it. Seriously."

Bitty took a swig of her coffee. She could see the river outside the Stitchery window, slogging on. For all her years of living with Craig, she felt like she'd been alone—that she'd been raising her children alone. She hadn't had a moment to give a thought to herself. But now, ensconced within the walls of the Stitchery again, and with her sisters ready to support her and her kids with everything they had to offer, she thought—maybe. Maybe she could go to law school. Maybe she could start again.

"So do you think we should wake her up?" Meggie asked, pointing with her spoon to the ceiling.

"Aubrey? No. Not yet."

"She looked like hell last night."

"Like the tenth circle of it," Bitty said.

"What did she sacrifice? Do you know?"

Bitty put down her spoon. She hadn't thought of what Aubrey might have forfeited to cast her spell last night. In the rush and panic and slapdash coordination, there hadn't been time. And now that Bitty was thinking about Aubrey's sacrifice, she worried. To Bitty's mind, even if Aubrey had given up nothing last night, she still would have sacrificed enough. "Well, whatever it was, I hope it was worth it."

"You don't think . . ."

"What?"

"Nothing. I guess we'll wait and see what happens."

"At this point, that's all we can do," Bitty said.

When Aubrey opened her eyes again, bright daylight was filtering into her bedroom. Her head ached—pain like she'd never known. The sunlight was an ice pick in her eye. Her bladder was stretched taut as a basketball. Last night, she'd cast the biggest spell of her life—perhaps the biggest she would ever cast. It had depleted her so fully and completely that *exhaustion* was not the word for what she felt. Her sleep had been so deep and opaque, it was more like death than slumber. But all in all, things could have been worse. She had not thrown up in front of the women of Tappan Square, as she had on the night of Craig's appearance—that was a blessing. And the fact that she was already awake was a good sign, too.

Slowly, she righted herself in her bed. She'd fallen asleep in her jeans and sweater. She sat with her bare toes on the cold wood floor a moment, waiting to get her bearings. She crossed the hall to use the bathroom and wash her face.

The sense of panic that had plagued her these last few days—the sense that her life was crashing down—was gone. Vic, and whatever happiness she might have found with him, was lost; she would never be with him again. She knew that her heart would not recover and that there would never, for the rest of her life, be another man she could love as she loved him. But Tappan Square, the Stitchery, the things that were bigger than she was—she was so certain that her neighborhood was saved, forever and truly, that she would have staked her life on it. She felt the truth of her optimism carried on the chill of the morning air. For the first time in her life, she felt glad of who she was. Unembarrassed and proud. She was a daughter of the Stitchery, and she was powerful, and confident, and generous in the most generous way she could be. She was not on the outskirts; she was essential. The possibility that her spell might not take, and that she had given Vic up for nothing, flitted through her mind. But it bore no more significance than a bird passing in front of the sun.

She opened the bathroom door when she was finished and made her way back toward her bedroom. Meggie and Bitty were there, in the hall, waiting. Meggie wore black denim jeans and an orange tie-dyed shirt. Bitty was in her workout gear. Aubrey supposed they must have heard her wake up.

"Good morning," she said. And then she laughed at how rough her voice sounded, as if she had been asleep for twenty years.

"Actually, it's afternoon," Meggie said.

"I slept late, huh? I haven't slept so late since—since ever." Her sisters did not so much as smile.

"Are you okay?" Meggie asked.

"I feel . . ." She stretched her back. "Stiff. Tired. Hungry. But . . . good. Really really good."

"Oh God, Aubrey—" Bitty gasped.

Aubrey felt suddenly self-conscious. Her sisters were looking at her. They were looking, and their mouths were open, and their eyebrows were high. Aubrey rubbed her cheek. "What? Did I sleep on my face? Do I have headlines?"

"No, it's . . ." Bitty peered at her. Aubrey resisted the urge to flinch away. "Do you see it, too?" Bitty asked Meggie.

Meggie squinted. "I see it. At least, I think I do."

"Jeez, guys," Aubrey said. She lowered her gaze to the floor. "Sorry. I forgot. This happened last time, remember? They got really bright. I'll go get my glasses."

"No—you don't understand," Bitty said. "They're . . . *normal.*"

Aubrey said nothing. She felt a tightness in her throat like a choked laugh. Maybe there was just some shift in the light. Some freak optical illusion. Maybe she was standing in a shadow. She returned to the bathroom. She looked into the mirror above the little sink. There was her face, her same old face, and there were her same old eyes.

"Are you sure you're feeling okay?" Meggie asked.

Aubrey stood straighter. "I think so. I'm just drained. It was a long night."

Her sisters exchanged a glance.

"Don't be worried, you guys," she said cheerfully. "We did the best we could with the spells. And all we can do now is just wait and see what happens when they vote tomorrow."

"Aubrey," Bitty said. "It *is* tomorrow."

She rubbed her eyes. "I'm not following."

"It's Monday," Meggie said.

Aubrey dropped her hands. A strange vertigo seized her. The Stitchery seemed to tip on its side. "Wait—it's . . . Monday?"

"Yes," Meggie said.

"I slept for . . ."

"Over twenty-four hours," Bitty said.

"Oh my God, Monday—what time on Monday?"

"Noon," Bitty said.

Cell by cell, Aubrey's body was waking up, flickering to life and full awareness. She'd been sleeping for ages. And there was something that her sisters didn't want to tell her, something they didn't know how to say.

"So does that mean . . . ?"

"They had the vote this morning," Meggie said.

Aubrey gripped the porcelain edge of the sink. She felt breathless. "And . . . ?"

Meggie was looking up at her with sorrowful, pitying eyes.

"It's no good," Bitty said.

"No!" Aubrey heard her own voice as if it were coming from outside of her. "That's not possible. There must be something wrong. A miscount. An absent voter. Something."

"I'm sorry, Aubrey," Meggie said.

She was too shocked to cry. The disbelief was a void the size of the universe, an awareness of something gone missing. She thought of Mariah, of all the names in the Great Book in the Hall, of the many battles the Stitchery had faced over the years, the many battles the guardians had faced before they overcame the odds. Aubrey could not envision what the end of the Stitchery would be like any more than she might imagine with clarity the end of the world. *The spell failed*, she repeated to herself. *The spell failed*. She could not fathom what it meant. *The spell failed*.

"Maybe it's not over," Aubrey said. "Maybe there's going to be an appeal. Or a recount."

"It's done," Bitty said. "It's all done."

It's done? Aubrey thought.

She listened, but the Stitchery had nothing to say.

From the Great Book in the Hall: *No gift is meant to last forever. Knitted projects are ephemera—meant to be used until they can be used no more. All magic fades. In a way, a magic spell is less like a castle than the scaffolding that helps to raise the stones. Our best hope is that the strength of our spells as we made them will be so effective in their time that the castle will continue to stand long after the bricklayers are gone.*

22

"Bind Off"

By mid-November, the beauty of a vibrant autumn in the lower Hudson had worn off. The leaves had become as brittle as mummified pharaohs. The first snow fell—unexpectedly violent—and Tarrytown was encapsulated in slick ice while the electric company struggled to restore power and the plows were rushed into the streets.

Aubrey moved about the Stitchery like a ghost of herself, oblivious to the ice tapping the windows, the whistle of a steaming kettle, the snowslides avalanching off the eaves. She did not pick up her needles. She did not even read. She went to her shift at the library, she played with Icky and cleaned his cage, she ordered her spicy dragon rolls, and all of it felt as if she were moving underwater. Sometimes, she cracked open the Great Book in the Hall, but rather than read it—the names of all the guardians, the lists of sacrifices, the notes and gentle guidance of the women who had gone before—she simply stared. Her heart in her chest was so heavy with guilt that it pulled her shoulders down. She had reached the fullest capacity of what she could handle; she could not withstand shouldering even one more particle of despair. She did not allow herself to think of Vic—of what he was doing or feeling at any given moment, of where he was while Aubrey was staring at the ceiling or standing in the shower until the water went cold. If she thought of him, his glinting eyes, his broad smile, it would shut her down.

Vic had been her only chance. It was Vic or it was no one. It was no one.

The only bright spot in her future was her sisters. Meggie had made herself at home in the Stitchery, and she'd found a job at a travel agency in Manhattan. On first glance she seemed to be dressing more conservatively—wearing pencil skirts and jackets. But her blouse was usually dotted with sequins, and under her skirt she wore a hot pink garter. In the evenings, she strapped on her roller skates and resumed her place among the Flying Dutchesses.

Bitty, too, remained in the Stitchery. Her children had transferred to Tarrytown's schools, and she'd begun to research going back to school herself. She was looking for an apartment but was in no rush to cut short her family's last weeks in the Stitchery. She made frequent trips to see her lawyer but found that she was even better at negotiating her divorce than he was.

As the winter wore on, Bitty and Meggie—even the children—were tightly strung, treating Aubrey with diligent gentleness and caution like women of ages past drying their wool on tenterhooks. Aubrey loved them for their efforts, even as she tried to shore herself up, to boost her own spirits, and to put on a better show.

They did not talk about the loss of the Stitchery, and what felt to Aubrey like the loss of magic. Each day, Aubrey discovered a flicker of irresistible hope that perhaps something would happen, someone would swoop in for an eleventh-hour rescue, and the Stitchery would be saved. And each day, she had to quash that hope for happiness. Because even if the

Stitchery was miraculously but belatedly saved, she still would never get back Vic.

Aubrey had stood in front of the people of Tappan Square and had staked her good word on the Stitchery. Yes, she'd warned them that the magic might fail. But in her heart she didn't believe failure was possible, and her actions told the true story of her feelings loud and clear, told it with more authority than the contradictory words she spoke. The women of Tappan Square dismissed her initial warning like boiler-plate legalese and instead clutched on to the core truth that Aubrey was offering them: that if they tried hard enough, the magic would not fail them. How horrible it was—Aubrey thought to herself at times—to have proclaimed her naked confidence before everyone, only to have it desert her. She did not know if she was a martyr or a fool. She did not know if there was a difference.

Every day, the council's plans to bulldoze Tappan Square moved forward. Properties were being sold one by one to the village, families were trickling out of neighborhoods, win-dows were boarded, doors nailed shut, houses condemned. The Stitchery's neighbors across the street, who had never been friendly toward the Van Rippers, had packed up their belongings, including the blue-and-white concentric *nazar* that hung on their front door. Old Mr. Hussein had always insisted that he would refuse to sell, that he would throw his body in front of the bulldozers if they ever came to knock down his home; but instead he'd taken the money the village offered and bought a trailer in Florida. Family by family, the neighborhood was being dismantled.

"It's just not fair," Aubrey muttered to her sisters on an unusually warm day in early December. They had gone out for gyros. As usual there were no open tables in the restaurant and so they shivered in the afternoon chill on cold metal chairs set on the sidewalk outside. Aubrey's hair was greasy. Her eyes, her dull normal eyes, were shadowed in blue. The real estate section of the newspaper was on the table, weighted down by a cell phone and luffing like a sail in the wind.

"I wish you would just go to talk to him," Bitty said. "Explain things. Give the man some credit. I'm sure he'd understand."

"I wasn't thinking about Vic," Aubrey said.

"But maybe you should," Bitty said.

Aubrey sighed. They'd been over this before. Bitty and Meggie wanted her to seek out Vic, to make things right with him. But even though the Stitchery had turned its back on Aubrey, she could not bring herself to turn her back on it. Rules were rules: Sacrifices could not, under any circumstances, be returned—even if a spell failed. If Mariah hadn't been cremated, she would have rolled over in her grave to know that Aubrey was entertaining the possibility of throwing herself at Vic's feet and begging for mercy. Because in fact Aubrey had thought, many times, of doing just that. She wanted Vic back. She wanted to go to his house and prostrate herself on his walkway. She wanted to see him look at her again like she was a living, breathing miracle—and not a woman who had stabbed him in the back. She wanted to wear his ring, and hold his hand at circuses, and scary movies, and funerals, and when they got old, she wanted to push his wheelchair down the sidewalks of Tappan Square.

No one could stop her from going to him. The Stitchery had abandoned her—why shouldn't she reciprocate? And yet, for as often as she'd been tormented by the idea of reclaiming her sacrifice, she knew she could not do it. She was too well trained. Too loyal to Mariah's teachings. But she wasn't certain of anything anymore.

"Tell him it was a mistake," Bitty said.

"It wasn't a mistake. I knew exactly what I was doing at the time."

Bitty spoke with a rasping irritation. "Don't you think it might be a little egotistical to think that this"—she gestured with her hand toward the newspaper, a move that was perhaps supposed to mean the loss of the Stitchery and the subsequent dilemmas—"is all about you and only you?"

"Of course it's not about me," Aubrey said, defensively.

"What about Vic, then? Is it about him? Because it sure as hell doesn't seem to be about *him*."

"It's not about him or me. Or him and me. It's about the Stitchery and its traditions."

"I think I get what Bitty's trying to say," Meggie said, her voice tight with forced patience. "What she means is, you're operating as if losing the Stitchery is about you, about us, about Tappan Square. Like you know what it's about. But at the end of the day, none of us knows what the big picture is."

Aubrey sat back in her chair. Until now, her only explanation for the failure of the yarn spell was her own bungling. Maybe she could have done things differently. Maybe having the group knit along with her had been a debilitating distraction. Maybe she should have given up more than Vic; maybe there was another sacrifice she might have made. Maybe she should have asked for bigger sacrifices from the women who had joined her that night. Her mind was full of maybes.

But now her sisters suggested an alternative possibility as to why the magic failed: Perhaps the result of the spell wasn't a failure but just a progression. A step in the life cycle. The next phase. Or—she took a bite of her gyro and angrily chewed—perhaps she was telling herself stories. She was trying to tease reason out of unreasonable things.

She lifted the straw in her soda up and down until it squeaked against the plastic lid. A chill wind blew down the street. "I guess I'll have to give it some thought," she said.

Christmas came and went, and the January freeze leached into Tarrytown's old bones. The days were short and hard. The reservoir was frozen along its edges. On the morning that marked the beginning of her final week in the Stitchery, Aubrey woke to find a dusting of snow on the streets and rooftops of Tappan Square.

She worked in her bedroom, packing the last of her boxes. Everything that she could live without—certain hairbrushes, certain sweaters, certain books—was sealed with packing tape in cardboard tombs. Her back ached, and she sat on her bed. Meggie, Bitty, and the kids had gone in the morning to the two-family house that Aubrey and her sisters had rented in Sleepy Hollow, cleaning it from top to bottom so it would be ready when they moved in. The new house was no Stitchery—just a vinyl-sided, nondescript Colonial with its gable end up against the sidewalk and its chimney little more than a tube like a straw in a glass. But the house would allow them to pool their resources and stay together while they each figured out what it was they were going to do.

The doorbell gave its asthmatic buzz, and Aubrey got to her feet. She went downstairs, her hand running along the banister. She expected to find one of the town's representatives at the door to bother her about whatever thing they wanted to bother her about this time. But when she tugged the old brass handle, and a smattering of dusty snowflakes blew in, it was Vic standing before her, rubbing his bare hands together in the cold.

"Oh," she said. "You!"

He looked contrite, as if he might apologize for being at her doorway. "Can I come in?"

She gripped the door handle. Her heart in her chest was pumping like a crazed steam engine. She wanted to shout at him *No! You shouldn't be here!* because what she wanted to do was throw her arms around him and drag him with her to the entryway floor, because she wanted to cry against his chest and say how sorry she was for everything—and it made her feel all kinked up and bent, not to be able to do those things.

"Please, do come in," she said.

He stepped past her, and she felt the chill coming off his jacket. She quickly shut the door. The snow had marked Vic's shoulders in little melting droplets. He took off his hat—it hurt that Aubrey had not made it for him, that it was a store-bought hat with thin mechanical stitches and elastic stretch—and his dark hair was mussed in a way that made her want to smooth it with her hands.

"It's cold out there," she said. She might also have said that it was daytime, or that it was snowing, or that her heart was a heap of rubble in her chest—or some other obvious thing.

"Yeah. It's snowing," he said.

"So . . . How are you?"

"Hanging in. You?"

"The same." She risked a glance at his face, then gave a laugh that meant nothing. She tried not to think of the last time she'd seen him, when his eyes had been so open and fathomless, and when he'd said he loved her, and when she'd kissed him and his lips were dead cold. "Did you, um, did you deed the house over yet?"

He fidgeted with his hat. "Almost. I have to be out next month."

"This is my last week," she offered. "My sisters and I are renting a place together over in Sleepy Hollow."

"That's great," he said. His eyes roamed the entryway, as if he wasn't quite sure what to look at and could not look at her.

"Where are you headed?" she asked.

"Now?"

"No, I mean, *after*—you know. After Tappan Square."

"Oh, right. My sister moved back in with my mom. And I rented a place across the river in Nyack."

Aubrey knew she should be thrilled. Vic might have said he was moving to the other side of the country; instead, he was moving only to the other side of the Tappan Zee. And yet, the idea that they would be separated from each other by the river—the great, wide reaches of the river—made her feel like she was in danger of breaking out in tears. She composed herself before she spoke.

"I'm sorry you have to move," she said. She pushed her hands down deeper into her pockets.

"Thanks," he said. "I'm sorry about the Stitchery, too."

"We'll get by," she said.

"Aubrey . . ." He looked at her for the first time since he'd arrived. Purple shadows had settled under his eyes; his mouth was drawn in pain. "I know what you did. I know about the Devil's Night spell. That *I* was your sacrifice."

"How?"

"Bitty came to the house and told me this morning."

"Of course," she said. She planted her feet on the Stitchery's boards and did not allow herself to move near him. "I didn't know how to tell you. If there had been any other thing I could think of—any other way . . . You *know* I would have taken it."

He narrowed his eyes. "Would you?"

She pulled herself up a little straighter. His doubt hurt her more than his absence had. He was the love of her life, her first and last and only. But she couldn't explain that to him. Not now.

"This is the twenty-first century," he said. "I think a guy should have a least a little say in it if he's going to be a human sacrifice. I mean, we're not barbarians anymore."

She wondered if he was trying to make her laugh, but she couldn't do it. She had no laughter in her. Each day that had passed since she'd last seen him, since she'd last felt the particular, nourishing energy that moved between them when they were alone, had been a low, long tolling. She wouldn't claim she had nothing to live for anymore—there was her family, after all. But she had lost her faith in magic. She had lost the very meaning and purpose of her existence. She had lost *him*. She could not see a reason to laugh.

"I wanted you to be able to keep your house," she said. "I know how much it meant to you. It was your dream."

"It was a *house*," he said, ice in his voice. "Don't get me wrong. I loved that house. But it's not my family. It's what I love, but it's not *who* I love." He looked at her; his eyes were dark. "I would have torched that house and a thousand more like it, if I thought that would have stopped you from doing what you did."

Her legs would no longer hold her; she lowered herself to the bottom stair. She put her face in her hands, then looked up again, careless of tears. "Why are you here?" she cried. "Why did you come here? To make me feel more terrible? To remind me of all the things that I lost when I walked out of your house that day? To make me wish for the ten thousandth time that I could take it all back and do it differently?"

He knelt before her, his hands bracing her forearms. She tried to pull away. "Why can't you?" he demanded. "Why can't you just take it back? At this point, what's the harm?"

"I don't *know*," she said. Her tears were ugly and falling. "Everyone keeps asking me, but I don't know. I have *no* answers. I have *nothing* to say."

"Then maybe that *is* your answer," Vic said. He took her hands, held them so hard it hurt. "Aubrey, these past months—without you—they sucked. I told myself that if I waited long enough, you'd come around. But I'm tired of waiting. The house I can deal with losing. It's replaceable. But you—you're *not*. I can't lose Tappan Square *and* you. I won't. Not over some stupid—"

She held her breath; if he said *spell* she didn't know what she would do.

"Shopping mall," he said.

She dropped her head; she didn't want him to see her crying and yet she couldn't stop. "I've missed you so much," she said. "I've thought of you a thousand times a day."

He sat on the stair beside her and gathered her close. She didn't resist; she pressed her face into the warm nook between his neck and coat. She held him like she was drowning, held on. She felt him kiss her hair. He told her: "I know you meant well."

She sobbed into his coat.

"Let's fix this," he said. "We can. I know we can."

"How?" She hiccuped. "The Stitchery's rules are very clear. Once a thing is sacrificed, you can't have it back."

He went quiet. She felt him stiffen. His hands, which had been roaming her back, her shoulders, her hair, went still. He pulled away. "I can't ask you to betray your principles for me. I *won't* ask. But if there's a way . . . if somehow—I don't know. If you could—"

An impulse crested within her and she followed it, riding the wave. She leaned forward, and she kissed him. His hands came around her back; she gripped the front of his leather jacket, still damp with cold and snow. She kissed him, and kissed him, and the bigness of it overwhelmed her. *This*, being with the man she loved, did not feel at all like it was a forfeit of her principles; instead, she felt it was a liberation— from all the confines and strictures and regulations about what magic was and was not, from theories about how magic worked or how it did not, from all the fumbling attempts at defining a thing that could not and would not be defined, from all the very small, very narrow, very human notions that had come to be called magic as the centuries had worn on. The Stitchery had made a thing very clear to her—a thing she did not see until now: Whatever the Van Ripper guardians had said magic was, was only a very small part of it, if it was part at all.

Vic ended their kiss abruptly. "I don't want you to regret this later."

"I won't."

"What about the rules?"

"The rules are what we make of them," she said.

She took Vic's hand, and with a feeling of triumph pulled him up the Stitchery's stairs to her room. She shut the door and kissed him again, until the walls of the Stitchery seemed to turn to rubber, until the floor beneath them bucked. They made love surrounded by cardboard boxes, and tied-up garbage bags full of blankets, and stacks upon stacks of books about knitting. Everything that had gone wrong had somehow made room for this—this *rightness*, the rasp of her breath and his, the old boards creaking with their movements, and the snow, tapping against the window, falling gently on the rooftops of a neighborhood that—whether they liked it or not—would soon make way.

* * *

Little by little, the winter forfeited its territory and the landscape softened and blushed. Purple crocuses clawed up between garden stones, and then daffodils assembled like a line of soldiers in front of Christ Episcopal, and then the forsythia bushes throughout Sleepy Hollow effused like a bottle of champagne. Tappan Square stood empty, and the work to clear the land began. The Stitchery did not go easily; it stood curmudgeonly and stalwart, so that the wrecking crew cursed its unusually stubborn porch spindles and its chimney that did not want to budge one inch off its foundation. But eventually, modern technology prevailed, and it was crunched into splinters by backhoes and bulldozers; some members of the crew said that as the dust rose up from the rubble, the shapes of human faces could be seen, hollow eyes and long, open mouths being stretched toward heaven. But others said that was ridiculous.

In Sleepy Hollow, the Van Ripper family settled into their new, albeit temporary, home. Although they had lost the Stitchery, they took pieces of it with them—Meggie had filched the doorknob of her bedroom, Bitty had loosened one of the foundation's stones, and Aubrey had preserved—with dexterity and care—the graffiti that some ancestor had scrawled on the tower's inside wall. They sold what relics were theirs to sell—the ugly brass guard lions on the mantel, the ancient rugs on the floor—and found that they had enough money to outfit their new house with new furniture. Some of what had been in the Stitchery stayed in the Stitchery until it was pulled down.

Aubrey was largely happy. Her heart was filled up: There were many people near her to love and who loved her in return. Vic traveled to her new house often from Nyack, and as the months had slipped by into spring, her love for him—

which had once felt like a butterfly dancing on a warm wind—
became deeper, more muscled and strong, less like a flighty
swallowtail and more like one of the hawks that surfed the
high currents along the Palisades. In the early mornings after
long nights, before her family began to rise, she dreaded to
leave him or have him leave; but the longing was sweet, and
she relished it, every pang, looking with anticipation toward
the day when they would sleep the whole night together, side
by side.

Since she was no longer running the Stitchery between her
shifts at the library, Aubrey had time. She knew that eventually she would need to attempt a job search—it was hard to
imagine an ad that said "Wanted: Spell-knitting witch/librar-
ian/hedgehog owner for administrative work"—but for the
moment, she was dedicated to enjoying as much of her sisters'
company as possible, and to returning the sacrifices that had
been stored in the Stitchery, one at a time. On any given day,
she and Nessa would wander across town to the storage unit
that she and her family paid a small fortune to rent—if it
weren't for the lack of running water, she could have lived in
the thing—and then she would pluck one random sacrifice
out of the many and sit with the Great Book in the Hall until
she found its owner. Sometimes, the process of locating an
object's owner was long and convoluted, full of dusty estate
proceedings and afternoons at the county surrogate's office or
genealogical society. Sometimes it was swift as the current
that flowed to her computer down fiber-optic lines.

It was a clear and gusty day in April when Ruth Ten Eckye's silvery jack-o'-lantern pin fell out of some hidden em-
placement and landed on the concrete floor of the storage
unit. Aubrey ran her thumb over its smug sneer, a pang of
nervousness shooting through her. *Ruth.* Although she no longer felt as confident about magic as she once had, she did feel

that there might have been some cosmic reason and order in how certain objects caught her eye and begged to be returned on a given day, while others seemed content to languish awhile more.

"That's a weird little thing," Nessa said, looking at the pin. "Do you know whose it is?"

Aubrey shook off her hesitation. There was no reason to be worried about going to see Ruth Ten Eckye. Ruth seemed, Aubrey thought, to have let go of some small piece of her resentment toward the Van Rippers, even to show some grudging support; she'd come to the Stitchery on Devil's Night after all. And even if Ruth did have some animosity toward her, there was nothing the old dame could do to hurt Aubrey— not now.

"I know who it belongs to," Aubrey said. "This will be an easy one today. We won't even need to look it up in the Great Book."

Nessa, who seemed to enjoy sleuthing and tracking people down, and who thrived on seeing the joy or bewilderment in people's faces when they had cherished or unknown old treasures thrust back into their hands, looked a little disappointed.

They drove from Sleepy Hollow and crossed into Tarrytown, the transition from one place to another demarcated only by the Hollow's orange-and-black street signs. Ruth Ten Eckye's house was high on the ridge; it was large, white, and impressive, with flat eaves and corbels that scrolled like elegant snails. Aubrey sat a moment in the car, gathering her courage. Ruth was going to give her an earful, a condescending and indignant earful, when Aubrey walked in holding the pumpkin pin. Also, there was the matter of the money; Ruth Ten Eckye had paid two hundred dollars for her spell. Aubrey didn't have two hundred dollars at the moment, and it would be a while before she could repay. Luckily, few people who had darkened the Stitchery's door ever sacrificed money.

Aubrey crossed the perfectly flat, round stones that led to the Ten Eckye family seat. The front door offered no doorbell; only a brass lion with a ring in its mouth. Aubrey knocked timidly at first, then more loudly. She stood for what seemed to be a long time before the door creaked open.

"You!" Ruth said, with surprising vigor. "You—it's about time. Come in!"

"I'm sorry—" Aubrey said. "Were you expecting us?"

"Yes, yes," Ruth said, waving her hand to dismiss the question. "But it doesn't matter that it took you so long. The important thing is that you're *here*."

They stepped into a central, clover-shaped hall; tiny white tiles covered the floor, and the ceiling was graced by a brass chandelier. Aubrey got a good look at Ruth in the light: She seemed tired and thin. Her beige dress hung slack from her shoulders. Her hair, normally in neat curls, was flat against her head.

"Wow." Nessa's eyes rolled as she took in the entryway's elaborate swags and festoons of heavy, carved wood. "Nice crib."

"I beg your pardon? And who are you?"

"You remember my niece," Aubrey said. "Ness—"

"I'm Vanessa," she said. "And your house is beautiful."

"Thank you—"

"In a mausoleum sort of way," Nessa said.

"Yes, well," Ruth said. "Come sit down."

Aubrey followed Ruth into a large overstuffed living room, which probably had some kind of fancy moniker like *sitting room*, or *entertaining room*, or *front parlor*. Certainly it was not a *rec room* or a *den*. She sat stiffly on a couch that felt like a hardened dish sponge. Any anxiety she'd felt about returning

Ruth's pin had vanished when she'd seen the war between expectation and exhaustion in Ruth's eyes. "Are you feeling okay?" she asked.

"Do I look okay?" Ruth said, laughing indignantly. "Of course I don't. I have cancer."

"Oh," Aubrey said. "I'm so sorry."

Ruth shrugged. "Might as well put my kids out of their misery. They've been waiting for years to divide up my estate."

"I'm sure they're not doing that," Aubrey said, but in truth, she knew they probably were. "I have something for you. I hope it will—I don't know—help." She reached into her large bag and rummaged until she found Ruth's pin. Then she held it faceup in the middle of her palm, her hand extended. Its liquid silver grin was all mischief and menace, and it seemed out of place among the softly blooming flowers of a Hudson spring.

"What's this about?" Ruth said.

"We're returning all the sacrifices," Nessa said brightly. "We don't need them anymore. Apparently returning them has no effect at all."

Aubrey watched the older woman, looking for Ruth's agitation, her disapproval and annoyance. Instead, Ruth sat perfectly still.

"It's okay," Aubrey said. "You can take it."

"No," Ruth said, the word a croak more than a whisper. "No, I can't."

Aubrey drew her arm back—it was getting tired—but she did not close her fist around the pin. "We're planning to return the money, too, as soon as we can. But it might be a while."

Ruth looked on the pin with a mix of longing and sorrow.

"I'm afraid it doesn't matter much now." She got to her feet. She walked around the chair, her back turned. Her normally square shoulders had stooped in a shaft of dusty sunlight. "I've made a provision in my will," Ruth said. "I have a building on Broadway. There's a tobacco shop in it, owned by a man I never liked. It's zoned for commercial business. When I pass away, that building will go to you to do with as you please. But my hope is that you and your family will reopen the Stitchery."

Aubrey could not quite process what Ruth had said—not for a long moment.

"Did you hear me, or do you have yarn stuffed in your ears?"

"I heard you," Aubrey said cautiously. "I just don't know what to say."

"*Thank you* is normally the accepted response for a gift of this magnitude." Ruth shook her head. "You Van Rippers have the manners of wildebeests."

"And you're one to talk," Nessa said.

Aubrey shushed her. She turned to Ruth. "What's the catch?"

"Catch?"

"What do I have to promise to do in exchange for your building?"

Ruth turned to face her, her whole face frowning. "Do what you always do for Tarrytown. Knit spells."

Aubrey sat motionless, but her heart in her chest was wild. Over the last few months, she'd grown very comfortable with, even *grateful* for, the idea that her future was no longer manacled to the Stitchery, that she was free to choose, to have the life she wanted, to perhaps be a normal—or at least semi-normal—member of her community. But here was

Ruth, making her an incredible and unexpected offer, and Aubrey felt as if the Stitchery were drawing her to it again, sucking her back into the circle of its power.

Ruth seemed to sense her discomfort. "What is it? What's wrong?"

Aubrey said nothing; she had no idea where to begin.

"You might as well tell me," Ruth said.

Aubrey took in a breath. "The magic . . . on Devil's Night, it failed. How can the Stitchery save anyone if it can't save itself?"

"Is that what you think?" Ruth laughed. "That's only because you didn't know I would be offering you a *new* Stitchery. But here I am, dying, practically on my last breath, and giving you the chance to start over—so it seems to me the Stitchery came through for itself in the end."

Aubrey rubbed her eyes and wondered. She looked to the large French doors that led to a stone patio behind Ruth's house. "I'm sorry. I—I'm just going to get some air."

Outside, the afternoon smelled of springtime—fresh and fragrant with sweet earth and flowers. Aubrey leaned her hip on the black iron railing and looked out at the river. It appeared calm and steady. She—on the other hand—didn't know whether to laugh or cry.

The Stitchery, back again.

Life was so unfair. Now that she'd finally gotten her feet under her—she knew who she was (more than just a guardian), and what she wanted from life (to spend it making memories with her sisters, her future family, and Vic)—all of a sudden she was supposed to return to her old way of life. She wondered, not for the first time, if the Van Rippers had not been gifted so much as cursed.

She wrapped her fingers around the cold black rail. Her knuckles turned white.

No. She would not revive the Stitchery. She felt as certain and sure of that as of her next breath. The old days were done.

"I'm sorry," she told Ruth as she walked back into the sitting room. "I can't do it."

"Why on earth not?" Ruth said. "You don't believe in magic anymore?"

"Of course I do!" Aubrey said, nearly yelling. And the moment she said the words she knew they were true. She did believe in magic, she always would—if only because she wanted to believe, and if only because—in the end—she'd come to accept that her belief in magic, the very heart of it, was and would always be a belief in questions. She would never know what Mariah had been trying to tell her on the day she died, but maybe that, too, was part of the Stitchery's message. Her shoulders slumped; she looked up at Ruth through the wisps of her bangs. "If I do this, *if* I do, I do it on my terms. The best way that *I* know how."

Ruth laughed. "As if that was ever in question."

Aubrey's chest rose and fell. "Okay."

"Yes?"

She closed her eyes. "Yes," she said.

"Woo-hoo!" Nessa, who had been sitting quietly, tackled Aubrey in a hug. "Hell, yeah!"

Aubrey laughed and tried to detangle herself. Nessa did not let her go. Even Ruth's face had softened.

"Does this mean I get to cast my own spells now, like a guardian?" Nessa asked.

Aubrey managed to get her arms out of Nessa's vise grip, only to wrap them around her niece again. "That's one you'll have to take up with your mother," she said.

Epilogue

"Yarn Over"

Just before the Van Rippers moved into their new brick home on Broadway, in the heart of Tarrytown, it was said that the mice in the basement and the bats under the eaves abandoned their nests and roosts even before the exterminator arrived—because they heard the Van Rippers were on the way.

It was Nessa who came up with the proper name for the new yarn shop, which occupied the first floor of a narrow brick walk-up not far from Jeanette's. In an evening of Merlot-infused bawdiness, she'd listened to her mother and aunts bandy about potential names, from the nostalgic (Whatever Wool Be) to the dyspeptic (Ewe Beginnings); from the reverent (Thy Wool Be Done) to the irreverent (The Wool Monty). But it was Nessa, stone-cold sober at thirteen, trying to hide her pinkening hair by tucking it under endless woolen hats, who suggested the winning name. And so when the yarn shop opened its doors in September, four months after Ruth Ten Eckye passed away, it was called, very simply, Honest Yarns.

To Aubrey's mind, the space was everything a yarn shop should be: cozy and warm, colorful and cheery. It smelled like clean wool and linen—and sometimes like cheap old-lady perfume that reeked of artificial rose. Some women who were new to Tarrytown or who were passing through on their visits to old houses like Kykuit or Sunnyside were drawn to the yarn shop strictly by its physical wares. Gorgeous fibers in every hue lined the walls—mohair, cashmere, self-striping, roving, cotton, bamboo, merino, angora, alpaca, thick–thin, hand-painted, hand-spun, and blends of flax, hemp, and even a few acrylics (because they served a purpose, Aubrey said, for baby clothes). But other women, Tarrytown natives, came for other reasons, more secret reasons. And it wasn't long before the women of Tarrytown had divided themselves into two factions: those women who attended the Thursday-night knitting circles at the Van Ripper yarn shop—women who sometimes smiled to themselves in the crush of grocery stores and day care centers, as if they had a secret on their minds—and those who did not attend.

As for Horseman Woods Commons, it was a success from the first brick to the last. Consumers came, and tourists came, and retirees came and set up their yoga classes and wine tastings and espresso machines on its upper floors. But it wasn't long after the bulbs began to need replacing and the sidewalks were covered with gum that Steve Halpern suffered the upset of his life: Dan Hatters—whom nobody outside of the Tappan Watch had even heard of before—rallied with the support of his former neighbors and took Steve Halpern's chair. Tappan Square had vanished, but the Tappan Watch had swelled. And the Van Ripper yarn shop came to be looked at as a place of foment, because women sitting in close circles with their knitting and crocheting, talking and drinking wine, were capable of big, dangerous things.

For as long as they lived—and for a long time after—it was said the Van Ripper sisters brought strange things into fruition wherever they went. The pink cherry tree in front of their yarn shop was always the first to bloom in the spring. Children swore that pennies chucked at the sisters always landed heads up, and they tested the theory regularly because once in a while it turned out to be wrong. And one cool day in October, on the day that would have been Mariah Van Ripper's hundredth birthday, when the skies were clear as blue crystal and the river was calm as glass, lightning struck the Tarrytown lighthouse out of nowhere and fried its circuits. Only the Van Ripper girls seemed not to be surprised.

Author's Note and Acknowledgments

When it comes to the Stitchery it's hard to know what to believe. You might say the same thing about Hudson Valley legends.

The Tarrytown in this book offers familiar landmarks, but its politics are imagined. One example: The real Tarrytown has a board of trustees as opposed to a town council. Also, Tarrytown is part of the township of Greenburg, a fact I've dispensed with in this story. There is no neighborhood within Tarrytown called Tappan Square, nor is there a specific neighborhood that served as a model. I've taken minor liberties with real Tarrytown settings.

The story of Mad Anthony's charge on Stony Point appears as I've read it in various sources, but minor bits had to be tweaked to accommodate the book's fictions (my apologies to the Lt. Col. François de Fleury, who actually won the top prize).

Regarding Bitty's claim about the real Headless Hessian's grave: Despite the "folklore" surrounding a gravestone at the Old Dutch Church that inspired Irving's tale, no record of such a thing exists. Bitty unwittingly participates in local myth-building. Of course, she isn't alone.

Theories about the evolution of left- to right-handed knitting can be traced to Richard Rutt's *A History of Hand Knit-*

ting, but it must be said that one knitting historian I met said she thought this might have been more folktale than fact. Either way, I loved the story for the Van Ripper's family tome.

Some of the hand-knits in this book were inspired by great crafts I saw on the Web, many of which have free patterns. So enormous thanks must go to all fiber artists who so generously share their work online. Links to this book's knitting inspirations are on my site (sorry, magic spells not included).

There are so many people vital (vital!) to this book. Great heaping thanks to my very gifted and inspirational editor Kara Cesare and the ever-diligent and insightful Hannah Elnan. Also thanks to Jane Von Mehren, Jennifer Hershey, and everyone at Random House who so ardently championed my writing. Thanks to Andrea Cirillo and Christina Hogrebe, who have never ceased to dazzle me with their warmth and sagacity, and to the entire team at the Jane Rotrosen Agency. And thanks to Sara Mascia of the the Historical Society of Tarrytown and Sleepy Hollow for helping me research one very obscure fact (that didn't even make the final cut of the book!).

Thanks also to Tia, for making me learn to knit even when I insisted nothing could be more boring. To my husband, for first bringing me to Tarrytown because he knew it would set me off. To my siblings and all the friends from my childhood who ran amok in Mom's backyard (and to Mom, for letting us do it). To members of my church for your support, particularly the ladies of the book club. And finally, to all people who love, read, buy, and talk about books. I mean this: You brighten my world.

The
Wishing Thread

A Novel

LISA VAN ALLEN

A Reader's Guide

A Conversation with Sarah Addison Allen
and Lisa Van Allen

SARAH ADDISON ALLEN is the *New York Times* bestselling author of *Garden Spells, The Sugar Queen, The Girl Who Chased the Moon, The Peach Keeper,* and the upcoming *Lost Lake*. She was born and raised in Asheville, North Carolina.

Sarah Addison Allen: *The Wishing Thread* is a delightful novel about the bonds of sisterhood, the transformational power of love, and the pleasures and perils of knitting. What sparked your idea for this novel?

Lisa Van Allen: It started with the knitting. When I knit a gift for someone, I always say a few prayers for the recipient. It's about sending deliberate thoughts of love and kindness, along with offering a gift. So it wasn't a far jump from there to "Wouldn't it be cool if somebody could knit a magic spell into the fabric of a hat or a scarf so that it rubs off on the wearer?"

Of course, in *The Wishing Thread*, the people who go to the Stitchery looking for magic never know what they'll get. Sometimes the spells don't work as expected. Sometimes they don't work at all.

Many people in the town think that the Van Ripper sisters are swindlers, preying on people who are desperate enough to turn to "magic" to fix their problems. But others think the sisters are the real deal and will defend the

Stitchery's magic, tooth and nail. Each sister in the story approaches the idea of magic in her own way.

SAA: The novel is set in Tarrytown, New York, the home of so much rich history as well as the legend of Sleepy Hollow. Is the Tarrytown of the novel the same as the real Tarrytown?

LVA: My husband gets full credit for the story's location. One day, he took me to Tarrytown and Sleepy Hollow, and he said "You're gonna like this."

So I rolled up my sleeves and dug into the local lore, including Washington Irving's charming legend of Ichabod Crane and the Headless Horseman. The book features many recognizable Tarrytown landmarks, and I hope I captured the town's busy suburban vibe.

But what I love about Hudson Valley folklore is that it's a living thing, always shifting and changing. Each storyteller brings her own spin. So yes, it's the real Tarrytown. But it's also quite stylized to suit my fancy.

SAA: Did you do any other research when writing the novel?

LVA: Oh, yes. I did a great deal of research on the haunts of old Tarrytown and Sleepy Hollow; the Headless Horseman is the tip of the iceberg. And I also did quite a bit of research about the history of knitting, which also has its share of rumor, myth, and legend.

SAA: The way you write about magic is so unique. What are your favorite books with magic in them that have influenced you?

LVA: I've always loved books that offer fun, imaginative plots along with a certain "makes you think" element—

going all the way back. As a kid I adored *The Little Prince* for its enigmatic characters, magical surprises, and emotionality. Recently I fell hard for Erin Morgenstern's *The Night Circus*. And, Sarah, your latest, *The Peach Keeper*, was one of those reads that had me sitting down thinking "just for a few minutes" and then realizing hours had gone by. This is always the sign of a great read.

SAA: Thank you! I'm glad to be in such great company! Magic is so wonderful to write but also so tricky. I think every writer approaches writing in a different way. What are your writing habits? How do you write best?

LVA: More and more, I find myself collecting things. I make a regular practice of writing lists with titles like "things you find that could change everything" and "reasons you might become stuck in a tree." Sei Shōnagon inspired this habit for me when I read her eleventh-century collection of writings called *The Pillow Book*. She makes beautiful, breathtaking lists.

I also keep random boxes in my office of things that seem to go together somehow: pictures, objects, bits of fabric or color, anecdotes, books and pamphlets, scribbles, etc. Each box has its own kind of ordered chaos. I like the idea of all these elements marinating for a while until all the flavors marry and become a cohesive story. I have Twyla Tharp's book *The Creative Habit* to thank for this.

SAA: I hear you have a hedgehog as a pet—is anything else in the book based on real life?

LVA: Ha, ha. Yes! My hedgie has quite a following. I guess you could say she was instrumental in developing the character of Icky Van Ripper, the main character's pet hedgehog in *The Wishing Thread*. I'm hoping my little beastie won't sue me for using her likeness or something like that. I'll have to pay her off with mealworms.

But seriously, I never have models for my (human) characters. That method just doesn't work for me. I do, however, expand on my own emotional experiences, like every writer.

SAA: How did you get started knitting? What do you love about it?

LVA: I actually outright *refused* to learn to knit for many years. I so was sure I'd hate it! But one day in my mid-twenties, an aunt finally took my shoulders and sat me down, and said "watch my hands." A few rows later, I was hooked. There's a scene in *The Wishing Thread* that definitely came right from that moment.

Of course, I had some false starts with knitting. My first scarf looked like a moth-chewed roll of lumpy toilet paper. One year, I made my brother three socks (one that was okay, one with holes, and one that could only have fit a hoof): But I'm better these days. Ravelry, a social networking site for fiber nerds, helped my technique a lot (find me as "lisava"). Knitting's a great creative outlet for when I'm away from my manuscripts. I'm not very good at sitting still.

SAA: Are you working on something new? Can you share anything with us about your next project?

LVA: I can tell you that my book-in-progress box is filled with bright red plastic berries, peacock feathers, beeswax candles, pictures of farm equipment, random info like "how to make a leech barometer," and writings about whether or not plants have feelings. It's gonna be fun!

Questions and Topics for Discussion

1. The three sisters, Bitty, Aubrey, and Meggie, are each very different and have spent a lot of time apart, but despite everything they all find their way back home upon the death of the aunt who raised them. What does the novel have to say about the bonds of sisterhood?

2. Each sister rejects, deals with, or embraces the idea of magic in her own way. Which sister do you relate to most? Are there themes in this book that run parallel with (or contrary to) the tenets of your faith community or your own personal ideas and beliefs?

3. At one point, Aubrey thinks "if the Madness was real, then the sacrifice of being a guardian of the Stitchery was a bigger, scarier thing than any single sacrifice made in the name of a single spell." What is the connection between the Madness and magic? Do you think the Madness will continue to follow the family after the Stitchery is gone?

4. Why do you think Bitty started out so rebellious, but was so quick to embrace a socially acceptable lifestyle in adulthood and to distance herself from her sisters and the Stitchery?

5. Aubrey struggles with confidence throughout the book. What do you think was the main turning point for her? What made her believe in herself?

6. Meggie drops everything to go looking for the truth about her mother. Is there anything from your past you'd like to get to the bottom of?

7. Why do you think Aubrey feels that she can't give in to her attraction to Vic?

8. The women of Tappan Square band together on Halloween Night to produce a feat of, if not magic, at the very least of remarkable artistry. What were the true effects of the yarn bombing? Do you feel the conclusion of the book indicates that magic is literally at work, that magic is something people choose to see, or that magic is what we make of it?

9. Were you upset by the fate of Tappan Square? What does this novel have to say about gentrification?

10. After Aubrey sacrifices Vic to save Tarrytown, she takes him back even though the Great Book in the Hall says she shouldn't. How does she justify her actions? Was she right to take him back or should she have stayed true to her legacy?

11. The old Stitchery is no more but something remarkable happens instead. What do you think is the legacy of the Stitchery and how does it live on?

12. In the end, Aubrey comes to accept uncertainty. She thinks "The Stitchery had made a thing very clear to her—a thing she did not see until now: Whatever the Van Ripper guardians had said magic was, was only a very small part of it, if it was part at all." Do you feel this is a step forward in her understanding? Or is it an excuse that allows Aubrey to reshape tradition according to her own ideas? What are your feelings about embracing irresolution and uncertainty?

13. What do you predict for the next generation of the Stitchery, Bitty's children Nessa and Carson?

14. There are many themes in this novel: sisterhood, love, civic responsibility, magic, and self-determination, among others. Which one resonated the most for you?

15. If the sisters of the Stitchery lived in your town, what would you ask them to knit, and for whom? What would you sacrifice for your spell?

LISA VAN ALLEN'S writing has been published in many literary journals and has been nominated for the Pushcart Prize. She currently lives in northern New Jersey with her husband and their pet hedgehog.

Want to meet Lisa? For information on how to schedule a call-in with Lisa for your book (and/or knitting) club, please visit www.WriterLisaVanAllen.com. Lisa accepts friend requests from fellow fiber arts fans on Ravelry.com, where she knits as "lisava." Find her on Facebook and GoodReads, too.

Chat.
Comment.
Connect.

Visit our online book club community at
Facebook.com/RHReadersCircle

Chat
Meet fellow book lovers and discuss what you're reading.

Comment
Post reviews of books, ask—and answer—thought-provoking
questions, or give and receive book club ideas.

Connect
Find an author on tour, visit our author blog, or invite one of
our 150 available authors to chat with your group on the phone.

Explore
Also visit our site for discussion questions, excerpts, author
interviews, videos, free books, news on the latest releases,
and more.

Books are better with buddies.
Facebook.com/RHReadersCircle

THE RANDOM HOUSE PUBLISHING GROUP